THE BIGGEST NAMES IN PALM BEACH HID THE BIGGEST SINS . . . .

THE CONTESSA—Consuela, the director of America's most chic jewelry house. The Kirsten could be her biggest sale or ultimate ruin . . . .

THE SENATOR—Mark, the New England politician who could be president if his wife's drinking and his sizzling infidelities stayed secret . . .

THE MISTRESS—Kate, the stunning, provocative "other woman," whose sexual desire for Mark was an addiction that threatened to destroy her . . .

THE RIVAL—Ben, the ambitious newsman who discovered why Kate didn't need to be loved as much as she needed to be used . . .

THE COLUMNIST—Reenie, the most feared woman in Palm Beach, who could turn the littlest sins into scorching scandal if she didn't get everything she wanted . . .

The Kirsten Diamond

Jacqueline Evans Wall

A DELL BOOK

Published by
Dell Publishing Co., Inc.
1 Dag Hammarskjold Plaza
New York, New York 10017

Dell ® TM 681510, Dell Publishing Co., Inc.

ISBN: 0-440-14593-7

Printed in the United States of America

April 1987

10 9 8 7 6 5 4 3 2 1

WFH

*To Louise
who loved life
and diamonds
and who is missed*

BOOK ONE

The Diamond

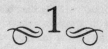

1

It rested on a bed of plain brown velvet.

"What do you think?" Contessa Consuela Constanza Perrugia asked, pulling slightly back in her chair. Her eyes remained riveted on the object in front of her.

"What else," Louis-Philippe Aumont said quietly. "It is superb."

The contessa nodded, then raised large blue eyes to meet Louis's brown ones. "Quite a coup," she murmured. "It is difficult not to be smug."

"Be smug, my dear. You've earned yourself a little gloat," he told her.

She smiled broadly, revealing the perfect teeth and dazzling smile that charmed counts, princes, dukes, a deposed king, and numerous others for over forty years. At fifty-four, she was still a remarkably beautiful woman. As president of the House of Graet (pronounced *great*), New York, jewelers to the crowned heads of Europe since 1736, she was a formidable figure in the international world of art and commerce she traveled in.

"Yes," she acknowledged finally. "It was a nice piece of work."

And that was a masterpiece of understatement.

The piece of work under discussion was the Kirsten diamond, named for its discoverer, Johannes Kirsten, who had brought it up in 1892 from the bowels of the South African earth where his diamond mines were located, not far from the famous five De Beers mines.

The Kirsten diamond was a rare garnet-red. Uncut, it weighed 115 karats. It had been cut, recut, and remounted over the years to suit the tastes of its various owners. Its current weight was 75 karats. The House of Graet paid $5 million for it.

Or rather, she had, thought Consuela wryly. As soon as her overseas grapevine informed her the diamond was available, she had flown to Zurich with a cashier's check, purchased with her own funds, not bothering to wait for approval from the board of directors. Not that she needed it. Still, $5 million out of her account was a temporary inconvenience. But timing was essential. Without a moment's hesitation, she had flown over with the check for the diamond merchant who had purchased the Kirsten from the estate of the last owner. Only after the deal was accomplished had she offered it to the House of Graet. They would ask $15 million for it when they put it up for sale. They expected to get it.

Consuela felt the price was reasonable. A record price for diamonds had been set at $111,000 per karat when the 41.3-karat Polar Star was sold in Geneva for $4.6 million in 1980. The Emir of Abu Dhabi purchased the 170.49-karat Star of Peace in 1981 for $20 million. Consuela was pleased. She had got there before Harry Winston, or Cartier, or Van Cleef & Arpels, or some rich Arab sheik who was racking his brain for some new way to divest himself of loose change. She had done it alone. Once more.

Nevertheless, she again asked Louis in the disarming way she had of sometimes seeming to defer, "I did right?" Louis recognized the illusion. He knew the will of iron the deference masked.

Consuela rose gracefully from her chair and moved closer to him. She was a tall, slender woman with thick blond hair, tinted now, brushed back from her face. Her eyes were very blue, well spaced in a mobile expressive face that had been painted and photographed by the most famous artists and photographers in the world. She was elegantly dressed in a white long-sleeved silk shirt and simply cut black wool skirt belted in black lizard that clasped together with an interlocking *HG* in 18k gold. Two strings of perfectly matched pearls and a piece of ivory tusk on a gold chain filled in the bare V of her neckline. The tusk was a memento of an African safari she'd been on. She had bagged the elephant. The pearls were a gift from the count. She had bagged him too.

She perched lightly on the corner of her Regency desk and crossed slender ankles. There was an energy, a vibrancy, about her that communicated itself. There was also an intense restlessness.

10

Consuela waited.

Louis-Philippe had been studying the long slender feet shod in sling-back black lizard. He wondered how even feet could be so beautiful. It seemed as if he had loved Consuela forever.

She tapped her foot impatiently. "Well?"

It was Louis-Philippe's turn to smile. It never failed to astonish him that someone as confident as Consuela could still need reassuring.

"You did absolutely right, Consuela. As always. It is indeed a coup for the House of Graet."

Gems were Louis-Philippe's business. A tall, taciturn man with dark, graying hair and soft brown eyes behind black-rimmed glasses, he looked like a college professor of the classics. His was the opinion Consuela valued.

Apprenticed at eighteen as diamond cutter to the House of Graet, Switzerland, home base of the firm, Louis had risen in stature with the company until, forty years later, he was chief jewelry designer for the House of Graet, New York. Of all the gems he handled, the diamond, the best known of the gemstones, intrigued him most.

Although diamonds were believed to go back 2300 years, the stone was rare until 1866 when a fifteen-year-old boy discovered a pebble near Hopetown that turned out to be a 21.25-karat diamond later known as the Eureka. That discovery started the South African diamond rush and diamonds became more plentiful. But not too plentiful. Shrewd diamond miners never flooded the market with the stones. Instead, they always withheld just enough of them to keep the purchase price high.

The diamond—a stone, Louis-Philippe knew, that captured the imagination of rich and poor alike. From the Greek word *adamis,* meaning "unyielding, hard." In fact, the hardest mineral known. Yet, nothing more than crystallized carbon.

Of all rough diamonds retrieved from the earth, 75 to 80 percent were fit only for industrial use—phonograph needle tips, cutting tools, abrasives. Most of these were handled by the CSO (Central Sorting Office) in London. But even gem diamonds went through an intensive sorting and grading process to classify them according to rareness and value.

The journey continued on to one of the chief diamond centers

—Amsterdam, Antwerp, Tel Aviv, Johannesburg, Bombay, San Juan, New York, where the diamond was studied and marked with india ink before the principal cut which produced the diamond's brilliance was made.

The value of the diamond depended upon its color, its clarity, its karat weight, its cut, and its rarity. Louis-Philippe leaned toward the Kirsten. Few gems like this existed outside of museums. How often could you come this close to one?

The Kirsten met all the qualifications of greatness. Its color, a deep garnet-red, glowed with richness. The "fire" it flashed, from its refractive powers, was dazzling. Colored diamonds, called "fancy" diamonds, were rare. The stone was flawless, without a spot or blemish. He had examined it with a corrected lens that magnified it ten times. Its brilliant cut with its fifty-eight facets, a cut invented in the late seventeenth century by a Venetian, Vincenzo Peruzzi, gave the diamond its added dimension and helped popularize it. Since then, other talented lapidarians had created a variety of cuts—the rose cut, the round brilliant cut, the square cut, the navette or marquise cut, the modified brilliant, and others.

The Kirsten had been given a modified cut in the pear shape, known as Kendeloque. The pear-shaped garnet-red diamond was framed by twenty smaller diamonds in white and the garnet-red that had been cut from the original stone. The pendant was connected by two diamond links to a necklace of forty white and garnet-red round-shaped diamonds.

Its weight, at seventy-five karats, classified it a gem of great magnitude. Larger than the Hope, as richly red as the Hope was deeply blue, it was, without a doubt, an exciting stone. Louis had no doubt but that Consuela would find her buyer and get her price. It wasn't often someone could own such a rare and beautiful gem, and the history of rare gems was studded with the names of people who coveted them.

Louis lifted it from its bed, holding it carefully.

Consuela watched him. "It's one of the world's legendary diamonds, Louis."

"Yes," he agreed, mesmerized by the stone he held.

He thought of some other legendary diamonds—the 186-karat Koh-i-noor, probably the oldest diamond in the world, with a history that went back to 1304. Given to Queen Victoria in 1850 by the East India Company on the 250th anniversary of its founding.

The Cullinan, at 3,106 karats, the largest diamond in existence. Discovered in South Africa in 1905.

The Star of Africa, cut from the Cullinan. At 530 karats, it remained the largest *cut* diamond in the world. Now on display in the Tower of London as the center portion of the Royal Sceptre.

The magnificent 112.5-karat blue diamond sold to Louis XIV by Tavernier, the French jewel merchant who brought it back from India. It was stolen during the French Revolution, and a 45.5-karat blue diamond, believed to have been cleaved from the French blue, turned up in the possession of a London diamond merchant. He sold it to Henry Philip Hope, a London banker. Its last and most publicized private owner was Evalyn Walsh McLean, daughter of a Colorado gold miner who struck it rich in 1896. The Hope was sold to her by Pierre Cartier of Cartier Jewelers. She paid for it on the installment plan. The Hope was probably the world's most famous diamond.

The 45.5-karat Hope was also the largest blue diamond in existence. It was now in the collection of the Smithsonian.

The seventy-five-karat Kirsten was the largest red diamond in existence. It was now available.

The Hope carried a legend of a curse for its owners. Anyone who owned it, or even touched it, would die, according to its curse. The Smithsonian disputed the legend.

The Kirsten had its own dossier that read apocalyptically. Louis wondered if Consuela had in part been tantalized by its history. No matter. Just as the supposed curse attached to the Hope failed to deter its buyers, he knew the Kirsten would fare as well. Size plus beauty plus price mixed with an element of risk was a combination that could only enhance its appeal. And glamour.

He placed the necklace back on its bed as carefully as he had picked it up. He turned to Consuela.

"You're not superstitious, I see."

"Hardly!" Consuela shrugged off the suggestion with impatience. Then, "Are you?"

Louis-Philippe shifted in his chair, stretched his legs. "No. I'm too practical a Swiss to believe in evil spirits."

Consuela smiled. "There, then. That makes two sensible souls in the midst of madness. Why people believe in magic and myths baffles me."

"It's easier to blame your misfortune on something else than to face up to it. Or to accept your good fortune. People feel guilty about that too."

"I suppose. But that's part of the Kirsten's mystique, isn't it? The thrill of the unknown. The thrill of daring to tempt fate." She laughed. "Did you know the curse attached to the Hope was said to be the invention of Pierre Cartier? He told Evalyn Walsh McLean that Marie Antoinette and Louis XVI lost their heads to the guillotine because they had worn the blue diamond. He invented other ignominious ends for past owners. He did it to titillate her. He was a salesman. A showman. And she was a woman who liked show."

Louis laughed too. "I understand that once, when she needed to hock the Hope, she invited the owners of the pawnshop to her estate in Washington. When they asked to see the Hope, she couldn't remember where she'd put it. Suddenly, she remembered. Mike had it. She went to the window and called him. A huge Great Dane bounded in wearing a magnificent blue stone round his neck. It was the Hope."

Consuela relished the tale, even though she had heard it before. "There, you see. It is the stories that embellish the stone, not the stone that enhances the stories. Where would the mystery that surrounds the Hope be without Evalyn Walsh McLean?"

"Or the Kirsten without the Contessa Consuela Constanza Perrugia?"

Consuela smiled at the compliment. She rose, walked to the sideboard, and poured coffee from the solid silver urn into a delicately flowered Limoges cup and handed it to Louis-Philippe. Consuela sat opposite him in a high-backed red velvet chair. She looked at him steadily, then let her eyes stray to the diamond.

"What we have here, my dear Louis, is a gem worth millions in publicity."

He agreed. The Kirsten would create a bigger press splash than the 69.42-karat Cartier-Burton diamond did when Richard Burton purchased it for Elizabeth Taylor from Cartier for $1,050,000.

Consuela paused, then spoke again dramatically. "I have special

14

plans for our latest acquisition. Before I am through with it, it is going to be even more famous than it is now."

Caught up in the excitement of her vision, Consuela rose again and restlessly walked about as she unraveled her plan. The color rose to her cheeks as she grew more expansive. The brilliant blue eyes sparkled. The restless body, graceful even in perpetual motion, fascinated Louis-Philippe as he sat there, the perfect captive audience.

She would, Consuela explained, send the Kirsten on tour. Just as the Hope had traveled thousands of miles making millions for charity, creating goodwill and bonhomie wherever it was displayed, the Kirsten would create its own aura. It would be exhibited at every House of Graet location across the country. Throughout the world. At every ball and benefit for every worthwhile charity on the books. It would represent the best of everything the House of Graet stood for—perfection and elegance. There would be buyers, of course, among the invited guests, but they would be put on hold. No one would be allowed to buy the Kirsten until the tour was completed.

Consuela paused only when she was directly in front of Louis-Philippe again. "Oh, Louis, can you see it?" She seemed dazzled by the image she had created. "One will be pitted against the other. They will be positively mad to own the Kirsten. But they will have to wait. Who could be so selfish as to interrupt a benefit for the babies of Biafra?"

Louis-Philippe was amused. "You'll be doing the buyer a favor by the time you relinquish it."

"Exactly." Consuela smiled, pleased that he understood.

"Where will the tour begin?" he asked.

A small dimple next to Consuela's mouth flashed. "Palm Beach. Our Christmas ball opens the season there. It is the perfect setting and the perfect time."

Of course, thought Louis. Palm Beach, one of the larger jewels in the House of Graet crown. The winter playground of the rich. The season was short but lucrative. And anybody who was anybody was there. With money. Partying.

"But, first," Consuela added, leaning toward him, "we have a project to undertake. And for this project, I need your special talents."

Louis-Philippe was not taken in by the use of the editorial *we*. "What project, Consuela?"

"We are going to redesign it. Create an entirely new setting." The dimple flashed again. "Or rather, you will."

"But it is already a masterpiece."

"You will improve it."

"Improve a masterpiece?"

"Only a true artist could. Like you, Louis."

He sighed. "Ah, Consuela, you always know how to offer me a challenge I am too vain to resist."

She tilted her head back and her eyes grew reflective. "The Kirsten needs a new look. Something romantic, perhaps. Nostalgic. Something no woman will be able to resist. We live in a bleak world, *caro mio*. Everyone craves a bit of elegance. And there is so little of it left."

"How long do I have?"

"How long do you need?"

He thought. "Three days for sketches. Then, if you approve, three weeks for execution."

"Splendid," approved Consuela. "And I am certain I will approve of your first sketches, Louis. I always do."

His mind was working already. It was the way it was with him. It was how he responded. And Consuela knew it.

Romantic. Elegant. Feminine. He mentally sketched a few designs, eager to get to his drawing board.

"Three days, Consuela," he agreed, rising.

Consuela beamed approval. "Ah, Louis, without you, I would be lost."

Louis smiled amiably. "I doubt that, Consuela. I doubt that very much." Although he would do anything he could to please her, he had few illusions about the contessa. Consuela would manage marvelously if she were stranded on an island in the Pacific with only the native population to work with. She'd be marketing their beads for them in no time at all. And they'd be loving it.

She walked with him to the door, holding his arm. "And when it is ready, Louis, we will have our first press conference."

2

Life, Consuela felt, had its lessons to teach. The trick was not to be defeated by them but to learn from them.

There were three photos in sterling frames on her desk. The first was a snapshot of Count Emilio Perrugia, tanned, handsome, and laughing as he boarded their yacht in Nice. It was taken two hours before the death he had not been expecting.

Death, Consuela rediscovered that afternoon, could be terribly swift.

The second photo was of a poor shelled-out village not far from Rome. All that remained of her family had been killed. Life was often bitter, Consuela reflected.

The lesson: It was still better than the alternative.

The third photo was of her daughter, Antonia, a plump, pleasant-faced matron frolicking on a Greenwich, Connecticut, lawn with three sturdy youngsters. Antonia's expression was one of maternal bliss. The scene was one of suburban enchantment. To Consuela, it represented everything she had rejected—motherhood, domesticity, and dullness.

The third lesson? Life was meant to be exciting. Filled with challenges.

The Kirsten was her latest challenge. She would fly with it. Consuela picked up the necklace from where Louis had left it, looked at it once more, then walked with it to the wall safe, placed the Kirsten inside, and swung the door shut.

She was pleased with the way things were going, excited about Louis's redesigning it. He would do it magnificently. She had no doubt about that.

She buzzed her secretary on the intercom. "Hold all calls for another half hour, Suzy. I want to go over the documents on the Kirsten."

She placed the folder in front of her and opened it. The dossier on the Kirsten was thick and thorough. There were photographs and sketches of the stone from various angles and in various settings. It had been redesigned and remounted four times. Louis's would be the fifth.

The file included the measurements of the diamond and its weight. It also included a list of its previous owners that read like a tale of splendor or a litany of woe, depending on the viewpoint of the reader. Consuela scanned the list.

The Kirsten had an international pedigree. It had been owned by an English earl, an Austrian archduke, a German baron, a Swiss banker, a French heiress to a perfume fortune, and an American playboy. Each had paid for the pleasure of possession and added to the legend of misfortune.

The English earl died in a hunting accident, the Austrian archduke was assassinated, the German baron was fatally injured when his racing car overturned, the Swiss banker was shot by his mistress, the French heiress to the perfume fortune committed suicide after a lovers' quarrel, and the American playboy died a bankrupt alcoholic.

The toll mounted. The diamond merchant who purchased it at auction was killed in a plane crash. A Texas oil baron who bought it from the diamond merchant's estate died of a stroke at fifty-two. An American actress, gifted with the diamond by her sixth husband as a wedding gift, was killed instantly with him when the Rolls they were touring Switzerland in missed a curve and plummeted down a Swiss mountainside.

"Dio mio," Consuela murmured. If she believed in bad luck or legends, she would be dead too.

But she didn't believe in luck. Except the kind you made for yourself. Or legends. Except the ones you created. Like the one she had created for herself.

The Contessa Perrugia was born Consuela Constanza Cafiera in a small village forty kilometers from Rome to a family of poor Italian farmers. She remembered only poverty, struggle, and drudgery from her childhood. She was the fourth child from the union of Raphael and Alfina Cafiera. Two of her sisters died at birth, the other in infancy during a smallpox epidemic. One brother was killed fighting for Mussolini's war. The other died fighting against it.

Mussolini's war for Italy's glory meant only more deprivation for most Italians. Consuela and her younger brother Sergio were always hungry. They went to bed cold from lack of heat, hungry from lack of food, and paralyzed with fear from the shellings.

Yet, through it all, Consuela always knew there was more in store for her. *She* was different. She believed that. She even *looked* different.

She was the only blue-eyed, blond-haired child Alfina Cafiera bore. Indeed, Consuela was the only blue-eyed, blond-haired child in the village. No one teased her. She was a *wonder,* an *awe* to the villagers.

"Gloriosa," they murmured when they saw her.

"Magnifica," they cried.

To Sergio, she was always the *principessa.* Princess.

To Alfina, who had had a blue-eyed, blond-haired father, Consuela was the new miracle sent by God in remembrance. She adored her.

"Bella figlia." Beautiful child, she would croon, petting this fair golden child of her womb.

Consuela was also a godsend to Raphael. She was *biondo.* Fair. *Bella.* She would bring him a good marriage price. If there were any young men left to want brides, that is.

"Guerra!" War, he complained. *"Basta!"* Enough! Life had taken so much from him. This child would help get some of it back.

But when she was fifteen, an incident occurred that robbed Raphael of his dream and changed the direction of Consuela's life.

Consuela was walking alone one afternoon through a deserted section of the village. Three drunken German soldiers careened by in a jeep. They spotted her. The wheels screeched to a halt. The jeep backed up.

"Seht an!" Look! *"Amerikaner!"* one cried out.

They got out of the jeep, circled round Consuela, then stood in front of her. *"Sprechen Sie englisch?"* one of the soldiers asked. To the other two, he said in German, "That's an ass I'd like to grab hold of."

Consuela wasn't frightened. She didn't understand the language but she was used to being admired. The blond good-looking soldier closest to her looked like a young god. She had never seen anyone so handsome. The other two were dark-haired, coarser. She looked only at the blond.

He smiled at her, staggering slightly as he fingered a strand of her golden hair.

"Eine yunge frau." A young woman, he said. *"Süsser wein."* Sweet wine. He turned to the other two. *"Sie ist mein erste."* She is mine first. They laughed drunkenly. They could wait. And watch, they told him.

Consuela smiled expectantly. Then the blond-haired one grabbed hold of her waist and began to fondle her breast. The others laughed, encouraging him.

Suddenly, she understood what they wanted. She broke away and started to run, but they caught up with her, twirled her from one to the other, then dragged her screaming and struggling into the nearby field.

The tall golden one threw her on the ground, dropped his trousers, and fell on her. *"Ich werde sie glücklich machen."* I will make you happy, he whispered drunkenly in her ear as he pounded away at her.

Consuela thrashed and fought to be free. The other two held her arms and legs. She screamed. But no one heard.

When the blond soldier was finished, he stood up, pulled up his trousers, and buttoned them. The other two took their turns. When they were done, the blond one looked down at the spent, twisted form lying before him. *"Verzeihung."* Sorry, he said. Consuela didn't understand. Or care.

Just as quickly as they had first approached her, they were gone and she was alone. She pulled herself up and tried to straighten her clothing. Her dress was torn. Her mouth was bleeding and her body was bruised. Her hair was disheveled. But she limped through the village past people she had known all her life.

No one came forward. She was no longer *gloriosa.* No longer *magnifica.*

When her mother saw her, she wept. *"Figlia mia. Non capisco."* Daughter of mine, I do not understand.

But her father understood. He was outraged. *"Disgrazia,"* he cried. She had disgraced his family. He would never get his marriage price. Who would want used goods?

Consuela never forgot the horror of those ugly sweating bodies with their rank foul breath over her and she never forgave her father for not comforting her or offering to protect her. Despite the pleadings of her mother and the tears of her brother Sergio, she left home the next day. She never returned until after the war. By then, they were all dead.

Consuela learned her first important lessons in the field that afternoon. That most people were only too willing to believe the worst. That the only person you could count on was yourself. And that what those men had taken from her she could get paid for. She never gave anything away after that.

She worked her way to Rome. She learned there was no shortage of men along the way eager to help her.

"Mangia." Eat, urged a farmer, putting a plate of pasta in front of her before he bedded her.

"Riposate." Rest, a cobbler insisted, stroking the golden hair after she had exchanged her favors for a cot to sleep in.

"Bella," sighed a young Italian soldier outside Rome who begged her not to leave him. Consuela sighed with him, but moved on.

In Rome, a German officer took her under his wing. When the war ended, the German officer was replaced by an American colonel. He in turn was succeeded by an American general.

The American general was bewitched. He had never seen a blue-eyed, blond-haired Roman before. He set her up in an apartment and vowed he'd leave his American wife for her. Consuela grew bored.

On impulse, she auditioned for a small part in one of the postwar movies that were beginning to proliferate on the Roman scene. She got the part.

She caught the eye of an aging Roman producer who saw in that short piece of film what audiences had begun to respond to—the magic marriage between Consuela and the pieces of celluloid that captured her image.

Her beauty was even more astonishing on film. The large blue eyes, framed by thick dark lashes, looked even larger. The mouth was full and well shaped, and a dimple at the right corner flashed beguilingly when she smiled. Her hair was a golden cloud framing her luminous face and her figure drew gasps from the Roman males in the audience. It was slender but lush with full high breasts, a tiny waist, and firm round buttocks. When she walked, the screen almost crackled.

But even more important than her beauty and sex appeal, Consuela could act. She had a presence, an authority, that only a few screen performers possess. The producer groomed her for stardom. Consuela left the American general and moved in with him.

Count Emilio Perrugia, heir to one of Rome's oldest titles, first saw Consuela in her third starring film on a home screen at the villa of one of his friends. The movie was titled *Donne e Guerra. Women and War.* It was one of the neorealistic films Romans were becoming known for.

From the moment of Consuela's entrance on film, Emilio sat upright. He had been slouched in his seat, distractedly stroking the thigh of the young brunette he'd brought with him. For the rest of the movie, while he stroked, his eyes remained riveted on the screen.

Consuela played a young war widow forced to beg, steal, and prostitute herself for food for her baby and herself.

Emilio became caught up in the performance. He laughed when Consuela played with her baby, raged when a soldier raped her, cheered when she retaliated by shooting him with his own revolver, wept when she was reduced to prostituting herself for food, and suffered when neighbors called her *puttana*—whore— and took her child from her. And, in the scene where Consuela ran maddened through the Roman streets searching for her lost child, soaked from the torrential downpour that beat upon her, Emilio lusted.

Never had he beheld such loveliness! The rain-soaked garment Consuela wore clung to her body, outlining the full high breasts, the rounded belly, and the long shapely legs. *Dio mio!* Those breasts! Those legs! His groin ached.

Emilio Perrugia who discarded lovers as easily as he changed his wardrobe was in love. His hand dropped from the thigh of the young brunette.

The following day, he arranged an introduction through the director of Consuela's new film, a friend of his. Consuela was on the set when Emilio arrived.

"Count Emilio Perrugia," the director announced. "One of your more ardent fans, Consuela."

Emilio was suddenly awkward. In his eagerness to greet her, he tripped over a cable on the floor and ended up on his belly in front of her. He grinned boyishly. "You see, Signorina Cafiera, I am already at your feet."

Consuela was amused. "See that you remain that way, Count Perrugia," she told him.

The courtship was swift.

The Perrugia family did not take the news well. A peasant! A movie star! Mistress to a movie producer! A *puttana!* Emilio must be mad!

His mother was horrified. She was also practical. "Sleep with her," she urged him.

But he had. And he was captivated.

His father applied pressure. "Buy her off," he threatened, "or I'll cut you off."

However, it was not a question of *buying* Consuela off. There was nothing Emilio had that he would not willingly give her. He wanted no one and nothing else. Even if he were disinherited, he would have her. In the end his family, who could deny him nothing, capitulated.

The marriage of Consuela Constanza Cafiera and Count Emilio Perrugia was the social highlight of the 1950 Roman season. The bride's family was dead but the groom's family was impressively present. Rome's *Vogue* and Roman newspapers gave the Cinderella story full coverage and Consuela began her finest role, that of the Contessa Consuela Perrugia. She played it with the consummate skill and concentration she gave to all her roles. Within three years, no one would have believed the beautiful and elegant young contessa was not born to the title.

To the surprise of many, the marriage was a success. Consuela was as madly in love with Emilio as he was with her. She promptly conceived their first child on their Paris honeymoon.

When she miscarried in her third month, Emilio was devastated. It was Consuela who transcended her own grief to comfort him.

"We will try again, *predilètto*. We shall succeed. You will see," she told him.

Three more miscarriages followed in quick succession. A series of visits to prestigious Roman gynecologists was not encouraging.

"Typical malformation of the female organs resulting from a childhood of deprivation," the last gynecologist said. "She will probably never be able to produce a normal child," he added gloomily.

Consuela mentally gave the Roman gynecologist the finger and diligently set about building herself up by adding twenty pounds to her slender frame. When she conceived again, she retired to bed and rose from it only after she was delivered of a healthy ten-pound baby daughter. Success. Consuela sighed with pleasure. She had put on a total of forty pounds. She viewed that with alarm.

Emilio was enchanted. *"Bellissima,"* he cried, standing in wonder before the perfectly formed replica of his Consuela. The child was named Antonia Emilia Consuela Perrugia.

Consuela quickly set about ridding herself of the unwanted poundage.

For the remainder of the ten years of the marriage, Antonia was left, except for occasional excursions, birthdays, feast days, and Christmas, in the care of governesses and nurses. Emilio and Consuela resumed their place as one of the international set's most attractive couples. With each passing year, they grew more in love. Until the only thing that could have interrupted the extended honeymoon occurred.

Lying on wicker chaises on board their yacht as it lay anchored in the waters off Nice, idly sipping iced drinks, their fingers loosely intertwined as they chatted, Emilio suddenly expressed a desire. He wished to go waterskiing. He was uncomfortably warm. He needed to cool off. Besides, he had been sitting too long.

Emilio told the captain. Within minutes, the boat was lowered from the yacht into the water. Consuela scrambled behind the wheel and waited while Emilio attached his skis.

The noonday sun was hot but the breeze from the sea as the boat flashed through the waters was refreshing. Emilio had been right, Consuela decided. The day was absolutely heavenly, too much so for them to remain confined on board the yacht.

Emilio called out to her. "Consuela! *Predilètto! Vede!*" Behold.

Consuela turned her head. Emilio grinned as he lifted his right leg and ski and with his left arm outstretched balanced himself on the remaining ski. *"Una gamba!"* he called out. One leg. *"Una mano!"* One hand.

Consuela smiled indulgently. Such a little boy, her Emilio. But the smile turned to horror as she watched Emilio lose his balance, twist crazily around, and topple into the water.

"Madonna mia!" cried Consuela.

They were the last words Emilio heard.

The newspapers gave as much coverage to the death of Count Emilio Perrugia of a broken neck at age thirty-five as they had to his marriage at age twenty-five. Photos of the bereaved widow and the fatherless heiress at graveside captured the emotions and sympathies of Romans. Even in her sorrow, the widow Perrugia was exquisite.

Consuela continued to grieve for one full year. During that year, in an excess of guilt and remorse, she lavished more attention on Antonia than the child had experienced in all of her six years. The attention confused Antonia.

At the end of the year, Consuela, in a burst of resolve, closed up the villa, dismissed the servants, bade farewell to her still grieving in-laws, and departed with Antonia for New York. *"Basta!"* To grieve forever was maudlin. Emilio would not have wished it.

Consuela temporarily established headquarters at the Plaza. Within a month, she purchased a brownstone in the East Eighties, put Antonia in private school, and set about the process of becoming American. In six months, Consuela's accent was charming, but her English was excellent.

Pictures of the transplanted contessa appeared regularly in New York City tabloids and magazines. *Vogue* did a four-page spread on the newly decorated brownstone. Gossip columnists predicted forthcoming marriages with each new alliance the Contessa Perrugia formed. But although the contessa proudly wore rings, bracelets, necklaces, and other concrete manifestations of devotion from each new admirer, she managed to avoid marriage. Consuela discovered she preferred the single life. It was one thing to share a bed with a lover for a night or a season. It was another to hand over your life. She had done that once. It had been perfect. But it was over.

Instead, she concentrated on giving and attending dinner parties for the most attractive people on the New York social scene. She appeared and was photographed at charity balls, benefits, theater and museum openings, and other celebrity events. She also attended to Antonia's needs, which were simple. Antonia was not a demanding child.

It was at a dinner party given by another expatriate, an Austrian baroness, that Consuela was first approached by the House of Graet's New York president, Simon Guest.

Would Consuela be interested in a position with the House of Graet? Simon inquired between the consommé and the trout *amandine*.

Actually, he was more discreet. He began by admiring the emerald and diamond necklace Consuela wore. "A perfect choice with your gown," he commented knowledgeably. Simon Guest was a man accustomed to excellence.

Consuela touched the necklace gracefully with one slender ringed hand. The necklace rested just above the scooped neckline of her pale green silk Dior evening gown. "A gift from the count," she reminisced fondly.

As Simon continued to study it, she added, "Emilio bought it for me on our honeymoon in Paris. From the House of Graet."

"Ah," said Simon, nodding his head. "I thought I recognized the piece." He noted, "But no woman, contessa, could wear it as magnificently as you."

Consuela tipped her head slightly and smiled in acknowledgment of the compliment.

When Simon Guest made his proposal, his timing, unbeknownst to him, was perfect. Consuela was bored with the New York social scene. She was ready for a challenge.

He repeated his offer once more. Consuela sipped her wine thoughtfully and narrowed her eyes. "In what capacity would I represent the House of Graet?" she asked.

"Meet me for lunch tomorrow at La Grenouille," Simon suggested. "We can discuss it better then." He raised his glass. "Is twelve agreeable?"

Consuela put her glass down. "Twelve is fine," she told him.

The plan, outlined over lunch the following day, piqued Consuela's interest. The Contessa Perrugia would be on the House of Graet staff in a new capacity. Her reputation as one of the world's most glamorous women, her title, her entree into the most select circles was, of course, invaluable publicity for the House of Graet. She would continue to attend and give parties, subsidized by the House of Graet, and she would wear House of Graet jewelry. The contessa could select the pieces personally. The House of Graet would suggest some. The option would remain hers.

The pieces would be admired, Simon forecast, as everything the contessa wore was admired. Psychology was an interesting phenomenon, he observed. Women were a fascinating study in the subject. They always wanted what another woman had, particularly when the woman was as beautiful and enchanting as the contessa, who carried everything off with such élan and distinction. Women expected those qualities to rub off on them—along with the pieces they purchased.

Consuela nodded. And listened.

Simon continued. Women were bound to covet the pieces the contessa wore. "It is a law," he told her. "Axiomatic. Immutable." Needless to say, the commission the contessa received on each piece would be handsome. Simon mentioned the amount.

When he was finished with his presentation, Consuela asked, "Would I have an office?"

"An office?"

"Yes. Would I be given an office at the House of Graet?"

The arrangement Simon Guest had considered had been a less formal one.

"I must have an office," Consuela insisted. "Some official recognition of my status with the firm. A place to call from and to receive calls. It makes everything so much more"—she smiled charmingly at Simon—"solid. *Sì*, you agree?"

Simon considered the request. The Contessa Perrugia was too big an asset to lose over trifles. He agreed.

Later, he decided he was right. The title and beauty of the Contessa Perrugia proved inestimable to the House of Graet. The jewelry Consuela wore to the balls and openings she attended was admired and inevitably purchased. Consuela had only to put a piece on to have some woman cry, "Darling, that necklace is divine, simply divine!" And then to the gentleman she was with, "Darling, I must have it. You simply *must* cajole Consuela into parting with it, before someone else does."

Simon once wryly observed that Consuela could have worn an ox yoke round her neck and started a stampede. As he had predicted, Consuela set styles and moved merchandise.

As he had not predicted, Consuela was not content to be a movable dummy. Over the years, her input increased with the size of her office. Or vice versa.

In late 1974, Simon Guest suffered a heart attack that temporarily curtailed his involvement with the House of Graet. In early 1975, he suffered a second heart attack that forced his retirement. By that time, the names of the Contessa Consuela Perrugia and the House of Graet had become interchangeable. Unanimously, the board voted her the next president of the House of Graet, New York.

Her innovations continued.

She recommended a network of nationwide boutiques promoting a new line of House of Graet merchandise. While retaining the elegance of the House of Graet name, the new line offered less expensive ware, making merchandise available to a type of client who might otherwise be too intimidated to approach the older House of Graet establishments.

Profits increased.

In searching out new products to market, Consuela suggested an eau de toilette and a parfum. She worked personally with House of Graet chemists until she was satisfied with the scents. A national media campaign, planned by and around the Contessa Perrugia, introduced the new products. The scents challenged Opium and Chanel in sales.

Profits increased.

Consuela initiated a series of small parties to which carefully selected guests with impeccable social credentials were invited for previews of special House of Graet pieces of jewelry. Privately, Consuela referred to these as her "Tupperware parties." They were exceptionally successful. People clamored for invitations. Everyone wanted to be among the first to view and purchase a new piece.

Profits increased.

She had the House of Graet exterior redesigned and remodeled. When that was completed, she concentrated on the interior.

The ground floor of the building was turned into an elegant bazaar where less expensive pieces of jewelry could be purchased by clients in a rush to do their gift buying.

The Gold Chamber was on the second floor, alongside the Silver Salon. Rubies, sapphires, emeralds, and other precious stones were on the third floor, along with the Pearl Parlor. The Diamond Door, a door encrusted with real and synthetic diamonds, opened onto the diamond collection on the fourth floor.

The fifth floor, splendidly furnished in Louis XIV through XVI, was reserved for very special clients for whom very select pieces were removed from vaults and discreetly brought forth for viewing by elegant personnel. Picasso, Klee, and Miró, eclectically mixed with Rembrandt, Turner, Cassatt, and a rare Giotto, hung in heavy frames on silk-lined walls. Champagne was served from frosted buckets into chilled tulip glasses or coffee from silver urns was poured into delicate china cups. The ambience was soothing. The sell was unnecessary. The client selected knowledgeably. And without hurry.

The House of Graet offices were on the sixth floor.

In the seven years since she had become president, the face and figure of the Contessa Consuela Perrugia graced the covers of most of the important publications in the country. *Fortune* called her, "One of the world's most important women." *Vogue* said she was one of the most elegant. *Harper's Bazaar* claimed she was "one of the world's great beauties." *Time* magazine referred to her as a "Woman of Her Time." And when she introduced a new line of House of Graet timepieces, *People* magazine did a spread of her, titling her, "The woman who creates Time—and makes it work for her."

The Kirsten was the latest coup Consuela had pulled off. She closed the folder. No, she didn't believe in luck or legends. Life was a plum, waiting to be plucked by those with will and imagination enough to dare to reach for it.

She rose, stretched, smoothed her skirt, and walked to the window. The first November snow of the season was falling, softening the starkness of the New York City streets.

There was nothing in her life she was ashamed of. She had

done what she had to do to survive. She would change nothing, even if she had the power to. Survival was what life was all about. The embellishments, the luxuries that made life more agreeable, came later.

It was nice to be rich. Money provided freedom and options. And, of course, there was the headiest aphrodisiac of all, power. Still, she was bound neither by money nor power. If, *Dio mio,* she lost everything tomorrow, she could begin again. She had the will. And the imagination.

Consuela suddenly realized she was hungry. For more than just food. She thought of the young man with the two-way name who, at her invitation, now shared her apartment. The brownstone had been sold long ago in favor of a Fifth Avenue penthouse duplex near the Metropolitan Museum of Art.

When she first met him, she teased him about the name, Derek Tracey. It could easily have been switched around.

"You made it up," Consuela suggested. "For the stage," she added upon learning he was an actor.

"No," he assured her. He had been born with it. He was the fourth Derek Tracey to bear the name.

"Indeed? Imagine!" She had laughed, studying him intently all the while. He was tall, thin, and intense, with a habit of nervously running his fingers through his curly bright red hair. His body was taut. Obviously kept in good condition. Trained to perform well.

What impulse had possessed her to invite him to share her place? She had never done that before. She preferred her lovers off the premises. Except when she wished them there. Nevertheless, she invited Derek to stay a month or two after she began sleeping with him. He was between roles, about to be evicted from his flat. She knew how desperate he was.

Through a friend of hers, Consuela arranged for Derek to test for a part in a new TV soap, *Webster's Cove,* about a summer colony much like the Hamptons. Derek got the part and within a month, the writer and producer expanded his role. Audiences loved him. Women of all ages responded to the lost, vulnerable, charm of Derek Tracey. And why not? thought Consuela. He was delicious. A young lover was a tonic. He kept *her* young.

She visualized him suddenly, settled comfortably in the large library chair, reading the dialogue for tomorrow's scene. Or perhaps rehearsing in front of the full-length mirror in his bedroom. She had caught him doing that once, oblivious to everything else. He had not been embarrassed at being caught. Only irritated at being interrupted.

Perhaps he was in bed studying his part. He rehearsed there too. She picked up the receiver from her private line and dialed home.

"Caro," she crooned when he picked up the phone. "I am coming home for lunch." The decision had been made impulsively.

Christ! thought Derek. He was in the middle of rehearsing his new scene. Trying to get the business down pat. It was crucial to get it right.

Consuela sensed his hesitancy. "You have something else planned, *caro?"*

Hell, how long could it take? "No, that's fine, babe. I'll be ready for a break by then."

"Good!" Who else would *dare* call her babe? Consuela smiled fondly and felt her flesh grow warm. "See you soon."

She replaced the receiver on its cradle, idly recalling Palm Beach and the plans she must make for the Christmas ball.

Palm Beach in December. The perfect time to escape New York cold or sleet. Palm Beach. Sunshine. Warmth. Heavenly scent of bougainvillaea. Starlit nights. Her Latin blood responded to the images formed in her mind.

She would take Derek with her. They could laze in the afternoon sunshine by The Breakers' pool, lie on the striped turquoise and white chaises on the pool patio, sip cold drinks and lunch at a table shaded by a turquoise and white umbrella, stroll along the Esplanade, gaze out at sailboats gliding over the Atlantic like brightly painted toys with their rainbow-colored sails.

They could make love in the moonlight. Or stroll in the moonlight and make love in the afternoon. Whichever. In between working, she would find time for pleasure. And it would be good for Derek too. He was much too intense.

A smile played round Consuela's mouth as she thought of lunch. A cold antipasto, prepared by Julius, her chef, served by Angelina. Some red wine. A relaxed hour of lovemaking. What more could a woman ask?

31

But because she was a businesswoman first, Consuela roused herself from reverie and began to plan the rest of the morning.

She must get hold of Kate Crowley in Palm Beach, have Kate send up a copy of the Christmas ball guest list and copies of the memos. Consuela had misplaced hers. Plans must be made, the stage must be set, the curtain raised for the production that was the Kirsten. It would be magnificent. Like no other extravaganza she had planned. Others would pale by comparison. Of that she was sure.

She leaned across the desk, reached toward the intercom, and buzzed her secretary. "Suzy, get me Kate Crowley in Palm Beach." Without being aware of it, she lapsed into her native tongue. *"Pronto! Per favore!"* Quick! Please!

3

Kate Crowley backed the five-year-old Mercedes out her graveled driveway onto Flagler Drive. The ride to work was a mood lifter. No matter what battles might be raging within, the drive from Flagler along Lake Worth and into Palm Beach from South Ocean Boulevard with the Atlantic on her right bolstered her spirits.

The convertible top was down, and the crisp November air felt good. Lake Worth, usually placid, was choppy this morning. She drove slowly, welcoming the unaccustomed chill, passing several brightly clad joggers. A lone male cycler grinned and saluted her. Kate smiled back, feeling suddenly expansive. It was that kind of day.

An intrepid septuagenarian fisherman concentrated on his catch, oblivious to the young woman driving past.

Several more fishermen lined both sides of the Southern Boulevard Bridge. Kate passed them daily. She wondered if they ever caught anything or if they were part of Palm Beach local color, planted there to lure tourists to the beguiling Florida life-style. They looked like Norman Rockwell still lifes posed artfully against the blue sky, peering into the aquamarine water.

Across the bridge, the sand-colored stucco tower of Mar-a-Lago loomed like the landmark it was. Mar-a-Lago, home of the late Marjorie Merriweather Post, Post cereal heiress and co-founder of General Foods. It was considered one of the most beautiful estates in the world. Or one of the most offensive. Depending on your point of view.

Palm Beach gossip traded stories on public reaction when it was first completed in 1927 for $8 million. One neighbor waspishly called it "early bastardized Spanish."

Socialite Harry Thaw, who killed the world-renowned architect Stanford White over White's affair with Thaw's show-girl wife, Evelyn Nesbit, was said to have been stunned when he first saw it. "My God, I shot the wrong architect!" he exclaimed.

Mar-a-Lago was so blatantly conspicuous it drew that kind of response. Yet, as Kate knew, it was one of the most famous of the Palm Beach estates, euphemistically referred to as "cottages."

Upon the heiress's death, Mar-a-Lago was offered to the government as a home for visiting dignitaries but the upkeep proved prohibitive. Now the fifty-eight-bedroom, thirty-three-bathroom "cottage" with its private golf course and under-the-road tunnel to a private bit of ocean beach had been sold. The original asking price of $20 million had been reduced several times, finally selling for $5 million to real estate tycoon Donald Trump as a part-time family retreat.

Kate steered the Mercedes past Mar-a-Lago's high shrubbed walls onto South Ocean Boulevard, past the massive estates of the very rich. The movement to designate the area an historic landmark was gaining momentum. The argument was persuasive. The area included perfect examples of Mediterranean-type architecture, probably never again to be duplicated in a similar setting.

Kate remembered how she had once thought such opulence obscene and tasteless. It offended her New England sense of thrift and propriety—one mansion bigger, more imposing than the next, the estates separated by a narrow two-lane highway from the Atlantic Ocean.

She was used to the grandeur by now. And as regional vice-president of the southern zone of the House of Graet, she had been to teas, buffets, and charity balls at many of the mansions. She was quite accustomed to the splendor by now and privy to enough of the problems of the very rich to know they were not immune to life's barbs.

Still, she had to admit the area made its statement boldly. Perfectly maintained estates with meticulously manicured gardens facing the seemingly endless expanse of sea. Towering palm trees lining the road. The road itself curved and unfolded as her car followed the scenic ocean pathway. Blue skies, blue sea, high green shrubbery—everything fastidious and flawless.

It was as though an experiment had been conducted on this narrow strip of island, an experiment in resplendent living, enjoyed only by a special few.

If it was all a bit unreal, that was probably part of its appeal.

Kate glanced at her watch, a slim, gold-banded House of Graet timepiece with its delicate white face set in a narrow 18k frame: 8:50. She had ten minutes to spare.

On impulse, she pulled the car over to the curb at a parking meter, turned off the engine, and stepped out, walking the few feet to the low stone ledge. She stood there, a tall, slender dark-haired young woman in a rust-colored Halston ultrasuede suit, and looked out at the expanse of sea.

Close to the shore, the water was green, changing farther out to a deep blue. Waves crested into white foam that splashed onto the sand. Seagulls soared, spread their wings, and swooped in and out of circles, forming configurations with startling grace. Kate felt her own spirit soar in response.

An early morning swimmer splashed his way out of the sea, spraying droplets of water as he bounded up onto the sand. He grabbed a thick towel and rubbed himself dry. He was tall, well built, with thick sand-colored hair, not so much handsome as interesting-looking, Kate thought. A strong face. Masculine. Without realizing it, she was staring.

The swimmer became aware of her presence. Generally, at this time of the morning, the beaches were empty. Surprised, he looked up, spotted the tall, slender figure standing at the stone ledge, the wind whipping the dark hair back from her face. A knockout, he observed. He grinned amiably.

"Hi," he said, knotting the towel loosely about his hips.

Kate turned quickly away, annoyed. Did he honestly think she was trying to pick him up? At this hour? She was angry with him for his presumption, angrier with herself for being caught.

It was November. Soon the season would begin. Hordes of part-time Palm Beachers would descend, fleeing the rigors of eastern and midwestern winters. They would party, entertain. There would be balls and benefits. Mostly they would buy. Designer clothes to wear to the splendid parties, expensive jewels to wear with their designer clothes. Van Cleef & Arpels, Cartier, and the House of Graet would compete to attract the fancy of its richest clients. And compete to attach their purses.

The Christmas ball introduced the House of Graet season. There were many things to be done. Guest lists. Caterers. Planning. Plus the supervising of the other House of Graet stores in the southern zone.

"Slow down, Kate," she warned herself. What was wrong with her? She was collecting anxieties like worry beads.

She glanced at the attractive stranger who was now watching *her*. She straightened her shoulders resolutely and with a cool look of dismissal turned her back on him. The stranger smiled amiably.

Kate got back into the car. Tilting the car mirror, she brushed her dark shoulder-length hair back into order, applied a light touch of lipstick, and was satisfied with the result. She readjusted the mirror.

What was it about the stranger that bothered her so?

He should be in an office somewhere, or at least on his way to one, instead of appearing so free and unencumbered. Bounding out of the sea like some young Adonis. Really!

She suddenly realized it was not so much the person as the memories he evoked that upset her. For some strange reason, although he looked nothing like him, the stranger had reminded her of her father. There was the same kind of reckless attractiveness about them both.

An image of her father flashed through her mind, an image she managed to banish quite effectively most of the time. Images continued to come now, a series of continuous flashes projected like bits of film on a distant screen as she sat very still behind the wheel of the car.

She was born Katherine Emily Crowley on July 4, 1959, to Nicholas and Caroline Crowley in Grafton, a sleepy Massachusetts village outside of Worcester.

When she was very small, her father told her, "You see how special you are, Kate. Every year on your birthday, there's a big blast."

Although she learned in time the fireworks, sparklers, and fanfare were not just for her, she was totally unprepared for the blast that accompanied her tenth birthday.

On that day, her mother shot her father, then turned the gun on herself, thus ending thirteen years of what appeared to be an unusually successful marriage.

The murder-suicide was given front-page coverage in the Worcester papers. The deceased were newsworthy; both were prominent Worcester attorneys.

Also noted was the information that the ten-year-old orphan was the first person on the scene. Kate had been in the garden playing with Scrabble, her wire-haired terrier, waiting for the birthday celebration to begin.

Shock ran through the New England town with its traditional village green and slumbering peace. *How* had been accounted for. *Why* was the question on everyone's lips.

The Crowleys had everything—good looks, popularity, a beautiful young daughter, a thriving Worcester law practice. Whatever possessed Caroline to do that to Nicholas, to herself, then leave a child behind to face that mess? It wasn't like Caroline, usually so tidy and controlled.

Whatever secret complaint Caroline had she took to her grave with her. The fact that she also took Nicholas compounded the mystery.

The child, Kate, coped with the tragedy the only way she knew how. She buried it along with her parents.

Neighbors remarked on how stoic she remained throughout the funeral service and burial. "It isn't natural," one whispered to the other. "The child should grieve."

"Shock," the other assessed. "The child's in shock."

The aunts, Caroline's two maiden sisters, called from Springfield to care for their niece, were less psychologically aware. They were unacquainted with Freud, Jung, and Adler. They attributed Kate's remoteness to New England reserve.

"Just like Caroline," one aunt observed. "Always in control." The other nodded agreement. Then they looked at each other as though suddenly aware of what Caroline's control had wrought.

The only time Kate almost cried was when the aunts prepared to take her back to Springfield with them. The wire-haired terrier was not invited. The aunts were allergic to animals.

Kate *wanted* to cry. The tears didn't come. Woodenly she handed Scrabble over to her friend Allison, avoiding the terrier's reproachful stare.

In Springfield the aunts changed Kate's last name to Winthrop, her mother's maiden name. "It's simpler that way," they explained. Only the school principal knew.

Kate understood. Springfield wasn't *that* far from Worcester.

"Where are your parents?" she was asked in school.

Kate had a standard reply. "They were both killed in an air crash. Years ago."

The response was always the same. *"How awful!"* As eyes widened in sympathy.

Kate didn't want their sympathy. She only wanted them to let her alone.

The aunts were kind to Kate. They fed her, clothed her, sheltered her, and paid for her education. The monies left by Kate's parents were kept in trust for her. But the aunts were both lifelong spinsters and years older than Caroline. Reserved themselves, they were not accustomed to overt demonstrations of affection. Their prescription for distress was simple. Sulfur and molasses for stomach upsets. Time, the great healer, for less easily defined complaints.

It was enough for Kate. She concentrated on being very, very good. "No trouble at all," she heard the aunts tell each other.

Kate was glad. She knew how important it was to be good. If she were bad, the aunts might shoot each other. And she'd be left all alone again.

"Invite your friends over, dear," the aunts urged. Kate had no friends. The aunts never noticed.

When she was in her first year at Radcliffe, one aunt died. Kate stood solemnly by the remaining aunt, stoic as she throughout the funeral. In Kate's senior year, the remaining aunt died. Kate attended to the funeral details, settled the estates, and returned to college.

The nightmares began with the death of the second aunt. Terrible, fearsome things that woke her up drenched with sweat, shrieking.

She began getting images, pictures of her parents that flashed through her mind. Once she had been able to switch them off and replace them with other pictures, much the way she changed channels on a TV set. Not so now.

Questions tormented her.

Why?

Why had her mother done what she had done? *What* had her father done to provoke such horror? She had thought them so happy together. Everyone thought that.

Was it something *she* had done?

Or not done?

She remembered Nicholas Crowley as tall, good-looking, with a sense of fun and adventure. She recalled the times he took her skiing, sailing, fishing, mountain climbing, and taught her that girls could do anything boys could do, only better.

Life was a feast, he told her.

See that you enjoy it, he instructed her.

Had *he?* Enjoyed *his* life? How would she ever know?

Once, when he took Kate to his Worcester law offices, he pointed to the sign that read CROWLEY AND CROWLEY and said, "When you're grown-up, Kate, and through law school, that sign will read CROWLEY, CROWLEY, AND CROWLEY."

"That's nepotism, Daddy," observed the child who had recently learned the word.

Her father laughed, tousled her hair. "A little nepotism is good for you. It cuts through some unnecessary grind."

Then, "Don't tell your mother I said that. She thinks struggle builds character. Not true. Struggle often defeats initiative. Character is a genetic gift. You have it or you don't have it."

Did she have it? The genetic gift?

She recalled her mother as almost as tall as her father, golden-haired and serene.

Only once had she seen her mother lose control. Caroline did the family bookkeeping. Nicholas's personal account was $2,000 overdrawn. The bank had called.

"Damn it, Nicholas," Caroline shouted. "When are you going to learn to balance your goddamned checkbook?"

It wasn't like Caroline to swear.

Surely, the tragedy hadn't been over an *unbalanced checkbook?*

But the nightmares were worse than the daytime images. She

was a child, lost, running frightened through a forest of high trees, searching, searching for someone, something.

She rushed on through a forest that never ended. Then, suddenly, it did end. She was at the edge of a cliff she hadn't seen. She fell. Down, down, down, into a deep pool. The pool wasn't water. It was blood. Bright red. Horrible. She was drowning in it.

Other images followed.

Her mother!

Her father!

As she had last seen them!

Then the shrieks that woke her up.

Her roommate, frightened for her and dulled from lack of sleep herself, insisted Kate see a psychiatrist. Kate made an appointment with Barry Tunis, an attractive dark-haired thirty-four-year-old psychiatrist with offices in Boston.

Dr. Tunis listened sympathetically to the account of the nightmares, the images, the trauma of the air crash that took the lives of both parents. Kate had told this version of the story for so long, she almost believed it.

He sat at his desk studying the delicate beauty of the young woman across from him. Elegant and tall, with a face that was startlingly beautiful. High cheekbones, narrow, slightly slanting clear green eyes, a thin aristocratic nose, and a well-shaped mouth. He found it difficult to concentrate on her story.

On Kate's third visit, Barry Tunis seduced her.

It was nice being with Barry, Kate had thought. She liked being held and comforted. Even the sex was nice. Like gentle waves that washed over her, cleansing her, soothing her.

She felt better. The nightmares had gone, the images were fading. Barry explained that the trauma of the early violence had taken a toll. Repressing it only pushed it underground. The death of the last remaining relative triggered the confrontation. Now she was facing it. Soon she would be well.

But Barry Tunis made an error in the seduction of Kate Crowley. He fell desperately in love with her. He wanted to marry her. He told her so.

When he proposed, Kate bolted. Pleasant as the relationship had been, the prospect of marriage was too terrifying to contemplate. Consider how marriage ended!

40

When Kate failed to keep her next appointment, Barry Tunis called the number she had given him. Kate's roommate told him Kate had left school. "Just like that. May have told the registrar, but not a word to me. Gawd, maybe I'll get some sleep now.

"No, no forwarding address," the roommate added to his next question.

Kate went to New York. She decided not to finish college, not now anyway. She certainly didn't want to go on to law school. The truth was, she didn't know what she wanted. She needed to find out.

She took a room in a women's hotel and scanned the want ads in *The New York Times.* The House of Graet advertised a sales position; Kate applied. Although she had no previous experience, she was hired. She had other qualifications. She was bright, extraordinary-looking, and obviously well bred.

She also changed her name back to Crowley. After all, it had all been so long ago. Who would remember?

Kate found sanctuary in the scented elegance of the House of Graet. The work made no emotional demands on her. She soothed clients who were testy, helped others with their selections, offered suggestions. The work was mindless but restful. It kept her from thinking.

Life was reduced to its utmost simplicity. Work, eating meals (alone), returning to her room, preparing for work again. She made no friends, neither at work nor where she lived, but she was satisfied. She was in control of her life again, pleased with the direction of her march into the future.

Where was she headed?

She had no idea. She only knew for the first time in her life she was on her own and managing. College hadn't counted. That was just another protected environment.

Everything was moving along splendidly until late one March afternoon about a year after she had begun working at the House of Graet. A client purchased a pavé diamond poodle pin with emeralds for eyes. Kate thought the poodle looked like Scrabble.

Except Scrabble had been a wire-haired terrier!

How could she have forgotten that?

"I know you'll be happy with it," she said, making idle conversation with the woman as they waited for the gift to be wrapped.

"Oh, yes," agreed the woman. "I just love it." Her eyes clouded. "I needed something foolish and expensive to distract me. You see, my dog died yesterday."

"Oh?" murmured Kate sympathetically.

"We'd had her for years," the woman explained.

Kate nodded, eyes wide, expression alert.

Responding to Kate's concern, the woman continued, words tumbling out. "She just ran out in the street, quite foolishly, you know. We'd tried to train her, of course—a dog in the city—one must be careful—but somehow, she snapped the leash out of my hand—she'd seen another dog on the other side and she just ran out and it was so quick—the traffic—so heavy—she never really had a chance. . . ."

"Your dog died?" Kate asked in disbelief. Tears began to fall softly down her cheeks. *"How awful!"* The rivulets turned into rivers as the tears coursed down, followed by racking sobs and wrenching shoulders while the woman, stunned by the bizarre reaction of the previously composed salesperson, stood helpless.

Consuela, who happened by on her way home to an early evening, took the scene in with one expert glance. She quickly motioned another salesperson to the counter; took Kate by the elbow; steered her into her private elevator and up to her office.

She seated Kate on a couch, handed her a box of tissues, and waited. When the tears began to subside, she said, "Perhaps you would like to tell me what *that* was all about?"

Kate looked up at the awesome, obviously annoyed contessa. "The dog . . ."

"Dog?"

"The lady's dog. It died." It seemed so simple to Kate.

Consuela's foot tapped impatiently.

Kate tried to explain, but the words wouldn't come. Instead, to her mortification she began to cry again, loud sobs beyond control. Her shoulders shook, her body almost convulsed.

Consuela felt as helpless as the woman downstairs had. Suddenly, she saw that this was no ordinary hysterical outburst. This was a pain that demanded attention.

She crossed over to the couch, sat beside the young woman, took one of the long slender hands in hers, and said quietly, "Tell me about it."

It all came out, all the things Kate had told no other living soul. *The actual deaths. The real tragedy.* Kate described it in detail.

The shots that rang out that clear July morning of her tenth birthday. Running into the house and discovering the bodies. The blood. The gore. The horror. The trauma, the guilt, the shame, and worst of all, *the most awful nightmare of all—never knowing why.*

Consuela sat perfectly still through the recitation, careful not to interrupt, careful only to be a supportive presence.

Dio mio! she thought. How cruel life sometimes is. She could relate. Her story was different, true, but horror is horror. The same always.

It was almost an hour before the story was unfolded. Consuela looked with compassion at the spent girl. "Ah, my dear, the violence done to us and around us can indeed be devastating." She took Kate's other hand. "Cry more if you need to, cry your heart out, *carissima.* Wash the sorrow clean with tears and then, when it is done, you will not cry again over it. You will see. So cry now, and then we will get something good to eat. Food is a very great comfort. Not too much so, of course, or we would get very fat. And that would be another misery."

Kate surprised herself. She laughed. The thought of food seemed so absurd. But she had no desire to cry. Somehow, she felt better.

Consuela realized she *was* hungry.

She took Kate home with her, fed her, and insisted she stay overnight in one of the guest rooms. Moved by the plight of the young woman who had had more than her share of heartache, she took Kate under her protective wing.

She helped her find a suitable apartment and took her to auction and specialty houses for furniture. She invited her to parties; saw that she met attractive young people; encouraged her to step out into a larger world.

She recommended a psychiatrist friend of hers to Kate, a man happily married for forty years whose reputation both professionally and socially was impeccable. Kate saw him three evenings a week for two years while together they traced the tenuous thread that held her life together so precariously.

At work, Consuela, recognizing Kate's flair and talents, and her obvious beauty, knew she would do well for the House of Graet. She shifted her around various departments until Kate was thoroughly familiar with the entire operation. Two years later, when a job managing public relations opened up, Consuela gave Kate a shot at it. As she'd foreseen, Kate performed magnificently.

A year after that, the regional vice-presidency of the southern zone became vacant. Consuela offered it to Kate. It involved advertising, community and public relations, and overseeing the shops in Miami, Boca Raton, St. Augustine, and Palm Beach. Kate would be based in the Palm Beach store.

"In the sunshine and warmth, you will complete your healing," Consuela predicted. "You will see."

She was right. Time, the sun, the work—they all helped heal. Kate was so grateful she would have done anything Consuela asked. She attributed her sanity to Consuela and Dr. Harper. Bless them both.

"You'll never know the whole truth, the *why*," Dr. Harper had told Kate. "You must accept that. You need only know it was not your fault. *Not your fault,*" he had repeated.

Not her fault. Not anything *she* had done. Or not done.

For the most part, Kate now felt good about things. Financially, she was independent. If she chose to, she could live the rest of her life on the interest from the estates of her parents and aunts. She chose not to. She preferred work. She valued her independence and her contributions to the House of Graet. She was doing a good job there. And that gave her a feeling of satisfaction.

Emotionally, she had come a long way, through a long dark tunnel that once threatened to engulf her. Her life was finally in order. *She* was in control now.

Except for one area, Kate thought ruefully. Senator Mark Hunter.

She glanced at her watch. She was late.

She put the key in the ignition, started the engine, and drove the Mercedes into her parking garage. She handed the keys to one of the parking attendants standing by, thanked him, and walked briskly the rest of the way to the House of Graet.

The attendant stared after her with a combination of admiration and lust. "That's one classy chick," he observed to the other. "You can bet your ass everything's come easy to her."

4

Ben Gately watched the gorgeous creature in the elegant suit get into her Mercedes and drive off. Whoever she was, she was a beauty. Not too friendly, though. The look she gave him could have frosted glass. Still, he'd caught *her* staring first. He grinned as he pulled a pair of jeans over his trunks and struggled into his sweatshirt. She hadn't liked that, he thought. So much for sexual equality.

He folded his towel neatly and put it down with the rest of his gear. Then, at a fair pace, he ran along the water's edge. He felt good. He'd enjoyed his swim, liked the bracing feel of cold water and the sting of cold air on his body when he emerged. He ran the length of the beach and back to where his gear lay untouched.

The beach had been empty when, on the spur of the moment, he'd decided to stop for his morning swim. Usually he swam closer to home.

Then he'd spied the girl—woman, he reminded himself, recalling his sister Joanna's insistent instruction. "Females are girls until they're twelve. After that, they become women."

Ben smiled, remembering. Big, bossy, beautiful Joanna. Who'd given him female consciousness-raising lessons for as far back as he could remember. He missed her. He missed them all.

He sat down on his beach towel and looked straight out at the expanse of water. God, he loved the ocean! He'd grown up next to one, the Pacific. Now he was clear across the country, facing the Atlantic. Different oceans. Different feelings.

He even lived on the water. His houseboat, the *Nellie,* was anchored at a dock on the Intracoastal. He'd shipped it from California lashed to the deck of a freighter that traveled to Florida

45

via the Panama Canal. When it arrived in the port of Palm Beach, it was put back in the water. Ben was there, waiting to take it to its permanent mooring.

The *Nellie* was his floating palace. It had everything he needed. A compact galley, a comfortable living-entertainment area with shelves to hold his books, stereo and video equipment, three separate sleeping quarters, two johns with showers, and lots of sundeck.

He'd named it the *Nellie-Bly* after Nell Baker, a lady he'd shared it with happily for two years. One problem. Nell hadn't understood naming a boat after her didn't mean he was making a life commitment to her.

Exit Nell. Amicably.

Ben decided it was time to make other changes.

He changed the name of the *Nellie-Bly* to *Nellie-By*, by altering only two letters.

He changed jobs.

He changed states. And he changed oceans.

He'd been working as a TV roving reporter on San Diego's KBSR-TV, channel 4. He could have applied for jobs in L.A. or San Francisco, or Houston, or Toronto. Instead, he chose West Palm Beach. There was an opening on WKBQ-TV, channel 9. Although he hadn't anchored before, he sent videocassettes of two award-winning pieces he'd done on the San Diego Zoo and the California prison system. He won out over 100 other candidates.

"It's Ben's face," observed his mother. "It's so open. And honest."

"It's because he appeals to the TV female audience," insisted his sister Jocylen. "Women control most of the buying power. God knows, they buy more toothpaste, more soap, more cake mixes, and more cereal than men do."

"Mother's right," argued another sister, Sabrina. "Ben *looks* honest. When he's up there on the TV screen, you'd believe anything he told you. But you're right, too, Jocylen. Women trust him."

Women *should* trust him, Ben decided. After all, they'd trained him.

Ben Gately could have written a book about women. A definitive treatment.

He grew up the only male in a family of five volatile, strong-willed, gorgeous sisters and a volatile, strong-willed, equally gorgeous mother. His father died when Ben was two. He never really knew him.

What he did know was women. That gave him an edge over most other males.

He was the baby in the family. Nurtured and encouraged by six powerful female presences.

There was Jocylen, the anthropologist; Joanna, the anesthesiologist; Jennifer, the congresswoman; Sabrina, the research chemist; Samantha, the Egyptologist; and Sybel, his mother, the publisher.

Finding a woman of equal strength and stature was not easy. It was a tough act to follow. Ben didn't even try.

But aside from learning women were achievers, Ben learned other things. He learned about their needs, their moods, and their methods. He learned what turned them on. And off.

He learned about female power. He spent his formative years watching a succession of suitors vie for his sisters' favors. He watched intelligent men turn stupid under the power of feminine pulchritude and capable men turn clumsy when confronted with feminine cunning.

Ben never bought the myth that women were the weaker sex. He knew better.

He understood them. He was sensitive to their nuances, in tune with their mystique. And, in turn, women adored him. They found him sympathetic, empathetic, a marvelous listener, an inspired lover, a delightful companion. And that rare creature—a man who understood women.

The trouble was, he understood them too well. At thirty, Ben Gately was a confirmed bachelor. He had nothing against marriage. Some of his best friends were married. It just wasn't for him.

Nor did he have anything against women. Hell, he loved them. Lots of them. He kept them as friends long after they ceased to be lovers. But permanence was not part of his working vocabulary. And the women who could change his mind and alter this decision simply did not exist.

His sisters chided him about his cavalier attitude.

Not true, protested Ben, defending himself. He was hardly cavalier. He was tender and true to all. And he made it perfectly clear at the outset there was no future to planning a future with him.

The sisters came back at him with infuriating female logic.

"He hasn't found the woman to light his fire," dismissed Joanna.

"When he does, the fire will start a blaze," decided Jocylen.

"Or an avalanche. The entire defense system will topple," predicted Sabrina.

"He's ripe for a fall," forecast Jennifer.

"A sitting duck," added Samantha cheerfully.

Ben shrugged good-naturedly. He had learned not to let the ladies rile him. He was used to their high-handed ways. Prophecies of doom did not shatter his confidence. Nor did predictions of impending entrapment.

His sisters weren't the only achievers in the family. He had a plan.

He was thirty. Part of the game plan was to be situated in a major market by the time he was thirty-four. Television was a field of new faces, young faces. He had it all mapped out. Nine months here in Florida, then back to the coast. Los Angeles, perhaps, or San Francisco.

New York was the focal point. He wanted to do some serious reporting, overseas stuff. Not just puff pieces on Palm Beach posh and local history like the one he was working on for his TV feature.

Ben stretched out on the sand, shaded his eyes, felt the Florida heat on his upturned face. There was a lot about Florida he enjoyed. Some things he didn't. It was different from California, that was sure. Flatter, for one thing. He missed the California hills, the feeling of openness, the option of mountainous terrain and the desert only an hour's drive from the ocean.

Still, Florida was where he was now. And he'd made progress in the short time he was here. The work was going well and his social life was developing nicely. He'd made friends at the station and he was dating. A stewardess based in Miami, an advertising copywriter from Fort Lauderdale, and an English instructor from FAU. No one from the station. He never mixed business with pleasure.

Suddenly a quick image of the young woman at the ledge

flashed through his mind. Something about her stayed with him. Yes, he thought, she definitely was memorable.

Ben glanced up at the rows of stately palms lining the road—the coconut palm, the tree that gave the town its name.

According to legend—and a number of books and articles he'd researched for the project—a sea captain in 1878 carried a cargo of 20,000 coconuts from Havana on a ship named the *Providensia,* destined for Barcelona. He also carried a cargo of 100 cases of Spanish wine, which, according to rumor, he sampled freely.

The *Providensia* never reached Barcelona. It wound up grounded on the beach near what is now the exclusive Palm Beach Bath and Tennis Club. Fifteen thousand coconuts spilled onto the sand. So, apparently, did the casks of Spanish wine. Local settlers collected on the spot and the first impromptu Palm Beach picnic took place.

Palm Beach began with a binge.

In a spirit of enterprise and under the influence of Spanish spirits, 15,000 coconuts were planted. Ah, *providensia!*

The trees that rose from those planted coconuts grew splendidly. In 1898, Henry Morrison Flagler, railroad magnate and founder (along with John D. Rockefeller) of Standard Oil, journeyed to this virgin spot from his newly built St. Augustine mansion. One look and he was seduced.

"I shall build on this spot a magnificent playground for the people of the nation," he prophesied. West Palm Beach became "the city I am building for my help."

Under the prophet Flagler's phenomenal drive and direction, Palm Beach became not so much a playground for the people of the nation as one big playpen for the nation's rich.

West Palm Beach became the home of its butlers. Flagler even built a bridge to connect the two. Despite social changes, and changes of social hostesses, Palm Beach continues to be one of the poshest winter playgrounds in the world.

Ben gathered his gear, mentally listing the things he had to do. He'd better get moving, he decided. He wanted to check out some more local lore and perhaps begin his tour of Worth Avenue.

Heading his calendar for the afternoon was a 2:00 P.M. meeting with a House of Graet vice-president named Kate Crowley.

5

The snow-covered hills of Connecticut provided a restful backdrop for the long, low white clapboard structure known as Greenhill Farms, home for the addicted rich. Its month-long program promised wondrous cures for those willing to make some elementary changes in their life-style. The recidivism rate was high. Not everyone was willing to make those changes.

Rosemary Hunter sat in the solarium applying a coat of nail polish to her toes as expertly as she would have liked to apply paint to canvas. Terrific Red. Surveying the results, she decided she liked it. Terrific!

Now, what could she do for an encore?

She could continue writing her autobiography. But that was nowhere near as soothing as painting her toenails. Besides, writing it was mandatory. And God knew she hated doing anything mandatory.

Why was it so unpleasant?

Dr. Broome asked her that same question last Thursday. "What's so unpleasant about facing yourself, Rosemary?" He had an irritating habit of trying to appear omniscient. He was also a recovering alcoholic. Like her?

His next question. "Are you an alcoholic, Rosemary?"

"Am I?" she countered.

"What do you think? Do you think you are?"

"I frankly don't know."

"Isn't that why you're here?"

"Is that why I'm here?"

"Well, I'm certain there are other places you'd rather be." His unfailing patience was another irritant. It had a reverse effect on her. It made her testy. She wanted to spar with him.

"Are you suggesting Greenhill Farms is not an ideal place for a month-long retreat, Dr. Broome?"

"You're not here for a retreat, Rosemary. You're here for an advance. Into a more constructive life-style. Don't you think you've done enough retreating?"

Rosemary was pleased. She had him on the defensive. Behind that pleasant facade, she could discern a small crack. If she continued as expertly, she could maneuver him off his favorite subject. Was she an alcoholic?

He was relentless. "The purpose of this autobiography, Rosemary, is to allow you to see your life, and your behavior, realistically. Once we see things, we can begin to change them."

Rosemary decided the meeting was at an end. She had no intention of waiting to be dismissed like an errant child. She preferred to control the options herself. She stood up.

Dr. Broome tilted back in his leather swivel chair. "Running away isn't the answer. You've done that before."

It was Rosemary's turn to be patient. "I'm not running away, Dr. Broome. I'm just going to do my homework. On the story of my life."

She picked up the tan lizard folder with the House of Graet emblem embossed on its cover. The autobiography, barely begun, was inside. Rosemary stopped at the door and turned back. "Tell me," she asked, raising a well-molded chin to the doctor, "do we have a publisher lined up?"

He smiled. "I'm sure we can rustle one up when we're ready for print."

Rosemary smiled too. "They'll be standing in line, Dr. Broome. Of that we can be sure."

John Broome watched her leave. Was he getting anywhere with her? He wasn't sure. There had to be some kind of breakthrough before he could penetrate the facade of Rosemary Hunter, the senator's wife, Rosemary Hunter, recognized Washington, New York, Connecticut, and Palm Beach socialite, and Rosemary Hunter, the woman. Had he achieved that breakthrough? He didn't think so. She was a puzzle. And he was not a man to be satisfied with puzzles. He liked all the pieces to fit.

Rosemary opened the folder. It had been four days since her conversation with Dr. Broome. She hadn't added a single word to paper since then.

She looked at what she had written. Good God, it looked like a résumé for a job. What job? Membership in the human race, maybe?

"Rosemary Schmittle Hunter."

Schmittle! Now, there was a name! No wonder she'd been so eager to change it to Hunter!

Forgive me, Daddy.

"Born. 1949."

1949! "That was a good year, Rosemary. The year you were born. The best year ever," Daddy often said.

Thank you, Daddy.

Was she having a midlife crisis? Well, she'd been having one for years. An identity crisis? Who in hell knew who anyone was?

"Education. Sacred Heart Academy, 1966. Marymount College, 1970."

Remember, Daddy? The day you and Mamma came to Tarrytown for graduation? Not only did I graduate magna cum laude but the class voted me Most Talented Artist, Most Beautiful Graduate, and Most Likely to Catch the Eye of the Most Eligible Bachelor.

1970. That was the year I met Mark at Newport. Wasn't he something, though? The most eligible man ever. And I won him. Over all the other contestants.

Cheer, cheer for Rosemary Hunter!

But what ever happened to Rosemary Schmittle?

"Married. Two children."

Well, for heaven's sakes, she'd done something right! Two healthy children.

"Husband. Mark Hunter. Choate, Class of '62. Harvard, Class of '66. Harvard Law, Class of '69." Senator Mark Hunter, up for reelection to his second Senate term. And burning up with presidential fever.

Oh, watch that thermometer, Mark!

The Mark Hunter of Greenwich, Newport, and Palm Beach. Only son of John Harper Hunter and Marjorie Raleigh Hunter, who was the only daughter of Wilson Raleigh III, who was the only son of . . .

Well, she was the only daughter of Carl Ernest Schmittle and Grace Gladys Ryan, for Pete's sake.

Raleigh money was old money. Hunter money was old money. Schmittle money was new money. But it was just as green and there was *so* much of it.

Daddy was Carl Ernest Schmittle, billionaire real estate tycoon and shopping mall developer whose malls from coast to coast offered one long, continuous shopper's paradise for millions of American women.

The Raleighs and the Hunters were snobs. The Schmittles were from the soil, even if Daddy had turned a good part of it into concrete.

Score one for Schmittles, Daddy!

Rosemary paused and lit a cigarette. No restrictions on cigarettes here. You could bloody well die from lung cancer but who the hell cared? So long as you didn't drink, you stayed in their good graces.

It had been a long time since she had been in anybody's good graces.

Except for Daddy's.

"Two children." Kimberly Allison Hunter, fifteen. Elizabeth (Beth) Hunter, twelve.

Both girls were at boarding school. *Sacred Heart girls, just like me.* Marjorie Hunter was definitely not thrilled over that choice. But then Marjorie was not Catholic. She was Episcopalian. High Episcopalian.

Kimberly will do very well in life. She has a hide just like her Grandmother Hunter. Polished to a blinding shine.

Beth is the one I worry about. She's like me. Soft edges. Vulnerable. Oh, hell, everybody's got to grow up sometime.

What about me? Must I grow up too?

But she was grown-up. Saints preserve us, in two more years she'd be forty. *How's that for a dose of reality, Dr. Broome?*

Rosemary closed the folder in disgust. So far she'd done an outline on someone who had no identity except as someone's daughter, someone else's wife, and mother to two others.

Who is Rosemary Hunter?

Nina Doyle, wearing her third stunning outfit of the day, marched out the double doors to the solarium, and spotting Rosemary, joined her.

"Darling," she said, sinking carefully into a chaise so as not to muss her sharply creased white wool trousers, "you missed group. And we missed you. You also missed an almost free-for-all between Carol and Louisa. Dr. Carlson practically used force to separate them, and you know what a little thing she is."

God, how she hated Nina! It wasn't only that she was thin and gorgeous, although, Lord knew, that was a tempting enough combination to test the charity of a saint. But she went on and on about such trivia. The only blessing was you could tune her out like a TV commercial. Except she kept coming back. Like another goddamned commercial.

"Honestly," complained Nina, "this place is the pits. There's absolutely nothing decent to do. And the people here are too tacky to be believed. I don't know how I'll ever last out the month. Why, if it weren't for you, Rosemary . . ."

"Excuse me," interrupted Rosemary, standing up. "I have to take a pee." She picked up her folder and strode off.

Why did she do that? Why did she alienate the one person who found her tolerable? Well, for one thing, *she* found *that* person intolerable. For another, she did have to pee.

Rosemary entered her suite, headed for her private bathroom, attended to the mentioned detail, washed her hands, and walked into the bedroom.

She picked up a brush from the vanity and stood before the long mirror, listlessly brushing her hair.

> *Mirror, mirror, on the wall,*
> *Who is the fairest one of all?*
> *Not you, Rosemary. Not you.*

She stared at her mirror image with repugnance. What ever happened to Marymount's Most Beautiful Graduate, 1970? Also voted The Girl You'd Most Like to Be Stranded With on a Desert Island by the 1970 class of Georgetown.

Rosemary could still see that girl. Nicely curved, long-legged, slim-hipped, with pale golden hair, large brown eyes fringed with thick gold lashes, a small straight nose, and a merry smile. A fun girl. A golden girl.

She studied the reflection with all the objectivity she could muster. Her plaid skirt was tight. Her tan cashmere sweater pulled across her breasts and gaped open at the buttonholes. She was fat, twenty pounds overweight. Her face was pudgy. She needed a facial. Her hair looked stringy. It needed a frosting. She lifted a strand of it, stretched it out, and sighed.

"Well," she despaired aloud, "you've gone and done it, old girl. You've let yourself go. Bad news, luv. There's nothing drearier than a middle-aged woman with a middle-aged spread."

Who would love you now, Rosemary?

Would you love you?

Rosemary threw herself across the bed and buried her face in the pillow. Damn! She was a mess. An utter and complete mess. And she'd done it to herself, all by herself. Another dose of reality, Dr. Broome!

No wonder Mark lost interest. Not true, she argued. He'd lost interest long before she'd lost her dazzle. He'd lost interest almost from the beginning, as though her dazzle were a fizzle. And so she found it necessary to prove she could collect as many lovers as he.

And the drinking? Well, the drinking had somehow got out of hand. Ah, but the drinking helped ease the pain.

What would she do with the pain now?

Rosemary raised her head from the pillow and looked around the room. What was she doing here anyway? On this godforsaken drunk farm.

"You're here," she told herself, "because Mark brought you here. Just as he brought you to all those others."

But I'm not an alcoholic, she insisted. *God knows, I've seen enough of them to recognize one when I see one. This place is full of them. Losers. All of them.*

Am I one of them?

Hardly! You drink, Rosemary, occasionally, when you are bored, or tired, or restless, or unhappy. Who doesn't drink then?

She rose from the bed, went into the bathroom, ran cold water onto a facecloth, and returning to her bed, lay down and placed the damp cloth over her eyes.

I hate winter, hate it. I hate being confined. I hate this goddamned godforsaken place. If I could thaw out my soul in the sunshine, I'd feel fine again. I know it. Sun. Warmth. That's what I need.

The Palm Beach house would be opened in a couple of weeks. Kimberly and Beth would be home from school for the Thanksgiving holidays. That would perk her up.

She thought of the Palm Beach house. Casa Miramar. House with an ocean view. Daddy had bought it for her and Mark as a wedding present. It was one of the early Addison Mizner houses on South Ocean Boulevard. Rosemary loved it. Just as she loved everything Daddy gave her.

She made a decision. She'd go to Casa Miramar. But first she'd call Deborah and make a reservation at The Golden Door in Escondido. California would be pleasant this time of year. Two weeks at The Golden Door and she'd be her old self again—slim, trim, and fit enough for anything. She'd look sensational again. Even Mark would notice.

On impulse, she dialed his Washington number. Kathleen Connelly, Mark's secretary, took the call.

"Senator Hunter is in session, Mrs. Hunter. Do you wish him to call you?" she asked.

"No. Thank you. It isn't important," Rosemary told her. What was there to say, anyway? He'd brought her here. He'd want her to stay.

But she wasn't a prisoner, for God's sake! She was a free, independent agent.

Wasn't she?

Rosemary rose, walked through the French doors onto her glassed-in terrace. Her easel stood facing her. A canvas with a barely begun watercolor of the Connecticut hills was propped on it. A jar of brushes and tubes of paint rested neatly lined up on a table next to it.

Too neatly. The Most Talented Artist, Class of '70, would never have been so tidy.

She looked at the snowcapped hills in the distance she had tried to capture on canvas. Ordinary. Christ, how ordinary it was! And bleak. How could she paint here? She needed something to nourish her soul before she could paint from it.

On another impulse, she went back to her bedroom and placed a second call. This time she got through.

"Daddy?"

"Princess!" Rosemary could hear the delight in his voice. Her father was never too busy for her.

"I miss you, Daddy."

"And I miss you, princess. Your mamma does too. Why, only this

56

morning over breakfast, she said, 'Carl, we haven't heard from Rosemary all week.' "

Rosemary sighed. "I know, Daddy. I'm so sorry. It's just been—" Sobs suddenly rose in her throat, choking her voice. "Oh, Daddy, I need to get out of here."

Carl Schmittle didn't answer at once. The call distressed him more than he let on. He couldn't bear it when Rosemary was like this. "Now, princess," he said soothingly, "you mustn't upset yourself. You know what the doctor said, honey. You've got to perk yourself up. My little girl mustn't allow herself to get this blue."

"Daddy, I hate this place."

"Of course you do, sweetheart. I said that to Mark. 'Mark,' I said, 'cooping that girl up is no answer. She needs to be where there's life, and fun, and people laughing, and things going on that interest her.' That's what I told him, princess."

"Oh, Daddy," wailed Rosemary, "Mark said I'm an alcoholic."

Carl Schmittle snorted. "Well, he's wrong, sweetheart. You're no more an alcoholic than I am. You tell him I said so. Tell him there are no alcoholics in the Schmittle family. A couple of rich drunks, maybe." He laughed, trying to boost her spirits.

Rosemary laughed too. She absently twirled a strand of hair around her finger while the other hand held the receiver. "Know what, Daddy? I feel better already. I always feel better when I talk to you. I can even see a rainbow at the end of this long dark tunnel."

"Of course you can. That's what Daddys are for. To make their little girls feel better."

"I love you, Daddy."

"And I love you, sweetheart. Always have. Always will. You can put your money on that. Okay, now?"

"Fine, Daddy. I'm fine." Rosemary lit a cigarette and blew out fat circles of smoke. They looked like hoops of hope she could float through. "I think what I need most, Daddy, is a change of scenery. I've been thinking of calling The Golden Door and going out there for a couple of weeks." She giggled. "I've gotten fat as a little piggy."

"Not you, princess!"

"It's true," insisted Rosemary. "I'm an absolute mess. Anyway, I've been thinking, once I get myself back in shape, I'll fly to Casa Miramar. I think I'd like that, Daddy."

"That's my girl. I can hear that old sparkle in your voice already."

"That will give me time to rest up before the girls and Mark come down for Thanksgiving. You and Mamma are planning on coming, aren't you?"

"Have we missed one yet? You can bet your boots we'll be there, darlin'."

"Oh, Daddy, you are a wonder. You do more for a girl than a new spring bonnet."

Carl chuckled. "Only for my girl, princess. You remember that."

Rosemary hung up the phone. She felt so much better. A tonic, that's what her father was. Why wasn't Mark more like that?

She sought out Dr. Broome almost at once to tell him of her decision.

"That's not the answer, Rosemary," he said, just as she knew he would.

Rosemary smiled sweetly. "Oh, yes, it is, John." She raised her eyes upward. "It's an answer from above."

Back in her room, she made reservations at The Golden Door and plane reservations to get there. Then she called a taxi to take her to the airport.

She called Mark's secretary and left the telephone number of The Golden Door should he wish to reach her.

She packed quickly, tossing clothes into suitcases. She'd have them pressed when she got there. She picked up her barely begun autobiography, removed it from the tan lizard folder, and slipped the folder into one of the suitcases.

Without a second thought, she tossed the autobiography into the wastebasket. Where she was going she wouldn't need it.

Besides, she was bored with that old story.

She was ready for a brand-new chapter.

6

For countless centuries, people adorned their bodies, content in the belief the gems they wore not only provided protection from evil but made them appear so invincible, those who beheld them were stunned by their splendor into submission.

The House of Graet functioned to perpetuate that myth.

The House of Graet, Palm Beach, was one of the more impressive jewels in the illustrious House of Graet crown. Centered on Worth Avenue, it followed the Spanish-Mediterranean-mishmash type of architecture dreamed up by Addison Mizner to beguilingly represent the elegance of Palm Beach.

The building was a two-story white stucco structure with wide windows and an orange-tiled roof. A teal-blue awning extended over the entrance and thick lush groupings of flowering bougainvillaea gracefully climbed its facade.

Kate Crowley hurriedly greeted the House of Graet's resplendently dressed doorman, and rushed through the massive carved oak double doors he held open for her. It was 9:20. She was late.

She walked quickly past the large pots of pale chrysanthemums, past the small banyan tree, the Japanese wisteria, past the sparkling cases where jewels were displayed, and briskly climbed the delicately filigreed black wrought-iron circular staircase to her office. She was annoyed with herself. She had stayed longer at the ocean than she'd planned.

Nancy Matthews, her secretary, was waiting. "The contessa has been calling. Since 8:30," she greeted.

"So early?" Kate looked concerned. "It must be important."

"So she claims. I'm to call back as soon as you arrive. Unquote."

She studied Kate quizzically. "Incidentally, what happened? You're not usually late."

Kate smiled enigmatically. "I was besotted by the sea." As she headed for her office, she paused. "Give me five minutes, Nancy, before you call. Okay?"

"Will do." Nancy Matthews was a slim spare woman of fifty-five with a manner as tight as her frame. She wore her thick straight salt-and-pepper hair in a short page boy with long bangs that reached the top of arched eyebrows. Large black-framed glasses covered small brown eyes, giving her the look of a wise old owl. Nancy, aware of the impression she created, rather enjoyed it. She pondered Kate's explanation of her tardiness and shrugged. There were more pressing matters at hand than attempting to decipher obscurities.

Kate removed her suede jacket, hung it on the mahogany coatrack, smoothed her skirt, and sat at her desk, idly rearranging papers. It wasn't like Consuela to call so early. Kate wondered what could be so urgent.

The intercom rang. "Your five minutes is up, luv. I'm placing your call."

"Thanks, Nancy."

Consuela's rich contralto voice vibrated over the wire. *"Carissima.* Where have you been? I have been trying to reach you for hours."

Kate smiled at Consuela's exaggeration. "Sorry. I got held up." She didn't explain further.

Consuela sighed. "Ah, the pace down there. Slow and easy. I love it. It is so—Roman."

Kate laughed. "Hardly, Consuela. It's as frantic here as anywhere else."

"No, no," argued Consuela. "It is marvelous there. Tell me. The weather is divine, *sì?"*

"As a matter of fact," Kate told her, "it's a bit chilly this morning."

"I will not listen," said Consuela. "We are having our first snowfall of the season. That is chilly." Her voice suddenly became less chatty. "But I did not call about the weather, Kate. I have some news I want to share with you. Hush-hush for now, but I want you to hear it from me first."

60

Kate listened attentively while Consuela told her about the Kirsten acquisition. Kate was impressed. However did Consuela manage these things? She operated as though everyone else had their hands and tongues tied, leaving the field wide open to her.

When Consuela finished speaking, Kate said, "Congratulations!"

"Grazie," responded Consuela modestly.

"In this business, landing the Kirsten must rate slightly below landing on the moon," observed Kate.

"Above, *carissima,*" crowed Consuela. "There are no Kirstens on the moon. All of the plundering is done right here on this planet."

Consuela continued, explaining to Kate about the Kirsten tour. Louis-Philippe was redesigning the Kirsten. A major press conference was scheduled in New York at the Plaza. Kate could then follow up with some publicity in Palm Beach. A feature, perhaps. Some press releases. Local TV coverage, especially when the Kirsten was brought down for the Christmas ball. And while it was there.

Security arrangements must be made at Kate's end. Arrangements had been made for the en route transfer. And she would like Kate to send her a copy of the Christmas ball guest list. She had taken Suzy's copy and misplaced it. Suzy was furious. She hadn't yet made a copy of the copy.

Consuela had some new names to add to the list. She knew it was late, but it must be done. Some important people had inadvertently been left out. An oversight. But inexcusable. Ah, well, she would have to blame it on Suzy. Fortunately, Suzy had broad shoulders.

Had all the invitations gone out? Good! Arrangements to hold the ball at the Wellington Arms country club were attended to? Good! And arrangements for party tents and other party paraphernalia? Good!

Consuela would be arriving with two guests. She hadn't told Derek about his tropical vacation but she was certain the writers could send his soap character on a trip to account for his absence. Or perhaps have him hospitalized with a temporary ailment. She hadn't told Louis either. But she knew he would be as pleased as Derek. How could they not be?

"We will arrive on the tenth of December, Kate. Please reserve two suites at The Breakers. That will give us time before the ball to relax and unwind."

Consuela did not know how long she would stay at The Breakers. Two weeks, perhaps. Polly Bowdin was flying to London to spend the holidays with her daughter and grandchildren and she had offered her cottage to Consuela. It faced the ocean, had a heated indoor pool, a billiard room, an exercise salon, was absolutely divine, and the place would be fully staffed. Perhaps she would move there and stay through Christmas. She adored Palm Beach at Christmas. And she just knew Derek would enjoy Palm Beach at Christmas too. All those Worth Avenue palm trees decorated with little green and white lights. *Bella!*

However, to be on the safe side, she arranged for two weeks at The Breakers. That would leave her free to decide whether to accept Polly's offer or not.

Consuela paused. "If I have forgotten anything, Kate, I will call you back."

"It sounds very grand, Consuela."

"But hectic, *si?* However, it will be great fun. A big bash for Palm Beach. After all, it is the first stop on the Kirsten tour." She laughed merrily. "Let's see who can top that for season openers!"

"You're not intimidated by the Kirsten curse, I see," observed Kate.

Consuela's laugh bellowed forth. *"Dio mio!* The Kirsten is a blessing, *cara*. It is going to shower gold over us all."

Kate laughed too. "If not gold, then gold dust."

"Stardust, *carissima*. Every famous pair of eyes will bulge with avarice when the Kirsten is shown. It is perfection. But even perfection will be improved with Louis in charge. He has the fingers of a genius."

Kate agreed. Louis-Philippe was without peer. She promised to get the new guest list off to Consuela today. Along with memos of all other pertinent information.

"Excellent," approved Consuela. I knew I could count on you. Until later, then, *cara, ciao.*"

"Ciao, Consuela," said Kate.

Nancy entered her office a few minutes after Kate completed her call. "That was a long one. Anything interesting?" she asked.

Kate told her about the Kirsten acquisition.

"Wow!" exclaimed Nancy, pushing her glasses up onto her forehead.

"Of course," explained Kate, "we take a vow of silence until we get the go-ahead. Then it's full steam ahead with publicity."

"Well, you can begin laying some groundwork with your two o'clock appointment," Nancy informed her.

Kate looked blank.

Nancy filled her in. "Don't you remember? There's a Ben Gately from WKBQ-TV coming in." Nancy sighed. "I cleared it with you three weeks ago."

Caught off guard, Kate was disturbed. Lately, she'd been forgetting too many things. She kept her voice casual. "Who is he?"

"The new anchorman on the evening news. Nice face. You know, the kind of face that tells you you could sit down and tell him all your troubles and he'd really listen."

Despite herself, Kate laughed. "You get all that just from watching him on the tube?"

"More," Nancy assured her. "Seems a lot of women feel the same way. His mail is coming in in bundles. There was a feature on him in the West Palm paper last week."

"Oh, Nancy, you're too much!"

"Not for me, luv. I'm old enough to be his mother. But someone young, good-looking, and unattached . . ." She looked pointedly at Kate.

Kate flushed. Nancy was one of the few people who knew about Mark Hunter. Kate was aware of her disapproval. Not for moral reasons, but because she cared for Kate and didn't want to see her hurt.

"What does Mr. Gately want?" asked Kate, steering the conversation in a safer direction.

Nancy was not unaware of the maneuver. "He's doing a series of TV features on Palm Beach ambience. Naturally, the House of Graet enters the picture. You *did* approve it," she reminded Kate. "Don't you remember at all?"

"Vaguely," replied Kate testily. It wasn't like her to forget things. Especially appointments. Her mind was elsewhere lately. Worrying about Mark. When he would call. Wondering why he hadn't called.

She looked directly at Nancy. "Fine. Two o'clock, then. Anything else on the agenda?"

Nancy checked the schedule for the day. "Mrs. Dawson is due at eleven. She wants to do some early Christmas shopping before the goodies are all gone and she needs to select 200 favors for a charity thing she's doing in January. Save the Children or something."

"Nancy!"

"Okay. But I get charitied out, don't you? And the season hasn't begun yet. Who can remember the names of all these charities? Animal Rescue, Cystic Fibrosis, Planned Parenthood, the Salvation Army, Mental Health, the . . ."

"All right, Nancy. I get the message."

Nancy grinned. "You know what Art Buchwald said? Two Palm Beach matrons meet for breakfast and wham, bang, they've come up with a name for another charity."

"He said that?"

"Well," laughed Nancy, "something like that. Anyway, luv, without all those charity balls, where would they wear all those jewels, and then where would we be? So I shouldn't bite the hand that feeds me, right?"

Kate ignored her. "Anything on for lunch?"

"Free day. We can dine in style in the kitchen. I brought an extra yogurt."

Kate nodded absently. "Sounds great. Now, we'd better get moving. And, Nancy, would you send a copy of the Christmas ball list to Consuela? She's misplaced hers. Also, any memos on ball arrangements. And please get me The Breakers. I want to reserve a couple of suites."

When Kate had completed making the arrangements for Consuela's stay at The Breakers, she sighed. The day promised to be a busy one. And a trying one.

She took her jacket off the hook, put it on, applied some fresh makeup, resolutely squared her shoulders, and walked briskly down the circular staircase to the main level.

7

If there was one word Consuela stressed to Kate as vitally expressive of the House of Graet, it was *image*. Consuela pronounced it *eee-mazh*.

Eee-mazh was everything, she explained. It was what clients expected. It was why they came. And it was why they never flinched when price was mentioned.

Except price was rarely mentioned until after the client made the selection, and then very discreetly. If the client couldn't afford the tariff, he or she would do better shopping elsewhere. The clients appreciated that unspoken understanding. In fact, they preferred it that way. After all, one could buy a piece of jewelry anywhere. But only at the House of Graet did the package include such elegance, luxury, and *eee-mazh*.

The House of Graet client list was extremely select.

Mimzee Dawson headed the Palm Beach list.

The much publicized, much married Mrs. Zinowsky Nolan Dragordo Turner-Smith Randolph, the former Miriam "Mimzee" Dawson, madcap heiress and enfant terrible of the thirties, had long been one of Palm Beach's social lions. When Mimzee roared, people paused.

Heiress to a Houston toothpaste and deodorant fortune—Dawson's Toothpaste . . . The Smile That Dazzles Longer, and Dawson's Deodorant . . . With Dawson's You're Always Secure —there was nothing Mimzee's money denied her, whether it was a million-dollar bauble to encircle her throat or an impoverished Polish count to decorate her arm. In her salad years, she had rushed through husbands like seasons—the dashing Polish count, a Hollywood cowboy movie star, a five-foot, three-inch Italian jockey, a Wall Street broker who was twenty years older, and a Palm Beach tennis pro who was twenty years younger.

At sixty-eight, she was a confirmed celibate. "Sex is *fine,*" she told one friend. "But everybody's doing it." To another, she explained, "In my day, when it was forbidden, sex was fun. When it wasn't discussed, it was worth doing. Now it's done in movies and TV right in front of you. Appalling!"

"Besides," she added, warming to her subject, "it dissipates energies. Think of those monks in the Middle Ages and their marvelous illuminated manuscripts. Do you think they'd have accomplished that if their sexual energies had been diluted? Never!"

Mimzee's sexual energies had long since been diluted and directed into the many charities she underwrote. Parties were the main vehicle for these pursuits, and Mimzee's parties were legendary. So was her disposition.

She insulted her guests with such blithe disregard for feelings that some were reduced to tears.

Her jewelry collection was world famous. And she was forever adding to it. Whenever a gem of significance appeared on the scene, Mimzee was alerted. She was one of the House of Graet's favorite clients. As such, her whims were attended to with consummate care. She was also one of the clients Consuela would approach when the Kirsten was ready.

Kate approached her gingerly. When Mimzee Dawson was in New York, Consuela took care of her personally. In Palm Beach, that task fell to Kate. Consuela, with her inimitable flair, handled Mimzee best. Kate fared less well. She found Mimzee Dawson an awesomely outrageous spectacle, even though she never allowed herself to show it.

For Mimzee's appearance was as outlandish as her personality. Hennaed ringlets framed a thin, sharp-featured face. Hennaed brows, arched and penciled in the style of the thirties, provided a look of perpetual flight. Brightly rouged cheeks provided the only color in a pasty face. Mimzee dreaded the sun.

She dressed in extravagantly voluminous capes or caftans outdoors and baroque costumes indoors. All were designed by Mimzee and stitched by the Japanese seamstress Mimzee maintained on the premises of whichever of her estates she was staying at.

But despite her flamboyant appearance, Mimzee always managed to look royal. As Consuela once observed, "The waters part for Mimzee Dawson."

Mimzee attributed her awesomeness to attitude. As she explained to a young interviewer from *Time* doing a piece on her, "People are impressed with imponderables. When you act as though you don't give a damn about anything, they think you've figured out something they haven't. That automatically puts you one step ahead of them."

Kate smiled, and stepped forward. "Good morning, Miss Dawson." Mimzee had resumed her maiden name some years before.

Mimzee nodded. A slight movement of the royal head substituted for speech. She pulled off one long black leather glove, then the other, stuffed them into the side pocket of the huge mink cape she wore, and scrutinized Kate boldly. "You've gotten thinner, Katherine. You look sick."

Kate felt the bloom on her cheeks fade. "Kate," she reminded Mimzee. "Please call me Kate, Mrs. Dawson."

"Nonsense," replied Mimzee. "Katherine is a splendid name. It suits you."

Kate shrugged. Some battles were not worth fighting. "Why don't we go into the sitting room where we can be more comfortable," she suggested.

Mimzee, who never followed anyone, swept forward, trailing her mink cape and Kate behind her. She marched into the sitting room and seated herself on a peach brocade sofa facing a blue-period Picasso over a Regency sideboard. She tossed her cape to one side and adjusted her huge emerald and diamond brooch.

Kate moved to the sideboard, where a sterling silver coffee service, Limoges cups, and a silver platter of bite-size Danish pastry lay waiting. "Coffee, Miss Dawson?" she asked.

"Yes, but hold everything else," directed Mimzee like a short-order cook.

Mimzee sipped her coffee with enjoyment. "Good," she said, drawing out the word until it fairly reverberated in the room. She looked over at Kate and confided, "You know, I've given up booze, except for one predinner martini, cigarettes, and sex, and never missed any of it, but I'll be damned if I can kick the coffee habit. Wouldn't even want to try, now that I think of it. Why bother? I can't think of one reason not to relax and enjoy it, can you?"

Kate agreed there was nothing like a cup of good coffee.

Mimzee sipped her coffee. "When's my good friend Consuela coming down?"

Kate told her Consuela would be down in mid-December, in time for the Christmas ball.

"Good," said Mimzee, shortening the word this time. "I was in Nice all summer, and London in early autumn, and just stopped by my New York apartment to pick up a few things," Mimzee continued, fondling the emerald and diamond brooch, "and I was in such a hurry to get down here and open up the cottage, I never had time to stop in to see her and buy a few things."

Mimzee's cottage, Elsinore, was a 110-room Mizner castle facing the ocean, one of the cottages Kate passed every morning on her way to work and again every evening on her way home.

Kate murmured she was certain Consuela would have been delighted to see Miss Dawson. She was also certain Consuela, more than most people, understood the demands of an exacting schedule.

Mimzee shifted position on the couch. "Which brings me to the reason I'm here. My New Year's Eve dinner party and concert—not to be confused with my Animal Rescue Foundation Ball on January thirtieth—will be small. Just 200 or so guests, and I need to select some party favors."

"Of course," said Kate.

"I also thought I'd do a little early Christmas shopping and look at anything special you have on hand for myself."

Kate told her some new things had just arrived from New York. "There's a particularly nice ruby and diamond . . ."

"Good," broke in Mimzee. She slapped her bony thigh and looked slyly at Kate. "You know, I learned a long time ago that if I didn't treat myself to some little trinket when I was buying for everybody else, I'd get blue, and, dearie, I never, never allow myself to get blue. I'm sure you've got something tucked away in back that will tickle my fancy and make all this shopping bearable."

Kate spent the next 2½ hours trying to tickle Mimzee Dawson's fancy. When the time was up, Mimzee had purchased 90 sterling silver pins and 110 sterling silver tie clips as party favors. She also bought three gold bracelets, one gold mesh evening purse, three sterling silver and lapis compacts with diamond clasps, one coral and pearl bracelet, one pearl and diamond brooch, four 18k gold watches, six sterling silver and 18k gold key chains, and seven tan alligator wallets embossed with the House of Graet insignia. The purchases totaled $200,000.

Mimzee did not care to charge it, she told Kate. Instead, she wrote out a check for the full amount. "Christmas!" she complained. "Why can't they keep it simple?" A little shopping trip. Nothing spectacular. But she was *exhausted*.

And she was definitely *blue*. She had found nothing to pique her interest despite the trays of jewels Kate had brought out to show her. "Nothing exciting, dearie," declared Mimzee, picking over each piece disconsolately.

Kate thought of the Kirsten. If jewels were Mimzee's passion, rare jewels were her obsession. Kate imagined how Mimzee would react if she knew a gem so rare, so beautiful, and so notorious it was assured a permanent place in gem folklore would soon be housed in this very building.

She said nothing. Instead, she helped Mimzee Dawson with her cape, assured her she would definitely let her know when something interesting came in, and walked her to the door.

Kate felt drained. She'd had little breakfast and nothing to eat since then. Now, she had time only for a quick swallow of something. Mr. Gately was due in fifteen minutes, and she needed to repair her face.

She also needed to repair her psyche. A morning of Mimzee Dawson fretfully pawing over trays of jewelry had put a strain on it.

8

It was 10:15 by the time Ben Gately arrived back on the *Nellie.*
By 11:15 he was back in his car, a red '69 Karmann Ghia he kept
in mint condition and refused to turn in for something flashier.

There wasn't time now to tour Palm Beach or stop by the Palm
Beach Historical Society.

Instead, Ben decided to concentrate on Worth Avenue, the one-
mile stretch of real estate where the rich shopped when they
weren't playing. Although, Ben understood, Worth Avenue's appeal was mainly to the tourists. The natives did buy there, but they
bought selectively. Tourists, on the other hand, purchased impulsively. A trip to Palm Beach, apparently, was not validated without
a Worth Avenue trinket or two as a memento.

Ben parked the Ghia in one of the two parking facilities the
avenue offered and began his walking tour. In two hours, he felt
he'd done it all. If he hadn't been in all the places, he'd located
them. And filed his impressions.

His Worth Avenue directory listed forty women's apparel shops,
and fifteen men's apparel. So much for sexual equality, thought
Ben. The disparity in numbers was certainly an indication of who
did most of the purchasing. There were twenty-one art galleries
since art was as much big business in Palm Beach as designer
clothing, twenty jewelry stores, two bookshops, eight leather goods
stores, including Gucci, Hermès, and Louis Vuitton, one hotel,
one liquor store, four restaurants of consequence, eight antique
stores, five bath boutiques, and five financial institutions, including
E. F. Hutton and Merrill Lynch Pierce Fenner & Smith.

He'd also strolled through the Vias, the charming little alleys
off Worth Avenue lined with quaintly charming shops, sat at an

umbrellaed table in the Via Mizner enjoying a boysenberry yogurt, and then he'd "done" the biggest and newest Via of them all, the Via Esplanade, a two-level span of forty-eight additional shops, including Saks Fifth Avenue.

Worth Avenue was, Ben supposed, impressive. It was meticulously maintained and spotlessly clean, said to be one of the cleanest streets in the world. And the only street with a daily garbage pickup.

The buildings were a polyglot mixture of Spanish-Mediterranean-Revival—white stucco with orange-tiled roofs, many of them designed by Addison Mizner, once Palm Beach's greatest architect, a gentleman who lived high and died broke, following the Florida land bust in 1925.

Mizner designed the Everglades Club on Worth Avenue, the Via Mizner, and a number of Palm Beach's more elaborate cottages. It was said he created such a demand for the bastardized Spanish style he made famous that Spain almost became a nation of tin roofs as Mizner attempted to import enough Spanish tiles to meet the demand for the Mizner look he had created.

The avenue was picturesque and posh. Colorful awnings covered shop entrances. Vines of lush bougainvillaea climbed archways in front of exclusive shops. Graceful palms lined both sides of the avenue. At dusk, green lights attached to palm trees turned on automatically, creating a mood of subdued elegance.

He looked down the length of the avenue once more and decided something else. The ambience, the elegance, the painstaking care, were calculated to awaken one response—the simple spending of cash.

Saks, Bonwit Teller, Cartier, Elizabeth Arden, Gucci, Brooks Brothers, Hermès, Louis Vuitton, Martha, Van Cleef & Arpels.

The House of Graet, impressive, imposing, and grand, was smack in the middle of the opulence. Ben glanced at his watch. It was time for his two o'clock appointment.

There were five House of Graet associates. All young, all attractive, and all carefully selected.

Sandy Stone was from Scarsdale. She was twenty-four, slim, red-haired, slightly freckled, with a pert tip-tilted Irish nose.

Sandy was Jewish. The nose was a twenty-first birthday present to herself, compliments of Dr. Gruber.

Sandy had just spent a morning to end all mornings. Granted, it was nothing like Kate's, who had to cope with Miss Dawson. Sandy always steered clear of her. They'd been at odds ever since the day Miss D. pointed a bony ringed finger at her in the middle of the floor and demanded, "You!"

Sandy hadn't moved. "You, there!" repeated Miss D., imperiously waving the same finger. Still, no reaction. "You, the redhead!" bellowed Miss D., completing the identification, although Sandy knew all along *who* was being addressed.

But for God's sake, she was a *person,* not a *thing.* She even had a name. Most persons do. Because she was annoyed, she had smiled and said brightly, "Hello, you too." Miss D. had been furious and reported her to management.

Miss D. apparently had dropped her umbrella. Since Sandy was closest to it, she expected her to pick it up. Sandy hadn't noticed the fall of the umbrella or she would have picked it up as a simple courtesy to an old lady. Not a rich old lady, mind you, but *any* old lady. But that witch had commanded her, and she'd got Sandy's Irish up. Sandy thought of herself as Irish. To match the nose.

Sandy was given a severe dressing-down by Kate and delivered a lecture on clients' rights, the gist of it being the client is always right, even when wrong, and an almost complete biography on Mimzee Dawson and how important a person she was. At the House of Graet, Mimzee Dawson could do no wrong.

Sandy had nodded, apologized, and translated the information into a syllogism: "Stay away from trouble. Miss D. is trouble. Stay away from Miss D." Whenever Miss D. came in, Sandy busied herself elsewhere, and let Donna, Blythe, Terri, James, the other House of Graet associates, greet her and attend to her needs.

Even without Miss D., it had been a bitch of a morning. Clients who were indecisive and either couldn't make up their minds what they wanted or never wanted anything in the first place. Just came in to browse on their way to the Colony or the Everglades or wherever.

Sandy categorized the clients. The regulars listed as Nice, Nice but Haughty, and Impossible and Haughty. With Miss D. reigning unchallenged.

There were tourists down from the northeast, over from the midwest, up from Miami, all eager to acquire some House of Graet ambience, preferably for under $50.00. Since not much was offered in that price range, most were disappointed.

All in all, Sandy concluded, it was a raw study in human nature. With human nature not coming off at its best.

Sandy had been in Palm Beach only a month when she decided it was like Disneyland. What was she doing, a nice Jewish girl from Scarsdale, servicing all these snooty WASPs? Except all of them weren't WASPs.

When she took the job on a whim while vacationing in Florida, her father, a Scarsdale ophthalmologist, had not been pleased. "Why do you want to do that? You'll be on the wrong side of the counter, Sandy. Go back to school. Get your degree. Do something important with your life."

Her mother was into a different kind of upward Jewish mobility. "Get married. Start a family. After all, you're almost twenty-five."

At twenty-five, you were washed up. Off the marriage market. Starting the downhill wind.

She could have married. There was Harlan, a nice Jewish boy with a practice in Mount Kisco, a doctor like her father. Only Harlan specialized in the other end. He was a proctologist.

How on earth could she climb into bed every night with a guy who had his fingers God knows where all day long? She knew. Scratch Harlan.

What she must do was figure out what she *did* want. She knew it wasn't Harlan, or Scarsdale, or Palm Beach, or the House of Graet. But before she moved on, she had to know which fork in the road didn't lead to another dead end.

As she suspected, Kate did not have time for a decent lunch. She poured herself a glass of milk, chewed on an end of one of Nancy's rolls, dashed upstairs to the john, and had barely sat down at her desk when Nancy buzzed her to announce Mr. Gately.

Damn! thought Kate. Wouldn't you know he'd be punctual? All that news training, no doubt.

"Send him in, please, Nancy," she said, and waited until the door opened and Ben Gately entered the room.

Afterward, when she had time to think about it, Kate decided Ben Gately had the edge on her. He recognized her first because she looked the same. She had all her clothes on.

At the moment, she studied him, vaguely discomfited, trying to place him, wondering why he looked so familiar. She concluded she must have caught him on TV.

"It wasn't TV." Ben grinned and waited. Kate looked confused. "This morning?" suggested Ben helpfully. Still no response.

He filled her in then. "The beach. You, standing at the ledge. I, bounding out of the surf. Same man. Different look."

Color flooded Kate's cheeks as she finally remembered. She became perceptibly cooler. "Of course. Please sit down, Mr. Gately."

Ben sensed her disapproval. "Look, I'm sorry if I embarrassed you. It was as much a surprise for me as it was for you." He smiled disarmingly. "Can we begin again?"

He rose, moved to her side, and extended his hand. "I'm Ben Gately of WKBQ. From La Jolla, California, until recently. There are six professional women in my family who'd be happy to attest to my character. If you'd still like some reassurance, the call's on me."

Despite herself, Kate smiled back and accepted the outstretched hand. "I'm sure that won't be necessary, Mr. Gately."

The rest of the interview went smoothly. Ben explained he was doing a series of five-minute features on Palm Beach—its history, how it developed as one of the world's most exclusive resorts, where it was now. He planned to devote one or two segments to Worth Avenue—shops, people, ambience. The House of Graet was a natural. Exactly what he was looking for. Ben said he wanted to catch the feeling of one of the avenue's most exclusive shops.

Kate listened attentively, and saw at once how all this could be used to her advantage. "Perhaps the filming could coincide with our Christmas ball. It's an annual benefit for several well-known charities and the official opening of the House of Graet Palm Beach season. It's really quite a spectacular event. You'd catch the full flavor there." She thought about the Kirsten and decided Ben Gately could prove to be an invaluable source for the kind of publicity Consuela wanted.

Ben looked interested. "When is the ball?"

"December eighteenth."

"The timing sounds good," he told her. "I won't be going on the air with the first segment until early December. This could work out very nicely."

Kate had another suggestion. "You might also be interested in interviewing the Contessa Perrugia, the president of the House of Graet. She'll be down for the ball, staying at The Breakers." Consuela, Kate knew, would be ideal. She was the best PR asset the House of Graet had.

Like almost anyone of reading age, Ben had read and heard countless lively stories about the glamorous contessa from the House of Graet. He'd also planned on doing a segment on The Breakers, one of the last great resort hotels in the world. That he could combine the two excited him. He said as much to Kate, thanking her for her suggestions.

Kate reached for a note pad and scratched out some reminders. "I'll speak with the contessa and set up an interview time. And I'll gather together some information on the ball and a little background on the House of Graet for you."

She rose. The meeting was at an end. Except for one thing. Kate smiled graciously. "How would you like to take the grand tour, Mr. Gately?"

Ben grinned. "I'd like that very much."

Ben's practiced eye assessed Kate. Cool. Competent. Professional. And fragile. Although most people would miss that. She was clever about concealing it.

She was also breathtakingly beautiful. Ben had known a lot of beautiful women. Had grown up in the midst of six of them. But Kate Crowley was something else. Beautiful *and* mysterious. That was the missing ingredient that intrigued him.

The matter, decided Ben, definitely required further exploration.

With Kate briskly leading the way, Ben followed, down the winding circular staircase and around the store, listening attentively to Kate's commentary.

Kate introduced him to personnel, explaining Ben's mission. He would be coming in, gathering material for his feature. And he would be covering the House of Graet Christmas Ball. They were to help him with anything he needed.

Ben smiled, shook hands, acknowledging each one individually. He had a way of looking directly at the person he addressed and his handshake was firm and strong. The women found that combination attractive. They found his looks irresistible. Observing them, Kate was amused.

Ben's eyes swept past the beautifully appointed rooms, his mind filing impressions. He noted the displays of jewelry—necklaces of diamonds, pearls, emeralds, rubies, sapphires, delectably draped on velvet throat stands—safely secured behind locked glass cases.

He noted the bracelets, earring displays, gold bangles, and was reminded of Andrew Carnegie's observation that jewelry wearing was a hangover from barbarian times. Ben looked quickly over at Kate, relieved she couldn't read minds. He had a feeling such irreverence would not sit well in an establishment that took its merchandising quite seriously.

When the tour was over, Kate walked Ben to the entrance door, smiled, and thrust out her hand. "Thank you so much for your interest, Mr. Gately. I'll call you as soon as I speak with the contessa."

Ben held Kate's hand for a fraction of a second longer than was necessary. "Thank *you*, Miss Crowley. You've been tremendously helpful. I'm really looking forward to working on this project with you."

He stood before her, smiling boyishly, still holding her hand. Kate carefully withdrew it. If the doorman hadn't opened the door to let Ben out, Kate had a feeling he'd still be standing there.

Nancy's request for a reaction was immediate. "Well?"

"Well, what?" queried Kate.

"Didn't I tell you he was gorgeous?"

Kate ignored the enthusiasm. "Nancy, you watch too much TV." She started for her office, opened the door, paused, then turned back toward Nancy. "However," she admitted, "Mr. Gately may turn out to be the find of the season. Now that, you must admit, is much, much more relevant than whether or not he is gorgeous."

This time, Nancy ignored Kate. She returned to her typing.

Kate sat at her desk, jotted some additional thoughts down, and decided again the meeting with Ben Gately was indeed fortuitous. He would fit quite nicely in with the House of Graet's promotional plans for the Kirsten. Kate was more than pleased with this turn of events.

Then, in the midst of the good feelings she experienced, the vague sense of disquiet that threatened her earlier returned. She was worried about Mark. It was that simple. She hadn't heard from him in a week. She had no idea why he hadn't called. Only worrying about it was futile. More important, it was interfering with her concentration. At a time when she needed every bit of it.

Resolutely, Kate pushed the concern from her mind, flipped through the rest of her afternoon calendar, and buzzed Nancy to tell her she was ready to place some calls.

9

Lord Victor Rothschild, British member of the international banking family, once observed, "A rich man is one who can live on the income of his income."

Mark Hunter could live on the income of his income. Except that he had a sense of public service. More than a sense, he had a mission.

He was one of the 101 most powerful men in the world (aside from the presidents of the United States and the U.S.S.R.)—men who controlled the purse strings to the fattest purse in the world.

He was Senator Mark Hunter, a member of an elite club of mostly millionaires responsible for forming the laws that govern the nation, and ultimately affect the world.

He was young, forty-three, good-looking, and independently wealthy. His political future was assured. Only his private life was a mess.

Mark Hunter spent the morning trying to gather Senate support for the new senior citizen mental health bill he was trying to push through. The bill, and the favorable political exposure, would give him the leverage he needed to cinch the Republican nomination for the presidency next year. He'd already been approached by the influential Republican Party leaders of several large states. He was the *numero uno* fair-haired boy. The prospects for passage of the bill looked promising, and would probably tip several more state delegations his way. His spirits were high.

They were not so high when he returned to his office and Kathy gave him the message that Rosemary had gone to The Golden Door in Escondido.

Holy Christ, she must really *be nuts!* He'd been so furious, he'd forced himself to remain still for ten minutes before he asked Kathy to get him Dr. Broome at Greenhill Farms. Even then, the anger flared.

"Why in hell didn't you keep her there?" Mark demanded.

"Really, Senator," replied the doctor, his tone placating, "we don't chain difficult wives to bedposts any more than you would chain an overadventurous daughter."

Mark was not pleased with the parallel. "You might have done *something!*"

"Oh?" Dr. Broome was equally open to suggestion. "What would you have done? Reason with her? I tried that, Senator, but your wife, I'm afraid, has a very strong will of her own. An admirable trait, at times. At others, an obstacle to a rational approach."

How well he knew, Mark conceded silently.

The doctor continued, somewhat more testily. "And, as I explained to you when you brought Mrs. Hunter here, we are *not* a miracle farm. We're not in the business of producing eight-day wonders. We're simply a drug rehabilitation center. One of the best in the country, I might add.

"However, we only consider ourselves successful when we can reach the client, and Mrs. Hunter, Senator, is not terribly reachable. In fact, she is not reachable at all. Not only does she not believe she is alcoholic, she doesn't even think she has a drinking problem. That, sir, is unreachable. Out of the realm of reality, and into the reaches of never-never land."

"Well, she *does* have a drinking problem, and she *is* alcoholic," snapped Mark.

"You know that, Senator, and I know that. But that makes the wrong two people with the information. Mrs. Hunter doesn't know it. More to the truth, she doesn't want to know it. She has, I'm sorry to say, one of the strongest cases of denial I've ever seen."

"I expected you to break through that defense," retorted Mark angrily.

"Not alone, sir. I told you when I first spoke with you that we at Greenhill Farms recommend what is called a confrontation by the entire family. Everyone who matters to her confronts Mrs. Hunter with specific dates and details on her alcohol-induced behavior and the upheaval it is causing in the family. *Then,* we might have stood a chance."

The guilt, the responsibility for failure, was now effectively transferred to Mark. Even if justified, he resented it. However, he held his tongue.

The doctor's tone became professionally encouraging. "We must never despair, Senator Hunter. Some other time. Some other place. Perhaps even here again. In fact, I must point out, even though I told you we're not a miracle-producing factory, I have witnessed some of those very miracles firsthand. People I was ready to write off who suddenly saw the light. Changed their lifestyles. Opted to live. Any way you want to put it, they finally stopped abusing."

Mark didn't find platitudes comforting. As far as he was concerned, Dr. Broome had wandered off the point into never-never land himself. The point was Rosemary. *She* hadn't been helped.

"Thank you for your time, Doctor," Mark said shortly.

"If I can ever be of help . . ."

"Thank you again." Mark hung up. He had Kathy call out for lunch and he ate it solemnly at his desk. Then he returned to the floor for the afternoon session.

By the end of the day, he was restless and still angry. Nothing seemed to go right. He returned to his office to change into dinner clothes for a party he was scheduled to attend, but he found himself brooding because there was nothing he could do about Rosemary, short of sending out a posse to lasso her and haul her back. But she was probably in midair by now, on her way to a suntan.

He felt guilty about the confrontation. Or lack of one. He knew all about the technique of uniting the family to face the patient with hard cold facts about her drinking in order to force her to accept the reality of her actions. But how could he have done that to Beth? She was only twelve. She wouldn't understand. It would frighten her. And Kimberly would find it humiliating.

Rosemary's parents? Grace Schmittle wandered about in her own fog. It wasn't alcohol-induced, but it was just as deadly. Whenever there was a crisis in the family, Grace Schmittle offered to show you her rose garden. She was oblivious to everything else on earth except those goddamned roses. She lived with them on another planet. And Carl Schmittle would never admit there was anything wrong with his Rosemary. He was too thick, too stubborn, too German, and too blind to see any flaws in his only child.

That left Mark the designated villain. So he had ignored the confrontation suggestion and dumped Rosemary on Dr. Broome. And waited for the miracle he was never promised.

Just get well, Rosemary, he desperately prayed. *So I can get on with my life. Please don't make any more waves.*

Like the last one. He'd hushed up the last drunk-driving charge, just as he'd hushed up the others. But how long could he keep that up? Even judges were getting picked up and booked on DWI's these days. Drunk-driving law enforcement was becoming more stringent. The public was incensed over the needless highway slaughter. Irate mothers were banding together into MADD chapters. Committees of citizens demanded action. No way could he continue to keep his image untarnished unless Rosemary shaped up. They were pushing new drunk-driving legislation through Congress all the time.

The odd thing was, Rosemary would be fine for a while. Especially after a bad binge. She'd be on her best behavior. Perfect wife, perfect hostess, perfect mother. Serene, sober, and beautiful. Until the next time.

Dr. Broome had told Mark that Rosemary was a type of alcoholic known to treatment specialists as a periodic. "The worst kind to be," he said, and went on to explain. "A periodic is the most difficult to help because he can stop drinking for a while. 'See,' they say, 'I've got it made. Whoever said I was an alkie? I can stop anytime I want to.' And it's true. They can. Often for good long periods. But sooner or later, something triggers them off and they pick up that *first* drink. Then, off they go. Sooner or later."

It wasn't much comfort, knowing Rosemary was a periodic instead of a daily drinker. Christ, the messes she created during one of her binges, it was just as well she wasn't a daily!

When had it been different?

In the beginning?

Mark remembered the first time he'd seen Rosemary that summer at Newport. When she'd just been graduated from Marymount. God, he'd never seen anyone so beautiful, full of fun, and just naturally sexy. The way she moved her body—unselfconsciously, yet filled with native sensual wisdom. She knew she turned him on. She turned them all on, all the horny young guys, hanging round, sniffing at the honey pot.

Mark had to have her. But Rosemary wasn't giving any away. All that Marymount training. "It's a sin to do it before," Rosemary told him with a look that drove him mad.

They did it afterward.

There wasn't anything Mark Hunter ever wanted he hadn't got. He wanted Rosemary, so he married her, Roman Catholic ceremony and all, much to the dismay of Marjorie, his mother, and her High Episcopalian distaste for Roman anything.

In the beginning, it had been great. Rosemary took to sex the way a natural swimmer takes to water. She was insatiable and inventive. The best pupil he ever had. Rosemary shucked her premarital modesty with postmarital abandon.

It was Mark who became uptight. The first time they stayed at her parents' house and slept in Rosemary's old room. Mark stared in horror at the collection of statuettes on Rosemary's dresser. "Who in hell are they?" he asked suspiciously.

Rosemary laughed. And introduced him. To St. Catherine of Siena, St. Teresa of Avila, St. Jude, St. Joseph, the Blessed Virgin, the Sacred Heart, and St. Ann, mother of the Blessed Virgin.

"They won't bite," cajoled Rosemary. "And they won't mind. It's all right, now." She reached out a hand toward him playfully.

All right or not, Mark insisted Rosemary wrap up the entire scene before he touched her. He wasn't *that* Roman.

At first, the marriage went smoothly. But Mark had his own philosophy about marriage. A philosophy that wasn't impeded by any austere Catholic indoctrination. Marriage, according to the gospel of Mark Hunter, was designed to perpetuate the family, stabilize society, and enhance his career. It was certainly not designed to cramp his style.

The trouble began when Rosemary found out about his first affair. Not his first, actually. Just the first she discovered.

She went mad. She ranted, shrieked, threw things at him, cursed him with a thousand dire predictions, until he began to question her sanity. When she learned it wasn't his first—or last—she went berserk. Rosemary spent a year in a sanatorium coming to terms with her marriage and herself. Actually, she informed Mark, she spent the year praying for his soul. Which she was convinced was damned.

But when Rosemary was released, she wasn't the same convent-bred, Catholic-instructed wife who had entered for treatment. Somewhere along the way, she shifted gears. When Mark's affairs continued, Rosemary decided to outdistance him. Christ, there were times Mark thought Rosemary would crawl into the sack with any available cock. It was a complete turn-off.

Still, he worked at the marriage as best he could. And he loved his kids. His daughters were the real prize culled from the wreckage of this ill-matched union. He'd do anything to spare them the pain and humiliation of a scandalous divorce.

Besides, there was his political career to consider. Nothing must jeopardize that. The plum was so close he could taste it. He'd earned it. He'd worked long, hard hours for it. And he owed his family this one.

The Hunters had been serving their government for generations. As senators, governors, ambassadors, even vice-president. None, as yet, had achieved the presidency. That prize remained for Mark to capture.

He would do anything—anything legal or otherwise—to keep Rosemary in line. Short of divorcing her. There were too many skeletons in Mark's closet. And Rosemary held all the keys.

Then there was Kate, his oasis of sanity amid the chaos.

Christ, he needed to be with her! He needed to hear her voice, see her, hold her, feel the length of that long, slim body against his own, coming to life beneath his probing fingers.

Mark picked up the phone and dialed Kate's home number. By mutual agreement, he never called at the store. He let it ring fifteen times. She might be in the shower. Finally, he hung up.

He tried every ten minutes for the next hour and a half. Damn! It was 7:30. Where in hell was she? He needed to talk to her. And he still had to shower, shave, and change for the party.

He took off his jacket, tossed it on the couch, loosened his tie, and sat at his desk. He swiveled around in his chair, stretched his long legs out in front of him, and stared moodily out the window. He felt as though he were strangling.

He rose quickly, strode the length of the room to the mahogany cabinet on the east wall. He pushed a button and waited impatiently for the bar to open. He put ice in a glass, splashed a generous portion of Scotch over the ice, and gulped it down.

He poured another Scotch and carried it back with him to his chair. He sat there, looking out the window, sipping more slowly this time.

He was so engrossed in thought, he didn't hear the door to his office open. Kathleen Connelly, his secretary, moved across the room to where he sat and stood before him.

"Long day?" she asked.

"Bad day." Mark looked up at her and managed a smile.

Kathleen smiled back. "That bad, huh?"

"Pour yourself a drink, Kath, and join me in my misery."

Kathleen went to the bar, poured herself a Scotch, added some water, and returned to Mark, pulling up a chair beside him.

"Nice," she said, sipping her Scotch.

Mark agreed. "Seems to help."

Kathleen picked a piece of imaginary lint off her dress. "I'm sorry about Rosemary, Mark. I know what a blow this is to you."

"Yeah. The best laid plans of mice and . . ."

"I'm sure it will all work out."

Mark swiveled around in annoyance. "For the best, right?" If he were offered one more platitude dealing with the subject of handling Rosemary, he would shove it down the offender's throat.

"Sorry," murmured Kathleen, embarrassed. "I just didn't know what to say to help."

"It's okay," Mark told her. "Just sit here. That helps." He looked over at her. "By the way, how come you're still here? You should be home by now, getting all dressed up for that new fella of yours. What's his name?"

He knew very well what his name was. "George," said Kathleen quietly.

"George. Right." Mark took another swallow of Scotch.

"I was just finishing up some correspondence that needs your signature," explained Kathleen.

"Christ, Kathy," lashed out Mark, "you could have finished that in the morning." Jesus, the last thing in the world he needed was more guilt. He wasn't *that* demanding with her. Noticing her expression, he softened, reached over, patted her hand, and grinned. "Anyway, I'm glad you stayed. I needed the company."

Kathleen nodded. George, Tom, Dick, or Harry? What did the names matter? No one else mattered. There was only one man who excited her and he knew it. She studied his profile as he stared out the window. What was he looking at? Not her, certainly. Why was she here? She knew why she was here.

He was so damned good-looking. More than that, he was so damned sure of himself. And of her. Except for now. Right now, he looked like a small boy who suddenly had his sand castle kicked over. Kathleen had a strong impulse to smooth the thick dark hair, brush away the lines of fatigue around the eyes, hold him close, and help make things easier for him.

Little Miss Fix-It, thought Kathleen. *That's one helluva lifetime goal!*

Still, she'd known what she was letting herself in for from the beginning. Mark was married. A family man. Pictures of the handsome senator and his beautiful wife appeared regularly in newspapers, magazines, on TV. Along with their beautiful young daughters. The Hunters on the grounds of their Greenwich, Connecticut, estate. The Hunters sailing in Palm Beach. The Hunters skiing in Vail. The Hunters entertaining in Georgetown. The very social Hunters doing very social things.

What wasn't common knowledge was that the senator's wife was a lush whose extramarital escapades were kept as discreet as possible. Not always possible when Rosemary was in her cups. And the senator's extramarital sex life would have strained the stamina of a twenty-two-year-old athlete. Not only was he built like a bull, he acted like one.

Kathleen entered the affair with her eyes wide open. In the nine years she was associated with Mark, she knew she was only one of a number of women who tried to bank the senator's fire. What she hadn't counted on was that she would fall in love with him. And feel used every time she accommodated him. Because it meant so little to him. Or that she would hate every other woman who ever touched him. Or that she would work so hard to keep his interest.

She kept herself trim and sexy for him. Three afternoons a week on her lunch break she worked out at a local gym. She kept her hair brightened, her eyes clear, her face and body glowing from massages so that, when he was ready, she would be there. Looking good. The Georges, the Toms, the Dicks, and the Harrys were just fillers in her life. For those times when the senator needed her. Like now.

Kathleen became aware that Mark was staring at her. "Penny?" he asked.

"Just mind browsing," she answered. "Not even worth that."

He laughed. "Now, who's feeling blue?"

He looked at her closely, as though she had just come into focus. She was wearing a sapphire-blue dress. Color of her eyes. Pretty. Contrasted nicely with her strawberry-blond hair. A good color for her, decided Mark. He watched as she stretched, finished her drink, shifted in her chair.

The fabric was silk. Soft. As Kathleen moved, Mark noticed the dress moved easily with her, outlining the full, firm breasts, the firm stomach, the pubis, clinging to the shapely length of leg and thigh. He felt himself reacting.

Kathleen noticed. She raised her empty glass. "Drink?" she asked.

"I don't think so," said Mark quietly.

She rose, put her glass down, walked over to him, and stood before him. Wordlessly, she slipped the sapphire-blue dress over her head and, folding it neatly, laid it carefully across the desk. She removed her bra, laid it on top of the dress.

She raised her arms and very slowly pulled out the pins that held the strawberry-blond hair neatly in place, allowing it to cascade gracefully over bare, full breasts. She stepped out of brief blue panties and tossed them carelessly on top of the dress.

She stood there, cream-colored and rosy in the soft light cast by the desk lamp, the red hair on her head and pubis seeming to catch fire, so breathtakingly lovely Mark felt the familiar desired response grip him.

Kathleen smiled, and gracefully, very slowly, she knelt in front of him. Slowly and deliberately, she unbuckled his belt, unbuttoned the top button of his trousers, and unzipped his fly.

She released him gently, took him whole into her mouth, and suddenly froze.

Mother of God! George! She'd forgotten all about him! He was due at her place in ten minutes! Now she'd be late! And George would be furious!

Mark, oblivious to any undercurrent of distress, stretched back in his swivel chair, his arms clasped behind his head, savoring the familiar sensation of Kathleen's expert touch. *Hell,* thought Mark, *things couldn't be all that bad!* Not with compensations like this so close at hand.

Suddenly, Kathleen pulled her lips away.

Good God, what was she doing down on her knees in this subservient position? She didn't even like doing it. She only did it because he liked it. What about all those consciousness-raising sessions she attended? Weren't they supposed to get her up off her knees? So she wouldn't be so damned eager to please?

Why in hell was she so friggin' accommodating, anyway? And what in hell did he care about her feelings? So long as he got his.

All at once, the accumulated resentments of the last nine years surfaced. Kathleen looked up at Mark and told him with unconcealed annoyance, "You know what, Mark? You really are a bastard."

He grinned down at her and pushed her head back toward his aching member. "Not now, Kathy. Tell me later."

10

It was Nancy's suggestion to have dinner out and take in a movie.

By the time Kate pulled into her driveway, she felt more at ease with herself than she had all day. But as she groped for the key to the front door, she heard the phone ring. She managed to open the door and reach the den phone by the sixth ring. The clock on the desk read 10:50.

"I've been trying to reach you for hours," complained Mark. "Where the hell were you?"

Automatically, Kate tried to placate him. "Nancy and I had dinner out." Then, because she was annoyed with the tone of his voice, she snapped, "Was I supposed to sit by the phone waiting for your call?" As she would have, had Nancy not insisted she join her for dinner.

Mark became instantly contrite. "Of course not. Look, Kate, I'm sorry. It's been one bitch of a day and suddenly, at the end of it, I needed to hear your voice. When you weren't there, I went a little wild."

Kate said nothing.

"Kate?"

"Yes?"

"I thought you'd gone off."

"No. I'm still here."

"I said I was sorry. Can we begin again?"

She almost smiled. It seemed everyone today wanted to begin again. "Where are you?" she asked.

"At some damned dinner party I had to attend. I sneaked off to call as soon as I could."

See, he cares. You weren't home, and he almost went to pieces. He needs you. Yes, but only when he needs you. What about when you need him?

"Tell me about your day, Mark. What went wrong?"

He began by telling her about Rosemary taking off for Escondido. "Can you beat that! She's really gone off the deep end!" He told her the rest of the day had gone steadily downhill from there. Any success he might have garnered earlier soured fast. He was at his wit's end. "I miss you, Kate. I need you."

"I miss you too, Mark."

"Fly up here for a couple of days. Or meet me in New York."

"I can't possibly get away right now, Mark. There's just too much going on."

He didn't push. "Well, then, I'll be down in two weeks. For Thanksgiving. I'll have to spend it with my family. . . ."

Of course. Every family man has to spend the holidays with his family. That's expected.

"But I'll manage some time off. For us."

"That will be nice, Mark," said Kate, an edge to her voice.

Mark picked up on it. "You don't sound terribly thrilled."

"Maybe I don't relish being sandwiched in among the festivities."

"Christ, Kate, what in hell *is* wrong with you?"

"Nothing, Mark. Only I had a trying day too. I'm tired, testy, and, suddenly, it all seems quite pointless."

"What's that supposed to mean?"

"Let's talk when we're together," suggested Kate. "Telephones are deadly for any real communication. And neither of us seems to be communicating tonight anyway."

"I called you because I needed to hear your voice. I needed you."

"For God's sake, Mark, you make me sound like a convenience store. I find that damned insulting." Very angry now, Kate slammed the phone down and disconnected it in case, as she knew he would, he tried to call back.

Mark tried the number again and couldn't get through. After several more tries, he gave up in exasperation.

Women. Who in hell could understand them? Rosemary, he understood all right. She was off-the-wall. But Kathleen. What in hell had been wrong with her tonight? It wasn't as though he ever had to twist her arm. Or force himself on her. Why the change in attitude all of a sudden?

And Kate? He'd never known Kate to hang up on him. Or be angry. She was his rock. In the midst of all the crises of these past five years, he could always depend on her to come through.

Kate wondered the same thing. In the five years she'd known Mark, she'd never hung up on him. Or shrieked at him. Or been anything but supportive, sympathetic, and sensitive to his needs.

What on earth was wrong with her anyway?

True to his word, Louis-Philippe had the Kirsten sketches ready for presentation in two days. He handed them to Consuela.

Consuela looked them over carefully, murmuring pleasurably over each one. "Nice. Oh, very nice, Louis. Mmm. Excellent. Ah, how unusual." There were five sketches in all.

When she had gone over each one, Consuela began again, more slowly this time, pausing to study the sketches, attending to every detail, lifting each board, turning it different ways, then placing it flat on her desk to study it once more.

Louis-Philippe sat facing Consuela's desk and waited patiently. He was satisfied. He knew the sketches were good. He also knew Consuela was pleased. He even knew which one she would select.

Finally, she looked up. "This one, Louis. Definitely."

He was right. She made the selection he knew she would make. "Yes," he agreed. "I thought that one too."

"It captures it all. Romance. Nostalgia. Femininity. You've managed it beautifully."

Louis nodded. "Only as you requested, Consuela."

She flashed him a smile and he was amply rewarded. It was worth everything—working late at night at his desk to complete the designs on schedule, postponing other activities, giving this project number-one priority—to witness Consuela's delight and pleasure.

Consuela clasped her hands together and leaned back in her chair. "Oh, yes, Louis. This is, indeed, the new Kirsten look I was searching for."

The look was romantic, nostalgic, and feminine. The Kirsten, sketched on the smooth throat of the headless creature Louis had drawn, was designed as a choker. Three rows of perfectly matched pearls alternated with marquise diamonds. The huge pear-shaped garnet-red Kirsten pendant, framed in a border of small round white diamonds, was connected to the pearl and diamond choker by three 4k diamond links.

The Kirsten, awesome even in the sketch, rested just above the creature's rosy cleavage.

As displayed in additional sketches, the Kirsten was detachable. It could be unclipped and worn as a brooch. Or it could be connected to a diamond link chain to form a longer pendant.

"Very functional," approved Consuela. "Besides being beautiful, Louis."

"I am happy you are pleased."

"Pleased! I am overwhelmed."

It was Louis's turn to smile.

Consuela picked up the mother-of-pearl–bordered calendar on her desk. "I have scheduled the press conference for the eighteenth—one month before the ball. Will that be agreeable?"

Louis nodded.

Consuela carefully put the sketches together and handed them back. "I want you present for the conference, Louis. The Kirsten is your creation. You must take the bows for it. I also want you present for the Christmas ball."

Louis objected. "You know I'm not comfortable at large affairs. I function better behind the scene."

"Nonsense," replied Consuela. "You will be lionized. That will be good for you. You are far too diffident. Besides," she teased, "all you have to do is stand there and let others do the work. And a few days in the Palm Beach sunshine will do wonders for you. You will see."

She scrutinized him. "You look tired, *caro.*"

She rose from her desk and walked around to him, studying him with concern. "And no wonder. Work, it is all you do. At least when Lenore was alive, she saw there was some balance in your life."

Louis-Philippe was uncomfortable. Although he missed Lenore, he enjoyed his solitude and managed quite nicely. The truth was, he felt himself better suited to the single life. However, he was more uncomfortable with Consuela's concern. He felt more at ease discussing the Kirsten or some other bit of impersonal business.

Consuela persisted. "It will do you good to get away," she repeated. And added, "I will not take no for an answer. A suite has even been engaged for you at The Breakers." She smiled. The dimple at the corner of her mouth flashed, and, once again, Louis capitulated to the velvet will. He was no match for her.

She continued to brood over him after he had gone. What was wrong with him? Ever since Lenore died, he had retreated further into that protective shell of his. Consuela understood the necessity of burying the dead once and for all and getting on with the business of living. *Dio mio,* she had adored Emilio. But life must go on. Only a fool dwelt in the past. And Louis was definitely no fool.

Had he loved Lenore so much? Strange, she had never received that impression.

Suddenly, Consuela realized that for all their years together, she knew very little about him. What were his interests apart from work? What type of woman did he find attractive?

What about his sex life? Consuela was an advocate of regularity in all life's basic functions. She attributed her own vigor to assiduously following her own advice. Sex was good. It toned up the skin, loosened the gait, lubricated the organs, brightened the eyes, did wonders for the complexion, added luster to the hair, and lifted the spirits. People who practiced often lived longer. That was a fact. Besides, it was pleasant.

Poor Louis did not look as though he had been engaging in any pleasantries.

Once more, Consuela ran through her mental file, searching for someone to match up with Louis. Why, he was young still, a few years older than she. He was handsome, quite charming, really. What a waste, thought Consuela, who abhorred waste of any sort. She must indeed take him in hand.

She thought of Derek. Impulsively, she picked up the phone on her private line and called home. Derek picked it up on the third ring.

"Carissimo," crooned Consuela throatily, thinking how marvelous it would be to drop everything for lunch at home with Derek. Until she realized that was quite impossible. She sighed. "I will

not be able to make it home for lunch. Louis has just brought in the Kirsten sketches. They are absolutely divine, but I have a million things to get ready."

"Oh?" replied Derek cautiously. He was in the middle of rehearsing his new scene. Consuela's home luncheons were wearing him out. Christ, how could she keep it up at her age? "That's okay, Connie," he said, with what, Consuela decided, was too much enthusiasm.

"Disappointment, *caro*. Always sigh with disappointment when the response requires it. Gratitude I never insist upon, but all that Actors Studio training should have taught you to recognize a cue when one is fed to you."

Derek bristled. "The American Academy, not Actors Studio." Then, relented. "Aw, hell, Connie, you caught me off guard. I was rehearsing a new scene and concentrating hard. You broke my concentration, that's all. Sure I'm sorry you're not coming home."

Consuela's rich contralto laugh rang out. "Better! Much better! That is much more pleasant to the ear than the bald truth. I will see you this evening," she said good-naturedly. *"Ciao, caro."*

Derek laughed too. *"Ciao,* Connie," and hung up. Whatever else she was, he decided, Consuela was an original. She let you know upfront when something bothered her. She was head and shoulders above most of the other women he knew. The bitchy actresses who stepped on your lines and hogged the best camera angles. The cloying females who smothered you with their dependency. The emancipated ones who got their kicks out of trying to emasculate you. Yes, Connie was an original.

Even if she did wear him out at times.

11

As soon as her conversation with Derek was finished, Consuela buzzed Suzy. "Has the folder from Kate Crowley come in?"

"It arrived this morning," she was told.

"Good. Bring it to me, please, Suzy. *Pronto!*"

Suzy Cranston, a tall, thin, chic twenty-four-year-old Barnard graduate with huge spectacles framing beautiful but nearsighted large brown eyes, was Consuela's right arm. She came into the office, folder in hand, and gave it to Consuela.

In exchange, Consuela gave Suzy a list of media names. "Contact these people and set up a 10:00 A.M. press conference for the eighteenth. Get the largest meeting room at the Plaza you can." The famous smile flashed wickedly. "We are about to launch the Kirsten, Suzy, my dear."

"Does that mean we can talk about it now?" asked Suzy, who had been in on the Kirsten coup from the beginning.

"Soon, *cara,* soon," promised Consuela. "Who ever said women cannot keep secrets? How little they know, eh?" She winked conspiratorially as Suzy exited.

Consuela opened the folder Kate had sent up and reviewed the ball arrangements. Kate had attended to all the details with her customary efficiency. Consuela was pleased.

She scanned the guest list. Anyone who was anyone of note in Palm Beach had been invited. Movie stars, socialites, TV celebrities, political figures, Palm Beach personalities. A happy mix.

She took pen and paper and listed the names of the people she saw as potential buyers for the Kirsten. Most of them were friends of hers. All of them were people she knew. She listed them according to interest level. As she determined it.

When the Kirsten was ready, she would make her first phone call. She rearranged a couple of names and numbers, then scanned the list once more.

1. *Mimzee Dawson.* Owner of one of the world's finest jewel collections. Acquisitive, avaricious, and compulsively competitive. Mimzee, Consuela knew, would do anything, *anything* short of murder, to acquire the Kirsten.

2. *Carl Schmittle.* Multimillionaire builder and financier. Now that he had almost completed the paving of America, Carl Schmittle was presented with another challenge—how to spend some of the millions acquired from the ungreening. Carl Schmittle adored his daughter Rosemary. He constantly showered her with *surprises.* Consuela had often helped him with his selections. What bigger, better *surprise* than the Kirsten?

3. *Sheik Abu Kahli.* The sheik, Consuela was aware, had recently plunked down 7 million bright crisp ones for a Palm Beach Urban-decorated cottage that ran from the ocean to the lake. He jetted around the world in his own custom-designed 747 that seated 154. Not too many years back, the sheik had huddled in a tent alongside other tribe members, eating couscous with his fingers. Now, even his silverware was gold. But the sheik still relied on experts to advise him. Consuela was one of the experts he sought out. Who better, then, to advise him about the Kirsten?

4. *Count Paolo Respighi.* Fellow countryman of Consuela's. A Roman, and a seasonal Palm Beacher. Renowned for his exceptional collection of paintings, antiques, and rare jewelry. Paolo was constantly scouting rare pieces. What was more rare than the Kirsten? Paolo would be intrigued.

5. *Bordon Granger.* Handsome, elegant, eligible owner and president of Cable TV-32. Self-made millionaire by thirty, billionaire by forty, rumored, at fifty, to be the next choice for governor of New York. Widowed in his mid-thirties, elusively single all these years, he was, Consuela had recently learned, engaged to Tami Hayes, Hollywood's newest rock star. What better wedding gift for a new bride than a nice little piece of jewelry? Bordon, Consuela knew, kept a house

in Wellington open for the season. Once they had been lovers. Today they were just good friends. It was time to call Bordon and congratulate him. And acquaint him with the fact that the Kirsten was available.

6. *Tony Owens.* Rotund, genial TV talk-show host who had joined the growing contingent of film and TV personalities buying homes in Palm Beach and Wellington—his competitor, Merv Griffin, the late John Lennon and Yoko Ono, along with longtime residents, the Douglas Fairbankses, Jr.

Tony was boastful of the material things he'd been able to provide his wife of thirty years with. Particularly after the early years of struggle. What more visible trophy of success could he offer her than the Kirsten? He would be delighted when she called.

Satisfied, she closed the folder. There was much to do in the days ahead. Feelers to put out, plans to set in motion, people to contact. That was the part she enjoyed most. The matching—the jewel to the prospective buyer. The process of arranging the marriage was a thrill like no other. It was a game of wits at which she excelled.

Oddly, there was, in Consuela, no desire for ownership. She could have owned the Kirsten. Indeed, once, for a few short hours, she had. Before she relinquished it to the House of Graet.

No, there was nothing in the world she was so attached to, she could not easily let go of. Emilio had been her attachment. With his loss came the lesson. Everything was on loan.

The secret to living successfully was to let go gracefully. Yet so few people understood that. They needed to accumulate, possess, clutch.

But the Kirsten, beautiful as it was, was, after all, just another stone. Larger than most, costlier than most, more rare than most.

It was also more durable. Without doubt, it would last longer than all the people who coveted it, laid end to end.

12

Ben Gately called Kate the day after their meeting to thank her. And ask her to lunch.

"There are a couple of points we didn't cover yesterday I'd like to check out with you." It was not quite true. He wanted to see her again. "We can lunch at Cafe Coconut," he suggested.

Kate was more receptive than she would have been ordinarily. She was still angry over her telephone conversation, or lack of one, with Mark. The thought of lunching with someone who was not only attractive but eager to be in her company was balm to her bruised ego.

She agreed. She'd meet him at Cafe Coconut at 12:30. Nancy, who had put the call through, stood in the doorway to Kate's office, nodding her head approvingly.

"It's only lunch, Nancy," cautioned Kate.

"Many a splendid future began with a simple lunch," observed Nancy sagely.

Kate thought she sounded like a Chinese fortune cookie.

Worth Avenue's Cafe Coconut, one of Palm Beach's newest restaurants, was becoming one of its most popular.

Ben decided Kate looked even more beautiful than she had the day before. Her dark hair was brushed back and twisted into a coil. The ruffled neckline of her starched white blouse framed her face, delineating its graceful planes—the high, carved cheekbones, the full firm mouth, the long, slightly slanting green eyes.

Kate saw that he was staring, was amused, at the total lack of self-consciousness with which he did it, and concluded it was an art. He made it seem more appealing than offensive.

They gave the waiter their order. Trout. A green salad with house dressing. A bottle of Riesling.

Under Ben's expert guidance, Kate relaxed her normal guard, enjoying his anecdotes on everything from the virtues of the California life-style to the intricacies of prime-time news gathering.

And under Kate's delicate querying, Ben talked more about himself than usual. Rule No. 1 was to let the ladies do the revealing. But here he was talking about plans and goals and his family.

He told Kate about Jocylen, the anthropologist; Joanna, the anesthesiologist; Jennifer, the congresswoman; Sabrina, the research chemist; Samantha, the Egyptologist; and Sybel, his mother, the publisher. Their influence had definitely left a mark, or rather, six marks, he admitted ruefully.

Kate allowed she wasn't surprised. "Not a nonachiever in the lot," she noted. But the vivid description of Ben's exuberant family caused her eyes to cloud momentarily and a small knot of envy to form inside her.

"Not a one," agreed Ben good-naturedly.

Kate added another observation. With a concentration of strong women around like that, most men would either be completely intimidated or thoroughly disenchanted. Which was he?

Ben smiled easily. He didn't know about most men. He, however, had nothing but the highest regard and admiration for the female sex. His intense look left no doubt Kate was included in this illustrious category.

She changed the subject. How was Ben adapting to the Florida life-style? She had discovered she needed to make some adjustments when she first came down from New England.

The maneuver was not lost on Ben. The changeover hadn't been difficult, he said. Particularly now that part of his California life-style had arrived to complete the transition. He told her about the *Nellie.*

"You live on a boat?" The announcement seemed to amuse her.

"Nothing like it," enthused Ben, extolling the advantages of houseboat living.

What a nice face he has, thought Kate. So open and attractive.

What is it about her? wondered Ben. One minute she was relaxed and receptive. The next she was all closed up. Like when he was telling her about his family. Her expression became guarded. The same look he'd noticed at the beach—startled, vulnerable. It made him want to reach out to her. That surprised him. It opened up a side of himself he was unfamiliar with.

The dessert cart was wheeled over. Kate selected Black Forest cake. Ben ordered banana cream. They ate with relish and dawdled over coffee.

Kate glanced at her watch. "I really must be getting back." She smiled. "Thank you so much for lunch, Mr. Gately."

"Ben," corrected Ben.

"Ben," obliged Kate.

He insisted on walking her back to the House of Graet. The way could be hazardous to her health. Wild animals roving the streets. Dangerous strangers on the prowl.

Kate laughed and allowed him to help her cross the sun-dappled "cleanest street in the world" and lead her safely to the House of Graet doors.

Ben wanted to see her again. The newsman in him needed to tidy up the enigma of Kate Crowley. The man in him was intrigued by the woman.

He'd spent most of lunch talking about himself, he explained. It was only fair to allow Kate equal time. In his business, that was a requisite. "What about Saturday? Dinner at seven?"

Kate hesitated.

Ben pushed gently. "Equal time? In the interest of fairness?"

Kate capitulated gracefully. "In the interest of fairness," she agreed. She reached for a card, scribbled her home address and phone number on it, and handed it to Ben. "Saturday at seven is fine," she told him.

She smiled, turned, and pushed through the double oak doors before the doorman could even open them.

She was amused at Ben's insistence, flattered by his interest, yet wary of involvement. The last thing she needed in her life was another complication. Whatever had possessed her to accept a dinner invitation?

Still, Ben Gately hardly seemed threatening. He was open and uncomplicated. Unlike Mark, whose deviousness and ploys were so familiar. Undoubtedly, Mark would call tonight in an attempt to mend last night's misunderstanding. He was expert at that.

Kate decided to be elsewhere.

Somewhat later in the day, she realized Ben had never mentioned the points he said he wanted to cover over lunch.

In fact, they'd never discussed business at all.

❧ 13 ❧

Kate Crowley first met Mark Hunter at one of Consuela's Sunday night suppers. Reenie Boyd, who wrote and syndicated "Reenie's Roster," one of the two top gossip columns in the country, called them "Consuela's Sing-for-Your-Supper suppers—the kind of party where everyone wants to pitch in and help, even though they don't have to, the *ambience* is that stimulating."

"Everybody was there, darling," she'd write the following day in her column. "That is, all the *everybodies* who *count,*" and Reenie would proceed to list celebrities, what they wore, who they came with, who they left with, and what they said or did, of note.

The Atlanta-born society girl–turned columnist and publisher was a household name, avidly followed by millions of readers who couldn't start their day without knowing how the rich struggled with sin in the midst of splendor.

Kate was due in New York for a week-long seminar to begin on Monday. Before she left Palm Beach, Consuela called Kate at home and extended the invitation.

"Come early, *cara*. Sixish, and plan to have supper at my place. It is open house, quite casual, only a few close friends who drop in from time to time, so come as you are."

"Not as I am, Consuela," protested Kate. "I'm in bed with a mustard plaster on my chest, in my faded old jammies."

Consuela sympathized. "Poor *bambina*. Take good care of yourself. I will see you on Sunday. Just a few old friends will be there. I am certain you will enjoy them."

The few old friends who just dropped in turned out to be a gaggle of people crowding the large airy rooms of Consuela's

Fifth Avenue penthouse. People from the various worlds she inhabited with consummate style. Politics, the theater, films, society, publishing. While Kate sipped a glass of champagne and chatted with a handsome House of Graet vice-president, she looked around.

Besides people she didn't recognize, there were those she did. Liza Minnelli, in a bright red silk Halston tunic over shiny black trousers, chatted earnestly with Gwen Verdon. Paul Newman and Joanne Woodward held a group enthralled as they enthused over their latest project. John Lindsay, former mayor of New York, was deep in conversation with Senator Mark Hunter.

Gloria Vanderbilt listened attentively to Leonard Bernstein, Lena Horne chatted with Bess Myerson. A publisher Kate had met at another party recognized her and waved. Kate waved back.

She watched Consuela gesticulate dramatically and enthusiastically with a small, pretty woman in a daringly revealing red satin dress. Nothing casual there, noted Kate.

"Who's that?" she asked. "She's very pretty."

"Reenie Boyd," Arthur Hale, the waspish House of Graet vice-president told her. "Her syndicated column seduces the gullible with half-truths and nontruths." Arthur, who kept his homosexuality as discreet as possible, had borne the brunt of a few of Reenie's printed barbs. "Don't let those disarming good looks fool you. She's got a typewriter in place of a heart and a cassette instead of a conscience. The only thing that turns her on is churning people up."

Kate grimaced. "Sounds awful."

Arthur Hale shrugged. "When you've got friends in high places, you can get away with just about anything, it seems." He laughed. "The lady's mean, I tell you. Real mean."

Kate studied the object of discussion objectively. Pale platinum hair cut short framing a small heart-shaped face. Large guileless blue eyes. A wide generous smile. She appeared anything but mean.

"She looks harmless."

"That's the worst kind," warned Arthur.

Consuela approached Mayor Lindsay and Senator Hunter and joined them in conversation for a while. The group expanded.

Kate observed Consuela take the senator's arm, murmur apologies, and drift off with him, arm-in-arm.

The next thing Kate knew they stood before her. "I need you for a moment, Arthur," Consuela said to the House of Graet vice-president. Turning to Kate, she explained, "I am not leaving you adrift, *carissima.*" She introduced her to Mark. And warned her, "You must watch him, Kate. He is a notorious charmer. And quite wicked, I am afraid." Her smile mitigated the warning.

Mark Hunter, decided Kate, was far more handsome than even his photographs or TV appearances allowed. From the charismatic smile to the unstudied casual grace, his charm was legendary. If he'd been Irish, they'd have said the leprechauns smiled at his birth, so easily did things come his way.

He was gifted with the astonishing good looks of a Hollywood movie star. If not the leprechauns, then surely the gods had bestowed Mark Hunter with more than the share allotted most men.

He wore faded denims, a white Irish fisherman's knit turtleneck sweater, and scuffed loafers. Consuela's Sunday night suppers were, after all, informal. "Come as you are" was the open invitation. Not everyone chose to. Mark Hunter did.

He might as well have worn the armor of Lancelot, so struck was Kate. He loomed over the room, dominating it with his presence.

Physically, he loomed over Kate, tall as she was. She had to raise her eyes to meet his. She looked up at him, noted the thick dark hair, the tanned quizzically smiling face, the clear gray eyes coolly appraising her.

The magic began for Kate even before he spoke.

"I instructed Consuela to direct me to the most beautiful woman in the room, and without hesitation, she brought me here. I see, as usual, she was right." The charismatic smile embraced her.

Kate felt her cheeks flush and experienced the familiar irritation at having feelings that so easily betrayed her.

Mark found it charmingly refreshing. He studied her intently. "I hope you're not going to be frightened off by Consuela's unfair warning?"

"A bit more guarded, perhaps," said Kate, recovering her wits.

Mark laughed. "An acceptable response. And understandable. A little wariness is always good. Especially in the young."

He was, Kate knew, teasing her. But before she could think of a clever response, Mark took her arm, led her expertly through a throng of chattering people, out onto the terrace overlooking the sweep of Central Park.

He asked if she was chilly. She wasn't, she told him. The September evening was pleasant.

He seated her on a white duck-covered wrought-iron settee, took her glass, and said, "I'll freshen these. Now, be a good girl and don't move until I come back. And don't talk to any other strangers. No matter how innocent they look."

Kate waited, somewhat overwhelmed. She longed to behave the way she looked—cool, poised, in complete control. Instead, she felt awkward.

She wore a loose V-neck silk tunic in emerald-green, the color of her eyes, over tailored ivory lightweight wool slacks. Her dark hair was parted in the center, falling gracefully to her shoulders. She knew she looked good. Always before, that knowledge made her confident. Now, nothing seemed to help. She fidgeted like a child at a party.

Naturally, she knew of Mark Hunter. From the papers, TV, Palm Beach gossip. Marjorie Hunter, Mark's mother, was a Palm Beach institution, involved in numerous charitable endeavors. And a favored House of Graet client. Rosemary Hunter, the senator's wife, was a popular Palm Beach hostess. Again, a favored House of Graet client.

The senator himself was often seen, in season, cycling around town, driving his red Ferrari, or striding down the avenue. Photographs of the senator and his family graced the pages of the *Palm Beach Daily News*, the *Shiny Sheet*, so called because of the paper it was printed on.

Yet Kate had not met him before. Or experienced anything like the impact he had on her.

Mark returned, handed Kate a freshened drink, and sat beside her. He leaned back, stretched out his long legs, turned to her, and gave her his undivided attention.

"All right, Kate Crowley, now tell me all about yourself," he instructed.

"Well," stumbled Kate, "I . . ."

Mark interrupted. "No, don't tell me. Let me guess. You're an actress."

Kate shook her head. "No."

He tried again. "A model?" He put his long lean hands under her chin and expertly moved her face about as he examined it. "You're certainly pretty enough to be one. Come to think of it, I do recall seeing that face in one of the magazines."

"No," Kate told him, smiling at last.

"A rich heiress? Escaped for a night away from a doting but demanding father?"

Kate shook her head again.

"A long-lost illegitimate daughter of Consuela's?"

Kate laughed. "Hardly!"

Mark spread his hands in defeat. "Okay, tell me, then. Tell me everything there is to know." He lifted one of Kate's slender hands and held it. He waited, as though nothing else mattered but the story Kate would unfold.

Somehow, even at the beginning, Kate sensed it would never do to burden Mark with the details of any past pain she had suffered. Of course, in the beginning, she never would have. But that insight helped set the tone of their relationship. *Keep it light, bright, and pleasant,* Kate told herself.

"See," she said when she had finished recounting her tale of a very ordinary childhood in Massachusetts, her schooling, and her job with the House of Graet. "Nothing world-shattering. No big waves. Only small ones."

"Why, you've just begun, girl," observed Mark lightly. "Your future's in front of you."

"And yours?" asked Kate.

"Mine too," said Mark. "That's what it's all about. Grand and glorious beginnings. After the beginning, it's all downhill." He took a long swallow of his Scotch.

Kate looked at him. She had yet to learn when he was serious.

Mark drained his glass and shifted restlessly. "You like soft-shell crabs?" he asked Kate.

Kate said she did.

"I know a spot where you can get the best soft-shell crabs in the country. Delaware. Right on the river." His tone was casual. "Care to join me?"

Kate smiled, certain he was joking.

"I'm serious," Mark told her. He leaned toward her. "Look, I happen to know what Consuela's serving tonight. Fettuccine Alfredo. She makes the damned noodles herself, from scratch. I don't know about you, but that stuff sits like lead in the pit of my stomach. I was going to sneak off early with an excuse." He smiled lazily at Kate. "You've given me a better one."

Kate said she didn't know. "Delaware?" That certainly wasn't around the corner.

"It's not that far," Mark said easily. He held both her hands in his and Kate felt wonderfully imprisoned. "I flew in from Washington this afternoon," he explained. "My plane's at Teterboro Airport. Ten minutes to get there and in no time at all you'll be enjoying the best soft-shell crabs you've ever tasted. Besides, I promise to get you back in one piece before bedtime."

"But Consuela . . ." began Kate.

"There's a roomful of people in there," Mark assured her. "You'll never be missed, Kate. I'll even give you a preview of the rest of the evening. *After* the fettuccine. And the cannoli. Liza and Lena will do a duet. Leonard will play the piano, and Gwen will do a soft-shoe." He smiled at her, the charismatic smile that won votes and maddened maidens. "Say yes, Kate. It's all part of your future, remember? But in order to experience it, you've got to begin."

Kate looked at him. No warning bells went off in her head. No label warned, This relationship might be dangerous to your health. No yellow caution light flashed before her eyes.

For all practical purposes, common sense and sanity were wrapped up tight in a package that read DO NOT OPEN AT THIS TIME.

"Yes," said Kate. "I'd like that."

Mark grinned approval. "That's my girl. I knew it the minute I saw you."

He stood up. "I'll go in and give Consuela my supper regrets. You wait fifteen minutes, and then follow me. I'll meet you downstairs."

He smiled and smoothly explained the need for caution.

"Reenie Boyd's in there. The last thing we want to do is give her an item for tomorrow's column." He bent gracefully, lifted Kate's chin, and kissed her lightly on the lips. "It's a red Ferrari. Out front. I'll be waiting." Then he was gone.

On the ride to the airport, Kate decided Mark had been right. Consuela was only sorry Kate would miss the fettuccine and the cannoli. "I made them myself, *cara*. Sunday is cook's night off."

However, Consuela insisted she understood. The residue of Kate's cold. That always leaves the stomach queasy. "Get a good night's sleep," she advised Kate at the door. "I will see you in the morning." As an afterthought, she asked, "I hope Mark did not ignore you completely?"

"Not at all," Kate assured her. "He was fine. Perfectly charming." She felt like a hypocrite.

But she also felt happy. In ten minutes, they were at Teterboro. In one hour, they were in Delaware. As the red and white twin-engine Cessna glided smoothly down the runway, Kate was reminded of adventures with her father. Impetuous flights of fancy Nicholas Crowley conjured up, then transformed into realities for an adoring, wide-eyed daughter. Being with Mark was like that. Not dull. Or ordinary.

A red Maserati was waiting when they landed. "Do you have cars waiting at all the airports?" Kate wanted to know.

"Only the ones I frequent," grinned Mark, taking her hand.

Kate was curious. "Are they all red?"

"It's my favorite color," he told her.

The restaurant with the best soft-shell crabs in the country was a rambling white clapboard country inn that overlooked the Delaware River.

The crabs were all that Mark promised, although Kate barely tasted them. Mark's voice, deep, resonant, with its definitive eastern accent, mesmerized her. As he recounted tale after amusing tale, Kate was completely hypnotized and wished only that age-old wish of wishers at special moments. That time itself could be freeze-framed into a now that never ended.

Over a glass of wine, Mark said, "I'm really enjoying this, Kate. What about you?"

Kate nodded. "Oh, yes. Very much." How could she tell him

she hadn't felt so free since those mythic times her father had transformed her world into an enchanted place? She hadn't realized until this moment how much she missed those times.

Everything was perfect. The inn was charming. The view from their table of the darkened Delaware, lighted only by the shimmer of reflected lights, was magical. Her escort was indescribably exciting.

Two hours ago, she'd been in New York. Now she was here. A genie named Mark Hunter had performed magic with a whisk of his wand.

Mark toyed with his onyx-lacquered lighter, lifted a matching cigarette case, opened it, and offered Kate a cigarette. She shook her head.

He lighted one for himself, inhaled, exhaled slowly, and looked at Kate. He smiled obliquely. "I could tell you my wife doesn't understand me, but I won't insult your intelligence. The truth is, she understands me too well."

Kate sat very still.

"There's a room upstairs, Kate. I'd like you to stay. I'd like that very much."

Suddenly, all the moments in her life seemed to converge into this one. She seemed left with no other choice. As she studied the handsome face before her, she understood that, somehow, her destiny was tied to his, and that whatever he asked of her, she would do.

"I'd like that too," she told him quietly.

Mark relaxed. "For a minute, you had me worried." He lifted her hand, turned it over, and brushed the palm gently with his lips. "I promise to get you up at the crack of dawn and fly you back." His smile, filled with promises, caressed her.

Like all beginnings, it was grand and glorious.

14

It could accurately be said of Reenie Boyd she did nothing without an ulterior motive. And, as her first husband once announced to a dinner table of their guests, "Reenie is no shy, shrinking southern belle. She's got a steel gut and a brass asshole. That's a combination that will do anyone in. Look at me!"

He then genially raised his fifteenth Scotch of the evening in tribute to Reenie's attributes. She chose to ignore him. It wasn't the first time he was insulting. Or drunk. What did he know about survival anyway? Of what it took to get where you wanted and needed to be? Rick Howland might have achieved some degree of power, but he was handicapped. Look at the way he held on to that glass of his. Reenie never held on to anything. Except herself.

Her second husband, Carter Flemming, the New York socialite, summed up his impression with more sober astuteness than he customarily displayed. "There's much more to Reenie than meets the eye. And for a lady who looks so pliable, she's got a will of steel. I expect that whatever Reenie wants, she'll get."

People magazine once did a profile on her titled "What Makes Reenie Run?"

"She looks like a protected, pampered southern belle—soft, feminine, malleable, conjuring up images of magnolia, wisteria, honeysuckle, and crinoline skirts swishing around the Old Plantation.

"She is anything but. She is determined, calculating, and ruthless. But then she's come far—from a genteel but impoverished southern background to co-publisher of *Moments Magazine* and syndicator of 'Reenie's Roster,' a column that offers her the opportunity to dip her pen in acid instead of ink. You don't come *that* far with sugar and spice, no matter how nice you are. Reenie Boyd would be the first to tell you, nice is unnecessary. In fact, *nice* gets in the way."

Reading only that far, Reenie shrieked across the breakfast table at her third husband, Harrison Boyd. "Sue the bastards!"

Harrison Boyd smiled benevolently back. "So far, my dear, they haven't maligned you. They've just told the truth."

Reenie looked over at him and suddenly laughed. "Not the whole truth, sugah. Just the bare outline."

The truth was, there were several factors responsible for the warping of Reenie's personality and a vocabulary of psychiatric jargon to explain it. Never impressed with jargon, Reenie sought no causes. Only results mattered. She concentrated on those.

What *did* make Reenie run? The untold story was a tabloid writer's delight. It remained untold. Reenie was closemouthed about her past.

But the past was what molded her.

Once an associate, observing her jockey her way up the ladder to success, asked, "Hey, Reenie, what's that bug up your ass that propels you forward?"

Reenie smiled, unoffended. "That's the bug called motivation, darlin'. Once you have that, there's no stoppin' you."

Motivation was what moved her. The forces that provided the motivation were the stuff of Greek dramas, child psychiatrists' case histories, and Tennessee Williams plays. Indeed, when Reenie saw her first Tennessee Williams play, a shiver of recognition shot through her. "Good Gawd," she gasped. "That's us. The Simmonses of Atlanta. Decadent and doomed."

Except for Reenie. She determined early not to be one of the doomed. She was a survivor. In a world filled with victims.

Beginning with her mother.

Daisy Morrow Simmons had her scenario written early for her. She was the soft and sheltered flower of young southern womanhood Reenie was often mistaken for. With Daisy, there was no error. The starch in her carefully laundered blouses was the only starch about her.

When she married Malcolm Simmons III, scion of an old aristocratic Atlanta family, she reasonably expected to continue in the affluent style of living she was accustomed to.

Malcolm had everything. He was handsome and rich, with a recent license to practice medicine. Not that he needed to practice anything. He was rich enough without it.

But Malcolm Simmons amended the old axiom, Shirtsleeves to shirtsleeves in three generations. He managed it in four. Whereas great-great-grandfather Simmons made the family fortune, great-grandfather Simmons increased it, and Malcolm's father nurtured it, Malcolm squandered it. Until they were all dependent upon the largesse of relatives to survive.

Daisy Simmons handled the situation by becoming dependent upon the morphine her husband liberally dispensed.

Wife beating was one way Malcolm Simmons dealt with his discontent. Alcoholism was another. Incest, a third.

From the time she was seven, Reenie's room was the scene of her father's drunken visitations. Why her mother never protested these violations troubled Reenie. She decided it was uninterest.

Only Delia, brought into the house when Reenie was an infant, provided care and a degree of normalcy during an abused childhood.

From her early years, Reenie understood she was at war. She was on one side. Everyone else was on the other side. She even understood the rules.

When you were small, you were dependent. When you were dependent, you had no control over what was done to you. The motivating goals of Reenie's later years were independence and full control of everything around her.

She learned early to feign, flatter, lie, cheat, manipulate, maneuver, all to outwit her adversaries.

It was in her thirteenth year that Reenie finally understood that the world was divided into victims and victors. Her mother was a victim of drugs. Her father, a victim of his appetites. Reenie was a victim of theirs. She decided to change roles.

The next time her father stumbled into her room and fell, grunting and groaning, onto her bed, Reenie was prepared. She reached for the long-bladed steel kitchen knife she had placed beneath her pillow. Carefully, deliberately, and with extraordinary strength, she thrust it halfway to the hilt into her father's shoulder. Startled, Malcolm Simmons screeched, lurched backward, and fumbled desperately at the knife protruding from his shoulder. While blood spurted from the wound, Reenie wiggled out from under him and calmly informed him, "The next time you come near me, I'll drive that knife all the way to the hilt into your rotten heart."

How her father explained away the wound was not her concern. The fact that he followed her explicit instructions was enough.

Shortly after what was euphemistically referred to in the family as "Malcolm's unfortunate accident," one of the still-rich Simmons aunts paid for Reenie's education at an eastern boarding school. Money was generously provided for holidays and vacations. Away from home. Scandal was to be averted at all costs.

Reenie didn't much care. She had no desire to go back. The only person she kept up with was Delia, sporadically sending her scrawled pages of information and promising to send for her when she, Reenie, got rich.

Delia responded with cards, letting Hallmark do the expressing for her. Thanks to her rural Georgia education, she lacked facility in writing.

At school, Reenie applied herself diligently and invariably finished in the top of her class. She made friends selectively, choosing only those who could be of benefit to her. But even they wondered about the real Reenie—the person behind the carefully cultivated facade of southern charm.

What made Reenie tick? they wondered.

Reenie wasn't concerned with speculations. She had her sights set on a future she orchestrated with a choreographer's passion for detail. Schooling. Connections. Marriage. A career. She would be rich and powerful. No one would be able to touch her.

Following prep school, Reenie went to the Columbia School of Journalism on scholarship. The written word, she decided, had power. Power was the most important part of the plan.

Her mother died during Reenie's first-year final examinations. Reenie ignored the funeral and took her finals. When word came her father had accidentally shot himself while cleaning his rifle, Reenie, preparing for graduation, opted for graduation exercises over funeral services, accepting both her diploma and her new status as orphan with equal insouciance.

Having graduated summa cum laude, it was not unexpected she would have no trouble landing her first newspaper job. It was expected she would rise on merit alone. Reenie took no chances.

Rick Howland was editor of the *New York Globe,* a hard-bitten, cynical newspaper man who had little to show for twenty years of labor except an ulcer due to years of frustration, a wife in Mamaroneck who bored him, two teenage children he couldn't relate to, and an aching sense of self-betrayal for never having disciplined himself enough to finish the Great American Novel he'd begun fifteen years before.

Comfort came from the bottle, specifically a fifth of Haig & Haig kept handy in his desk drawer. There was always a succession of sweet young things with literary aspirations who were intrigued by Rick's brooding John Wayne introspection and Charles Boyer angst. Besides, Rick Howland decided what assignments female reporters got.

Reenie drew Rick's attention almost at once. The platinum-haired puff from Atlanta with the big blue eyes and big round tits promised to provide new amelioration from his midlife crisis.

He invited her out for drinks after work and, surprisingly, found himself telling her things he'd never even told his wife— dreams long forgotten, aspirations laid to rest. Reenie listened, nodded, sympathized, and, when appropriate, interjected her thoughts. Rick discovered that, in addition to her tits, she had a brain.

But the first time he bedded her, he was undone. Never in all his years of screwing broads had he had such a lay. Reenie had talents far beyond her ability to string words together. She had fingers that danced, lollipop lips that sucked, and a body that gave him a hard-on just to look at her.

And she was sexually insatiable. More than that, she made him feel the same way. Never before had he performed so well or so long. Even with the booze.

"The best, darlin'," breathed Reenie in admiration. "You are the best. Evah."

Gone was the inadequacy from the unwritten novel. Up was his self-esteem, rising with the organ that drew Reenie's lavish praise.

Rick Howland divorced his Mamaroneck wife and married Reenie Simmons. She didn't want a big honeymoon, she told him. They could stay in the city, fix up their new apartment. "Just bein' with you is honeymoon enough, lovah," murmured Reenie. Rick expanded. He had confidence enough to write a dozen novels.

There *was* one little thing he *could* do for her, Reenie offhandedly informed Rick, after a more improvisational and fulfilling evening of lovemaking than he had ever before encountered.

"What's that, doll?" asked a satiated Rick, anxious to do anything.

"The Gretchen Grant column, darlin'. I'd love to do that."

Gretchen Grant did the social and celebrity news of the city in her daily column, "Social Jinks." Reenie had decided it would provide a good power base to begin.

Rick laughed easily. "Christ, Reenie, she's been doing that goddamned thing for years. You couldn't pry her loose from it with a crowbar. I couldn't. Wouldn't even want to."

"But, sugah," insisted Reenie, "she's a mess. Why, everybody knows that. All that booze and Valium has taken its toll. I bet she can't even see the typewriter keys these days."

"Don't kid yourself, sweetheart," said Rick. "Gretchen's a pro. Blind drunk, she can make those keys sing."

"Besides," observed Reenie as though she hadn't heard, "she's old, darlin'."

"Old? Jesus, Reenie, she's only forty-three! Three years younger than I am!"

"You? Poo! You're young, darlin'. You're my young stallion. But Gretchen Grant is over the hill. She looks and acts more like sixty than forty-three. Don't you ever compare yourself to her again. You heah?"

Rick tried another tack. "Why do you want that old column anyway? That's shit work. Not newspaper writing."

"I want it," replied Reenie stubbornly.

The sexual euphoria was wearing off. "Well, you can't have it," Rick told her. Softening his tone, he added, "Besides, Gretchen's on the wagon. Has been for six months."

"Wagons break down," noted Reenie. Suddenly, she smiled at him meltingly and any irritation he'd felt was dissipated. "You just asked me what I wanted, sugah, and I told you," she pointed out.

114

Had he? Funny, he couldn't remember having asked her. He thought she'd brought up the subject. Still, he wanted to keep her happy.

He had an inspiration. "Reenie, how's about taking the job of Gretchen's assistant? The one she has is due to leave. She suggested some young guy on her staff but I think I can change her mind. You could step right in in about a week."

Reenie's eyes widened with anticipation. "If you think so, darlin'. Whatever you say."

Gretchen Grant wasn't thrilled. She had a young twenty-eight-year-old male staff member she'd planned to insert into the vacant spot. Also into her bed. God knew she needed some comfort in her aging years. And this one was just what the doctor ordered when he told her to stay occupied and keep her spirits up.

Rick's smile was even. "Give it a try, Gretch," he cajoled. "If you don't, you'll wreck my sex life."

"What about mine?" countered Gretchen.

He grinned. "I have full confidence in you. You'll improvise."

Surprisingly, Gretchen hit it off at once with Reenie. As with Rick, Reenie listened to and sympathized with Gretchen's recounting of endless masculine betrayals, followed by endless depressions, suicide attempts, pointless sessions with psychiatrists, and enervating bouts with booze and pills.

Only work provided satisfaction, Gretchen railed. Everything else was shit.

Reenie understood, she told Gretchen. It was rough going for a sensitive woman in an insensitive world. Scrap and struggle. Pretend to be one thing. Fight to be another. Good Gawd, no wonder women needed some help along the way, a little drink to ease the pain, a small pill to counter the stress. Lordie, who on earth could make it all the way without anything?

She was trying to do just that, noted Gretchen proudly. Six months already. Although, to be completely honest, she had to admit she was just about ready to jump right out of her goose-fleshed skin. But she heard it got better as you went along.

Reenie obtained the Valium by sleeping with an intern she'd met when he was a premed student at Columbia. The booze required only a cash outlay at the local liquor store.

She liberally provided Gretchen with both chemical aids and assurances that requesting a little help along the way was hardly a sign of weakness. Lordie, no! It was practical to accept help where you found it. Sensible.

When Gretchen Grant was discovered dead on her couch from an overdose of Valium and alcohol, Reenie was as distraught as everyone else. She had learned so much from Gretchen, she told Rick, in just the six months she'd worked with her. God only knew what toppled her off the wagon. What could have possessed her? Reenie hated to say it, but once an alcoholic or a pill head . . . at least, that had been her experience. . . .

Reenie changed the name of "Social Jinks" to "Reenie's Roster" and dedicated her first column to the memory of Gretchen Grant, who was beloved by her loyal readers and an inspiration to Reenie.

Almost at once, the tone of the column changed. Where Gretchen had been arch, Reenie was bitchy. She concentrated more on celebrity news—big names in the theater, movies, TV—while still covering the international social scene. Gradually, little bits of gossip that titillated, teased, and tantalized in their suggestions of who was doing what to whom, were introduced.

"Careful," warned a wary Rick Howland. "We don't want to bring on lawsuits."

"Shoot," dismissed Reenie. "All's we're doin', sugah, is raisin' circulation. Everybody enjoys readin' about someone else's nastiness. Don't you know that?"

It was true. "Reenie's Roster" not only raised circulation but developed a following much larger than Gretchen's. Letters poured in bagfuls.

It was Reenie's suggestion to syndicate. When Rick said he would have his salesmen present the package to 105 editors nationwide, Reenie was outraged. Why, she, personally, would go to meet them. Imagine! Trusting to salesmen the task of explaining what "Reenie's Roster" was all about. Lordie! There was only one person to do that properly. Reenie herself.

She visited each of the 105 newspapers, striking up personal relationships with 105 editors countrywide. When she returned to New York, she had in her possession 105 contracts to carry

"Reenie's Roster." Rick was impressed with his wife's powers of persuasion.

It wasn't until two years later that Rick Howland, attending the newspaper editors' convention in Boca Raton, learned just how persuasive Reenie's powers were. They included, he discovered, bedding and bestowing the full repertoire of her sexual skills upon 105 grateful editors.

It was over drinks in the bar at the Boca Raton Hotel that Rick learned the truth. An editor from the Midwest raised an eyebrow when he heard Rick was editor of the *New York Globe*.

"Christ, laddie, you must know Reenie Simmons."

"As a matter of fact . . ." began Rick, anxious to proudly establish his connection.

Instead, he got a knowing nudge in the ribs. "What a piece of ass! I tell you, friend, when she went down on me I would have signed my name to anything she shoved in front of me. Just so long as she didn't stop. Seems a lot of other guys felt the same way."

The editor from the Midwest wore dark glasses for the rest of the three-day convention to hide his shiner. "Christ," he wailed to a friend, "how was I supposed to know he was her husband?"

Rick said nothing to Reenie. Instead, he nursed his fury for weeks by drinking more heavily than usual. His self-esteem plunged at the idea of being cuckolded on such a grand scale. The adulteries hit him where it hurt. Rick couldn't get it up for even the sweet young things in the office. The more he thought about Reenie, the more he wanted to kill her.

Finally, at a large dinner party they were hosting, Rick rose unsteadily to his feet and drunkenly offered a toast to his wife. Twenty smiling faces focused on Reenie.

"To my wife," toasted Rick. "Miss Twinkle-Cunt. The lady with the golden box. It winks, it blinks, it dazzles. It screws everything in sight and converts it to gold. A regular Fort Knox muff. Isn't that right, sugah?" asked Rick, drunkenly drawling out the *sugah*.

Reenie paled visibly. But the steel of generations of genteel southern aristocracy fortified her. She rose, walked carefully down the length of the table, glass in hand, to the sounds of ice tinkling and skirt rustling. When she reached Rick's side, she looked at him scornfully and threw the contents of the glass in his face.

"You lie down with pigs, you get covered with shit. Mah daddy taught me that." Without another word, she left the party and went to bed.

Fortunately, there was no one there who dared to immortalize the scene in print. The story, however, made the rounds until everyone who was anyone in town knew Rick Howland had been cuckolded on a scale massive enough to impress the most jaded.

The marriage ended, but not fast enough for Reenie. Rick Howland, never recovering from the blow to his self-esteem, bathed his battered ego in drink until he lost his job. Reenie later heard his ex-wife found him in Skid Row, took him back to Mamaroneck, and nursed him back to some semblance of health. He never finished the long-abandoned novel.

Reenie's second marriage was briefer. She wed a New York socialite, Carter Flemming, who also had a predilection for the bottle, and who, blind drunk one rainy night, drove his car off the Triboro Bridge, mistaking it for the Forty-ninth Street exit on the West Side Highway. His bride of six months was left a bereft rich widow.

But it was in her third marriage that Reenie hit pay dirt. She married Harrison Boyd II, publisher of the *New York Globe,* and owner of six television stations across the country and an about-to-be-born magazine called *Moments. Moments* preceded *People.* It promised to capture in print those memorable moments in the lives of the great and the about-to-be great.

Harrison's wedding gift to his bride, along with some expensive jewelry and property, was to list her on the magazine masthead as co-publisher. He also allowed her to retain her increasingly popular column, "Reenie's Roster." She certainly didn't need it, but she wanted it. Harrison indulged her.

Harrison Boyd was all the things Reenie's first two husbands weren't. He was a nonsmoking, Bible-reading, born-again Christian teetotaler. He was also a hardheaded realist with few illusions. "Jesus knew what was in man," he'd scowl to anyone who tried to con him. "Not much," he'd add. And although he enjoyed a frolic in the sack, he was an old-fashioned man. He insisted his wife confine her sexual expertise to one man—him.

"I know all about that 'grand tour' of yours, Reenie. From now on, no more traveling."

His meaning was unmistakable. Reenie nodded wisely. She was so busy helping get *Moments* launched, plus continuing her column, there wasn't *time* to travel. Despite his sixty-two years, Harrison kept her exhausted in the sack. Who had energy left?

But Harrison's years caught up with him. At sixty-six, in the midst of a session of nocturnal lovemaking, at the peak of climax, a startled look crossed his face, his eyes bulged, he gasped, grabbed at his chest, and fell, all 204 rock-hard pounds of him, flat across Reenie's firm 112-pound body.

For one wild moment, Reenie feared Harrison was taking her with him. Instead, she found herself a widow again. Albeit, a richer one. And only twenty-nine.

In the ten years since Harrison Boyd's death, Reenie Simmons Howland Flemming Boyd had become a force to be reckoned with. One of the world's most powerful women, there was nothing she wanted she didn't get.

What she wanted most was Senator Mark Hunter. She'd wanted him since she first laid eyes on him. She was not a patient woman. And she'd waited long enough.

Her designs, not unknown to Mark, were not honorable. The bastard knew exactly what she wanted from him.

Finding themselves paired at a party recently, Mark, taking in the vision of Reenie sensuously shapely and seductive in ivory satin, complimented her. "You look fantastic, Reenie."

Reenie ignored the praise. She held Mark's eyes with hers and smiled coolly at him. "I do it better, you know."

Mark looked momentarily perplexed. "Do what better?"

Reenie's smile was bland. "Whatever it is you like, sugah."

He smiled back. "I'll keep that piece of information filed where it's handy."

"Don't file it, darlin'. Use it." She handed him one of her personal cards. "Tuesday. Eight o'clock. And bring your jammies, sugah. You'll be too exhausted to leave afterward."

Mark's eyes appraised her carefully, measuring the explicit promise. He'd heard all about Reenie's sexual prowess. Why not find out firsthand? "I don't wear jammies, Reenie."

She patted his hand. "Good. We'd only have to take them off anyway."

She had waited until midnight, still not believing the bastard had actually stood her up. Not a phone call. Not an explanation. Not an apology. But before the anger and the humiliation came the disbelief. How dare he! How dare he think he could do this to her and get away with it! Before she was finished with him and his precious reputation, he wouldn't be fit to run for county dog-catcher. He could kiss his entire career good-bye. Because Reenie Boyd would rustle up skeletons in his closet Mark Hunter didn't even know were there.

15

Derek Tracey, for all his nervous intensity, was a creature of habit. Extremely methodical. His sweaters lay in lined plastic boxes, labeled according to color and fabric. His shirts were also labeled and individually boxed.

Derek had taken great pains to explain to Consuela's maid precisely how he wanted his socks done.

Each sock had to be turned inside out, with the toe tucked in. Then the sock was to be ironed. It rolled on easier that way.

His suits, sports jackets, and trousers were in separate garment bags. His shoes were in labeled boxes with color and style noted. Even his pajamas, laundered and pressed, were placed according to color in his dresser drawers. Dark ones on the bottom, lighter ones on top. Neatness was a reaction to a disorganized mother who couldn't care less what got washed, cleaned, or folded.

"Oh, wear it that way, Sonny," she'd say when he complained. She always called him Sonny, even though she knew he hated it.

When he continued to fuss, she cried, "Jesus, Sonny, you sound like a fag! Do it yourself if you don't like the way I do things."

So, from an early age, Derek Tracey did for himself. The habits he cultivated were his protest against the fatherless household he lived in under the grudging largesse of a mother who, despite her good looks, was, in his opinion, a slob.

He wasn't a fag. Not then. Not now. He just, for God's sake, liked things to be where they were supposed to be.

Like now. Where was his white silk pajama top, anyway? He was certain he'd put a clean pair on the chair next to his dresser the night before. This morning, he had showered. Now, he wanted to flop on the bed and run through his script.

He'd found the bottoms. He had them on. *Where the hell was the top?*

His concentration was interrupted by a knock on the door, followed by the entrance of Consuela. *"Buon giorno,"* she beamed. "You are up. The last time I looked in, you were fast asleep."

Derek stared at her.

Her cheeks were flushed, her eyes sparkled, there was flour on her chin, flour on both her arms. She'd been in the kitchen again, making that goddamned pasta. Wearing *his* pajama top. The sleeves were rolled high on her arms, the bottom reached midthigh.

"Damn it, Connie, that's my top you're wearing."

"Of course it is, *caro,"* she admitted. "I needed something loose and comfortable while I rolled out the pasta." She recited the evening menu for him with delight. "Ravioli stuffed with ricotta, braciola stuffed with *riso* and pignoli, and cassata siciliana for dessert. All homemade."

His stomach lurched. The national trend was toward lighter food, but Consuela ignored it. She poked his ribs playfully. "You need fattening up, *carissimo.* Too many ribs are visible."

Consuela had given up her Sunday night soirees long before Derek met her, but Sunday was still cook's night off. The only opportunity Consuela had to take over the kitchen. For all her sophistication, there remained, thought Derek petulantly, more than a little of the Italian peasant in her. Why else would she choose to spend Sunday up to her elbows in pasta dough? It was a miracle she wasn't fat. The way she cooked and ate, any other woman would have turned to blubber years ago.

As though she read minds, Consuela mourned, "One day, *caro,* it will all suddenly collapse. The chin, the bust, the thighs. And then, no one will love Consuela." She seemed amused at the prospect. Not for an instant did she believe it.

Derek refused to be put off. "I really hate it, Connie, when you take my things."

"You have so many, Derek. Drawers full. I took only one." Long slender fingers stroked the fret lines at his mouth. "Surely you are not going to spoil Sunday over a silly pajama top?"

"It isn't the top, it's the principle," persisted Derek.

Consuela shrugged. "Of course it is. I did a wicked thing. Forgive me?" She reached up and kissed him lightly. "After my bath, I will fix you a superb breakfast. *Squisito*. It will improve your temper. Food is a great neutralizer of emotions."

When he started to protest, she raised her hand firmly. "No. No more arguing. Sunday is a day of rest. And I am on my way to my bath. I will not let you spoil another minute." She swept from the room before Derek could rebut.

Granted, it was childish to argue about a pajama top, but he was right. The *principle* mattered. Why couldn't Consuela grasp that simple concept?

He flopped on the bed and propped up some pillows behind him. His legs were hunched up, his arms wrapped around them. The script lay beside him.

There were times Consuela definitely reminded him of his mother. The comparison didn't please him.

Bobby would do that. Borrow his good shirts to wear around the house because she was too lazy to launder her own. But Consuela didn't do her own laundering. What was her excuse?

Did all women appropriate? Or just the ones he knew.

Like Bobby.

Bobby Baker was sixteen when she married Derek Tracey III. She explained the circumstances to Derek early on. "I had a bun in the oven, Sonny. You."

As she never hesitated to remind him, "I had great plans for my future. You came at the wrong time."

All male Traceys suffered from poor timing. All arrived prematurely. All left the same way.

Derek Tracey the first met his end at twenty-two in the worst Wheeling, West Virginia, flood in history. Derek Tracey II died in a hunting accident from his own rifle. He was twenty-one. Derek's father, Derek Tracey III, two days past eighteen, was thrown from the motorcycle he was riding over the West Virginia hills at the exact moment Derek Tracey IV exited Bobby Baker Tracey's womb.

"The son of a bitch soared off in style, Sonny," Bobby was wont to explain. "Even if he did leave me holding the bag."

For the rest of his life, even though he chose a profession of risk, Derek remained cautious. His genes didn't look too promising. At twenty-eight, he never tempted fate. He didn't walk under ladders. Never flew DC 10s. Never traveled by water. And checked the skies before planning his day.

Consuela's bath was a pagan ritual of devotion and delight—the perfect place to indulge all her senses—touch, taste, sight, smell, and sound.

Ambience was imperative. But it had to be created.

The ten-foot sunken tub in the thirty-foot-long bathroom was pale pink Carrara marble. Shipped from her palazzo in Rome, it provided a comforting feeling of familiarity.

The bathroom windows that looked down on the evergreens and bare-branched deciduous trees of Central Park provided a feeling of space.

Hanging baskets of geraniums, ferns, philodendrons, and clusters of potted African violets created an indoor garden look.

Sterling silver baskets filled with pastel ovals of scented soaps imported from France gave off delicious fragrances. Tapered white candles in sterling silver candlesticks that were lighted when Consuela bathed at night added subtlety.

A House of Graet crystal bud vase with a single yellow rose rested on a sterling silver tray, alongside a bottle of chilled Pinot Chardonnay, a Baccarat crystal wineglass, a bowl of Beluga caviar over cracked ice, and wafer-thin slices of toast.

The bath water was run to a precise temperature of ninety-six degrees, established by her Hammacher Schlemmer thermometer, the temperature recommended by Consuela's favorite dermatologist.

Before submerging herself, she carefully lathered her body with the dermatologist's specially prepared moisturizer.

She could lie here forever, so content was she. But she allotted herself only thirty-five minutes of indulgence.

She almost dozed. Until she remembered Derek and his fret. Such a fuss. Over nothing. Over a *pajama top*. Why, look at the things she had on her mind. The Kirsten. The press conference. The Christmas ball. And a host of other details, too numerous to mention. But Sunday—Sunday was a day of rest. Nothing should mar its perfection.

It was all in the attitude, decided Consuela. Knowing what was important. Knowing what to let go of. For thirty-five marvelous minutes, Consuela let go. Of Derek, the Kirsten, the press conference, the ball, and anything else that threatened to interfere with the ultimate pleasure of her bath.

From the beginning, Derek's life had been chaotic.

In the first eighteen years of his life, he lived in eight cities, nine states, and two countries. He may have interrupted Bobby's grandiose plans for her future. He certainly didn't eliminate them.

"One day we'll hit the big time, Sonny," she promised. They never did. They lived from hand to mouth, one step ahead of the sheriff, while Bobby collected three more husbands and a string of lovers in her search for security and Derek collected allergies.

He was a shy, lonely, and introverted child until they landed in Toronto and he found himself. On stage. In the part of the young male lead in the high school production of Robert Anderson's *Tea and Sympathy*. Derek was seventeen.

On stage, he wasn't shy, introverted Derek Tracey. He was Derek Tracey IV, actor. Reborn. Confident.

The high school drama coach took an interest in him and arranged for an audition at the American Academy of Dramatic Arts in New York. She helped him with his selections, coached him, paid for his plane ticket and hotel stay, and recommended him for a scholarship.

Derek thought of the ground he had covered since then. His first Broadway part, playing Biff in a revival of Arthur Miller's *Death of a Salesman,* opened to excellent reviews. And a rave from Walter Kerr in *The New York Times*.

He received the Tony for the role of Biff. His first. And last. So far.

He'd been on a high roll back then. Twenty-three. The Tony. The accolades. Then, when everything should have been a breeze, the rhythm changed. And the long slow period that stunned him and everyone else began.

An actor's life is a crapshoot.

Relaxed and renewed, Consuela stepped from her tub, toweled herself dry, slipped into a hooded white terry-cloth Pratesi robe, pulled the pins from her hair, brushed it until it shone, and applied a light touch of makeup to her face.

Filled with fresh resolve, she strode out the bathroom door through her bedroom and down the hall to Derek's room. What he needed was more than a good breakfast. She had been right. He needed a vacation. This was the time to tell him about Palm Beach.

He would, she knew, be delighted with the arrangements she had made.

He was less than delighted.

Consuela began by sitting on the bed beside him and announcing she had something very exciting to tell him. A surprise!

Derek found himself tensing. Surprises made him nervous.

He preferred to be prepared. More important, he preferred to do the preparing himself.

But he listened attentively as Consuela told him about the Palm Beach trip which would double as a vacation for both of them. He discovered he was growing very angry.

Oblivious to his mood, Consuela blithely extolled the virtues of palm trees, the Florida sun, the balmy breezes off Lake Worth, and the soothing sound of the Atlantic surf slapping against The Breakers' shores. "Just talking about it excites me," she enthused.

Derek stared at her. "You must be nuts!"

"Nuts?" Consuela looked blank. *"Che sè dice?"*

"How in hell can I get away for a week in the sun? I'm an actor, a *working* actor, not the goddamned president of a trinket shop who can take off whenever she pleases."

"The House of Graet is hardly a trinket shop," retorted Consuela huffily. "Besides, I *am* going to Palm Beach to work."

"Exactly. And I'm staying here to work."

"But it has all been arranged, *caro,*" explained Consuela, getting excited.

"What's been arranged?" he wanted to know.

She told him.

Greg Gillman, the producer of *Webster's Cove,* of which Consuela owned a sizable share—a fact of which Derek preferred not be reminded—came up with the perfect solution.

Blaine Blandings, Derek's soap character, would be lost at sea.

A boating accident. After a week, he would be found. The new diversion would add increased dimension to his character. Not to mention a ratings boost. All in all, a marvelous happenstance.

"I see." He was angrier than he'd been in a long time. The incident of the pajama top paled in comparison. It was just like Bobby all over again. Managing. Manipulating. Moving the chess pieces around on the board.

"Did it ever occur to you, Consuela, that *I* was the one to consult? *Before* you made all the arrangements?"

"I thought you would be pleased," she reproached him. "I thought a little vacation would do us both good."

"Even if I don't want it?"

She sighed. "We do not always know what we want. Or need."

Derek's voice grew menacingly calm. "I am an actor, Consuela. A working actor. As I mentioned before. Not an international playboy. You don't seem to be able to grasp that simple concept either. Perhaps it's because you don't understand the profession of acting."

"*I* do not understand?" flared Consuela. Her hands flew out in outrage. "*I do not understand?*" she repeated incredulously. "I was an actress of distinction before you were born."

"You were a movie star, not an actress, Consuela. A sex symbol. A screen personality," noted Derek stubbornly.

Consuela jumped off the bed and glared at him. "I was an actress, *caro*. A-C-T-R-E-S-S." She spelled out the word, enunciating each letter with precision. "I still am. I have never lost touch with my art. Never." She spread her arms wide. "Only now the whole world is my stage."

She circled the room in a fury. "You think what I do isn't acting? It is theater, pure theater. Divine comedy. Tragic theater. It takes every ounce of my energy and imagination to keep my performance at top pitch."

She stopped pacing, glared at Derek with scorn. "Why, had I remained in films, I would today be one of the world's great actresses. As it is, my work is still being shown in theaters and TV and discussed in film seminars thirty years later. Do you think, my dear Derek, you will be able to say the same of yours?"

Before he could respond, Consuela rushed on. "And another

thing. You are a spoiled, petulant child. You sulk and complain and you have at last given me a headache."

She stopped in front of him and looked at him in utter disbelief. "I tried to do something nice for you. Out of the goodness of my heart, I thought it would be good for you to get away. One week. One silly week or two, and you carry on as though your lifetime career is in jeopardy. You make scenes over pajama tops and other nonsense."

She gesticulated wildly, accenting each word with force. Finally, she threw her arms up in despair. *"Basta!* It is Sunday, and I will have my day of rest even if I have to have it alone." She swept out of the room, slamming the door behind her.

Derek was speechless. She had completely taken over and played the scene center stage like some goddamned Italian diva spraying notes into a captive audience.

She hadn't heard or understood a goddamned thing he was saying. Not about principles, or practices, or rights.

Just like Bobby!

Bobby followed him to New York his first year at the academy. She was between husbands.

"I missed you, Sonny," she told him, suitcase in hand. She moved right in.

She got a job at Henri Bendel's behind the perfume counter. Three months later, she married Herb Halpern, a wealthy garment manufacturer with a mansion in Scarsdale. This time, Bobby landed a survivor. Her financial future was secured.

Derek's wasn't.

When he'd just about decided poor was forever, the life script introduced a new character. Enter Consuela. Taking charge. The role of Blaine Blandings in *Webster's Cove* saved his professional and financial life. And the part was opening doors.

A film executive approached him recently about the male lead in a new film being shot in England. A TV series with him as the star was in the discussion stage. Derek hadn't mentioned either to Consuela.

What he was most interested in was finding a play with a part in it that would land him another Tony.

He hadn't discussed that with Consuela either.

He needed to make it on his own.

Inconsistencies gnawed at him. Why was his professional life so intact and his personal life such a shambles?

Why did he allow women to manipulate him? First, Bobby. Now, Consuela. Consuela even had the gall to say he'd ruined her Sunday. *Her* Sunday!

Sunday! Jesus! That was the day Bobby liked him to call. "It's not a duty call, Sonny," she instructed. "A mother just likes to hear from her son."

Derek remembered all the years Bobby couldn't care less. But she had her own way of doing things. At forty-four, she had skipped menopause and discovered motherhood.

Matchmaking was high on Bobby's priority list of things to do for Derek. And she objected strenuously to his relationship with Consuela, citing the age difference. "You want a mother, Sonny," she told him, "come to Scarsdale."

She had even extracted a promise from him to spend Thanksgiving with Herb and her in Scarsdale. Without Consuela. "It's a family day, Sonny. She's got her own."

Actually, Consuela *was* spending the holiday with her family in Greenwich.

Derek had planned to spend his holiday alone.

There must be a way to gain control of his life.

There had to be.

Bobby Halpern was distressed to learn the beautiful young model in Herb's shop was unable to come for Thanksgiving dinner. Her mother took sick in Ohio. The model was flying out.

Bobby was sorry about the mother, sorrier about the situation. She had high hopes for the model and Derek.

A temporary setback.

She remembered Herb's friends, the Stones. And recalled they had a pretty daughter named Sandy.

With the resilience she always displayed when confronted with potential disasters, Bobby flipped open her telephone book to the names of Dr. and Mrs. Arthur Stone, and dialed Ruth Stone's number.

Derek should be grateful he had a mother to look out for his interests.

~16~

Sandy Stone spent Sunday recuperating from Saturday.

Saturday had been a grueling day at the House of Graet. Mimzee Dawson stopped by and Sandy ducked in the back, leaving her to Celia. Kate was off for the day. Miss D. was looking for something to pique her fancy. Nothing did. There had been no new deliveries since her last appearance. She left, as she had come, feeling blue.

Sandy spent 2½ hours with Mrs. Dean Oliver, of the banking Olivers, who bought a number of small gift items, totaling $3,000. Mrs. Oliver called them stocking stuffers. To herself, Sandy referred to them as *tchotchkes*.

Saturday afternoon consisted mostly of browsers on their way to or from lunch at The Breakers, Café L'Europe, Cafe Coconut, or the Colony. Wearing Lilly Pulitzer prints, the Ralph Lauren prairie look, Halston ultrasuede eastern chic, or Palm Beach eclectic. Anything but shorts. Shorts were frowned upon on the avenue.

They were bored or indifferent, demanding or dissatisfied. They fondled objects listlessly, searching for panaceas to unexpressed longings. Sandy called it the consumer dilemma. Will buying this make me feel better? If I pay this outrageous sum, will my life be improved?

They weren't buying. It was one of those days when Sandy wondered why she was in retail. One thing she knew. She would never enjoy shopping again.

By the time the day ended, she was drained. And Saturday night had been even worse. A blind date with a Fort Lauderdale lawyer, a friend of a friend of Sandy's in Scarsdale.

"He's darling, Sandy. You'll see," promised the Scarsdale friend. "And he's Jewish too."

Well, Jewish he'd been. Darling, he wasn't. When would she learn not to be so obliging to friends with matchmaking proclivities? At best, it was a gamble. At worst, a disaster. Still, as her mother kept reminding her, you never know.

So how come Sandy always knew?

The Fort Lauderdale lawyer was thirty-six, divorced, with two preteen children. He was tall, trim, with curly brown hair, brown eyes, perfectly capped teeth, and a perfect Florida tan.

He was also perfectly coordinated and accessorized. Ralph Lauren pink polo shirt under a dark blue Brooks Brothers suit, Christian Dior red print tie, black Gucci loafers, an 18k gold Rolex day-date oyster chronometer, with the day and date conspicuously marked on the face of the watch, on one wrist, and an 18k gold Cartier love bracelet on the other.

Two 18k gold screws held the bracelet in place, he explained. It was a "commitment" bracelet. Didn't come off easily. Came with its own screwdriver, he told Sandy. Sandy said she knew.

The Fort Lauderdale lawyer was a walking-talking demonstration of label validation. To cement this impression, he drove a 1987 white Porsche. The evening was not destined to improve.

They agreed to meet in Boca Raton. The lawyer lived closer to Boca than Palm Beach. Boca, he pointed out, was approximately halfway for each of them. Fair.

He was an eighties man, he told Sandy—free-spirited, independent—no holds barred. Eager to meet an eighties lady.

That's when she should have hung up.

The initial phone conversation:

"Hi! This is Russ Gold. May I speak with Sandy?"

"This is Sandy."

"Hi, Sandy. I'm a friend of Rhonda Stern's. In Scarsdale."

"Yeah? I know a Rhonda Stern. From Scarsdale too."

"Ha! Ha! Rhonda said you were a card!"

Pause.

"She also said you were a real looker. Red hair. Green eyes. A regular spitfire."

"That's me. The Jewish Scarlett O'Hara."

Russ Gold laughed. Then he asked, "What about me?"

"You?"

"Yeah. Didn't Rhonda tell you about me? Didn't she give you my phone number?"

"As a matter of fact, Rhonda did."

Russ Gold hesitated. "When you didn't call, I decided to take the initiative."

It was Sandy's turn to hesitate. *He had expected her to call him.*

"So, I'm calling you."

"Well, that brings us up to date," noted Sandy.

He laughed again. "I thought we might meet, get acquainted. See how it goes, you know. Have a few drinks, dinner. Get a feel for each other."

Sandy waited.

"Sound okay?"

"Sounds okay," she answered warily.

"How about Saturday?"

"This Saturday?" she answered even more warily.

"Sure, this Saturday. Sooner the better."

Like a vaccination, thought Sandy.

"You booked?"

"No, I'm free," said Sandy, then paused, deciding to watch her language more carefully from here on in.

"Great," enthused Russ Gold. "We're on then for Saturday night. Now, look, Sandy, ordinarily I'd be gung ho to hop up to Palm Beach to pick you up, but I've got a fivish meeting with a client that'll take an hour or so. So, I thought if we could meet in Boca, that would be halfway for each of us. Sounds fair to me. What d'ya think?"

Before she could reply, Russ added, "Besides, they have this terrific restaurant in Boca. Eating there's an experience."

"Okay," agreed Sandy, who wasn't especially into experiences.

That's when he told her he was an eighties man. And that's when she should have begged off.

"You know the Wildflower?"

"The pink palace on the Intracoastal? I know it."

"Meet you there at seven. Okay?"

"How will I know you?"

Russ Gold chuckled. "I'll be the good-looking one at the bar. With the eager look in his eye. And a pink camellia in his lapel."

My, God, was he serious!

"I'll wear a red rose. To match my red dress. That matches my red hair."

Russ Gold's laughter boomed into Sandy's ear. "Like Rhonda said! Great little kidder!"

The evening, like the phone conversation, had nowhere to go but up.

Yet it continued to plunge.

The Wildflower was a two-story pink stucco structure on the Intracoastal Waterway. According to Russ Gold, it won the best architectural design award for 1981.

It looked like a gigantic pink marshmallow. It had a busy bar surrounded by lusting trendies, a free hot and cold hors d'oeuvres table, a circular staircase leading to the second level, an abundance of green plants, piped-in rock music vying with human gurglings, and wide windows that provided a sweeping view of the Intracoastal. Boat traffic created a colorful background as drinks were lifted and assignations made.

Sandy wondered why she had come.

As promised, Russ Gold recognized her. He stepped out from a crush of people at the bar and approached her. "Sandy?"

"Yes?"

"Russ Gold." He pointed to the pink camellia. "Where's your red rose?"

"I left in a hurry." Sandy stared, stunned by teeth, tan, and perfection. She had rushed from the store to her apartment to the shower.

She had dressed quickly—a black wool skirt, white silk top with spaghetti straps, black wool bolero jacket, black pumps, a single pearl necklace, and pearl earrings. She was winded. But her red hair blazed and her smile was bright. She was, if anything, the eternal optimist. Willing to withhold judgment.

"I recognized you right away," Russ Gold told her. "Even without the rose. Rhonda sent me a snapshot of the two of you taken at the club last year."

"Ah," said Sandy, tilting her head provocatively so he could get the full impact of Dr. Gruber's nose job. How else could she compete with his effulgence?

Russ steered Sandy to a small table he had reserved facing the

133

Intracoastal. He ordered Chivas Regal on the rocks, Sandy ordered white wine.

A small yacht passed by. A young blonde in a black satin jump suit toasted a white-haired sixtyish gentleman in impeccable white slacks and navy blazer.

"See," approved Russ. "Everybody's making it."

Sandy held on to her smile.

Three drinks later (having covered the first eighteen years of the story of his life—growing up in Westchester County, New York), Russ Gold checked his Rolex. "Time to move on. I've made dinner reservations at La Vieille Maison. You're going to love it, Sandy. People don't eat there. They dine. Like I said, it's an experience."

La Vieille Maison was approximately a two-minute drive from the Wildflower. They drove there in Russ's new white Porsche. Sandy's red 1979 Renault was left in the Wildflower parking lot.

La Vieille Maison was a beautifully restored, elegant Addison Mizner gem with typical Mizner touches of old Spanish charm. From its handsome entrance gate of iron, old Spanish courtyard with tile accents, fountain banked with flowers, to the bright airy interior rooms with beamed ceilings, highly polished antique tables, and ornately carved high-back chairs, it was impressive.

Reidel stemware from Austria and porcelain d'Auteuil china from France were used throughout the several rooms of the restaurant.

Awarded the Mobil Travel Guide Five-Star Award (given to only twelve restaurants in the country) and the Holiday Magazine Dining Award, La Vieille Maison is considered one of the finest restaurants in the country. With one of the best wine cellars.

Fresh-cut flowers exploded in displays of color. Carts overflowed with fresh fruits and wheels of French cheeses. Fantastic desserts tantalized from dessert carts.

The food was excellent. The service, sublimely sophisticated. The ambience, unmatched. Eating there was, as Russ Gold promised, an experience. Unfortunately, he led Sandy through it with absolutely no flair. Throughout the various courses, he talked only about himself.

Exception. He asked one question of her. How did she enjoy being in the midst of Palm Beach chic? When she opened her mouth to answer, he rushed back to his favorite subject. Himself. Sandy concentrated on the food. There was so much of it.

The menu was prix fixe—$33 each for a complete dinner that included hors d'oeuvres, entrée, salad, selections from the cheese cart, fruit, and dessert.

They had escargots poached in wine, French Brie, and fresh strawberries. Sandy had pompano sautéed in butter with pecans, white wine, and cream. Russ had *Selle de Chevreuil Grand Veneur* —saddle of Scottish venison with wild rice. The wine he selected was important enough for the waiter to decant it with ceremony at their table.

Under the influence of food, wine, and ambience, Russ Gold expanded even more. While he spoke, Sandy ate.

He told her of the frustrations of being married to Sybil Gold. "What can you do when one person in a marriage grows, and the other stands still?" There were his kids, Brucie and Kendel, ten and nine. "Great little kids. I miss them like hell. Maybe I'll fly them down for a weekend." There was his work. "Financially rewarding. Emotionally satisfying." There was his life in Fort Lauderdale.

He was, he told Sandy, playing the field now. No more long-term relationships for him. He watched to see if she got it. She got it.

He was dating an actress from a local repertory company, a model from Miami, a computer analyst from Delray Beach, a socialite from Hobe Sound, a widow from Orlando, and a divorcée from Phoenix.

He was into "expansion"—developing himself to his full potential. When he thought of the years wasted, stifled and stalemated by middle-class values—the house in the suburbs, the two cars, the boats, the private schools for the kids, the charge accounts for the wife—he thanked his lucky stars he had finally come to his senses and walked out.

What about her? asked Russ.

"Mousse," said Sandy.

"What?" asked Russ.

Sandy explained. "The waiter. He wants to know what we want for dessert. I'd like the mousse." The waiter stood discreetly by. They ordered.

She must have gained ten pounds during dinner. She had eaten everything that wasn't nailed down, shoving things wildly into her mouth, while her eyes glazed over and her mind dozed. When she got her hands on Rhonda, she'd kill her!

Dessert done, Russ checked his Rolex. Sandy studied the love bracelet. Russ motioned for the check, read it carefully, added 20 percent, and submitted his American Express card. He studied Sandy with the same intensity he gave to the check. "Didn't I tell you this place was an experience?"

"You were right," said Sandy.

He helped her on with her jacket. They walked outside, waited for the attendant to bring round the Porsche.

Russ put an arm around Sandy's waist. "I know the greatest little spot for a nightcap and dancing. Like to dance?" His look was intimate, sated from food and conversation, but ripe for adventure.

Sandy wiggled out of his embrace, lifted his wrist, and looked in horror at the Rolex. "My God, Russ, it's 10:30. I've got to get back."

"Back?" He looked stunned.

"I'm expecting a long-distance call from my mother. My father's very sick. I only came tonight because my mother insisted I go out for a while. I didn't mention it earlier because we were having so much fun, and I didn't want to spoil it. But I can't tell you how worried everyone is. I was going to call and cancel, but I couldn't find your number, and, as I said, my mother insisted it might do me good to get out. After all, it wasn't as though I could do anything constructive except sit by the phone and worry, and God knows, that wouldn't have helped anyone."

Russ Gold stared in disbelief. Sandy Stone hadn't spoken that many words the entire evening.

Sandy grabbed his hand, shook it enthusiastically. "Listen, I had a great time, and I can't thank you enough. Like you said, it was an experience."

"Why can't you call home from here?"

"Oh, I couldn't. My mother called from the hospital. My father was rushed there from the house."

"Call the hospital from here, then."

"I don't know which one they went to," stumbled Sandy.

"They were in such a rush. . . ." Her voice trailed off. But her eyes reflected back a mixture of wild concern and sincere regret she hoped would satisfy him.

She knew from his expression he didn't know whether to believe her or not. She also knew, after spending an entire evening with him, rejection was beyond his comprehension.

The attendant waited patiently for his tip.

"Look," complained Russ. "I had *plans.*"

"Oh, I know," sympathized Sandy, "and I *am* sorry."

"This evening cost me over two hundred bucks," whined Russ.

"That much," said Sandy weakly. She smiled brightly. "Well, it was worth it. I mean, it certainly was an experience."

He wasn't listening. "I thought we might go back to my place. It's not that far from here. Have a nightcap. Play some Brubeck. You could drive back tomorrow."

Her sigh was as sincere as she could make it. "Any other time I would have loved it."

He became petulant. "I had the entire evening planned. If I'd known, I could have made other arrangements."

The model from Miami?

The socialite from Hobe Sound?

The divorcée from Phoenix?

The widow from Orlando?

The computer analyst, perhaps, from Delray Beach.

Sandy sighed once more, this time in earnest. "Russ, I'm really sorry. Look, I don't want you to trouble yourself anymore. I mean, heavens, you've done enough. The Wildflower's out of your way. I'll call a cab and pick up my car. So, you go on ahead, and thanks again."

Before he could respond, she smiled her brightest, tilted the nose, shrugged in apology, turned on her heels, and walked briskly back inside.

She chewed on a cuticle, tapped her foot, and waited five minutes. When she looked outside, the Porsche was gone.

She walked the five-minute walk to the Wildflower, got into her car, and drove the dark, winding A1A home, her headlights piercing the deep night shadows. She could have taken the brightly lighted I-95, but A1A suited her mood better. Black and bitter.

She had just spent the most horrendously dreary evening of her twenty-four years with the most offensive oaf she had yet encountered.

Imagine—3½ hours boring her to tears, and he expected to be rewarded. They were all alike, eighties men. She hadn't met one yet who wasn't focused exclusively on himself. *His* needs. *His* desires. *His* requirements. *His* demands.

If she were Catholic, she'd join a nunnery. Except even nuns were leaving them. If she had guts, she'd stay at home. At least her own company was less predictable.

She might be the only twenty-four-year-old virgin in the state of Florida, but she certainly wasn't about to relinquish that status for a jerk like that. When she was finally deflowered, it would be in style. With rockets bursting, balloons soaring, music crescendoing, and someone she could look at the following morning without retching.

17

The work on the necklace was done. It lay on the worktable in the studio Louis-Philippe maintained at the House of Graet. It was beautiful. Incomparable. Truly magnificent.

Louis stared at the stone before him, lost for a moment in the depths of its garnet-red color. No one was sure precisely why diamonds are colored, what or which elements present create the coloration, although experiments had been conducted to duplicate the process.

No matter. The rich color of the Kirsten was sufficient justification. It didn't matter how or why it got that way. It was enough that it was.

As he had promised Consuela, the necklace would be delivered ahead of schedule. He had spent all day Sunday at his studio working on it.

He hadn't minded coming in. Sundays to him were much like other days, only quieter. With no distractions. Work, he learned a long time ago, was his main satisfaction in life. Without it, he would be lost.

Consuela was wrong. He had no desire to learn how to play. All his energies and desires were directed into and fulfilled by the gratification and stimulation provided by good work. It was too late in life for him to shift gears. Besides, he didn't want to. Another thing he had learned: the man who finds his place in life is fortunate indeed. He considered himself an extremely fortunate man.

He had come far from his humble Swiss beginnings, both as a jeweler and as an artist. A signed Louis-Philippe piece was considered a treasure. His whimsical pieces—a pavé diamond ladybug with ruby markings, a diamond grasshopper with movable emerald legs, a pavé diamond elephant with pearl trunk and ears, a pearl dolphin with sapphire eyes—were coveted pieces cultured women throughout the world refused to part with.

Fashion awards and design awards lined the shelves of one bookcase in his study at home. His lectures on the history of jewelry were standing room only. Last year, the Metropolitan Museum of Art held a forty-year retrospective of his work.

His had been a long and fulfilling journey to the Kirsten.

The Kirsten, too, had traveled a long way from its beginnings in a South African mine. In a few short weeks, its journey would begin again. Until at last it rested, fair and resplendent, around the throat of its next fortunate owner.

Or unfortunate—if one believed its legends and predictions of doom. He did not. He was intrigued by beauty, not by omens.

However, the Kirsten would find no more resplendent resting place than around the neck of the Contessa Perrugia. He had designed it with her in mind. Consuela would wear it with great style. And relinquish it with equal grace. He knew her well. Better than she was aware.

How strange that beside his work he should have only one consuming passion. Yet, the object of this emotion was as oblivious to it as she was to the fact that his work *was* his play.

He knew her so well; she didn't know him at all.

Louis-Philippe tore his gaze from the necklace, reached for the telephone, and dialed Consuela's home number.

"Louis?" She sounded surprised to hear his voice. "Where are you?"

"At work. The Kirsten is ready, Consuela."

"Really! Sunday, and you are at work! You are incorrigible, Louis. What am I to do with you?"

"I thought you would be pleased."

"Of course I am pleased. But you have become a source of major concern to me. That does not please me."

Louis laughed. "Well, you need not concern yourself any longer. The work is done. Once I put it in the safe, I will go home, have a warm bath, and settle in for the rest of the evening."

"Have you eaten?"

"As a matter of fact . . ."

"See! Just as I thought. Come for pasta, Louis."

Louis thought of Derek Tracey. How was Consuela to know it was painful for him to see them together?

"Some other time, Consuela. I'm simply too tired to make an agreeable companion this evening."

Surprisingly, she understood. "Of course, Louis. It is selfish of me to insist. Naturally, you are tired. Some other time, then."

"I would like that."

"*Ciao,* then, Louis. And go right home. *Capisce?*" Do you understand?

He laughed again. "*Capisco,* Consuela. *Ciao.*"

Consuela approached the telephone the same way she entered into a love affair. Expectantly. Expertly. And in full command.

Her first call was to Mimzee Dawson. She reached her at her Palm Beach cottage.

"*Cara mia,* I wanted you to be the first to know."

"What's that, dearie?"

"A treasure you would not believe possible is available. Something so *magnifico,* you will weep with wonder." Consuela told her of the House of Graet's acquisition of the Kirsten.

"I thought that relic was in a museum," said Mimzee.

"You are perhaps thinking of the Hope," suggested Consuela. "That is at the Smithsonian." She saw her opportunity and seized it. Alas, the Hope could now be viewed *only* in a museum. No longer available to those with a fine appreciation for rare gems. Ah, but the Kirsten would be presented at their Christmas ball. "However, it is not at the moment for sale," explained Consuela. "After our tour, it will be." She mentioned the price she expected to get for it.

Mimzee ignored the price information. "Tour?"

Consuela explained the worldwide tour, creating goodwill and making millions for charity.

"How long are you planning to extend the road show, dearie?" queried Mimzee.

Consuela wasn't certain. "A year, perhaps." She sighed.

"That long, huh?" Mimzee sounded worried.

Consuela sighed again. She understood how Mimzee felt. The Kirsten would be the perfect addition to the Dawson collection. A museum piece that comes along once in a lifetime. If we are so blessed.

Mimzee decided it had nothing to do with blessings. "Consuela, I want to see that diamond *before* the ball. Before people start slobbering over it."

"How is that possible, *cara?*"

Mimzee explained how. She'd fly to New York tomorrow to see it. And she wanted to be kept posted on all interested parties.

"As you wish, Mimzee," soothed Consuela.

"Good," barked Mimzee. "See you tomorrow. Does two o'clock suit you?"

Consuela assured her two was fine.

Mimzee hung up and fondled her double strand of matched pearls thoughtfully. She wanted that diamond. She was hell-bent to have it. And no piece of Italian baggage would stand in her way.

For the first time since purchasing the 200 party trinkets, Mimzee Dawson definitely did not feel blue.

Consuela reached Bordon Granger at his farm in Wellington.

"Caro," she crooned, "how are you?" Then, with a sigh, "Why we allow so much time to pass without reaching out to old friends, I do not know."

Bordon didn't have an answer to that one. But, yes, he was fine. And delighted to hear from her.

They chatted about his forthcoming marriage. Consuela was thrilled for them both. She and Bordon had been friends for years. She had also met Tami Hayes. And adored her. "She is divine, *caro.* Perfect for you."

She was deeply glad for his happiness, she told him.

Now she was going to add to it. She told him about the Kirsten.

Bordon chuckled appreciatively. "So, that's where it is. Last time I heard, it was in Geneva. Next time I inquired, it was gone."

Consuela was sympathetic. She just happened to be in Geneva when it came on the market. A happy circumstance.

"Quite a coup," acknowledged Bordon.

"We are very pleased," replied Consuela modestly.

Bordon's laughter roared into Consuela's well-shaped ear. "I'll bet we are. That's a gem I dearly wanted, Consuela. Only you beat me to it."

It was an ideal lead-in. "As a matter of fact, Bordon, the Kirsten is again up for sale." She explained about the tour, and that it could be seen at the ball.

Bordon was silent as he seemed to chew on the information. Then he admitted he was interested. "It would make a nice wedding gift," he mused.

"What a marvelous idea," enthused Consuela. "Trust you to think of something grand like that."

He laughed again. "I'm certain it occurred to both of us, my dear."

"Only in passing," she allowed.

"Consuela, you haven't changed at all. You're still the prettiest carpetbagger on the scene."

Consuela accepted the observation as a compliment. *"Naturalmente, caro. Ciao."*

A tall broad-shouldered, handsome man of fifty, there was nothing Bordon Granger wanted he hadn't got. Now he wanted the Kirsten. He wanted it for Tami.

He didn't know what there was about Tami Hayes that made him long to take care of her. Certainly she never appeared to need taking care of. Or even to want it.

Orphaned while still in her teens, she'd even managed to raise and educate her fifteen-year-old kid sister while still making it to the top of her profession by twenty-five.

He loved everything about Tami—her spunk, her talent, her beauty. He felt that the Kirsten was a rare gem that required another rare gem to wear it with distinction—someone like Tami. Consuela was right. It was the perfect wedding gift.

Derek knocked on the study door.

"Avanti!" called out Consuela, her hand over the mouthpiece of the telephone.

"I thought you were through," apologized Derek.

"Almost," she smiled, waving him toward the couch and pointing to the pot of steaming fresh coffee on the sideboard. Their earlier misunderstanding had been resolved. Consuela was not one to harbor grudges.

Derek poured some coffee, sat on the couch, and listened, fascinated, as Consuela spoke with Count Paolo Respighi in Rome, Sheik Abu Kahli in London, and Tony Owens in Beverly Hills.

All were apprised of the availability of the Kirsten.

All were interested.

Watching the performance, Derek conceded Consuela had a point. She hadn't given up the stage. She'd merely extended the area she performed on. And she performed magnificently.

Consuela found Carl Schmittle at his home in Greenwich, Connecticut. Ever so deftly, she got round to the Kirsten. "Louis-Philippe has designed the most exquisite setting for it. I immediately thought of Rosemary."

Carl responded quickly to Consuela's enthusiasm. "Roe would certainly go for something like that, Contessa. What's the tariff?"

She told him.

He whistled. "That's no ordinary Christmas trinket, is it?"

Consuela concurred. It was not ordinary. Nor would it be available for Christmas. She explained about the tour. And why she had called. "I would not have felt right, Carl, not to let you know about the Kirsten. How often does such a gem come upon the scene? Once in a lifetime? If we are lucky?"

Carl assured her he was definitely interested. And made an appointment to see it on Tuesday. He chuckled. "Mark would split a gut if I got that diamond for Roe."

"Oh?"

"He's sensitive about any display of wealth now that he's got his eye on the White House," explained Carl. He chuckled again. "Oh, hell, Roe can always wear it in the tub when she's taking one of those damned bubble baths she's so fond of."

Consuela laughed with him. And said she was looking forward to their meeting.

Carl thought of Rosemary. That diamond was sure to bring a sparkle back to those big brown eyes.

It bothered the hell out of him to see his Roe so down. If Mark concentrated more on his wife and less on every piece of ass that brushed against him, Rosemary wouldn't be in the mess she was in.

Well, if it took a diamond to raise those spirits, a diamond it would be. He had the wherewithal to do it.

Hell, wasn't that what fathers were for?

When Consuela completed her last call, Derek asked her, "What are you trying to do, Connie, start World War III?"

She shrugged. "This little exercise is called—how do you say it? Hedging your bets? So many claim interest in the first flush of enthusiasm. But when it comes to parting with a check"—and here she paused, dramatically reached into the air, and pulled on an imaginary chain—"flush, there goes the enthusiasm."

Derek laughed. "What if you're wrong? And they all want it?"

The famous dimple flashed. "I will think of something. I always do."

Bordon Granger reached Tami Hayes on the set of her new film. She was on a break.

"I miss you," he told her. "And I have a surprise for you."

"Oh?" She sounded excited. "What is it?"

"If I told you, it wouldn't be a surprise," he pointed out.

"A hint," she pleaded.

He relented. "It's big and dazzling and quite spectacular."

"The Taj Mahal!"

He laughed. "Not quite." He knew she would love the Kirsten. "You'll have to wait to see it."

"You're a terrible tease, Bordon."

"No, I'm terribly in love with a woman I see too little of."

She sighed. "There's Christmas. I'll be in Wellington then."

"Too far off."

She agreed. But as soon as the film was wrapped, she had some bookings to fill.

"Come here for Thanksgiving," he urged.

How she would love that. "I'm booked in Vegas then."

Bordon made a quick decision. The way to Tami's heart was through her kid sister, Erin. "I'll come there. I'll rent a house, hire a cook, and we'll have an old-fashioned Thanksgiving Erin won't forget."

Tami was touched. Erin would love that. "Sounds great, darling," she agreed.

"Good. I'll call tonight."

She laughed. "Again? You're burning up the wires."

"No," he said. "I'm burning with desire for my woman."

Tami's voice was soft. "You're distracting me, Bordon."

"Good. That was my intention."

A rap on the door beckoned Tami back to the set. "Sorry, sweetheart. I've got to run."

She hung up, smiled to herself. Bordon always made her feel so good. Loved. Protected. Safe from harm.

Bordon Granger was the best thing that ever happened to her.

Correction. Erin was the best.

Then came Bordon.

∽18∽

Rosemary Hunter had never felt better. Or looked better. Thanks to Deborah Szekely and her Japanese-style inn, The Golden Door, Rosemary had a hold on life again, her life. She was back in control. And all it took was a bit of endurance.

She'd been weighed, measured, and fed spartanly. She'd exercised inside the spa and huffed and puffed her way around the rugged southern California terrain. And, when wilted, she'd had her face and body pampered with facials and massages. She'd had the works—Swiss showers, water-exercise classes, acupuncture massages.

It was worth it. The excess poundage was gone, along with the facial bloat. The face reflected back from the Lindbergh Airport bar in San Diego was tanned, tight, and glowing with health. The large brown eyes glistened with clarity; the thick blond hair, newly cut and styled, was springy and youthful. She looked ten years younger; she was twenty pounds thinner. Marymount's Most Beautiful Girl, 1970, had been resurrected. And she, Rosemary Schmittle Hunter, had done it all.

She had done more. She hadn't had a drink—a real drink, that is—in four weeks. Whoever said she was an alcoholic? Rosemary smiled sagely at her mirror reflection. So much for Dr. Broome! So much for Senator Mark Hunter! What did they know?

"Something I can get you, ma'am?" The thin, dark-haired thirtyish bartender stood politely by.

"Perrier with lime, please. In a frosted glass." Rosemary smiled as she turned from her mirror image.

She liked bars. She enjoyed the conviviality they offered. Old identities were abandoned in bars, new ones created. A bar was a separate world that enveloped everyone in its own special glow. Offering promises of deliverance from the dull and the dreary. With the suggestion of excitement and the possibility of something more as replacements.

She even liked bars when she wasn't drinking. Ordinarily, she preferred them dimly lighted. They seemed more romantic that way. Today, she didn't care. Today, she looked good enough to withstand even merciless sunlight. And today, alcohol wasn't necessary. She felt so good, she didn't need any artificial help.

She glanced idly around. Several men sat opposite her, and a lady-executive type, approximately the same age as Rosemary, but not pretty. Not even stylish, really.

Rosemary was aware of the looks of interest from the men. Although their admiration was pleasant, she ignored them. She was accustomed to male admiration.

The bartender placed the frosted glass with its sliver of lime on the polished wood surface of the bar. "Will that be all, ma'am?"

"Yes, thank you." Rosemary lifted her glass, sipped demurely, and smiled again. She was happy with her new image, gratified by her self-control. "Umm," she said. "Good. Good for you too."

"So they tell me." The bartender grinned. "Me, I'm a Scotch man myself."

Rosemary nodded, not bothering to comment. She took a silver cigarette case from her Hermès purse, pressed the emerald clasp, released the catch, and took out a cigarette. The bartender quickly withdrew a Bic from his shirt pocket and lit her cigarette.

She inhaled, blew smoke out through delicately carved nostrils, and smiled once again. "Thank you."

"Pretty," he noted. Although his eyes indicated the cigarette case, they implied more.

"Yes," agreed Rosemary, choosing to ignore the implication.

"On your way into the city or out?" he asked, making conversation.

"Out. I've just come from Escondido."

Of course. One of those Golden Door dolls. Rich and pampered. But this one was a looker. Classy. Great build. What could they possibly do to improve her?

"On your way to New York?" he asked.

"Palm Beach, via L.A. I'm picking up a connecting flight there."

As he suspected, a rich one.

"I'm going home for Thanksgiving," Rosemary said, wondering why she volunteered the information. But her mood was so expansive, why not? she decided.

"Nice," commented the bartender. He'd never been to Palm Beach. One sunspot was the same as another. Personally, he preferred Thanksgiving in Vermont. Only he was going to spend it tending bar in San Diego.

They chatted impersonally about the merits of San Diego versus Palm Beach. The weather, of course, was nearly perfect in San Diego, admitted Rosemary. In Palm Beach, one stayed only for the season. Not that she really stayed in San Diego. In and out of Escondido for a quick overhaul.

She didn't look as though she needed an overhaul, he told her gallantly. He meant it. Rosemary smiled.

She had another Perrier. The bartender served his other customers and returned.

He had, noted Rosemary, beautiful blue eyes, fringed with thick dark lashes. A pity to waste those lashes on a man. Most women would have killed for them.

She was aware she was mildly flirting with him, and he with her. No harm. She wasn't going to be here long enough to get into trouble. Besides, she wasn't looking for trouble. It was just pleasant to enjoy his admiration. It was a validation of her attractiveness, far more satisfying than a mirror.

But more heady was the knowledge that she held the controls. She could encourage a relationship or terminate it. She chose to terminate this one.

She glanced at her solid gold House of Graet watch with its matching 18k gold mesh bracelet. "Oops! I'd better get moving if I want to catch my plane." She smiled, slid gracefully off the barstool, and several gold bracelets jingled prettily against the watch as she searched for her wallet in her Hermès bag. She laid four crisp bills on the bar, and walked out, cool, elegant, and ladylike in a wheat-colored silk suit, long-legged, slender feet shod in ivory calf sling-backs.

Her hips swayed gracefully, her blond hair bounced. The bartender's eyes followed her until she disappeared from sight. Under that cool rich facade lay one hot lady. He could always tell. If only he'd had a little more time, he knew he could have scored.

Rosemary boarded her PSA flight to Los Angeles and settled into her seat. Her luggage—such as it was—was checked through L.A.'s Eastern flight #405, arriving in Palm Beach at 4:44 P.M.

The PSA flight, thank God, lasted only thirty minutes. The other, four hours. Rosemary had an absolute terror of flying. No matter how often she did it, it never got better. Mark couldn't bribe her up in his plane. At least these larger ones looked secure.

"There are more accidents on highways," Mark told her.

"Balls!" shot back Rosemary, not about to be converted by that absurd piece of information. If you were lucky enough to step out of a crashed car, at least you stepped out onto God's solid earth. If you crashed from 30,000 feet, forget it! Or if you crashed on takeoff. Or on landing. Or whatever. She had no confidence in planes. Or in pilots. Only in prayer. It was the grace of God that got her there.

She fingered the delicate jet rosary beads in the pocket of her silk jacket. Sister Mary Alice had given them to her when she graduated Marymount. Rosemary was never without them.

She began with the five decades of the Joyous Mysteries. The Annunciation. The Visitation. The Birth of Jesus. The Presentation, and the Finding in the Temple, filling her mind with images of Mary, the Mother of God, and the Infant Jesus. That always relaxed her.

Halfway through the third decade, she remembered the short impromptu prayer she always said on takeoff and landing. She interrupted the decade to say it. "Dear Jesus, get me there safely and I'll never take another drink again. And I'll always be good." Feeling more confident, she resumed the decade she had interrupted.

She did the same thing from her first-class seat on the Eastern flight from L.A. to Palm Beach.

When the plane's engine revved up, Rosemary's hand slid into the pocket of her jacket as she said the short promise to Jesus, followed by the Our Father.

Once in the air, she relaxed somewhat. When the stewardess came round offering cocktails or wine, Rosemary shook her head.

150

When lunch was offered, Rosemary refused again. She was determined not to add one ounce to what she and The Golden Door had accomplished through perseverance and sheer will. She accepted only coffee. Black. Without sugar.

She stared out the window at drifting cumulus clouds. Then, hand in pocket, fingering the jet beads, she began the five decades of the Glorious Mysteries. The Resurrection. The Ascension. The Descent of the Holy Spirit. The Assumption of the Blessed Virgin Mary, and the Coronation of the Blessed Virgin Mary.

She skipped the five Sorrowful Mysteries. The Agony in the Garden. The Scourging at the Pillar. The Crowning with Thorns. The Carrying of the Cross, and the Crucifixion. She preferred a triumphant Jesus to a suffering one.

These completed, Rosemary allowed her mind to wander. She had telephoned Mrs. Swanson, her housekeeper, informing her of her arrival. Everything was ready. Rosemary's beautiful Mizner house was waiting for her. Peter, her chauffeur, would meet her flight.

She couldn't wait to get there—to relax in the sun, swim in the pool, paint in her studio, shop on the avenue, lunch with friends.

The girls would be home from school for the Thanksgiving holiday. She hadn't seen them since September. Thanksgiving dinner would be just family. Her parents. Her children. Her husband. And her husband's mother.

Unfortunately, Marjorie Hunter had accepted Rosemary's dinner invitation. Surprising Rosemary.

Mark would be down Wednesday night. Flying his own plane from Washington. He couldn't make it before then, he'd told her.

Rosemary had called him from The Golden Door. The first time, she hadn't reached him. She had reached his secretary, Kathleen what's-her-name, the one with the big tits.

Mark thought she didn't know he was screwing that red-headed bitch. But she knew. Mark would screw anything that wasn't bolted to the floor and made of wood, stone, or steel. He was sick, that's what he was. God only knew who or what else he was screwing.

She'd reached him on the second try. The conversation had been stiff and awkward. Not that she hadn't tried to be pleasant.

Telling him how wonderful she felt, what marvels The Golden Door had performed, how she felt like a new woman.

"You're not a new woman, Rosemary," Mark insisted. "You've got the same old problem. Only you're not facing it."

To hell with you, buster, replied Rosemary, midair between L.A. and Palm Beach. Mark was such a mood breaker.

Why did she stay with him anyway? She'd had so much potential. So much promise.

Sister Mary Alice had such high hopes for her.

Rosemary's mood shifted. Purposefully, she cleansed her mind of all negative thoughts and concentrated instead on what she would wear for Thanksgiving dinner.

A good-looking man in his mid-fifties, well-dressed, obviously well-bred, sitting across from Rosemary, tried to make conversation. Rosemary discouraged him. Instead, she took her silver cigarette case from her Hermès purse and smoked three cigarettes in a row.

When Daddy arrived in Palm Beach, everything would pick up. Daddy always made her feel marvelous.

The stewardess announced that Eastern flight #405 would be landing in Palm Beach in a few minutes. Would everyone smoking please extinguish their cigarettes and fasten their seat belts? She wished them a pleasant Sunday evening.

Sunday! In all the flurry and excitement of leaving Escondido, Rosemary had forgotten mass!

She put out her cigarette, fastened her seat belt, said a quick apology to Jesus, and silently uttered the prayer that would help the pilot land the goddamned plane.

It was, she knew, the only way to go.

Early in adulthood, Julia Sheffield realistically assessed that she could not live on the trust fund left her by an adoring father. Not in the manner he had accustomed her to in the years before he, through a series of poor speculations, lost a goodly amount of his fortune.

In order to survive with any style, she had to supplement her income.

She did this in a number of enterprising ways.

She provided services. Discreetly advertised and efficiently expedited.

Since she possessed spectacular good taste, was an inspired coordinator, had entrée to all the best clubs through the accident of generations of good breeding, and possessed a vast roster of influential friends, she capitalized on these assets.

A number of Palm Beach nouveau riche, intimidated by the social skills of the entrenched rich but anxious to enter their ranks, unable to properly coordinate a complete outfit without glaringly advertising their lack of expertise, or cope with an unfamiliar collection of silver set before them at dinners out, sought and utilized the talents of Julia Sheffield.

For a flat fee and a percentage of what they purchased, Julia helped launch them.

She trotted them about to Martha's, Sara Fredericks, Saks, selected their wardrobes, waltzed them to the House of Graet, Cartier, or Van Cleef's for the jewels to complement their outfits, entertained them at the Everglades or the Bath & Tennis, and arranged parties where they could meet some of the older rich.

After the initial launch, they were on their own. Unless they wished to avail themselves of Julia's longer plan. Services for the entire Palm Beach season.

Since she was privy to so much of what was going on in town, Julia was able to convert this knowledge into additional cash.

For another fee, she fed Reenie Boyd, and a couple of other columnists, fodder for their files—information on who was doing what with whom, and where.

Julia understood Reenie Boyd's needs perfectly.

The dirtier the morsel, the better Reenie liked it. And the larger the check Julia received.

She wintered comfortably in Palm Beach, summered in the Hamptons or Europe.

During the winter, she shared a Palm Beach condominium facing the Atlantic. Cissie Morgan, who had been her lover for the past four years, was her roommate.

Cissie was a realtor in town. One of the best. She knew everybody. And everything.

What information Julia didn't pick up on her own was provided by Cissie.

So, two hours after Rosemary Hunter was settled at Casa Miramar, Cissie made the fact known.

"Hear your friend's back in town," Cissie informed Julia. "Recovered from her last binge. Tanned and fit, I understand."

"Really!" Julia and Rosemary often lunched or shopped together. Julia was well aware of Rosemary's drinking problem, and of Mark's sexual wanderings.

Mark Hunter would screw anything that walked. Almost. He'd passed up an opportunity she offered him once when she was between female lovers and a bit high at a party they were both at.

"Sorry, Julia," refused Mark with a grin. "I don't do dikes."

"And fuck you too," retorted Julia. "On second thought, why bother?"

She never forgave him.

Now, she called Rosemary at home. "Darling, I heard you were back in town."

"My God, Julia, if I didn't know better, I'd swear you were on the CIA payroll. How did you find out this fast?"

Julia giggled. What could she say? It was a small town.

Rosemary agreed. "You pee here and everybody hears the john flush."

"I hear you look divine, darling," gushed Julia. "So tell me. Where you've been, what you've done, and with whom."

Rosemary laughed. She felt so good. It was so marvelous to be home. She didn't even mind Julia's nosiness. "Why don't we have lunch? Tomorrow. Give me a buzz in the morning and we can decide where. I'll fill you in then."

Julia agreed. She was certain there'd be some piece of information she could pick up and convert into cash.

19

Ben Gately woke Sunday morning to the sun streaming through the window above his bed on the *Nellie.* He had, as he did most nights, anchored out away from the dock. He liked waking to the freshness of a new day surrounded by water, away from the hubbub and commerce of the world. His TV career depended upon his immersion in that world, yet an essential part of him yearned to reduce life to its barest essentials. An odd duality.

He dressed quickly in cut-off jeans and a crew-neck sweater, didn't bother to shave, made his breakfast, and carried it on deck where he ate, sipping his coffee reflectively.

He thought about last night. And a woman named Kate Crowley. A tall, slender, excitingly beautiful woman with a disturbing duality of her own. She had a face that was expressive one moment, guarded the next. She was unlike any woman he'd ever known.

They'd spent Saturday night together. They had dinner at Chuck & Harold's. At the sidewalk café. Under a wide canvas awning.

The café faced out onto Royal Poinciana Way. Four rows of massive, majestically erect 40-feet-high royal palms with thick cement-gray trunks tapering to slender shafts, topped by feather-shaped ten- to twelve-foot-long green palm fronds, lined both sides of the avenue. The sight was impressive.

The night was mild, more like an early northeastern spring. The sky, a deep purple, was cast with pink. The evening was still, its peace broken only by cars turning the corner on North County

Road onto Royal Poinciana Way, headlights and directional signals impatiently flashing their course.

Ben smiled across the table at Kate and, indicating the royal palms, asked, did Kate know that Addison Mizner, the architect, and Paris Singer, his millionaire benefactor, the creators of Palm Beach as we know it today, attempted to have the royal palms moved to and transplanted in Boca Raton? They envisioned creating another paradise under the sun there. They gave the town board some cockamamy story about the uselessness of the trees. The board, of course, voted down the request. Much to the chagrin of that incorrigible pair.

Kate smiled. No, she hadn't heard that story.

They ordered. Filet of sole Véronique for Kate, Norwegian salmon for Ben.

Ben urged Kate to talk about herself. Kate hedged, but politely related her own history—the early tragedy, the aunts, the college years, working at the House of Graet, transferring to Palm Beach.

Ben listened to Kate describe the tragedy, noticed the same hesitant look cloud her eyes, saw it disappear as quickly as it had come, replaced with the familiar poise and control.

He was puzzled again by the enigma that was Kate Crowley. An ice maiden. Yet vulnerable. Hurting.

He longed to reach out and hold her. Protect her. He was startled by the intensity of the emotion he felt.

Oh, if his sisters could see him now, Ben thought wryly.

Watch it, he warned himself. The lady sitting opposite him affected him like no other lady ever had before.

But what a sight she was! Magnificent green eyes. Fine cheekbones. The slender nose. The sensitive mouth. And that cloud of dark hair framing her exquisite face.

She wore a dove-gray thin wool sleeveless dress with a matching jacket lined in emerald-green silk, draped over her shoulders.

Ben found himself so mesmerized by her eyes, he lost track of what Kate was saying. With effort, he pulled himself together.

Did Kate know the other Palm Beach palm tree story? The one about the coconut palms? Kate shook her head and Ben recounted the tale of the *Providensia*.

"Just think," he mused, "if they'd never gotten loaded on all that free wine, we wouldn't be sitting here having this rewarding conversation."

Kate laughed and Ben watched her face brighten. She needed more brightening in her life, he decided. He knew the perfect place for this happening to take place.

He told her he was planning to celebrate his first Florida Thanksgiving on board the *Nellie*. How would Kate like to be his first official guest?

Kate smiled. "What a lovely invitation. Unfortunately, I already have a commitment." *If waiting for Mark's call could be called that,* she thought to herself.

Ben tried again. "I should let you know I'm a marvelous cook. Trained by six gorgeous gourmets. You won't have to lift a finger."

Kate looked hesitant. "You make it hard to resist."

"Don't resist, then," he suggested easily.

But Kate retreated to a safer place. "I'm really sorry," she said again. There was no point, she decided, in prolonging the relationship with her attractive escort. It had every danger of creating a problem.

Ben knew when to surrender gracefully. "It's an open invitation. If you suddenly find yourself uncommitted, just leave word on my answering machine if I'm not there."

When the dessert cart was wheeled over, they passed. Ben suggested a nightcap at The Breakers. "There's a good trio there I think you'll enjoy."

He didn't want the evening to end.

He wasn't accustomed to women resisting the Gately charm and he was determined to find out why Kate was resisting.

Well, he thought to himself, he didn't yet understand Kate Crowley, that was for sure.

A long, low, crowded bar faced the entrance to the Alcazar Room at The Breakers. And from wide windows, Ben and Kate had a sweeping view of the stone walkway and the waves of the Atlantic crashing on the breakwaters.

They ordered drinks. And rose to dance while they waited. The Don Chattaway Trio provided the music. The dance floor was postage-stamp small. Intimate. The trio played "Stardust." Ben pulled Kate closer.

In her heels, she was almost as tall as he. The match was

perfect. The fit was perfect. He bent his head slightly and his lips brushed against Kate's hair.

They finished their dance and dawdled over their drinks. Kate said, "That view is quite glorious."

Ben suggested they explore it up closer. He motioned for the check, paid it, led Kate down the corridor, through the double doors, and down the stone steps onto the walkway. A 3-foot-high stone ledge ran the approximate 400-foot length of the walkway.

They walked it in silence, stopped, stood at the stone ledge, and looked out over the Atlantic. A three-quarter moon cut a path across the water. Hotel lights reflected back irregular shapes. The sounds of splashing waves mixed with the haunting strains of the vocalist's rendition of "Send in the Clowns."

Kate shivered.

"Cold?" asked Ben.

She shook her head. Remained silent. Suddenly she said, "Problems seem so minute at moments like these, don't they?"

"Have you such weightsome problems to warrant such philosophical reflections, Miss Crowley?" he teased.

She turned to him. "No. Of course not. Only the small nagging concerns that trouble us all. But at times like these, they don't seem to matter much."

"I couldn't agree with you more," said Ben, bending to kiss her.

Startled, Kate drew back. "You didn't have to do that."

"That was something I wanted to do, not something I had to do," he informed her.

"I don't want to complicate things, Ben," Kate said.

"We won't complicate them," he assured her. "We'll just let them develop naturally." He brushed her hair back from her face, lifted her chin, and, cupping her face in both hands, kissed her once more. Then he took her firmly by the elbow. "C'mon. I'll take you home now."

When they pulled into her driveway, he turned the engine off, walked around to Kate's side, and helped her out. He walked her to the door.

Kate extended a hand. "Thank you, Ben. For a lovely evening."

Ben accepted her hand. And held it. "You make it sound like an ending. Instead of a beginning."

She withdrew her hand. "Good night, Ben."

"Good night, Kate." He waited until she was inside.

He thought about his words on the way home. *A beginning.* That's what he had called it. That's what it was. How long it would take to develop into something more was another matter.

But develop it would.

The lady was a challenge.

And Ben Gately loved challenges. He was persistent and competitive, qualities that served him well professionally.

And he was definitely determined to unravel the mystery of Kate Crowley.

~20~

Mark Hunter landed his twin-engine Cessna at Palm Beach International Airport forty-five minutes after Eastern's flight #405, with Rosemary on board, landed.

The last time he talked with Rosemary, she was too busy euphorically describing the wonders wrought by Escondido's Golden Door to mention anything so prosaic as when she would be arriving in Palm Beach.

He'd told her he'd be there Wednesday evening. This Sunday flight of his was a spur-of-the-moment thing.

He kept a car, a highly visible Maserati, garaged at the airport. He rented a less conspicuous Buick from Avis.

The Avis girl recognized him. A cute little brunette with a button nose, huge brown eyes, and breasts about to burst forth from her uniform jacket.

Mark took her into his confidence. "I'm only here for the evening. Surprising my wife. Don't want anyone to know I'm in town."

The Avis brunette enjoyed the game. She flashed a smile and assured the senator his secret would remain her secret.

After Mark left with the key to the Buick, the fortyish blonde who worked beside her scoffed, "Wife, my eye! Knowing him, he's got some tootsie on hold nearby!"

The young brunette looked shocked. "Evelyn, you're a terrible cynic."

"Damned right," affirmed Evelyn. "Years of practice."

She was right. Mark was on his way to see Kate. And he had no intention of checking at the house to find out when Rosemary was expected.

He'd made his decision impulsively. Sunday, instead of offering a respite from his Senate chores, threatened to stretch interminably before him. He was restless, charged up, Georgetown seemed stifling, and his last conversations with Kate were less than satisfying.

He had a sudden need to smooth things out. He knew he'd be home for Thanksgiving. He also knew he'd be tied up with family matters. Not an ideal time for mending relationships. Rosemary undoubtedly had scheduled his entire holiday so he'd have no free time.

He called Kate from Georgetown. She was, he thought, less enthusiastic than he had anticipated. He told her he'd called several times before. Kate didn't volunteer information on where she'd been.

Mark frowned as he drove, noting that traffic was getting heavier. After Thanksgiving, and throughout the season, it would be impossible to maneuver around.

He cut over to Flagler Drive and drove along, enjoying the view of the Intracoastal Waterway on his left. Boat traffic was heavier, too, boat enthusiasts out in force. It was that kind of day—mild suddenly, in the mid-seventies, after a cool spell. Gentle breezes blowing in off the lake lifted his spirits, took away the edginess he had experienced earlier.

What was wrong with him? Generally, he had a handle on things. Usually, he was able to juggle the different parts of his life —career, family, personal affairs—with the ease of a circus performer.

From the beginning, he had always had a plan and a direction. He knew who he was, knew where he was headed, and knew how to get there.

From the time he was a small boy, his father, his mother, his uncles, had prepared him. A Hunter for president. He was the Hunter chosen to fulfill the destiny.

It was because of Rosemary he was feeling unglued. Her behavior was so erratic that it was taking a toll.

Only Kate expected nothing from him. She accepted what they had together and demanded nothing more. For five years their relationship had flourished until it had developed into something he could depend on. He needed Kate to provide sanity. Whatever was bothering her, he knew he could straighten things out.

He patted the flat, handsomely wrapped package he'd placed on the seat beside him. It was an expensive peace offering he'd picked up yesterday at the House of Graet, Washington. Kate would love it. He'd planned to give it to her for Christmas.

He decided this was a more politic time.

Kate Crowley tucked the white silk blouse into her white silk pleated skirt and added a wide ivory lizard belt. She brushed her dark hair, parted in the center, until it fell in a smooth shimmer to her shoulders. She touched up her lipstick and pushed the earrings Mark had given her last Christmas into her lobes, anchoring them securely.

They were exquisite. Flawless pear-shaped emeralds, surrounded by pavé diamonds. They had cost a fortune. She knew. But didn't *he* know, she asked, he didn't have to buy her expensive gifts? She loved him anyway.

He liked buying her expensive gifts, he told her. End of discussion. Except to say it gave him pleasure watching her wear them. Emeralds. To match her eyes. The perfect choice. For his perfect love.

Facing her mirror image, Kate wondered absently why Mark was coming today. She'd planned a quiet Sunday to unwind and tend to the household chores that had accumulated during the week.

She walked out of the bedroom, down the stairs, into the kitchen. She took two glasses from the cabinet and set them in the refrigerator, alongside a bottle of white wine and a pitcher of martinis, prepared the way Mark liked them—chilled Beefeater gin, a whisper of vermouth, a sliver of lemon peel.

The salad was prepared but not mixed. The steaks were ready to throw on the fire, along with two foil-wrapped potatoes. There was peach sorbet for dessert.

"Nothing fussy," instructed Mark. "I just need to see you."

At one time, that simple declaration of need would have sent her into orbit.

She walked out of the kitchen, through the house, into the sunroom facing out onto the lake. Small craft drifted by. A sail-

162

boat with rainbow-colored sails, a good-sized yacht, a speedboat cutting through the water, leaving behind a path of foam.

Kate stretched out on a chaise and stared out the windows at the perfect view. It failed to nourish her and she wondered why.

She was accustomed to Mark's impromptu visits and demands. Mark rarely asked her her preferences. Rather, he took it for granted she would want what he wanted. Generally, she did. And generally, she found security in his authority.

From the time Mark flew her to Delaware for those renowned soft-shell crabs, her life had been lived solely, it seemed, to accommodate him.

Few people knew about their affair. She had taken great pains to protect their privacy, knowing Mark was paranoid about the press. Theirs was not a relationship designed to blossom in the light. She knew that. But, then, so much of her life had been shrouded in secrecy, it didn't feel unusual.

Why, then, did it suddenly disturb her?

How different her date with Ben had been. Surprisingly, she had enjoyed her entire evening with him. Except when he kissed her. Why had he complicated things?

And why had she lied to him? Told him the story of the plane crash and her idyllic childhood? Ah, but she knew why. When you exchanged truths with someone, you handed over pieces of yourself. The truth implied trust, and trust implied commitment.

Even Mark didn't know the truth about her. After all this time, he had no idea of what she had been through. Kate preferred it that way. She suspected Mark would too.

She heard a car pull into the driveway and stop near the rear of the house. Mark always buried his car under the protection of the fullest trees, free from prying eyes and away from the probing lenses of paparazzi he suspected lurked everywhere, waiting to entrap him.

Kate rose and opened the front door. She stared at the sight of him. His cap was pulled down to the top of his sunglasses. The collar of his jacket was pulled up, hiding most of his face. How had he seen to drive?

Mark grinned. "Can't be too careful. Paparazzi everywhere." He pulled her to him, kissed her hard and hungrily, buried his face in her hair, and whispered, "God, it's good to be here, Kate. You've no idea how much I missed you."

He drew back, placed his hands on her shoulders, and held her eyes with his. "This is where I needed to be."

Suddenly, as quickly as they'd come, Kate's doubts vanished. She was glad he was here. She felt safe in the protection of his arms. She belonged there. "I'm glad you came, Mark," she told him.

He held up the handsomely wrapped package. Kate recognized the paper. He took her hand. "I've brought you a surprise. Now, follow Santa, like a good girl."

He led Kate up the stairs to her bedroom. He turned, pulled her to him, kissed her again, and handed her the package. "Open it now," he insisted.

She carefully unwrapped the familiar gold paper, too well instructed in how much care went into the wrapping of a package to rip the paper off heedlessly, no matter how eager she was.

Mark never took his eyes off her.

She withdrew the long gold leather box with the embossed *HG*, released the clasp, and stared at the emerald and diamond necklace resting against its white velvet cushion. Pear-shaped emeralds, breathtakingly beautiful. Flawless in cut, color, and clarity. Interspersed with round and marquise-shaped diamonds, flashing brilliantly. A match to the earrings Mark had given her last Christmas.

She raised her eyes. "Oh, Mark," she gasped, "it's exquisite!"

Mark lifted her chin and gazed into her eyes. "Emerald eyes. My Kate has emerald eyes. It's the stone that most makes me think of you."

Not a word did Kate say of the outrageous price she knew he had paid for the necklace. She was too touched by his gesture. How could she ever doubt his love? Or be cross because she felt he treated her carelessly?

She handed the necklace to him. "Put it on for me, please, darling." She turned her back to him, lifted her long dark hair, and waited.

"I have a better idea," Mark told her. "Undress for me. I'll put it on then."

Obediently, she turned to face him, and slowly, gracefully, undid the buttons of her white silk blouse. She unzipped her skirt, stepped out of it, tossed it on the bed. She slipped out of her blouse, undid her bra, and tossed them both over. She slid down her silk bikini pants and left them on the floor.

She stood before him, tall, slender, naked, except for the emerald and diamond earrings, and her high-heeled lizard sandals. She turned slowly away from him, walked to the threefold mirror of her vanity, lifted the long dark hair once more, and waited.

Mark walked over, put the necklace around Kate's neck, secured the clasp, covered her breasts with his hands, and studied their reflections.

"Nice," he said, his lips against her neck.

"It's beautiful," breathed Kate.

"You're beautiful," Mark insisted, his voice rough. He pressed himself into her back, quickly unzipped his trousers, released himself, and turning Kate around, grabbed hold of her buttocks and raised her slightly so he could enter her.

"God!" he cried. "Oh, God, that's more like it!"

It was over in a second or two.

Mark apologized easily. "Sorry to act like a sailor who hasn't had shore leave in a month," he said, looking chagrined.

He took Kate's hand, led her back to the bed, laid her down, and quickly undressed. Then, slowly and expertly, he brought her to climax.

He grinned, kissed her lightly, and circled her nipple with his finger. "What do you say we try another one, darling, this time for the both of us?"

They lingered over drinks on the patio while their steaks sizzled on the fire. For the first time in days, Mark felt thoroughly relaxed. He lifted his martini, sipped it appreciatively, and smiled at Kate. "I made it into Palm Beach with no one recognizing me except the Avis girl. And she's sworn to secrecy."

Kate smiled back as her hand strayed to the emerald and diamond necklace. "In that outlandish outfit of yours, darling, who would recognize you? You were completely disguised."

21

Kate was wrong. So was Mark. Julia Sheffield was certain she recognized Mark Hunter when he pulled up alongside her at the red light on Flagler Drive. Even in that absurd cap and jacket, even with those wraparound sunglasses, and driving that dinky Buick, she knew it was he.

Or thought she did. He was so preoccupied, he didn't even notice her. She was in the left lane, preparing to cross the bridge over to Palm Beach. To satisfy her curiosity, she switched suddenly to the right lane, maneuvering her yellow Jaguar behind the Buick, infuriating the driver next in line, who glared at her. Julia Sheffield glared back.

She followed the Buick along Flagler until it signaled a right turn into a driveway. She drove a few feet ahead, pulled over to the curb, and turned around in her seat.

Sure enough, the figure striding toward the front door was Mark Hunter. No one else walked like that, as though the entire universe were his.

She watched as the front door opened, framing a tall, slender, dark-haired woman dressed in white. Julia Sheffield thought she looked familiar. With a slight frown, she watched the door close behind them.

Whoever she was, she and Mark Hunter certainly looked as though they'd been cozy for a long, long time.

Julia made a U-turn, and drove the Jaguar slowly past the white stucco house until she spotted the number. She kept it firmly in mind until she was able to stop the car and scribble it down on the corner of a past-due Bonwit's bill she found in her purse.

As soon as she reached the oceanfront apartment she shared

166

with Cissie, Julia started dialing. After a few phone calls, she reached Cissie at the Bath & Tennis. Julia explained her problem. Cissie knew exactly whose house that was. She had just sold one two doors down from there, and had run into the owner of the one Julia was so curious about. That house, explained Cissie, belonged to Kate Crowley. That long, gorgeous House of Graet vice-president.

So, that's who it was!

Julia thanked Cissie and placed the phone back on the receiver.

Well, what have we here? A little love nest, right across the lake. Cozy, folksy, and just about as harmless as a teacup filled with TNT.

Apparently, Rosemary didn't know a thing about it. Nor was she aware Mark was in town. She certainly hadn't mentioned it when they'd talked on the phone.

Wait until she told Reenie Boyd!

This little tidbit should certainly merit a respectable sum.

Every call that came in on Reenie's private line was taped, then filed.

Reenie, for all her wealth, power, and public image—or because of it—was zealous about her privacy. Each employee of hers was required to sign an affidavit, contingent upon being hired, that nothing personal about Reenie Boyd would be disclosed, either in print or spoken word, should said employee leave his or her designated post.

A Japanese houseman, a Swedish cook, and a British secretary attended Reenie's needs in her fourteen-room duplex. They were dismissed at night, except when certain functions warranted their presence. Only Delia, who took care of Reenie's personal needs, lived in, and only Delia was privy to Reenie's private doings.

The answering machine to Reenie's private line was off limits to everyone but Reenie and Delia. The British secretary had strict instructions not to touch it. The Swedish cook spoke little English, and the Japanese houseman couldn't have cared less.

Reenie walked across the room in her study-office to the bar, fixed herself a bourbon straight, and taking a large swallow, glanced at her notes.

Most of the messages were from stringers calling in with items for "Reenie's Roster." Reenie had stringers throughout the country. She also had friends who contributed information on who was doing what, where, and with whom. After all, Reenie couldn't be *everywhere*.

She paid the stringers by the inch, a practice that went back to early newspaper days. The friends were rewarded differently. Theater tickets to a current Broadway hit, a scarf from Hermès, a trinket from Tiffany's, the House of Graet, or Cartier, or Joy or Bal à Versailles from Saks or Bonwit's.

The gift was proportionate to the value of the information received. Sometimes Reenie rewarded a friend with cash.

Julia Sheffield was a friend, but only because it was expedient to keep her as one. Actually, Reenie despised her. Julia was useful, however. She had a nose long enough to pry into everyone's business and a hide thick enough to insulate her from rebuff. And she was always in need of cash. The combination of character deficiencies suited Reenie's purposes perfectly.

She answered her other calls, saving Julia's for last. She reached her about nine.

"Darlin'," drawled Reenie. "Sorry to take so long gettin' back to you, but I just got in."

Julia made annoying small talk until Reenie cut in nicely. "Sugah, my other line's lightin' up. Hold on a sec." She put Julia on hold, lit a cigarette, buffed a fingernail she had snagged earlier, freshened her drink, took a deep swallow of bourbon, and got back to Julia. "Sorry, luv. I have an emergency on the other line. What's up?"

Julia told her. She sounded like a child who had just unearthed a treasure.

As indeed she had. Reenie understood the child required praise. "Well, well, well, well, well," crooned Reenie in approval. "You've outdone yourself, darlin'."

Julia expanded under the praise. "It was just by the sheerest of coincidences I saw him. And Rosemary's in town, I just heard."

"That's it, darlin'. That's how the best things come to us. Sheer accident. A bonanza when you least expect it."

Before Julia could launch into another monologue, Reenie cut her off. "Sweetie, I must run. My other call's probably peein' in his pants by now. You've done well, sugah, real well, and Reenie

168

wants you to know you'll be receivin' somethin' very special by express mail. Talk to you soon, darlin'. In fact, I'll see you soon. I should be in Palm Beach right after Thanksgivin'. Now, remembah, give my love to Cissie, and you take care, heah?" She hung up quickly.

"Well," said Reenie aloud, "what do you know!" Everyone on God's green earth knew Mark Hunter's reputation as a womanizer, but cavortin' right in his wife's backyard was not terribly smart. Especially for a man positioning himself for the presidency.

This little revelation of extramarital high-jinks would certainly add fuel to Rosemary's drinking problem. Mark Hunter thought he'd kept the secret neatly under wraps, but there was little Reenie didn't know about other people's messes. Celebrity news was her business. But celebrity *bad* news was her specialty.

Besides, she and Senator Hunter had a very personal score to settle!

"Reenie's Roster" was syndicated coast to coast and read avidly by 30 million loyal readers over breakfast coffee. Many drab lives were temporarily uplifted by the knowledge that the rich got theirs too. Even if it happened only in Reenie's column. She always had the last word. Generally, she printed it.

That Sunday night, Reenie added the blind item about Mark Hunter and Kate Crowley to her column. Then she called her messenger service and had them pick it up and deliver it to the wire service.

Neither Mark Hunter nor Kate Crowley was named. But Reenie knew her readers enjoyed a good guessing game. And most of the beautiful people who read "Reenie's Roster" would have no trouble identifying the mystery figures.

How could they?

The blind item read: "What handsome eastern senator with presidential fever was caught sneaking into what beauteous Palm Beach jewelry exec's West Palm pad when his wife, just settling into Palm Beach for the season, didn't even know he was in town?

"Reenie has eyes everywhere, Senator, or didn't you know?"

<center>22</center>

Most little girls like to play dress-up. At sixty-eight, Mimzee Dawson liked to play queen. She'd been playing it for years.

One of her upstairs walk-in closets housed the queen costumes. Gowns she had made to represent her favorite queens of history—Cleopatra, Catherine the Great, Marie Antoinette, Mary Queen of Scots, Empress Eugénie, and Elizabeth I of England.

Queen Bess was Mimzee's favorite. Even though Mimzee herself had had four husbands, she identified most with the red-haired Virgin Queen, who ruled over an expanding empire with imperial unpredictability.

The wig room, an antechamber to one of the walk-in closets in Mimzee's bedroom suite, housed the wig collection.

Displayed on white marble wig stands, on shelves built to her specifications, stood the high powdered wigs of Marie Antoinette, the jet-black wigs of Cleopatra, the short curly red wigs of Queen Bess, and the elaborate concoctions of miscellaneous figures from seventeenth- and eighteenth-century European royalty.

Mimzee's personal collection of wigs, separate from the others, blazed in the famous "Dawson red." Mimzee was bald as a cue ball, a fact kept hidden from everyone but her doctor and her wigmaker.

Mimzee's walk-in safe was in another antechamber. Part of the fun of playing queen was donning a queen's jewelry. Necklaces, bracelets, pendants, brooches, rings, tiaras, and other ornaments once owned by royalty were to be found in Mimzee's safe, the combination known only to Mimzee and the safemaker.

Included in the famous Dawson jewel collection were:

170

An emerald and ruby rivière, or chain, belonging to Catherine the Great.

A diamond stomacher worn by Marie-Louise de Bourbon.

A gold and baroque pearl pendant that once belonged to Anne of Austria, mother of the Sun King, Louis XIV.

The renowned Renaissance Rianini baroque pearls—huge pear-shaped pearls set in diamond mounts and fashioned into pendant earrings.

A Sévigné brooch, belonging to Maria Amalia Christina, queen of Spain.

A demiparure, pearl necklace and brooch, former jewels of the queen of Naples.

Jewels from the collection of Marie Antoinette, including a diamond necklace, not, however, the one reputed to have sparked the French Revolution that resulted, for the queen, in the loss of her head.

Revolutions served Mimzee well. During the upheaval preceding and following them, jewels disappear, find their way into other countries, are cut, restyled, and sold to begin their new odyssey to new ownership. When a piece of significance came on the market, Mimzee wanted to be the first to know. Her "finders" kept her posted.

Mimzee's tiara collection was also legendary. Mimzee wore tiaras the way some women wear hats. Unlike most women, Mimzee wore hers to breakfast. After all, how could you play queen without a tiara?

Not that Mimzee *played* queen, so much as she *was* queen. At least in her own mind. Save for an accident of birth, the heiress to the toothpaste and deodorant fortune saw herself as royal-born. How else explain how *right* she felt arrayed in all her imperial splendor?

Thus, bedecked and bejeweled, wearing her queen-of-the-day costume, Mimzee entertained. Her guests viewed her eccentricities quietly. To comment was to risk censure in the form of being crossed off the Dawson guest list. No one wished to risk exclusion.

For Mimzee was the last of the flamboyant hostesses. There were no parties to equal hers since Eva Stotesbury, known as Queen Eva, retired and relinquished the social mantle to Marjorie

Merriweather Post. It was not likely there would be another. Times change. Styles in hostesses change. Mimzee Dawson might be an anachronism, but she was the only one left. And she was still hanging on.

The Kirsten diamond was the perfect adjunct to the Dawson jewel collection. Granted, it had not been owned by a queen. That honor belonged to Mimzee. She was determined to have it. Nothing would satisfy her until the Kirsten was in her possession.

There was only one obstacle. The contessa.

Mimzee flew to New York in her private jet and presented Consuela with a certified check for $15 million.

Consuela refused it. The Kirsten, she patiently explained once more, was not for sale. At the moment. When it was, she would, of course, give Mimzee's desire top priority.

"Balls!" replied Mimzee. "Of course it's for sale. You're nitpicking about a technicality."

Consuela pointed out that *technicality* included others who had expressed interest. Their wishes must be respected too.

"Horseshit!" Mimzee told her bluntly. "Money talks, and mine's right here." A bony jeweled finger thrust the $15 million cashier's check across the desk toward Consuela.

A slender finger eased it back. *"Cara,* if I *could,* I *would.* But there are other things to consider. Ethics, for one."

"Ethics, hell, Consuela. You and I are a couple of old horse traders. You showed me your Kirsten, and I'm showing you my check. That's a good enough horse trader's exchange for me." Mimzee looked shrewdly across at Consuela. "If you want more money . . . ?"

"It is not a question of money, *cara."*

"Well, of course it's a question of money, dearie. What else? We're not a couple of Indians trading beads. I can bid higher."

Consuela looked strained. "It is not a question of a bid, *cara amica.* If I could accommodate your wishes, I would. Nothing would please me more. But right now that is impossible. I am in the midst of preparing for a major press conference. The Kirsten tour is already scheduled. Others have made appointments to view the Kirsten." She spread her hands wide. "My hands are tied."

Mimzee thought of Oliver Cromwell. "A man never goes so far as when he does not know where he is going." Well, Mimzee

172

knew where *she* was going. She was going in the direction of the Kirsten. If she had to follow the goddamned thing around the world to get it, she would do it.

She decided to change tactics.

She reached across the desk and patted Consuela's hand affectionately. "Dearie, we're getting absolutely nowhere, and I don't want to hold you up any longer. I know you have a busy day."

Consuela smiled gratefully. "Thank you, *cara*. It was good of you to come all this way."

"Nonsense. I wouldn't have missed it for the world," insisted Mimzee.

Consuela rose and came round the desk, the $15 million certified check in her hand. "Your check, Mimzee."

Mimzee brushed it aside. "You hold on to that, dearie. I'm staking my claim on that diamond. I want it, and you know I want it. We'll tidy up the details later."

Before Consuela could reply, Mimzee said, "Don't bother to see me to the door. I know the way by now." She gathered up her voluminous mink cape from where she had flung it and strode out, dragging the cape behind her, an awesome but comic figure in her embroidered wool caftan, her face made up to its continually startled look, bright red curls poking out girlishly from under her high mink hat.

Only the eyes, bright and steely blue, indicated that Mimzee Dawson knew exactly where she was going and how long it would take to get there.

Consuela forced herself to remember that weeks that began disastrously could end gloriously. Thursday was the Kirsten press conference. All her energies had to be channeled toward that.

Dio mio, who would have thought she would come armed with money? And be so persistent?

Really! She had burst into Consuela's office, barging past Suzy, whom she rudely brushed aside, demanding what she called a "look-see" at the Kirsten. Then she plunked down an unexpected $15 million cashier's check on the desk.

Money talks, she had said. Well, money talked only when Consuela decided it had a mouth to speak.

* * *

A more pleasant bit of business on Monday restored Consuela's good spirits.

Suzy had left a copy of the Sunday *New York Times* ad introducing the new House of Graet miniature calculator on Consuela's desk. A goodly amount of House of Graet money had gone into creating the calculator and promoting it. The *New York Times* ad ran concurrently with double-page full-color *Vogue* and *Harper's* spreads and a series of thirty- and sixty-second TV spot commercials.

The name of the calculator was L'Aventur. The adventure. It carried a $20,000 price tag.

Consuela picked up the ad and studied it.

L'Aventur was being presented in time for the Christmas market. The miniature calculator was palm-size. "A great little stocking stuffer," one ad suggested. The case was twenty-four-karat gold. The cover was pale gold Moroccan leather. Consuela had sent a House of Graet representative to Morocco to personally select the hides at the tannery. Louis-Philippe had designed the case and the cover with its embossed *HG* symbol.

L'Aventur was a printing calculator. It printed out information like a cash register or an adding machine. It could be read item by item. Its calculator memory remembered, even after the machine was turned off.

But besides its utilitarian advantages, L'Aventur was a thing of beauty. Precious stones that served as keys—diamonds, rubies, sapphires, emeralds—studded the twenty-four-karat gold face. It was delectable enough to ensure instant attention to its delighted owners.

The campaign, Consuela knew, was timed well. L'Aventur was a luxury piece. For a select few. They could expect interesting results.

Consuela smiled amiably, her spirits completely restored.

Carl Schmittle arrived a bit after 2:30 on Tuesday. Consuela showed him the Kirsten. He was overwhelmed. "My God, Contessa, it's beyond description!"

Men, reflected Consuela, had so much more finesse. When a

woman wanted something badly, she allowed her greed to show. Greed was never attractive to witness. Especially in someone else.

She smiled graciously. *"Sì.* As I told you."

Carl shook his head. "More so. Louis-Philippe's done a magnificent job. It's absolutely breathtaking."

Consuela agreed. "Breathtaking!"

Carl asked permission to hold it. Consuela nodded assent.

He held the necklace carefully in his large hands and examined it. "I can picture it on Rosemary," he said, turning to Consuela. She nodded wisely. *"Magnifico!"*

Carl continued to study the necklace. "Rosemary needs a little perking up right now. She's been a bit under lately."

"Oh?" Consuela's eyes expressed concern. "I am sorry to hear that, Carl. I did not know."

He carefully returned the necklace to its presentation box. "Nothing too serious, thank God. I'd just like to give that girl of mine a boost and, by George, I think this necklace of yours might just do it, Contessa."

"How could it not?" acknowledged Consuela graciously.

"So I've decided to take it. One look, as you can see, and I've fallen under its spell." He grinned as he removed his wallet from his breast pocket, took a cashier's check from it, and offered it to Consuela. "I believe the amount is correct. You said 15 million?"

Consuela nodded dumbly. The prospect of two $15 million cashier's checks in two days was unnerving. But she smiled charmingly and spread her hands in distress. "Ah, but, Carl, as I explained to you Sunday, the Kirsten is not for sale at the moment." She launched quickly into repeating the account of the Kirsten tour and all it entailed.

Carl Schmittle was a man whose phenomenal success was achieved by hurdling obstacles most men stumbled over. He was also a realist, with tremendous patience when needed. He knew he could afford to wait.

He thanked Consuela and smoothly eased her embarrassment. "Certainly, Contessa. I understand." He laughed good-naturedly. "I just like to put my money where my mouth is. I hope I won't be faulted for anything more than enthusiasm."

"Of course, of course," Consuela assured him. She extended the hand holding the $15 million cashier's check.

Like Mimzee Dawson, Carl Schmittle waved it aside. Only much more graciously. "No, Contessa, you hold on to that."

"But, Carl . . ."

"I understand your position perfectly," he told her. "But I also want that necklace. So, whenever you're ready to talk, you just let me know."

23

As soon as the blind item in "Reenie's Roster" appeared in the *New York Globe,* it began to attract attention.

Kathleen Connelly, Mark's secretary, spotted it at once. A mass of anger formed in the pit of her stomach.

So that's who that son of a bitch was seeing!

Furious, she scissored the item out of the paper, slapped some rubber cement on it, and positioned it carefully on a sheet of white typing paper. Then she centered it on Mark's desk over the correspondence that awaited his signature. Only a blind man could fail to see it there.

She did several other things in quick succession. She canceled her Wednesday lunchtime exercise class, made a decision to resume her consciousness-raising sessions, and called George Baxter to tell him she'd be delighted to spend the weekend with him in the Poconos.

Kathleen Connelly wasn't the only one to call Mark a son of a bitch. Carl Schmittle called him that and several other choice names. He wasn't aware he had spoken out loud.

"What's that you said, Carl?" asked Grace Schmittle absently.

Carl snapped the paper shut. "Nothing important, Mother." He'd take the paper with him so she couldn't see it. Not that she was likely to connect it with Rosemary and Mark. Grace was naive about things like that. Still, you never knew.

"You're taking the paper with you? I haven't seen it yet." Grace Schmittle raised her eyes from her book, *Roses—Their Nurturing Effects.*

"Sorry, honey. I need to check out something in it. I'll bring it home this evening." By evening she'd have forgotten. He bent,

177

kissed her on the cheek, and quickly walked out of the breakfast room.

Sitting in the back of his chauffeur-driven Rolls limousine on his way into the city, Carl fumed and planned his strategy. He would make that bastard son-in-law of his toe the mark if it was the last thing he did on this earth.

All of his fury was directed toward Mark. Absently, he tried to fix a picture in his mind of the House of Graet vice-president mentioned in the item. He failed. He thought about calling Consuela, then decided against it. He'd handle this thing without assistance from anyone.

Mark noticed the clipping when he stopped by his office on his way to lunch. Notice it! How could he not notice it? All cemented and centered on top of everything else on his desk.

Kathleen was out of her office. Mark vaguely recalled an exercise class she attended several times a week.

He experienced varied reactions to the article. His first impulse was to strangle Reenie Boyd. That bitch had it in for him ever since she'd set up an assignation at her apartment and he had failed to show up. Easy ass never tempted him. He preferred to pursue his. Besides, there was so much easy stuff around, Reenie Boyd was the last piece of it he'd go after. Not with her mouth. But a woman scorned had other resources. Reenie's were unique. He read the item again.

And worried about Rosemary. She'd called him Monday morning at the office. After trying to reach him, she said, all over the goddamned globe. Where in hell had he been? She'd arrived in Palm Beach early Sunday evening.

Mark lied easily. Charlie Paultzer was in Washington for the evening. They'd gone out on the town. Charlie really tied one on, Mark told her, forcing a laugh.

"And you tucked him into bed after an evening of good-natured boyish revelry?"

"As a matter of fact, I did."

"I bet!"

"The truth is rarely believed, Rosemary."

"You can say that again! Especially when the source is so suspect."

As always, their ability to fail to communicate got in their way. Mark said he'd be down for Thanksgiving.

"Are you certain you can squeeze us into your schedule?" Rosemary asked. Mark thought of Kate, who had registered the same complaint.

"There's no need for sarcasm, Roe."

"On the contrary," countered Rosemary, "sarcasm can be very comforting. Particularly when you're left with little else." She hung up on him before he could respond.

Now Mark wondered if Rosemary had seen the item. And if she'd connect the two figures described. And how she would react. He discovered he was perspiring. He loosened his tie and unbuttoned his shirt collar.

Then he broke one of his cardinal rules for caution. He called Kate at work. Her secretary put the call through.

Kate was surprised to hear his voice.

"Listen," said Mark. "There's an item in today's *Globe.*"

"Yes. I've seen it."

"Christ, Kate, if I could get my hands on that bitch, I'd kill her."

"That's hardly a viable solution, Mark. Besides, it's against the law."

"So is lousing up other people's lives—or it should be, anyway." He paused. "Look, Kate, there's going to be a ruckus over this and I'm going to have to come up with something plausible. I think it best meanwhile to stay close to home and hearth and repair some personal and political fences."

Mark's tone was reasonable and conciliatory. Kate had an image of him as a general mapping out a campaign, moving the pins representing his battalions around on the board.

Which pin was she?

Where would he move her?

She waited.

"Kate?"

"I'm here, Mark."

"Which means any chance of seeing you over Thanksgiving holiday is out."

"I see."

"You do see, don't you, darling?"

"I said I did, didn't I?"

"Kate, it's only for a little while. Until it's not news any longer."

She saw her future unfolding in a series of scenes while she waited for new news to become old news so their relationship could be resumed. She saw herself, for the first time, as something of a joke, the grade-B Hollywood movie version of the back-street wife: expendable, replaceable, removable.

It was not a pretty picture.

"Kate?"

"Yes, Mark?"

"You haven't said anything."

"I'm looking for my lines in the script."

"Don't be like that, Kate."

"Mark, do me a favor. Don't tell me what to be like anymore." She placed the phone firmly down on the receiver.

She buzzed Nancy. Without pretense she said, "If he calls again, Nancy, tell him I'm in conference."

"I'll tell him you're in Taluti."

"Taluti?"

"It's a place he'll never find. I made it up."

Despite herself, Kate laughed. "It sounds pleasant, Nancy. Book me some space there."

"Only if you promise not to tell anyone else about it. Otherwise, it'll be so jammed, you'll never be able to get in."

Kate sat quietly at her desk thinking about the ramifications of Reenie Boyd's item. How it would affect her and Mark.

Mark's major concern was himself. As usual. Or what his wife would do. Not with Kate's welfare at all.

What's new about that? brooded Kate.

She wondered about Rosemary. Was she likely to play the irate wife? The thought of Rosemary Hunter storming into the House of Graet in search of Kate was not exactly cheering. It was downright depressing.

How had her life become so complicated?

The need for simplicity suddenly seemed urgent.

Kate thought of Ben Gately, remembered his invitation to Thanksgiving dinner, recalled the attention he had showered upon her, and felt a desperate need for more of the same.

She picked up the phone and dialed Ben's number. The machine informed her Ben was not at home. It pleasantly requested the caller to leave a message.

Kate gratefully complied.

Ben listened to his messages played back when he returned to the *Nellie*. Only one interested him.

"Ben? Kate Crowley. About that offer of a home-cooked Thanksgiving dinner. I'd love to come. If the offer's still open, that is. And, incidentally, if it is, what can I bring?"

Ben wondered what had changed her mind. Whatever it was, he was glad. He wasn't aware his good fortune was due to a lady he had never met who had sought release from humiliation by venting her wrath in a column he never read.

In New York, Consuela read the item with distaste.

What a way to make a living! On other people's weaknesses! Thank God, she catered to the simple needs of people. They wanted a piece of jewelry; she, Consuela, provided it. She felt disgust for such a trade as Reenie Boyd's and unparalleled loathing for a woman whose livelihood fattened on the failings of others.

The maternal part of Consuela knew how Kate must be hurting, longed to console her and reassure her that this, too, would pass. The practical part of her won out.

She placed the call to Palm Beach.

"Kate, how are you?" Consuela asked cheerfully.

"Fine, Consuela," lied Kate.

Consuela ignored the strain in Kate's voice. "*Cara,* I do not like circumlocution. I will come directly to the point. I trust you have seen the item in this morning's paper."

"Yes, Consuela. I and most of the country, I'm sure."

"At the moment, I am only concerned with you."

"Look, Consuela . . ." Kate began.

"No, you look, Kate. I did not call to scold you or to rub your nose in grime. What I wanted to suggest is that you do a tour of the southern branches. Work out your itinerary so you can leave

181

tomorrow. A week or so should do it. It has to be done anyway and this is as good a time as any. By the time you return, this will have blown away nicely. Disasters, fortunately, never last long. Otherwise, we would all collapse. They are temporary inconveniences."

Kate's voice caught. "I want you to know, Consuela, it's all over between me and Mark."

"Oh? Good! Just in time, I would say. Now, start that itinerary, Kate. And keep your spirits up. *Ciao, carissima.*"

"*Ciao,* Consuela. And thank you."

Consuela put the phone down and gave the conversation no further thought. She had other things on her mind.

The Kirsten press conference was tomorrow.

24

Rosemary Hunter read the *New York Globe* over her morning coffee. She spotted the item almost at once.

If she were in doubt about the participants in the drama, which she wasn't, they were fully identified in the morning telephone call she received from Julia Sheffield.

"Darling," cried Julia, "you didn't tell me Mark was in town when we talked. And, incidentally, I adored lunch. It was simply marvelous getting together again."

Rosemary agreed lunch was fun. And deliberately ignored the subject of Mark.

Julia was not so reluctant. "Of course, I thought Mark must be at Casa Miramar when I saw him. At least, I thought it was Mark. I spotted him just as I was waiting to cross the bridge into Palm Beach. Then, when I read that dreadful item in Reenie Boyd's column, this morning . . ." Her voice trailed off.

But not for long. "I understand that house belongs to Kate Crowley. You remember her, Rosemary. That gorgeous House of Graet vice-president. She spoke at the Everglades luncheon last season. On the investment value of good jewelry. The luncheon for the undernourished children of Ethiopia. Remember?"

Rosemary said she remembered.

"Well, darling, I feel simply dreadful for you. If there's anything I can do, anything at all . . ."

"You've already done it, Julia," snapped Rosemary, hanging up the phone.

Damn dyke! Hers was probably the first of the condolence calls. People panted in ecstasy over someone else's pain.

De la Rochefoucauld said it: "In the adversity of our best friends, we often find something not entirely displeasing."

Rosemary didn't read de la Rochefoucauld, but Mark quoted him. Funny, the things you remember. At the most appropriate times.

Shit! She was hyperventilating! Hyperventilating from fury, that's what! Rosemary forced herself to breathe normally until she was calm.

She rose from the breakfast table, ignoring the maid who was serving her, and walked out the dining room, across the wide tiled hall, into the paneled library. She perched on the edge of the massive eighteenth-century Spanish mahogany desk and stared with unfocused eyes at the long mahogany bar with its shelves of glistening bottles.

Her eyes focused, coming to rest on a quart bottle of Wolfschmidt. Now, if she were *really* an alcoholic she could drown in that stuff. Isn't that how alcoholics operated? Betrayed wife seeks solace in bottle! Humiliated wife hits the sauce! Wouldn't they all love that? Rosemary Hunter, flat on her ass, on the blue and green Karastan rug in the mahogany-paneled library of her beautifully decorated Mizner house.

Fuck them!

The more she brooded, the madder she got. It was one thing for Mark to screw that big-busted red-headed secretary of his on his office desk, another to screw anything else available, so long as he was discreet.

But right here in town? Under her very eyes? In the place she had come to find some peace?

More than the hurt of the betrayal, Rosemary dreaded the scorn and pity of others. Within twenty-four hours, everyone in town would know the names of the unnamed senator and the latest piece of ass he was screwing. And she, Rosemary Hunter, the senator's wife, would look like that most ludicrous of all God's creatures, the rejected wife who didn't have enough sexual savvy to keep her stallion husband in line.

Rosemary looked at the Wolfschmidt again. Well, she wasn't about to get drunk. But she did have other options.

The more she thought about them, the calmer she grew. Until, eyes bright, lips pursed, shoulders squared, Rosemary Hunter prepared for battle.

She checked her watch, noting it was 9:30. She raced upstairs, showered quickly, and thoughtfully selected her combat clothes. A sheer ivory lace bra, sheer ivory lace bikini, and sheer pale hose.

She chose a white silk front-buttoned Halston blouse, easy to remove in a hurry, and slipped into an ivory silk Halston skirt. She pulled the matching jacket off its hanger.

She slid her feet into pale lizard high-heeled Charles Jourdan shoes.

She brushed her hair until it shone, applied makeup with the skill of the artist she had hoped to become, and grabbing an ivory leather Hermès purse, walked calmly down the stairs.

She walked out the front door and around back to the garages. When the chauffeur polishing the gray Rolls limousine spoke to her, Rosemary didn't answer. She hadn't heard.

She opened the door to the white Rolls convertible Daddy had given her last Christmas, slid behind the wheel, put the key in the ignition, and drove the white Rolls past the gray one, missing it and the chauffeur by a mere three inches.

She drove down Ocean Boulevard to Worth Avenue, turned, drove down to Hibiscus Street, pulled into the parking lot, and handed the attendant the key to the Rolls.

"I'll be about two hours," she told him. She checked her watch, the only piece of jewelry she was wearing. A thin 18k gold Cartier Tank L.C. Two minutes to ten. She'd be there when the House of Graet opened its doors.

And she was. Harvey Matthews, the doorman, opened the massive oak doors for her, greeting Rosemary by name. She nodded and swept past him.

If they thought she was here to make a screaming scene over that bitch of Mark's, they were wrong. Rosemary Hunter had style, and style, damn it, is what they would get.

A red-haired associate approached her.

"I'd like to see L'Aventur," said Rosemary, sleek, sophisticated, and in full control.

"It just came in," the redhead told her.

"Good," said Rosemary coolly. "Then you can show it to me."

Sandy Stone took the calculator from the glass-fronted cabinet and placed it on a peach velvet tray in front of Rosemary.

Rosemary picked it up. Palm-size, the calculator was a cunning work of art. The pale gold Moroccan leather cover with its embossed *HG* was butter-soft to the touch.

She opened the cover. The calculator was twenty-four-karat gold. The numbers were pavé diamonds. The function keys were precious stones.

The plus sign was a ruby; the minus sign, a dark green emerald; the equal sign, a sapphire; the percent, a pale topaz; the decimal point, a yellow diamond. Other signs, other stones. The calculator glittered in Rosemary's hand.

L'Aventur. The adventure. She was delighted. A whole new world lay before her, awaiting her discovery. A golden, jeweled talisman would chart the journey.

A cunning object. With a cunning price: $20,000. Rosemary loved it. She pressed the appropriate pavé diamond numbers, pressed the ruby plus sign, pressed the pavé diamond five, pressed the emerald percent sign, touched the sapphire equal sign: $20,000 plus $1,000 tax = $21,000.

The machine tape printed out the same figure.

For the first time that morning, Rosemary smiled. "I'll take it," she said.

"Shall I gift-wrap it?" asked Sandy, straight-faced.

"No," Rosemary told her. "I want to keep it near me." She smiled again. "Now, show me something in pearls." She checked her watch. It was 10:05.

By 10:15, Rosemary was out the door of the House of Graet carrying only L'Aventur with her. The rest of her purchases were to be delivered, with instructions on where to send the bill.

She had bought a sapphire and diamond-link bracelet for $10,000, a double-strand cultured pearl choker with a cabochon emerald center stone for $30,000, and a few small leather pieces for $3,000. Total: $63,000 plus tax.

In only fifteen minutes!

Rosemary headed for Cartier. Twenty minutes later, she was out. The twenty minutes were spent efficiently. Fingers flying over diamond numbers and jeweled signs, Rosemary purchased one black suede evening pouch with gold chain details for $1,080 and a gold lizard evening purse with a 24k gold clasp. The 24k gold chain was set with four oval cabochon sapphires. Only $1,430. The matching gold lizard belt was $500.

She bought a solid gold large Santos sports watch for $8,200, and a Tortu cultured pearl watch in 18k yellow gold with pavé diamonds set around the face and on the clasp. The winding stem was a diamond. $28,000.

L'Aventur totaled the purchases: $39,210. The tape printed them, item by item.

Rosemary scrawled her signature for the purchases. Again with instructions. "Deliver them," she said breezily.

She crossed the street to Bonwit's for a brief visit totaling $15,000, and stopped at Van Cleef & Arpels for miscellaneous baubles at $30,000.

Time: eleven o'clock.

Crossing Worth Avenue again, Rosemary walked toward the new Gucci complex, past the two huge female nude bronzes by Emilio Greco of Rome, to the Ladies Fashion Salon in the rear patio.

As Rosemary began purchasing, excited sales personnel, recognizing her, fussed about her, eager to please. Fingers busy, Rosemary totaled sums faster than they could.

She purchased an antelope suede outfit in blueberry, slacks and tailored jacket for $1,835. She admired the scarf draped across the mannequin wearing the outfit. She purchased the scarf for $140. She bought the same outfit in raisin.

And another in gray, suede gaucho pants and suede-and-leather–trimmed jacket. She purchased a dozen scarfs. "Send them," she instructed, scrawling her name.

In the Gucci shops fronting Worth Avenue, Rosemary bought six pocketbooks, including a darling Bordeaux crocodile shoulder bag with a gold link chain and lapis end beads, for $3,800. And a dozen pairs of boots in suede, leather, and leather and suede. In brown, blueberry, raisin, and black. With low heels, high heels, and medium-height heels.

She also purchased some luggage.

"Deliver them," directed Rosemary pleasantly, slipping L'Aventur into the pocket of her Halston jacket.

Total purchases: $58,815.

Time: 11:50 A.M.

The mannequins gracing Martha's Worth Avenue windows caught Rosemary's eye. Their heads were swathed in high puffed gauze turbans in delicious ice-cream shades. The gowns were enchanting. Romantic, feminine, ecru-net, embroidered fantasies. Low-necked, fitted waists, short puffed net-embroidered sleeves, and miles of net-embroidered floor-length skirts.

Rosemary was greeted warmly when she entered Martha's.

The ball gowns were by David Emanuel of London, who had designed Princess Di's wedding dress. Prices: $6,000 to $8,000. Rosemary bought one in white for $7,000. She adored the turbans. The turbans were not for sale, she was told. However, if Mrs. Hunter wished . . .

Mrs. Hunter wished. The gown and the turban were ideal for the House of Graet Christmas Ball.

She also purchased an iridescent silk taffeta evening sheath by Mignon for $700 and a Chantilly lace cocktail dress with a perky peplum for $790.

Total expenditure: $8,490.

In Martha's International Boutique, Rosemary bought a Judith Leiber red and white hand-beaded evening purse with gold chain for $1,700. She was so taken with it, she purchased $6,000 worth of other Judith Leiber bags.

In Sara Fredericks, Rosemary fell in love with a Geoffrey Beene black sequined tunic for $5,400 over black silk-satin evening trousers for $800. She bought it. She also bought one in white with a huge center-design beaded red rose and green leaves.

She bought a Halston, a Bob Mackie, and a Michael Navarese gold bugle-beaded and satin evening gown.

Rosemary's L'Aventur was admired.

"It's brand-new," explained Rosemary.

"It's darling," commented the saleswoman.

"Works like a dream," purred Rosemary, engrossed in the process of calculating.

They both watched, entranced, as L'Aventur performed, the printout sheet itemizing, the numerals and signs glowing. Total: $30,000.

"Amazing," observed the saleswoman.

Rosemary agreed. She fingered the calculator fondly. It was comforting to have so trustworthy a friend.

Time: 11:57 A.M.

In Hermès, Rosemary bought a natural linen and nutmeg calf purse with braid shoulder strap and trim for $1,595.

In Saks, she selected a dozen cashmere sweaters in yummy pastel shades, two Neil Bieff hand-beaded sequined dresses with matching jackets, two Ultrasuede Anne Klein outfits, some Bill Blass sportswear, six pairs of Saks shoes, several silk blouses, a fleece-lined wheat-colored trench coat, lingerie, Germaine Monteil makeup and one piece of Louis Vuitton luggage.

She packed the Louis Vuitton piece with one pair of shoes, one pair of hosiery, several pieces of lingerie, some makeup, and one of the Bill Blass outfits. She carried the trench coat. She requested Saks to deliver the remainder of her purchases. She scrawled her signature and gave instructions on the billing.

Time: 12:20 P.M.

Total Saks purchases: $16,580.

Total morning expenditures: $277,575.

Humming, Rosemary walked briskly to the Hibiscus Street parking lot, picked up the Rolls convertible, added the $2.50 parking fee to her total, and made Palm Beach International Airport in ten minutes. She arrived at La Guardia three hours later.

She repeated the adventure in New York in one hour and fifteen minutes; L'Aventur tallied it: $787,943.88.

She took a cab to Kennedy, flew to Los Angeles, and spent the night in bungalow 8 of the Beverly Hilton Hotel. She began her shopping at 10:00 A.M. the following morning at Georgio's on Rodeo Drive. She completed it by noon. Once again, L'Aventur produced the calculations: $921,431.40. Somewhat sated, Rosemary took a cab to Los Angeles International Airport.

On the flight from L.A. to Palm Beach, she did her favorite relaxation exercise. She mentally planned which fetching costume she would wear to which marvelous gala during the upcoming Palm Beach season. The exercise was interspersed with prayers for safe takeoffs and landings.

She arrived in Palm Beach at 11:00 P.M. with mixed emotions. She was exhausted. She was exhilarated. She felt as though she'd been on a three-day drunk. But she felt vindicated. Gloriously vindicated.

In two days, she had spent $1,986,952.78. Almost $2 million. As per her instructions, all the bills had been sent to Mark's office.

Let his fucking secretary break the news to him.

Let him learn there was more than one way to get screwed!

On the way through the airline terminal, Rosemary paused before a trash receptacle. She reached into her Hermès bag, withdrew the Moroccan leather, twenty-four-karat gold jeweled calculator, and tossed it in.

She had no further use for it.

It had served its purpose.

25

The House of Graet press conference for the Kirsten diamond was held on Thursday, November 18, in the largest meeting room of the Plaza Hotel. It was attended by 200 people from the media, here and abroad. The House of Graet picked up the tab.

Among the Americans present were Eloise Treat from *WWD*, Françoise Dupree from *Harper's*, Jeanne Boslow and Sally Cole from *Vogue*, Cybel Chimes from *The New York Times*, Ed Sims from NBC-TV, Lewis Elliot from ABC-TV, Brian Shaw from CBS-TV, Bea Barry from *Time* magazine, Graham Sill and Eldridge Foster from *Life*, Tom Haney from *Newsweek*, and Reenie Boyd from *Moments*.

Diamond talk ran rampant.

"How much is that diamond?" asked Brian Shaw from CBS.

"Fifteen mil, I hear," replied Bea Barry from *Time*.

"*That* much? Whatever will the peasants do for kicks?" wondered Eldridge Foster from *Life*.

"Let 'em eat zircon," dismissed Françoise Dupree from *Harper's*.

In another group, diamond talk continued.

"Ever read the dossier on that gem? Everyone who ever owned it ended up dead," said Ed Sims from NBC.

"What a way to go," chimed in Cybel Chimes wistfully.

"Hell, I don't believe a word of that crap. It's all a big hype," commented Graham Sill from *Life*.

Eldridge Foster, also from *Life*, wandered into the new group at the tail end of the conversation. "Yeah? Well, I don't walk under ladders. And I don't buy jinxed jewels."

Reenie Boyd patted his hand. "Not to worry, sugah. You

191

couldn't buy that rock if you saved up twenty years worth of paychecks."

And in another group, diamonds were still the focus of attention.

"According to *WWD,* diamonds are *in.* Isn't that right, Eloise?"

"Mmm," replied Eloise Treat. She took a swallow of her Bullshot. "So are rubies, emeralds, and sapphires."

"What's *out?*"

Eloise took another swallow. "People who say *ciao.* Like the contessa."

Sally Cole from *Vogue* hooted. "She's so *out,* she's *in.* Besides, I don't think she gives a shit. Do you?"

"Probably not." Eloise took one more swallow. "With her dough, you can afford to be camp."

Suzy circulated among the guests, gossiping easily and smiling brightly. The smile was somewhat strained. The conference was scheduled to begin at 10:00 A.M. It was almost that now. Where was Consuela? Where was Louis-Philippe? And where was the Kirsten?

At precisely that moment, Consuela swept into the room, a House of Graet jewel box clutched in one leather-gloved hand. Two Pinkerton men flanked her. Louis-Philippe trailed behind.

Consuela, smiling broadly, waved to a few familiar faces; paused to chat briefly with one or two others. The Pinkerton men remained close to her side. Louis-Philippe waited patiently.

The contessa had never looked more radiant. She wore a full-length pale sable coat, which she shrugged off quickly after removing the Italian-made leather gloves. Beneath the coat, she wore a garnet-red velvet suit. The waist-length jacket was fitted. Tiny velvet-covered buttons served as fasteners. A high white lace ruff, attached to the round collarless jacket, framed her face. The jacket had a yoke detail three inches down from the collar that ran from front to back. The skirt was full, midlength, with side pockets. It covered the tops of the garnet-red suede boots she wore.

Diamond earrings glittered from her ears and jewels sparkled from her wrists and fingers. A pale sable hat covered the famous blond tresses.

She paused, walked to the front of the room, removed the sable hat, patted the smooth blond chignon, and placed the House of Graet jewel box on a table beside her. The Pinkerton men stood discreetly by. Louis-Philippe took a seat.

She spoke. "I wish to welcome all of you and thank you for coming." The smile flashed once more.

Nikon shutters clicked, TV cameras rolled, and notes were scribbled on pads as the much-publicized press conference began.

Consuela continued. "You are here today because of a diamond —a magnificent diamond with a most intriguing lineage." Eyes strayed to the House of Graet jewel box on the table beside the contessa.

"We have prepared press packets for you. These contain photographs, origin, size, dimensions of the diamond, its pedigree, and other information we trust you will find helpful. Suzy, would you please have these passed out?"

Suzy handed the packets to eleven young, attractive House of Graet associates recruited to help host the conference. The packets were passed to the press.

Consuela waited until each press member had one. "I must confess there was heated discussion as to how to carry the Kirsten here." She paused. "Naturally, I won out." Her smile included them all.

As she was talking, she casually reached behind her neck as if to smooth her chignon. "It was my feeling, a very strong feeling I should add, that the only way to present the Kirsten to you was to show it as it was meant to be displayed—around the neck of a woman."

With a sudden dramatic gesture, she released the Velcro closure holding the yoke to her jacket and pulled away the lace ruff and three inches of velvet fabric.

"This is not a strip," she announced with a brilliant smile. "Just a small tease to demonstrate my point."

The garnet-red seventy-five-karat Kirsten surrounded by twenty-one small white diamonds and attached by three diamond links to the pearl and diamond choker designed by Louis-Philippe lay revealed, glowing above the rich garnet-red velvet of Consuela's suit jacket.

The response was automatic—a few involuntary gasps, a burst

of spontaneous applause, and a shuffling of chairs as press members, one by one, stood and cheered.

Contessa Consuela Perrugia and her Kirsten diamond received a standing ovation. Jaded, sophisticated, and inured to tricks as these press members were, they still loved a show. And appreciated showmanship.

When the furor died down, Consuela spoke. "Now, I would like to introduce the gentleman responsible for the new look the Kirsten wears. Then we will be happy to answer any questions you may have. May I present Monsieur Louis-Philippe Aumont, a man whose talents have been compared to Cellini, Fabergé, in this century to Schlumberger, but who actually is incomparable. He stands alone. His work speaks for him. As you can see." Consuela extended a hand. "Louis? Come join me, please."

Louis-Philippe rose to hearty applause and joined Consuela. In his gray wool custom-tailored suit, white shirt, and dark blue Christian Dior tie, he looked handsome and imposing, but more like a prosperous Swiss banker than a jeweler.

"Thank you," he said, acknowledging the applause. "It is good to be here. Like the rest of you, I am enjoying seeing the Kirsten so splendidly displayed." He paused. "Are there any questions?"

"Brian Shaw, CBS. Monsieur Aumont, I understand the interest in colored stones is growing. Can you tell me why?"

"These are rare stones, much more rare than colorless diamonds. That in itself makes them more valuable. And expensive. Of course, they are also very beautiful."

Louis-Philippe responded to several more questions with low-key expertise, then turned the meeting back to Consuela.

Reenie Boyd stood up. "Consuela, the Kirsten's been compared to the Hope diamond. And everybody knows what a hex the Hope was."

"The Hope hoopla as I like to call it, Reenie, was a carefully nurtured myth. No one took it seriously. Least of all the people who bought it."

"But there was a curse on it. Everybody who owned it—even touched it, they say—died."

"*Cara,* no one dies from *touching* a diamond. Perhaps over grief from never having touched one." Consuela was joined by the press in laughter.

Reenie persisted. "I'm looking at the Kirsten dossier, Consuela. Ten owners. Ten deaths. How do you explain that mystery?"

"We all die, *cara*. That is no mystery."

"But, sugah, these deaths were *tragic.*"

Consuela shrugged. "Coincidences. That made good copy. And although we do not take the Kirsten curse seriously, we, too, as you can see by your packet, publicize it. People enjoy danger. And everyone loves a fairy tale. Even one with a wicked ending."

"Tom Haney, *Newsweek.* One more question, Contessa. The Hope has a copy. Harry Winston valued it at $25,000. Will the Kirsten have one?"

"Ah, Mr. Haney, you anticipate me." Consuela lifted the House of Graet jewel box from the table, opened it, and removed the Kirsten replica Louis-Philippe had thoughtfully provided.

She held it between both hands and raised it for the cameras. "Ladies and gentlemen, allow me to present the Kirsten replica."

"Wow! Looks real to me," Ed Sims said. "What's that worth, Contessa?"

"$50,000."

"But the one you're wearing—that's the real one?"

Consuela smiled broadly. *"Certamente."*

She explained the replica would travel on tour with the Kirsten original. The replica would be used primarily for publicity purposes. As all could witness, it was a magnificently executed duplicate, painstakingly detailed, with a beauty of its own. Again, thanks to Monsieur Aumont. Consuela extended a hand toward Louis, who acknowledged with a slight bow in her direction.

She turned back to her audience. "And now, ladies and gentlemen of the press, thank you again for sharing this momentous occasion with us. I am certain by now you are thirsty and hungry. Sadly, neither Monsieur Aumont nor I will be able to join you, as we have another meeting scheduled on the other side of town." She glanced at her watch and smiled ruefully. "One, I might add, we are already ten minutes late for. However, Suzy and others of the staff will be delighted to see to your needs. *Buon appetito! Ciao!"*

On the way out of the meeting room, Consuela pressed Louis-Philippe's hand. "It was a tremendous success, Louis."

"Beyond expectations," he agreed.

She nodded. "Without you I could not have done it, *caro.*"

He smiled. "Whatever you say, Consuela."

26

The week following the press conference, astonishing things began happening for the House of Graet—and Consuela.

Thirteen more certified checks for $15 million staked claims on the Kirsten diamond. They came by registered mail from Bordon Granger, Sheik Abu Kahli, Tony Owens, and Count Paolo Respighi.

Checks also came from a king from a small African nation, a Texas oil baron, a Seattle conglomerate, a German princess, a French count, a Washington, D.C., newspaper publisher, a Washington, D.C., congressman, an English earl, and a prince from a tiny European principality no longer in existence.

Consuela was devastated. What had begun as a pleasant little promotion was threatening to turn into a Molière-like farce. The task of attempting to placate and pacify fifteen eager purchasers of one necklace was formidable.

She and Suzy drafted a letter explaining the situation, describing the Kirsten tour and its intent, and thanking each one for his or her interest. The letters and the certified checks were returned by registered mail to each potential buyer.

The checks came back with letters to Consuela, instructing her to hold them. Each person was interested. Each was willing to wait. Each was determined to have the Kirsten.

Dio mio, who ever said the economy was faltering!

The press conference had been successful beyond her wildest expectations. The Kirsten diamond was news, big news. Not often did a diamond of such magnitude come upon the scene. Pictures of it were flashed around the world on television screens and in newspapers. Names of potential buyers were leaked to the press,

197

probably by the buyers, thought Consuela grimly, certainly not by her or the House of Graet. It added glamour and intrigue to a situation that was promising to take on the proportions of a major debacle.

The Kirsten curse enhanced its appeal. Listed in newspaper articles and recited by commentators were the names of the previous owners, and their untimely ends.

"Some timid souls might tremble at the prospect of tangling with the legendary Kirsten curse," noted a BBC commentator, "but not the Earl of Effingham, who claims to have already sent in a check for the diamond that's taking the mind of the British off Prince Andrew and Fergie, Princess Di's wardrobe, and the sagging British economy. Ah, well, c'est la vie! We'll keep you posted as the saga unfolds."

Consuela thought of Derek. "What will you do if they all want it?" he had asked. Her reply: "I will think of something. I always do."

It was time to do just that. She used the time-tested technique she had used so often before. She filed the problem in the back of her mind and went about her business as though no problem existed. The solution would come to her.

It came in the middle of the night in the form of a dream. Consuela woke, turned on the bedside light, blinked at the sudden break of darkness, and scrawled some words on the House of Graet pad she kept on the Louis XIV table next to her bed. Satisfied, she turned off the light, turned over, and immediately fell asleep.

She told her dream to Suzy the following morning over cups of Brazilian coffee served from Consuela's Georgian silver urn and poured into pale pink porcelain cups.

"We shall have a raffle," announced Consuela.

Suzy sputtered. The coffee was hot. "A raffle?"

Consuela beamed. "It came to me last night in a dream." She waved her hands expressively as she warmed to her subject. "A grand party, yards of exquisite gowns worn by beautiful ladies. Heavenly gentlemen in black-tie. A large hand-cut, hand-etched crystal bowl of unimaginable beauty and clarity, with the light from thousands of candles casting color on its polished surfaces. . . ."

"Consuela . . . ?" interrupted Suzy.

Consuela raised her hand impatiently. ". . . and in the center of the beautiful crystal bowl float small bits of colored paper.

"A tall, handsome gentleman dips his hand into the bowl, followed by a roll of drums in the background. Everyone hangs suspended with anticipation as the gentleman's hand selects one of the scraps of colored paper. Then—*voilà!*—the scrap of paper is removed from the bowl and extended to the hand of another gentleman who stands by. And in the ensuing hush, the second gentleman reads the name. . . ."

"The name?"

"The name of the winner of the Kirsten diamond, Suzy. Do you see? The solution. We shall hold a raffle for the Kirsten at the Christmas ball in Palm Beach."

"But the Kirsten tour . . ."

"Oh, we shall have the tour, *cara*. We shall merely adjust our plan a bit. It will be understood the winner of the Kirsten must permit the tour to take place. Too much planning has gone into it to cancel. Besides, for such a good cause, who would dare object?"

Suzy blinked. "Who'll participate in the raffle, Consuela?"

Consuela lost patience. "Suzy, are you not paying attention? 'Who will participate in the raffle?' she asks. Why, the people who have already sent in their checks. *Dio mio, cara,* one necklace cannot be divided into fifteen pieces. The raffle is the only viable solution. Anyone with a sporting sense will appreciate the fun of it. And enjoy the publicity."

"But . . ."

"First, we will hold a new press conference, Suzy. Nothing so elaborate as the first. *Piccolo.* Small. I have drawn up a list of names. Call them, please, and set up something as quickly as possible. And we must draft another letter to the buyers, explaining the entire situation again and informing them of our solution." Consuela paused briefly and looked delightedly at Suzy. "Do you not think it inspired, Suzy? The solution, I mean?"

Suzy hesitated. "Unusual."

Consuela smiled approval. "Yes, unusual," she agreed. "Like the Kirsten."

"You think it will work?" asked Suzy curiously.

"Of course it will work. The people who do not agree to our

conditions will have their checks returned. Their names will not go into the crystal bowl. How can it not work?"

The new Kirsten press conference was set up for two days before Thanksgiving. But before that event took place, an additional unexpected development occurred.

Reenie Boyd followed up her blind item about Mark Hunter and Kate Crowley with another blind item.

Captioned "What Hath Wrath Wrought?" the body copy read: "Hell hath no fury like a woman scorned but armed with a fat checkbook and a tiny calculator. The House of Graet's new bitesize jeweled calculator, a steal at $20,000, darlings, called L'Aventur, was put into remarkably imaginative use the other day when one determined lady toted hers around the country, running up a tab of almost 2 million—dollarinos, darlings—on what might yet turn out to be the world's most lavish and vindictive two-day shopping spree.

"Now, what could have activated the splendid wrath of the lovely lady? Could it have been her spouse's involvement with another lovely lady from a famed Palm Beach jewelry emporium? At any rate, L'Aventur—the adventure—was certainly that. More power to R.H., our anonymous friend. And happy shopping to all you other ladies with similar displeasures."

Across the nation, women responded to the clarion call with alacrity. Sales of the calculator increased—again beyond Consuela's expectations. What was being promoted as a Christmas stocking stuffer for the very rich promised to become an emblem of female revolt.

There was no question on anyone's mind who the R.H. of Reenie Boyd's column was, or to whom to give thanks for the sudden increased exposure.

Suzy looked over at the L'Aventur figures displayed on the sales chart positioned behind her desk and observed, "Rosemary Hunter's become a modern-day heroine."

Kathleen Connelly reacted to the item by slapping it on Mark's desk, along with the first of Rosemary's bills to come in and her own typed letter of resignation.

Mark spotted the item at once.

He picked up the piece of paper, sat down, and read through it quickly. He reread it slowly, digesting the content. Finally, the full impact hit him.

Jesus Christ Almighty God, Rosemary really *had* flipped. *Almost $2 million!* What in hell was wrong with her? *Two million dollars? In two days?* She had to be out of her fucking gourd! God damn it, he'd have her committed! Better still, he'd strangle her with his bare hands! Then he wouldn't have to bother to commit her! Jesus, she must have been tanked! She must have gotten herself all sauced up out of her fucking mind!

Almost insensate with rage, he buzzed Kathleen. He'd have her call Dr. Broome. He'd tell Dr. Broome he was shipping Rosemary back to Connecticut. Let the good doctor fix her up. He had lots of experience with drunks, even periodic ones.

Kathleen didn't respond to the buzz. Impatiently, Mark rang again. When there was still no answer, he rose from his desk and strode out of his office to Kathleen's. Her desk was neat and tidy. Her chair was empty. He strode back into his office.

Still fuming, he saw the pile of bills Kathleen had stacked for him. He opened them and studied them, one by one. He put them back down, forcing himself to remain calm, and spotted the number 10 envelope with his senatorial insignia in the upper left-hand corner and his name scrawled across the front. He opened it and read Kathleen's less-than-terse notice of resignation.

> *Dear Mark,*
> *This is to inform you I am no longer able to work for you. Under the circumstances, I do not feel required to give advance notice. Nine years is advance enough.*
> *I'm being married shortly to George Baxter. You don't know him. We're leaving Washington right after the ceremony. George has a job in Columbus which is far enough away from Washington to suit us both.*
> *Give my best to Rosemary. As for you, Mark, if you ever do run for president, don't expect my vote or George's.*
> *Kathleen.*

Jesus H. Christ. Kathleen was as nutty as Rosemary! For nine years, his easygoing, accommodating secretary had been gathering grievances like daisies. And he'd had no idea.

He strode to the bar, poured himself a hefty Scotch, and swallowed it quickly. He followed it up with another and drank it just as fast. He poured a third. No matter, he was too mad to get drunk.

He went back to his desk, shoved the bills into a drawer, tore up Kathleen's letter of resignation, and reread the item from Reenie Boyd's column as slowly and thoughtfully as he drank his third Scotch.

He made a decision about Reenie. Another situation demanded his attention first. He had to do something about a new secretary.

There was a little blonde in the secretarial pool who'd pinch-hitted when Kathleen was out with the flu. She was young, bright, eager to learn, and grateful for the opportunity to work for Senator Hunter. She'd told him so. She also had the best pair of knockers around.

Mark put the item from Reenie's column down and did two things in quick succession. He put in a call to the supervisor of the secretarial pool requesting the young, bright, eager-to-learn, and grateful-for-the-opportunity-to-do-so blonde.

Then he called Reenie Boyd.

27

Reenie was not surprised to receive Mark's call. She knew sooner or later he would capitulate. One had only to know where to apply the pressure, and Reenie Boyd knew all the tender points.

She planned the evening with consummate care. She dismissed the Japanese houseman, the Swedish cook, and the British secretary for the evening and gave Delia cab fare to visit her sister in Queens, instructing her to spend the night there.

Delia eyed her suspiciously. "You look like Delilah all ready to shear off Samson's locks in that outfit."

Reenie smiled, pleased with the imagery. "Do I? Do I, now?" She ran her hands along the hipline of the floor-length gold tissue lamé gown cut outrageously low, front and back. The firm round breasts that had enchanted Rick Howland—and innumerable others—were visibly outlined. The dress fit like a second skin, and was slit to the crotch. Nothing was left to the imagination. But then, for the price it cost, nothing should be. The dress, after all, had a specific purpose.

Reenie twirled around. "Maybe I just want to even up a score."

"Vengeance is mine, saith the Lord," quoted Delia, scowling.

Reenie laughed. "He was wrong. It's mine. And despite what anyone else says, it's very sweet." She directed Delia gently but firmly toward the door. "Go on, now. I know how much you enjoy bein' with your sister."

"Except for worryin' about you."

"Well, don't worry. I can take care of myself. You ought to know that by now."

Unconvinced, muttering under her breath, Delia allowed herself to be eased out.

Reenie closed the door behind her and walked back through the hall to the huge cathedral-ceilinged living room. A fire crackled comfortably in the brass-lined fireplace. A large Jackson Pollock dominated the wall above it. Low lights from crystal lamps cast soft shadows on two six-foot-long ivory satin sofas flanking the fireplace. Flowers in tall crystal vases flashed color and filled the room with delicate scent. Not entirely satisfied, Reenie fetched an atomizer from her bedroom and sprayed the living room with her favorite fragrance.

On the wide black marble coffee table between the sofas, a bottle of Dom Pérignon chilled in a Baccarat ice bucket. Crystal champagne flutes rested on a heavy silver tray alongside a crystal bowl of Beluga caviar over ice, thin toast slices on a silver dish, and crystal-lined silver bowls of chopped onion and chopped egg. A fifth of Mark's favorite Scotch rested unopened on another tray.

A Cole Porter medley played softly from the stereo. Reenie planned to make Samson's shearing memorable. A night Samson was not likely to forget.

Mark needed to exorcise the furies that threatened to consume him. The objects of these furies were women, two in number. Rosemary, and Reenie Boyd. Since he held Reenie and her vitriolic column pieces accountable for triggering the entire mess, she was the one to bear the full brunt of his anger. He could cheerfully dismember her. Since she clearly seemed to want something else, he decided to accommodate her.

Maybe once he got her on her back, she'd get off his.

He called her, set up a time, flew the twin-engine Cessna to Teterboro Airport, picked up the red Ferrari garaged there, and drove into the city. He parked the red Ferrari a block from Reenie's Park Avenue apartment.

The doorman recognized him at once, called upstairs, and expansively gave Senator Hunter directions to the penthouse. He also volunteered the information he'd voted for the senator the last two elections and planned to keep on doing so. Mark flashed the charismatic smile that won him countless votes of confidence, and headed for the elevator.

It opened up onto Reenie's penthouse apartment. Mark stepped inside.

A wide smile welcomed him. "Why, Mark," exclaimed Reenie as though his presence was a total surprise, "how nice to see you. Come on in."

He stood still for a minute, taking in the vision of Reenie's calculated loveliness—the gold tissue lamé gown—what there was of it—that clung to and outlined breasts, stomach muscles, pubis, the soft round bare arms, the platinum hair feathering out from the heart-shaped face, and the ingenuous large blue eyes.

She watched him form impressions, then turned and led him inside, the back of the gown plunging to the division between buttocks, the fabric revealing the full firm shape of twin globes moving irresistibly as Reenie walked. It had its desired effect. Mark could feel himself hardening.

Reenie seated herself on the couch, crossed her legs, the slitted skirt of the gown parting, leaned back, and patted the cushion beside her. "Come join me, darlin'. It's been a long uphill struggle encin' you here. Now that you are here, I want to make certain you're comfortable."

Mark said nothing.

Reenie smiled encouragingly. "Champagne? Scotch? Caviar? What'll you have, sugah?"

Mark's eyes raked her over insolently. "How about a piece of ass, Reenie? Isn't that what this is all about?" Without waiting for an answer, he reached over, grabbed hold of the fabric of her gown, and with one wrench, ripped it from bosom to crotch, the tearing sound of tissue lamé blending with the Cole Porter refrain "Anything Goes."

He stood up, dropped his trousers, stepped out of them easily, took off his shorts, and, fully erect, mounted a startled Reenie whose mouth was open in outrage at the condition of her expensive new gown.

Mark smiled grimly. "You've got a big mouth, Reenie. How about putting it to good use?" He tore the rest of her gown, grabbed her by the buttocks, and thrust his engorged penis in her open mouth.

Reenie's eyes widened.

Then she went competently to work.

* * *

He planned to leave as soon as he'd finished. Instead, he stayed the night. They tried each of the fourteen rooms in the penthouse duplex, fourteen different ways. Mark, who considered himself an expert on sexual ingenuity, was given an education. By dawn, he was more exhausted than he let on. Especially since Reenie looked remarkably refreshed.

They ended the expedition on the custom-made king-size bed in Reenie's surprisingly feminine bedroom. Mark stretched his arm from where he lay to the edge of the bed, not nearly making it. "You could entertain an army in here," he observed with cool detachment.

"Not quite an army," corrected Reenie, "but enough."

"And do you?" he queried. "Get enough, I mean?"

She stroked his thigh lazily. "Let's say I make certain I never go hungry, sugah."

Mark roared. "I'll bet you do." Impulsively, he reached over, lowered his head, and slipped his lips around one rosy protruding nipple while he rolled the other between his thumb and forefinger. Then just as impulsively, he stopped, rolled out of bed, and stood up. "I'd better collect my things and get moving if I'm to be as bright and bushy-tailed as I'm expected to be in this morning's session."

Reenie smiled, stretched, purred, and frankly admired Mark's long, well-muscled naked body.

He grinned. "Don't be greedy, Reenie." He strode out of the bedroom, picked up his clothing, and dressed quickly. He glanced at his watch: 6:15. He'd be in Washington in an hour and a half with time to stop by his Watergate apartment, shower, shave, and have a bite to eat before he left for the Senate.

Fully dressed, he walked back to the bedroom and stood framed in the doorway. Reenie rested contentedly against three down pillows.

"One more thing, Reenie. Do me a favor. No more stuff about me in that column of yours. You're making life difficult for me."

Reenie looked offended. "Why, sugah, we're friends now. Why on earth would I evah write anything to distress a friend?"

God only knows, thought Mark. "Just don't. You've been whipping up a broth that's a little too rich for my blood." Then he smiled the charismatic smile that melted female hearts from Bangor to Olympia. "Thanks for the orgy, Reenie. And you're right. You do do it better." He turned to leave.

Reenie raised herself slightly from the pillows. "Oh, it's not over, darlin'. It's only beginnin'. I'll see you next week."

Mark whirled around. "Next week! Christ, Reenie, I don't know if I can make it."

"Oh, you'll make it, sugah. I have no doubt about that." She smiled, stretched, and feigned fatigue. "If you don't mind, darlin', I won't get up to see you out. I'm sure you know your way around the place by now."

Surprisingly, the second Reenie Boyd item did not distress Rosemary. It was read on one of her I-couldn't-care-less-about-Mark's-antics days.

What did distress her was the loss of the high she'd experienced from her shopping binge. She was tense and uptight.

Not even the arrival of the girls from school helped, although she managed not to let on.

Beth had grown so. Rosemary hugged her, marveling over the sight of her. At twelve, much of Beth's chunkiness was gone. All of her good nature remained.

At fifteen, Kimberly was a beauty. Elegant to the fingertips and more like Marjorie, Mark's mother, every year.

Kimberly didn't approve of her. Rosemary could feel the disapproval. The feeling made Rosemary clumsy. And made her do dumb things.

Like now. In the midst of pleasant chatter over tea on the terrace, Rosemary accidentally knocked a floral teacup off the table. The cup was one of six Marjorie had received as a gift from the Duchess of Windsor, who had spent a week with the duke at Marjorie's Palm Beach estate thirty years before.

Marjorie had given the tea set to Rosemary and Mark as one of the many wedding gifts she lavished upon them.

Rosemary stared stupidly at the shattered pieces, and immediately bent to retrieve them.

"Hilda will do that, Mother," said Kimberly, ringing for the maid with authority.

Hilda promptly appeared and discreetly wiped up the offense.

"Save the pieces, please," instructed Rosemary. "We may be able to have it mended," knowing full well the cup was beyond repair.

"I won't tell Grandmother Hunter," Beth said stoutly. "What she doesn't know won't hurt her."

"Of course grandmother must know," decided Kimberly. She looked across the table at her mother, and Rosemary knew exactly what she was thinking.

She thinks I've been drinking. She thinks I'm drunk and I knocked over the goddamned teacup because I'm sozzled. I know that look of judgment.

Beth rose, went to her mother, and put her arms around her. "Don't feel bad, Mom. Accidents happen. Besides, it's only a teacup."

"Only a teacup!" echoed Kimberly, ice in her voice. "It just so happens to have been a gift from the Duchess of Windsor to Grandmother Hunter."

"I don't care if it came from the Queen of Sheba," Beth told her sister. "It's still only a teacup. Besides, it belongs to Mother now, not Grandmother. And since you're so all-fired superior, Kimberly, how come you don't know it's just plain rude bad manners to make someone feel rotten over something they couldn't help?"

Rosemary took hold of the situation with some of her old spirit. "Girls," she said firmly. "No arguing." She picked up a cigarette and nervously tapped it against the table before lighting it. "Beth, thank you for your vote of confidence, darling. Kimberly, for God's sake, don't look so stricken. Beth is right. It's only a goddamned teacup. No matter who it came from."

28

The second Kirsten press conference was not so splashy as the first. Invited members of the media were given a quick briefing on new developments, and the House of Graet decision to hold a raffle at their Christmas ball in Palm Beach to determine ownership.

Louis-Philippe stopped by Consuela's office before leaving for home. He seated himself in the chair opposite her desk. "How did the conference go?"

Consuela shrugged. "A bit anticlimactic, perhaps." She smiled. "It cannot be helped."

It was his turn for concern. "You look tired."

Another shrug. "I suppose I am."

Knowing her boundless energy, he found it an alarming admission. He searched the face lovely to him beyond description, whether animated or in repose. But rarely in repose. More often alive and responsive as a dozen or more emotions lighted the eyes, lifted the corners of the lips, and illumined the face he thought the most beautiful of any he knew.

"You are burning the candle at both ends," he reproved.

Consuela burst out laughing, then clapped her hands over her mouth, lest he be offended. "I am sorry, Louis. But you sounded so intense just then, I hardly knew you."

He refused to be put off. "You really must slow down."

With a sigh, she agreed.

"You're not getting any younger, you know," he said, expecting the comment would irk her into some sensibility.

"Nor am I teetering about on a cane," responded Consuela tartly. Then, in recognition of his very real concern, she softened.

"In Palm Beach, Louis, we can all slow down. Rest in the sun, delight in the roll of the surf, expand with indolence." The images that flitted across her mind lighted her face, taking away the lines of fatigue that had distressed him. "Besides, I am going to spend Thanksgiving with Antonia and her family in Connecticut. I shall rest there."

Satisfied, he nodded. "Good. You need to rest more."

His carping about her age annoyed her more than she let on. "And you, Louis?" she asked, deliberately changing the subject. "Where will you spend the holidays?"

Consuela waited. Nothing more forthcoming. Again she realized how little she knew of his personal life. "It would make me unhappy to think of you alone," she told him finally.

"It is not the worst thing in the world to be alone, Consuela."

The eyebrows arched. "No? And on a holiday? Ah, *caro*, we are different. I should consider it a disaster."

Louis-Philippe laughed, the laughter creasing his face attractively, making him look years younger. "A minor one, I hope."

"Not so minor, Louis. When I am dead, I will be alone. Until then, I prefer to be occupied."

"One can be occupied and alone at the same time, you know."

She rose and walked around to where he sat. "That is because you, *carissimo*, have so many superior inner resources. I, alas, have few."

He saw she was teasing him. But at least her mood was lighter. "Not true, Consuela. I suspect you have even more than most of us give you credit for."

Impulsively, she reached across and kissed him lightly on the cheek. "Do you know, Louis, you are a very nice man?" The dimple flashed. "But of course you know. How could you not when I am forever telling you so?"

29

Derek prepared himself for Thanksgiving in Scarsdale with Bobby by telling himself he would not react to her baiting, bantering, or matchmaking.

Everything was fine. Until he sat down to dinner.

Derek recognized the fine hand of Bobby the matchmaker almost at once.

The redhead on his left at the dinner table was a plant. Bobby's feelings about Consuela were made known to him often enough. "She's older than I am, Sonny. For chrissakes, get yourself someone your own age."

Agewise, the redhead fit the bill. But Derek wasn't ordering. He was taking charge of his own life, thank you. Ordering from his own menu.

He was polite but hardly encouraging.

Sandy Stone smelled a setup. She was being paired off with the guy on her right, the hostess's son. What else could it be with a table full of marrieds?

She decided to finish him off before dessert. The way to do that was to be the opposite of everything she was expected to be.

She turned to Derek. "I think they should erase all holidays from the calendar, don't you? I mean, the suicide rate soars over holidays. Expectations are never met and people can't seem to handle the disappointments without doing themselves in. It's all such a holy mess. Don't you agree?"

Derek's fork was midway to his mouth. He put it back down. "Are you a sociologist?"

"No. I'm in sales. What about you?" Sandy had a deep distrust

211

of good-looking men. They were self-centered, demanding, and invariably spoiled silly by women.

"Excuse me?"

"What do *you do?*" repeated Sandy.

"Oh. I act. I'm an actor. On a soap."

"You make a living doing that?" Sandy had a deeper distrust of actors.

Derek smiled. "As a matter of fact, a very good one."

Sandy delivered her zinger. "I don't watch soaps. I mean, we have trouble in life sorting through the garbage we collect without subjecting ourselves to more."

Derek studied her. "You sure you're not a sociologist?"

"No," pondered Sandy, "but maybe I should become one."

Derek searched for neutral ground. "Where do you sell?"

"Disneyland," Sandy told him.

"Sounds like fun," Derek said.

"Oh, it is," Sandy assured him.

"Well, if I ever get there, maybe I'll look you up."

"Do that," said Sandy coolly. "Just ask for Little Bo Peep. Everyone there knows me." She turned away, giving Derek the full benefit of Dr. Gruber's nose job.

Later, Derek learned from Bobby that Sandy Stone worked at the House of Graet, Palm Beach. He wanted to tell her that he'd be there soon himself and that maybe they could get together.

He went looking for her, couldn't find her anywhere.

It was almost as though Sandy Stone never existed. As though she'd been a figment of his imagination.

Outside Las Vegas, Bordon Granger, Tami Hayes, and her sister Erin were finishing the dinner prepared by the cook Bordon had hired in the house he had rented for the holiday.

He had done what he told Tami he would do. Provided Erin with an old-fashioned Thanksgiving. And some more of the family stability Tami was so anxious to give her.

It was only fitting. After all, soon they would be a family.

"Now, that was a typical New England Thanksgiving dinner," he announced with a broad smile. "Even if it did take place in Vegas."

212

"It was terrific, Bordon," Erin told him. "Wasn't it, Tam?"

"Terrific," echoed Tami absently.

"Nothing but the best for my women," Bordon said. He looked fondly at Tami, noticed again a tension he'd become aware of since he saw her last. She was doing too much, damn it. "You need to take a good long rest, sweetheart."

"I'm fine," Tami said defensively.

"I disagree. I think you need Wellington more than you realize."

"Bordon, don't push me," she snapped.

It was so unlike her, he was startled.

She noticed his expression, forced a smile, and apologized.

"Sorry, darling. I guess I am getting pretty testy in my old age."

"Old age," he scoffed. "A kid like you. You'll have to find a better excuse than that."

She rose swiftly from her seat, crossed over, and kissed him lightly. "You're right. Age is no excuse for rudeness."

He was so dear, she'd do anything rather than hurt him.

And so decent, she had no right to hurt him.

How then to protect him from the nightmare that had suddenly surfaced and threatened to engulf her?

Once she thought Bordon could protect her from all harm.

Now she knew there was one thing Bordon couldn't protect her from. Her past.

And her past had recently risen from its shadows to become part of her present.

Settled in the cabin of his private jet on the flight from Greenwich to Palm Beach International Airport, Carl Schmittle alternated between swearing under his breath and rubbing intermittently at his chest.

"For heaven's sakes, Carl, what on earth is wrong with you?" Grace Schmittle asked. "You'll have me a nervous wreck before we even get there."

"Sorry," he apologized. Then he felt a sharp pain and his face contorted.

Alarmed, Grace turned to him. "Carl? Are you all right?"

He managed a smile even as he reached for the small vial in his jacket pocket. "Fine, Mother. Just fine."

Grace eyed the vial suspiciously. "What's that?"

"Something Harry Barton gave me for tension, Mother. Nothing for you to fret about."

Grace Schmittle's lips tightened. "See! Exactly what I've been telling you. You've got to slow down and relax, Carl, for your own sake. And for mine. Or you'll be the death of me yet."

Carl patted his wife's hand distractedly, no longer listening to her.

More likely he'd be the death of himself. That's exactly what Harry predicted. "Unless you drastically alter your personality and start getting sensible, Carl, I won't be held accountable."

Well, he would. Once he got Rosemary settled in his mind, and once he attended to that son of a bitch she was married to, he would change. But he didn't want to worry Grace. Grace was the kind of worrier who worried about what she'd worry about next. That he didn't need.

"Do you hear me, Carl?"

"Yes, Mother?"

"This weekend, I want you to do nothing but rest. Just sit in the sun, rest, get lots of sleep. And no arguing with anyone."

"Yes, Mother."

"Promise me, Carl."

"I promise, Mother."

Satisfied, Grace returned to her book, *The Residual Effects of Rose Breeding on the Grower.*

Grace hadn't read the newest item in Reenie Boyd's column. Carl had seen to that. Grace would only fret about Rosemary's extravagance and insist upon a full explanation of what triggered the incident.

Son of a bitch! Did Rosemary really spend that much money in only two days? Despite the pain, which was subsiding now, thanks to Harry's prescribed pills, Carl found himself chuckling. That girl of his really had style. She knew how to zing someone where it hurt the most.

"Son of a bitch!" he repeated. He had spoken aloud.

Grace lifted her eyes from her book. "Carl, I must insist you stop that swearing. It's bad enough Rosemary has picked up on all those cuss words of yours, but I won't have you setting a bad example for the girls."

214

He reached for his wife's hand. "Yes, Mother," he assured her. "I promise to overhaul my character and mend my ways until I'm acceptable to the most effete of sensibilities."

"There's no need to overdo humility," his wife told him. "It doesn't become you. Besides, it makes me suspicious." She smiled at him, becoming almost pretty. "And I love you just as you are—ornery and feisty. I only want you to slow down and stop cussing. Surely that's not too unreasonable a request?"

Carl smiled back, brought her hand to his lips, and gallantly kissed it. "No, Gracie," he said, "it isn't. And I do promise to mend my ways. Honest."

30

Carl wasn't able to see Mark alone until Thanksgiving, when he met with him before cocktails in Mark's study.

Carl got quickly to the point. "Listen to me, you son of a bitch, and listen good. You cause my daughter any more pain and I will personally string you up by those golden balls of yours until they shrivel up into leather."

Mark took a sip of his Scotch and kept his gaze steady. "There's no need to be quite so graphic, Carl."

"No need, my ass! You hear me out, boy. You clean up your act or you're finished. Not only in the Senate, but with any other grandiose plans for the future you may be nurturing. I'll see to it your name is mud throughout this land, no matter how much Rosemary is hurt by it or how much it costs me. If I have to spend my entire goddamned fortune finishing you off, I'll do it. Gladly!"

Mark put down his glass and took a cigarette from his onyx and gold cigarette case. "Are you threatening me, Carl?" he asked mildly.

"Not threatening you, fella. Promising. I'm promising you. One more piece of publicity about your extramarital sexual antics and you're through! Finished! Kaput! *Capisce?*"

Mark lit his cigarette. "Everything's been taken care of, Carl," he explained smoothly. "You needn't concern yourself any longer. There won't be any more publicity."

"Don't tell me I needn't concern myself. Someone sure as hell has to be concerned. And it obviously isn't you."

Mark rose, walked to the bar, and freshened his drink. "That piece in the *Globe* was a deliberate attempt to intimidate me. Nothing more. Don't exaggerate its importance."

"Well, if it isn't true, sue the bitch!"

"I told you, Carl. It's been taken care of. There won't be any more pieces."

Carl laughed shortly. "Yeah? What did you do, screw the bitch's mouth shut?"

Since this was closer to the truth than he cared to admit, Mark grew angry. "Don't be absurd, Carl. Gossip is Reenie Boyd's stock in trade. She likes to stir up trouble because trouble sells newspapers. It's that simple. I spoke to her. She listened. She's not, after all, completely unreasonable."

Carl remained unconvinced. "I bet! Just remember what I told you. And what about that vice-president at the House of Graet? Don't tell me there was nothing to that . . . ?"

Mark held onto his patience with an effort. "It was nothing. Blown out of proportion. Carl, if we remain calm, it will pass. And if we keep our perspective . . ."

"I'm calm, boy," interrupted Carl, "and my perspective's just fine. But I'm putting you on notice. Anything that upsets Rosemary so she ends up in one of those nut farms you ship her to every so often, I will hold you personally responsible for."

Mark finally lost patience. "They're not nut farms, Carl. They're drug rehabilitation centers. And I'm hardly the cause of Rosemary's drinking problem. She's an alcoholic. Alcoholism is a disease. Like cancer, TB, mental illness. Your daughter can't drink, Carl. She's allergic to the stuff. That's the absolute truth of the situation."

Carl's face tightened with rage. "My daughter never drank until she teamed up with you. And she never had a problem with booze until you started catting around. She was a beautiful good girl who never gave her parents a moment's sorrow."

"I'm afraid you tend to view Rosemary through rose-colored glasses," said Mark with barely disguised irony. "She's a woman with many complex problems."

The veins in Carl's forehead became more pronounced. "And I tell you she never had those problems until she married you. Once you clean up your act, she won't have them anymore. And clean it up you will, or I'll fix it so you won't be able to get that cock of yours up again for anyone, anytime!" He spoke with such quiet contained fury his skin grew mottled, his breath grew short, and, once more, his face contorted with pain as he grabbed at his chest and groped for the vial.

Mark froze, then collected his wits, moved quickly to Carl's side, reached for the vial, and handed him the pill. He loosened Carl's tie and unbuttoned his shirt.

Carl swallowed the pill and waved him away. "It's okay. For Christ's sake, don't fuss over me like an old hen. Just let me breathe a bit. And don't panic. I'm not going to drop dead in front of you."

Mark's face was ashen. "Good God, Carl, what in hell is wrong? You scared me out of a year's growth."

Carl managed a bitter chuckle. "Scared myself more, boy. Just a small problem. Nothing serious. Nothing erasing twenty years wouldn't cure."

Mark reached for the phone. "Let me call a doctor."

"Shit, no," said Carl, stopping him. "What in hell could he do? Tell me to calm down, change my life-style, take up needlework?" He looked shrewdly across at Mark. "Don't let this little incident lull you into a false sense of security, sonny. I'm ornery enough and determined enough to be around for a good long time. Long enough to keep an eye on you."

Mark relaxed. Hearing Carl threaten him again was oddly reassuring. For a moment there, he was afraid he was going to have to cope with a corpse. He managed a rueful grin. "That's more like it. You're beginning to sound like your old self." He sat down next to Carl. "If you'd like to be excused from dinner, I'll explain to Rosemary."

Carl buttoned his shirt and straightened his tie. "Hell, no. Wouldn't miss this shindig for anything. Besides, I don't want to worry Grace."

Mark extended his hand and grinned ingratiatingly. "Then how about declaring a truce? Through dinner, anyway?"

Carl ignored the outstretched hand but agreed. "Through dinner. But remember what I said. I've got my eye on you. And I expect to be around for a long time."

Rosemary knew she looked good. And when she looked good, she felt good. It was simply that simple.

She also knew the McPhersons, Patti Shaw, and probably everyone else in the room was speculating about her gown. Which one was it? Was it one of the ones bought on Rosemary's binge? Here in Palm Beach? New York? Rodeo Drive?

No one was gauche enough to ask, but Rosemary could feel the questions as she circulated. She enjoyed the speculation enormously.

The dress was a Pauline Trigère. White silk organza with hand-painted bouquets of flowers on the ankle-length skirt. With a full tucked capelet that formed a ruff to frame her face, then reached just below the bosom. It was a feminine, utterly romantic look. And, yes, angelic too. Wearing it, Rosemary decidedly felt angelic.

Ruby and diamond earrings sparkled on her ears, ruby and diamond bracelets shone on her wrists, and her large brown eyes glistened with undisclosed secrets. Her hair in its new short full cut bounced as she moved about the room, greeting guests, laughing happily.

Carl Schmittle thought his daughter never looked more beautiful. And wondered why he had ever worried about her. He should have known his girl had spunk. Bounced right back, his Roe, just like that glorious golden hair of hers. A real fighter, she was. Not one to lie down and stay down.

He slipped an arm around her waist and steered her aside, apologizing to the Emberleys, claiming his right to claim his daughter, even in the midst of festivities.

"You look mighty fetching, sweetheart," he told her.

Rosemary glowed, rose on the toes of her white satin slippers, and kissed her father affectionately on the cheek. "Thank you, Daddy."

"Had me worried there for a while," he admitted.

For a moment, a strained expression crossed Rosemary's face. "Oh, Daddy, I am sorry. I was just feeling gloomy back then."

"Well, thank God, you don't look gloomy now."

Rosemary's expression brightened. "I'm feeling wonderful now."

"Good," smiled Carl in approval. "See that you stay that way. I don't want to see another worry line on that beautiful face of yours, princess."

She laughed and squeezed his hand. "Daddy, you don't know

219

what a tonic you are. Just knowing how much you care gives me a boost."

"Well, see you remember that, girl. Because that's something you can count on from here to forever." He gave her a good-natured nudge. "Now, go spread some of that glow round your other guests."

Watching her glide gracefully around the room, his own mood lightened. God, but it did his tired old heart good to see her this way. Sometime this weekend, he'd get her alone and tell her about the Kirsten. How those brown eyes would sparkle over that piece of news!

Rosemary chatted with the Emberleys and the Lorings, then excused herself and moved toward another group. Midway between groups, Mark stopped her.

"Ah, Rosemary, we meet at last."

"Hello, Mark," said Rosemary, smiling sweetly. "You know how it is at these things. I circulate. You circulate. Occasionally we bump shoulders."

Mark looked around the room. "Nice party," he concluded. "But, then, you always were a splendid hostess."

Rosemary was caught off-guard. "Why, thank you."

"When you're not sloshed, that is," said Mark, turning back to her.

She stiffened. "Why is it, Mark, you always follow a compliment with a zinger?"

"Sorry." He looked embarrassed. "I shouldn't have said that. You have done this up superbly." To make amends, he added, "And you look positively radiant, Roe. New dress?"

"As a matter of fact, yes," admitted Rosemary warily.

"It suits you," said Mark with no further comment. Instead, he changed the subject. "The girls look great, don't they?"

On safer ground now, Rosemary relaxed. "Wonderful."

Carl and Mark crossed paths several times during the course of the evening. They were affable and cordial with each other, demonstrating for all to see a harmony necessary for a healthy father-in-law, son-in-law relationship.

There was no sign of discord between them. It was as though the incident in the study had not occurred.

Rosemary couldn't sleep. Like an actress conscious of the power of her performance, Rosemary knew she had done her hostess bit perfectly. She also knew she had to come down.

Because the play was over. The curtain was rung down. Her guests had gone, while she, at two in the morning, was maddeningly beyond sleep.

Tomorrow it would begin again. Guests for breakfast, guests for lunch, guests for dinner. And if she had bags under her eyes, she'd look miserable. If she looked miserable, she'd feel miserable. It was simply that simple.

In the old days, thought Rosemary wryly, a drink, a pill, or both would hurry the transition from insomnia to wonderful blessed release. The new Rosemary denied herself such indulgences.

A book might help. The new John Le Carré in the downstairs library might just do it. She'd already tried meditation, counting lambs leaping over fences, and repeating the word *one* until she was ready to shriek. None of it worked.

She kicked back the covers; slipped her feet into ivory satin mules; put the ivory tulle peignoir over her spaghetti-strapped ivory satin nightgown, a Rodeo Drive outfit; brushed her hair. You never knew who you might meet on the stairs, even at this ungodly hour, she thought, and went downstairs to the library.

She opened the massive oak library doors and stepped inside, soft light from the desk lamp flooding her. Startled, she discovered she was not alone. In the huge leather chair facing the still-glowing embers from the fire in the fireplace sat Mark, shirt unbuttoned, long legs stretched out before him, a glass of Scotch held loosely in his hand. A half-full bottle rested on the floor beside him.

He looked up, his eyes sweeping drunkenly over Rosemary. He managed a lopsided grin. "Welcome to Casa Miramar, Rosemary." He swept his hand out loftily. "Come join in the festivities."

Rosemary looked in disgust at Mark, the glass, the half-full bottle of Scotch on the floor. "Thank you, no, I don't drink," she said stiffly.

Mark sighed. "What a pity." He lifted his glass and took a large swallow.

Rosemary drew her peignoir more tightly around her. "Are you aware, Mark, that drinking alone is one of the first signs of alcoholism?"

He burst out laughing. "Ah, the expert speaks!"

Defensively, Rosemary shot back, "Well, you're the one who sends me to all those places that give courses in the subject." Somewhat hostilely she added, "Maybe you ought to go yourself next time."

Mark studied her quietly over the rim of his glass. "Rosemary, there is no one quite so tiresome as a self-righteous ex-drunk. Don't you know that?"

"All I know is, I came down here for a book, not an argument," Rosemary told him.

Mark waved a hand toward the 8,000-book stacks, probably the only Palm Beach personal library not stocked by a decorator. "Help yourself, then. What shall it be? Toynbee's a bit heavy at this hour. As are Wells, Proust, Stendahl. A little light Hemingway, perhaps? Better still, some Thurber."

"I thought I'd try the John Le Carré, thank you," said Rosemary coldly.

Mark shook his head. "I'm not certain that's the wisest choice, Rosemary. A thriller might keep you awake. On second thought, take the Toynbee. You'll be asleep in no time at all."

"If it's all the same to you, I'll take the Le Carré," snapped Rosemary.

He shrugged. "Suit yourself."

She moved to the shelf of current fiction, looked under mysteries and spy tales, found the Le Carré, and started to leave. Mark called out sharply, "Rosemary!"

She turned. "Yes?"

"C'mon over here a minute," he said, his words slurred.

Rosemary hesitated, then crossed over and stood before him, the light from the embers flickering across her hair, her face, her gown.

Mark looked up at her. "Tell me something, Rosemary. To satisfy my curiosity. Did you really spend almost $2 million?"

Rosemary never flinched. "As a matter of fact, I did."

"In three cities?"

"In three cities."

"In just two days?"

"In just under."

Mark threw back his head, slapped his thigh, and roared. "Holy Christ, Rosemary, that takes balls!"

Rosemary lifted her chin. "I thought so."

Mark looked at her oddly. "Next question. Was it worth it?"

"I thought so."

"That thing you're wearing? Part of the trousseau too?"

Rosemary paused, then whirled slowly around so Mark would get the full effect. "Rodeo Drive," she announced. "A little boutique."

Like a cat, he rose swiftly from the chair, placed his glass on the floor next to the bottle of Scotch, grabbed Rosemary around the waist with one hand, the other circling her throat. She never once cried out. Releasing his hand from her throat but still holding her fast, he quietly asked, "Aren't you afraid you'll try my patience, Rosemary?"

Rosemary held his eyes without fear. "I tried everything else, Mark. I thought this time I'd try your patience."

Marveling at her gall, excited by the intensity of his rage, and suddenly stimulated by the feel of tulle and satin, the familiar shapely body, the familiar scent she wore, the quickening of her pulse, and his own rapid breathing, Mark expertly undid the fastening on the peignoir, rubbed his hands across her breasts, and pulled her closer into his embrace. "Ah, Rosemary," he whispered, smiling strangely at her, "it's been a long time since you got laid in the library."

He pushed her down on the library carpet, pulled the peignoir and gown off her, and thrust his tongue into her mouth while his fingers rediscovered the spots that caused Rosemary to move and moan with pleasure.

"Oh, Mark," cried Rosemary, "what a magnificent bastard you are."

"Hush," he instructed. "Don't talk. Fornicating in the presence of some of the great minds of all times is intellectually enriching. You'll get a vicarious education, Rosemary." His fingers found the moistest spot. "Besides, this will help you sleep better than the Le Carré."

31

It was with some misgiving that Kate boarded the *Nellie*. The last thing she needed in her life, she reminded herself again, was another complication.

She could almost hear Nancy's practical comment. "Since when is one dinner a complication?"

"Welcome aboard," said Ben, greeting Kate.

She noted his cut-off jeans, chef's apron covering his bare chest, high chef's hat, and smiled.

He grinned back. "Cook's attire on the *Nellie*." He held her eyes with an approving stare. "You look properly nautical. And improperly pretty."

Kate surprised herself by blushing. She wore white denim jeans, a red cotton-knit, short-sleeved, scoop-necked shirt, and the obligatory white sneakers to observe deck etiquette. Her long dark hair was tucked up into a navy Greek captain's peaked cap, and her emerald eyes were covered by sunglasses.

Ben took her canvas-and-suede–trimmed House of Graet satchel containing, she told him, changes of clothing for any changes in weather. "Follow me," he directed.

He led her below deck to the guest bedroom quarters, complete with adjoining bathroom. "There are hangers in the closet, soap and fresh towels in the head. Anything else you need, just call your captain." He kissed her lightly and left.

Kate put her satchel on a bench, took out and hung up a jacket and a blue and green floral print evening skirt, a last-minute choice she'd made should she decide to change for dinner. She folded a pale lime V-neck cashmere sweater and matching shawl and placed a pair of lime-green ballet slippers neatly on the floor. Then she freshened up and went in search of Ben.

She found him in the ship's galley, basting the chicken. "That smells marvelous," she said, and asked what she might do to help.

"Not a thing," Ben told her. "Houseboat rule number one. Guests guest. I do all the work." He grinned. "When you cook for me, it'll be my turn to relax."

Kate's green eyes glinted. "I don't recall having made the offer."

"You haven't yet. But you will," Ben assured her good-naturedly.

He lifted a tray of crackers, cheese, pâté, olives, chopped vegetables, and a spritzer. "Let's take these on deck so you can begin your relaxing officially."

He led her topside to the sundeck and directed her to a white wicker yellow-cushioned chaise.

He placed the tray on a low round table and pulled it close to her. "I'm going to raise anchor and move us out some, away from the dock. It'll be more restful out on the Intracoastal." He pointed to a nearby rack. "Magazines. Papers. Today's *New York Times.* I won't be long. So don't go away."

Kate stretched out on the chaise and smiled contentedly. "Where would I go, captain?" She reached for her spritzer, sipped it, and rested her head against the cushioned back of the chaise.

As she watched the shore recede, her gaze swept over the surrounding scene. Blue water. Blue skies. Sprawling mansions lined the opposite shore. Tall, tapering pines interspersed with palms and sea grapes. Small craft and large yachts moored to private docks.

Every muscle in her body seemed to be unknotting. She felt herself drift with the boat and, under the drifting, all the accumulated tensions of the past weeks disappeared. It was as though there were no Mark, no House of Graet, no Kirsten, no demands on her. Only this peace in this present. She closed her eyes.

When she opened them, Ben stood before her, a fresh spritzer in one hand, a Heineken in the other. He handed Kate her drink, pulled up a chaise, and sat beside her, sipping his beer. Neither spoke for a long while, but the silence was companionable.

Ben broke it first. "You know something? You fit into this kind of life."

Kate's look was quizzical. "You mean I pass the test?"

He nodded. "One hundred percent. I've never seen you look so relaxed."

For some reason, the comment irked her. "Let's not build an entire scenario on the basis of one mood," she said tartly, and then flushed at her rudeness.

Ben chose to ignore it. *Move slowly,* he cautioned himself. *Don't crowd her. There's something here that needs healing.*

In time he would find out what it was.

None of his knowledge of women prepared him for someone like Kate. His sisters were extroverted. The women he had loved and bedded had not been troubled by any secret traumas he could recall. Still, they were women. And he was an expert on the sex.

Kate folded one arm behind her head and groped for sunglasses with the other. She put them on and looked out at the tranquil scene. She wanted to make amends for her rudeness. She turned and smiled at Ben. "It is wonderful out here," she admitted. "An entirely different perspective. Problems that seem magnified on land are reduced to insignificance."

Ben forgot his resolve not to probe. "That's the second time we've been together you've mentioned problems, Kate. Are there that many?"

"Everyone has problems, Ben," said Kate, testy again.

Impulsively he reached over, lifted her chin, and moved her face closer to his. "Yours seem to burden you. That bothers me." It did bother him. That surprised him.

Kate sat up, brushing her hair back from her face with startling intensity. "I'm sorry. I didn't mean to sound burdened." She attempted a smile. "If I did, I'm certainly not being a very good guest, am I?"

Ben watched her struggle for composure, saw that he had pushed too close to the source of discomfort, and cursed himself for his clumsiness.

His turn to make amends. "There's no such thing as a bad guest, Kate. Only a poor host." He grinned sheepishly. "I'm not usually so oafish. In fact, if I may boast a bit, most ladies generally find me fairly appealing."

227

Kate, restored to composure, smiled. "I'm sure they do, Ben."

"So," said Ben decisively, "let's start over. My name is Ben Gately and there are six intelligent, articulate females in La Jolla who'll attest to my general good character and customary sensitivity. If you like, I'll call them."

Kate laughed. "That won't be necessary," she said.

The awkwardness between them was dispelled.

Kate dressed for dinner in the blue and green floral print evening skirt and pale lime cashmere sweater. She brushed her hair, applied makeup, buckled on a narrow gold chain belt, slipped her feet into lime-colored ballet slippers, and went topside.

Ben whistled his approval. "You add class to the *Nellie,*" he told Kate. He wore wheat-colored jeans, a blue crew-neck sweater, and a navy sport coat. Kate thought he looked quite handsome.

She looked at the table appointments with surprise. She hadn't expected anything quite so grand on a houseboat. Tall silver candlesticks and pale yellow candles. A crystal bowl filled with daisies. A deep blue linen cloth. Napkins in mahogany rings. White china. Silver flatware and crystal wineglasses.

If she was impressed by the table appointments, she was stunned by the food. "You didn't!" she exclaimed over each course. "Not by yourself!"

Ben accepted each compliment modestly. One of his minor talents, he pointed out. Wait until she discovered some of the major ones.

Later, sitting topside, listening to the water lapping lazily against the side of the boat, breathing in the fresh air, looking at a sky studded with stars, Kate sighed with contentment. She wrapped the shawl Ben had gone below to get her closer.

"Cold?" he asked.

"Not really. Just pleasantly and thoroughly relaxed." She looked over at Ben and smiled. "This is the nicest Thanksgiving I can remember in a very long time."

He looked at her. Guard down, face relaxed, she looked more serene than he'd ever seen her look.

Kate turned and smiled again. "You're staring."

"Guilty," he admitted pleasantly.

"That's pretty bold," teased Kate.

"I was thinking bold," Ben told her.

"Oh?"

"I was thinking of the first time I kissed you and wondering, Was it really as great as I remembered? Or was it a fluke? A onetime phenomenon?"

Kate remained silent.

Ben rose, reached for her, pulled her to her feet and into his arms, tilted her head back, and kissed her long and lingeringly on the lips.

She didn't resist.

"Well," he said, assuming a studious expression, "what d'ya know? No fluke."

Kate pulled away. "I don't want to complicate things, Ben," she said, as she had said before to him.

"It's too late. They're already complicated," Ben told her. "I'm falling in love with you, Kate."

She stiffened. "Don't be absurd. You know nothing about me."

His fingers traced the line of her lips. "Then teach me. Tell me what you think I should know." He grinned at her. "It won't make any difference. I think I loved you from the moment I saw you standing at that ledge."

"Oh, Ben . . ."

"It's true. Everything my sisters said is true. It's like an avalanche. The entire denial system goes under. The truth emerges. Ben Gately loves Kate Crowley. He may not understand her. But he sure as hell loves her."

"It isn't true. You don't know me," repeated Kate.

Ben looked at her steadily. "I know you need to be loved and cared for. I want to do that. I see something that hurts you, and that hurts me. I see you frightened, and I want to fix it for you." His eyes teased, even though his tone was serious. "That's gotta be love, Kate. Unless I'm coming down with some bug. And I feel pretty healthy."

She didn't laugh. She wasn't amused. Ben's kiss disturbed her more than she cared to admit. His concern discomfited her. She wasn't accustomed to it. Her entire relationship with Mark was based on making him comfortable.

"Don't be too good to me, Ben. It might backfire on you," she warned him.

He turned serious. "I'll take that risk. You could do with some spoiling." He pulled her close again; raised her face; kissed her. "I don't know what it is that troubles you, Kate, but I want to help if I can."

Suddenly, she stopped resisting. She let herself go slack in Ben's arms, rested there, safe for the moment.

It was as though at long last, after a raging storm at sea, she'd come into port.

The relief was too intense.

It broke through the reserve. The emotions tapped were too powerful to stem, and the tears came. Her body heaved and shook while Ben held her, trying to soothe all the terror and anguish accumulated over the years to produce such pain.

"Ah, Kate," whispered Ben, stroking her hair, "I do love you."

She raised her tear-streaked face in disbelief. "Ben, you don't know about me—where I came from, where I've been. . . ."

"It doesn't matter," he assured her.

"It matters to me," she insisted. Then, slowly, haltingly, with Ben's arms still around her, Kate began to trace the tale for him, tugging at the roots of her pain as she had done only for Consuela and Dr. Harper. Only this time, going deeper, revealing her relationship and dependency upon Mark.

Ben listened quietly.

When she finished her story, he kissed her softly on the lips. "Now that you've told me something of yourself, I love you even more."

He couldn't change one ugly scene in the story Kate told him, but he could change the quality of the rest of her life. He intended to do that.

He couldn't do anything about her past involvement with Mark Hunter, but he could affect her present involvement. He intended to do that.

He lifted Kate up in his arms, carried her below quarters, placed her gently on the bed, and looked down at her. Her eyes were puffy and red from weeping. Her makeup was streaked. Her hair was damp. She looked strangely small and defenseless lying there, and he had never thought her more beautiful or desirable.

But because she looked so vulnerable, he turned to leave.

Kate stopped him. "Ben. Don't go." She reached out a hand to him.

All resolve fell from him. He felt such love for her and he was engulfed by it. Oh, how he wanted her!

He lay beside her and gathered her into his arms. With trembling fingers he stroked her, caressed her lovingly, kissed her tenderly, murmured to her, and undressed her until, naked beneath him, she clasped him closer and cried out as, for the first time, he entered her.

~32~

A New York *Daily News* cartoon depicted a two-headed Contessa Perrugia wearing two Kirstens. Question marks hovered over each head. The caption: "We know she will, but which she won't is the question."

It was a question that aroused the curiosity of others.

Noting the cartoon lying face up on the table, Suzy inquired, "Well, which one will you wear to the ball, Consuela?" They were busy labeling, ticketing, and boxing selected House of Graet gems for the journey south. Consuela would entrust the task to no one else.

The dimple flashed. "How did you know I would wear one?" she asked.

"The same way *they* did," said Suzy, motioning with her head toward the *News* cartoon. "How could you resist? Better still, when have you ever?"

Consuela shrugged expressively. "What can I say? I only just decided to wear the Kirsten. I have not yet decided which Kirsten to wear."

At last they were finished. When all the pieces had been boxed and placed in vaults ready to be shipped south, two opened House of Graet presentation boxes remained on the conference room table. Within them rested the two Kirstens, the real and the fake —the stars of the House of Graet Christmas Ball.

Suzy studied them with interest. "For the life of me, Consuela, I can't tell them apart."

Consuela laughed. "They are twins, *cara.* Only Louis could have produced such a miracle." Her long slender fingers lovingly touched each necklace. "Now, I have two *bambinos,* Suzy. What do you think of that?"

"I think you're right. Louis is a magician. Well, at least we know by the inventory number which is which."

"Ah," said Consuela slyly, picking up the real Kirsten. "We have another way of knowing. Not only is Louis a magician, he is a genius. Look, Suzy. Look closely." Consuela picked up the Kirsten replica and held the necklaces side by side.

Suzy looked closely, somewhat bewildered. Both large red stones, surrounded by smaller white stones, glittered and blazed.

"You see nothing?" queried Consuela.

"I see two gorgeous hunks of rock. I know one of them isn't a real diamond, but I'm hard pressed to tell which is which."

Consuela nodded, satisfied. "You are supposed to find it difficult. Louis planned it that way. Only"—she paused for effect—"he added something to the *real* Kirsten." She waited for Suzy to absorb that vital piece of information. "An extra white diamond has been added around the center red diamond. There are twenty-one diamonds around the Kirsten, Suzy. The replica has only twenty. An expert could spot the real one right away. The ordinary person will find it a stunning mystery. Also"—another dramatic pause—"the clasp on the replica is slightly different from the clasp on the real Kirsten."

Suzy studied them again. "I'm only a secretary, not a gemologist, but I tell you, Consuela, I'm still spooked by the uncanny way they look alike."

"Good," approved Consuela. "So shall everyone be."

The other person who expressed curiosity over which Kirsten Consuela would wear to the ball was Louis-Philippe.

He stopped by her office the night before she was due to leave for Palm Beach.

"You have created another tempest," he observed, referring to the New York *Daily News* cartoon.

"Only a minor one," granted Consuela. "It will enhance our efforts."

His look was speculative. "Which one *will* it be?" he asked.

"Once my decision is made, Louis, you shall be the first to know," she responded provocatively.

"It might be wiser to wear the replica," he suggested mildly.

"I will be surrounded by guards. Perfectly safe," she assured him.

"Still, it's quite a responsibility."

"More of a challenge. One that will heighten the drama," she insisted.

Louis-Philippe saw that he would not budge her. He changed the subject. They discussed the many details that needed to be attended to. Ball procedures. When Louis would arrive in Palm Beach. Press coverage for the Kirsten.

The press was not aware of when or how the Kirsten would arrive in Palm Beach. Security measures were tight. Only Consuela, Louis-Philippe, Suzy, and Kate knew it would travel with Consuela and her Pinkerton men on board the House of Graet company jet.

The Pinkerton men could accompany her and the Kirstens to the House of Graet, Palm Beach, where the real Kirsten and the replica would be stored in the store vault. Pinkerton men would guard them day and night. The night of the ball, both Kirstens would be transported, under guard, to the ball site.

Once business was completed, Consuela fixed them each a brandy. She handed Louis his, and raised her glass in a toast. "To you, Louis. You are a treasure house of strength to me. How would I ever manage without you?"

"Very well, I fear," he said.

"You are wrong," insisted Consuela. "You do not know the thoughts that plague me. Things that could go wrong with the Kirsten, the ball, the entire project." Her eyes clouded at the images she conjured up. She pulled herself together resolutely. "Naturally, I do not allow myself to dwell on such happenings."

"Naturally."

"We must hope for the best."

"Of course."

"Expect the best."

"Always."

"You humor me, Louis. You think I do not know your tricks, but I see right through them."

He smiled. "I'll try not to be so transparent in the future."

Consuela nodded approval. "How was your holiday?" she asked, studying him shrewdly.

"Very fine. And yours?"

"Mine was spent with the family. As I told you." Consuela waited, her eyes narrowing slightly. When he supplied no further information, she continued. "You were with friends?"

He smiled. He knew she was fishing. "With good friends, Consuela," he said.

Incredibile! He was not going to tell her a thing. "It is good to have friends, Louis. In one's old age," she added, somewhat testily.

He laughed outright. "Since we're on the subject of age, Consuela, it might be a good idea to close up shop. A couple of old-timers like us should be in bed by now."

Consuela's eyes narrowed even more. "I do not know about *your* bed, Louis, but mine is not a place to retire in."

BOOK TWO

The Place

1

Ben's first TV feature on Palm Beach aired early in December. Ben narrated.

"It was first a sandbar. Sun, sea, sand, and simplicity attracted its first settlers. They named it Palm City.

"But once Henry Morrison Flagler was seduced by those *Providensia* palms, it became something else. He built his hotels there; built a railroad bridge that crossed Lake Worth to facilitate the arrival of his guests. And he renamed Palm City, Palm Beach.

"It was the day of the big resorts, documented by Cleveland Amory in his book *The Last Resorts*. Saratoga. Newport. Bal Harbor. Tuxedo. The Springs. Social life revolved around resort hotels.

"It was Flagler's dream to add Palm Beach to the illustrious list.

"He built the Royal Poinciana Hotel, the largest wooden hotel structure in the world. Six stories high, 475 rooms. He painted it bright yellow with white trim. The dining room seated 1,600. Four hundred waiters attended them. The menu was extensive, the service superb. Suites cost $100 per day.

"The hotel opened February 11, 1894. Flagler invited his illustrious friends to add tone.

"They came with their families: Vanderbilts, Cushings, Pierponts, Morgans, Astors, Stewarts, Wanamakers, Whitneys, Harrimans, Rhinelanders.

"They came in style, to see and be seen. With servants to tend their luggage, nannies to tend their children, and wardrobes to proclaim their status.

"They changed clothes. For breakfast, bathing, lunch, sightseeing, tea, dinner, dancing, and for the casino.

"The social agenda was full. Golf or bathing in the morning. After lunch, a trip in an Afromobile to shop, or to Alligator Joe's to watch Joe wrestle a gator.

"The Afromobile was the only transport permitted on the island. Horses were banned. Afromobiles, invented in Palm Beach, were white wicker two-seaters, attached to the rear half of a bicycle. Guests rode in the two-seater. A Negro steered and pedaled from the rear.

"Originally, the Negro pedaled from up front. Until it was discovered this position blocked the view. Moved to the rear, the view became unencumbered.

"Afternoon tea was a main event. It took place in the Royal Poinciana's Coconut Grove, a huge outdoor tea garden with tables and chairs invitingly placed under the protection of the now-ubiquitous Florida palms. An orchestra provided music for listening or dancing.

"Dancing also followed dinner. And once a week guests gathered to observe the cakewalk. It was so popular that, later on, it was changed to twice a week.

"Six colorfully dressed servant couples strutted, shuffled, and soft-shoed in competition for the huge iced cake awarded the winner.

"So successful was Flagler's venture, the following year he built the first Breakers Hotel on the shores of the Atlantic Ocean. He called it the Palm Beach Inn.

"And one year after that, Colonel Edward Reilly Bradley opened his Beach Club. It became the most exclusive gambling club in America. Never once raided, Colonel Bradley operated it until his death in 1946.

"The Beach Club rivaled the casino at Monte Carlo. Its restaurant, with its French chef who was paid $12,000 for the three-month season, equaled any in Paris.

"Bradley's Beach Club was the place to be seen. If you qualified for admission. It was carpeted with millionaires. It wasn't unusual to see someone lose several hundreds of thousands of dollars in a night without visible signs of discomfort.

"The code of a gentleman gambler is to accept your losses and smile.

"The season was short. It lasted from mid-December until February twenty-third.

"The February twenty-second Washington's Birthday Ball, held in the Royal Poinciana Ballroom, signaled the season's closing. It was the high point of the Palm Beach social season. It was also a benefit, its proceeds going toward charitable causes. Perhaps it was the inspiration for the Palm Beach penchant for lavish charitable events.

"On February twenty-third, all guests left the hotel. In style. Just as they had come.

"Who were they, these American aristocrats? They were the men who made their fortunes from things so diverse as cereal, soap, patent medicines, tobacco, cookies, candy, department stores, oil, sewing machines, steel, banking, the stock exchange, the railroads, steamships. And any service or product the public wanted badly enough to make the offerer rich.

"Most of these men didn't inherit their fortunes. They created them. They weren't handed titles. They claimed them. They became the kings, princes, lords, and dukes of American industry. And they crowned their wives and daughters queens, princesses, ladies, and duchesses.

"Some of these titans and their spouses had manners not always as polished as their purses. That detail would be corrected by later generations.

"They flocked to Palm Beach as they did to Newport, Bal Harbor, Tuxedo, Saratoga, and the Springs.

"Later, they began to build resort hotels of their own, palaces they euphemistically called 'cottages.'

"They built, or assembled, like the aristocrats they were. Sprawling Italian Renaissance palaces. Fortresslike castles. Splendid homes that proclaimed their privilege as blatantly as any crown perched atop a royal head.

"No longer need they go abroad for culture. They were rich enough to cart culture home. Even if they had to dismantle it, brick by brick, stone by stone, and ship it across an ocean.

"Italian palazzos, English castles, Spanish courtyards, Italian marble, stained-glass windows, circular iron staircases—all found their way into the new framework for this resplendent style of living.

"These men were admired, envied, feared, held in awe, and held up to others as examples of the rewards obtainable from a little American ingenuity, a little hanky-panky, and a lot of shrewd hardheaded American know-how.

"In Palm Beach, they had come upon an island in the sun. They basked in it, and savored the fruits of their rewards.

"But what of the man whose vision began it all? Like most visionaries, Flagler was a man with a quest. And like most men whose personal life left something to be desired, his energies went outward.

"The son of a poor preacher, Flagler teamed up with John D. Rockefeller, co-created Standard Oil, and became a multimillionaire.

"When his first wife became ill, Flagler took her to St. Augustine. He built his first hotels there. When she died, he married her nurse.

"The marriage suffered stress. As indicated when Flagler's second wife announced one morning she was betrothed to the czar of all the Russias. She spent the remainder of her days committed to an asylum.

"Flagler courted his third wife for ten years. Twenty-four-year-old Mary Lily Kenan spent a Cinderella-like existence living in the attic of rich relatives. To stifle gossip from Flagler's attentions, and to placate Mary Lily, Flagler married her.

"But, first, he needed to divorce his second wife. Flagler pushed the Florida divorce law through the Florida legislature. Two weeks later, he married Mary Lily. He was seventy-one. She was thirty-four.

"Four years later, the law was repealed.

"Mary Lily had one simple bridal request. 'Build me a marble palace,' she instructed her groom. As bridal gifts, she also received from her groom a $500,000 pearl rope necklace and $1 million in cash to play with.

"In 1902, to the tune of $4 million, Whitehall, now the Flagler Museum, was ready. Europe had been scoured for treasures in an effort to prepare it for its debut.

"Its 110-foot-long, 40-foot-wide hallway was done in seven shades of Carrara marble. A forty-foot-long, twenty-seven-foot-wide millefleurs Kerman carpet, the largest of its kind to be loomed, partially covered the floor. A twenty-foot frescoed dome ceiling rose overhead.

"Whitehall had an Italian Renaissance library, a Swiss billiard room, a Louis XV ballroom, a Louis XVI salon, a Francis I dining room, an Elizabethan breakfast room, an Italian courtyard with a Florentine fountain.

"It also had a master suite and sitting room, baths, and fourteen guest chambers.

"It was once called 'the Taj Mahal of North America.'

"The roots of Mary Lily's obsession with bigness might be traced by modern psychiatric interpretation to snubs endured at the hands of insensitive rich relatives. It's said she never wore a gown twice, and she owned over fifty complete dinner sets.

"The roots of Flagler's preoccupation with bigness might be traced to his early poverty. But, then, these were the years when bigness was not suspect. Or tasteless. Bigness was what America was all about.

"Was Flagler content, now that Mary Lily was? When asked that question, he replied, 'I'd trade it all in for a shack.'

"He died in 1913, never recovering from a fall down three of Whitehall's Italian marble steps.

"Generous beyond the grave, he left an estate of $100 million.

"Right to the end, it remained a Palm Beach fairy tale.

"Next," Ben Gately told his viewers, ending his first TV feature on Palm Beach, "we'll look into the Mizner-Singer influence on Palm Beach, the years of the fabulous twenties."

Kate's call was the first to reach Ben. "I love it," she told him. Ben glowed. "You can show me how much when I get there."

Earl Blakely, watching the TV feature on Palm Beach from the bar in Palm Beach's Peter's Pub, agreed this was indeed the place where fairy tales could come true. Where a good-looking stud with some savvy and style could get it on in no time at all.

With a few natural assets and a little bit of luck, a guy could strike gold here.

Especially a guy with a way with the ladies. Christ, he'd only been in town a few days and opportunities were falling into his lap.

He'd come cross-country, all the way from Hollywood, to collect on something due him. Only to discover the place was alive with women eager for a little southern comfort.

Like the broad down the bar. Classy-looking. Rich-looking too. A lot of mileage there, but what the hell. She wore it well. And the cool invitation in those silvery blue eyes left nothing unsuggested.

Earl Blakely picked up his drink, eased his way down the bar, smiled disarmingly, and moved in for the hit.

Bordon Granger, comfortably settled in his Wellington house thirteen miles from Palm Beach, watched the feature on the five-foot-wide screen in his video room. He turned to Tami Hayes seated beside him. "Nice piece of work."

Tami smiled and nodded absently, her mind on other things.

It could only happen in Palm Beach. . . .

Rushing through Saks on her lunch hour, Sandy Stone was greeted by a slender blonde wearing a dazzling smile and a green knit dress. "Have you seen the Castleburys?" beamed the blonde.

Sandy stopped short. Who were the Castleburys? Should she know them? Were they lost? Should she help find them?

Only later did she realize Castlebury was a knitwear line. The dazzling blonde in the green knit was modeling one.

On her way home from work, Sandy passed one woman offering another a ride home. "It's my old Rolls. The brown one," apologized the woman.

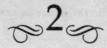

2

The media covered the Contessa Perrugia's departure from New York with interest. They hurled questions and snapped pictures. Derek Tracey was visibly annoyed. The contessa was visibly gracious. She smiled endlessly.

"How long will you stay, Contessa?"

"Until the work is done. Perhaps I shall visit longer and play a bit." Another bright smile. "The climate there is so perfect this time of year. Who could resist it?"

"The big question on everybody's mind, Contessa, is what you're wearing to the ball?"

The famous smile broadened. "A divine Geoffrey Beene. Designed especially for the occasion."

"I think what my colleague means," interjected a TV reporter, "is which Kirsten?"

The laugh was disarming, as was the shrug that accompanied it. "What can I say? I have not yet decided."

Derek sulked the entire way down to Palm Beach. He thought the fuss over the Kirsten was obscene. "The thing that gets me, Connie, is you take all this hoopla seriously."

"It is show business, *caro*. You of all people can surely appreciate that."

"All I know is, if this keeps up, we won't get a chance to relax," complained Derek.

"Hush," soothed Consuela. "You will have plenty of opportunity to relax. Trust me. Consuela knows what is best."

Derek wasn't so sure.

Dio mio! brooded Consuela. Out of bed, Derek was becoming an absolute chore to have around.

* * *

Bordon Granger and Tami Hayes were having their first argument. A serious one.

Bordon couldn't believe what was happening. "You can't mean it!"

"I mean it, Bordon."

"But why?"

"I can't explain."

"Tami, the whole goddamned wedding is arranged. Down to flowers, flower girls, ring bearer, minister, church, guests, guest housing, caterers, photographers, media people, and God knows what else. The least I am owed is an explanation."

"You're right. You are. I just can't give you one."

Bordon cared nothing about wedding arrangements or wedding paraphernalia. He cared only for Tami. Without her, nothing had meaning.

He pulled her gently into his arms. "I love you, Tami."

She rested there. "I love you too, Bordon."

He tilted her chin and looked steadily into her eyes. "Well, then, that's all that matters."

"No, it isn't," she said with a deep sigh.

"Why?"

"I can't tell you."

In Connecticut, Grace Schmittle, fretting over Carl's insistence on pushing himself beyond reasonable and rational limits, made a decision.

She called Rosemary.

"Mamma?" Rosemary was surprised to hear from her mother. Generally, it was her father who called to chat. "Is anything wrong?"

"Everything is wrong," Grace said. "Rosemary, I want you to contact some realtors and find a house for Dad and me."

She told Rosemary about the sorry condition of Carl's health. She had spoken with Harry Barton, who had not minimized the seriousness of the situation. It was imperative that Carl begin to take care of himself, according to his physician.

All her life, Rosemary's father had seemed invincible. Almost immortal. The thought of his mortality was terrible. And more frightening than Rosemary cared to admit.

"Rosemary? Are you still there?"

"Yes, Mamma."

"I want you to attend to this at once. If you can't buy something we can move into immediately, rent something. You and I can look around once we're down there. You know the kind of place Dad likes."

Rosemary rarely heard her mother so decisive. It served to reinforce the gravity of the situation and frighten Rosemary even more.

"I'll get right on it, Mamma, and call you back."

"That's a good girl," said Grace Schmittle absently.

Rosemary sat by the pool, phone and phone listings at hand. She had tried three realtors so far. Nothing suitable.

She chewed on a cuticle absentmindedly, still trying to absorb the information her mother had given her. Why hadn't she been told at once? No matter how many goddamned houseguests decorated the weekend, why didn't her mother take her aside and confide in her?

Because her mother never told her important things concerning her father. It was as though she were jealous of the special bond he and Rosemary shared.

Not as though! She was. Simple fact. *Digest it, Rosemary. Digest it all over again.*

Her husband and her goddamned roses! Those were the only things Grace Schmittle ever cared about. She didn't give a shit about Rosemary. Rosemary learned to nibble on that truth very early in her life.

The discovery came in small ways. Small criticisms that made her unsure of herself.

On her fourth birthday, her father gave Rosemary a Shetland pony. Safely mounted but frightened, Rosemary surveyed her parents, the grounds, the pony beneath her. She felt anxious but free. Exhilarated but unsure. Until her mother spoke.

"Rosemary, you look so awkward on that pony, I think we'd better take you off."

Rosemary never rode the pony after that.

Rosemary's sexual instruction was given her by her mother. When she considered Rosemary old enough, Grace told her about the "holy act." The nuns had explained it to her, she said.

What was it? wondered Rosemary.

The "holy act," her mother told her, was what happened between a man and his wife. Now that Rosemary was bleeding every month, it meant her body was ready for the "holy act," even though she wasn't. She must be very careful from now on.

What was it? persisted Rosemary. What must she be careful of?

She must be careful never to allow a boy to touch her. Rosemary had attributes boys liked. Rosemary wondered what they were.

The "holy act," continued Grace, was designed for marriage. In marriage, Rosemary would discover things she would not particularly enjoy. The "holy act" was one of them. It was, however, what God made women for. *He* would provide Rosemary with the strength she needed when the time came.

When Rosemary was older, Grace would tell her more about it. Just as the nuns explained it to her.

In Rosemary's fourteenth year, her mother caught her necking on the solarium sofa with Shawn Patrick O'Malley. Grace decided the time had come.

After sending the O'Malley boy home, she sat Rosemary down and continued the instruction.

Nice Catholic girls did not permit familiarities.

When Rosemary was married, she would perform the "holy act" with her husband. She would go into the bathroom and lock the door. She must never allow her husband inside the bathroom when she was there.

She would remove her clothing, put on a long high-necked nightgown and, when she was decently attired, she would return to the bedroom, slide between the sheets, pull the blankets up around her, and turn out the lights.

That was her cue to her husband that the "holy act" could begin. Grace described the procedure in detail.

Rosemary made no further comment, but for some time she found it difficult to look at her mother and father together. And she found herself at the oddest moments staring at people and thinking they wouldn't be here at all if it weren't for the "holy act."

Still, the maternal warning persisted. Rosemary remained a virgin. Despite pleas and protests, her hymen remained intact.

On her wedding night, Rosemary let go. No long-necked nightgown, no locked bathroom door, no cumbersome blankets, and no turned-off lights. Rosemary wanted to see, feel, enjoy, and experience everything.

Afterward, lying on the wide bed, blankets kicked to the floor, staring blissfully up at the bedroom ceiling of their Plaza Hotel suite, Rosemary giggled.

"What's so funny?" Mark wanted to know.

Rosemary rolled toward him. "Let's do it again," she whispered.

"Do what?" teased Mark.

"The 'holy act,' " said Rosemary with reverence.

"What's that?"

Rosemary reached down. "You'll see," she promised.

As usual, her mother had been wrong.

Rosemary was C-R-A-Z-Y about the "holy act."

When Rosemary first learned of Mark's infidelity, it was as though the "holy act" was no longer holy. Mark had desecrated it.

He was still doing that. He hadn't been near her since Thanksgiving night when he all but raped her on the library floor. And that had been the first time he'd touched her in months.

Mark was never around when she needed him. And she needed him now.

She needed to tell Mark about Daddy.

So Mark could tell her what to do.

3

Of all the seed spilled into Mimzee Dawson, B.C. (Before Celibacy), by five husbands and countless lovers, only one batch produced sperm potent enough to fertilize an ovum, form an embryo, and develop into a full-term child.

The donor of that successful connection was Mimzee's second husband, Hollywood's sexiest cowboy movie star of the late thirties, Branch Nolan.

"Sexy my butt," observed Mimzee in rebuttal. "Branch was as surprised as I was by the pregnancy."

Truth was, only after the wedding ceremony did Mimzee learn Branch preferred cowboys to heiresses. And that before cowboys came love of his horse. Not that Mimzee suspected any hanky-panky there. Only Branch never would get off the goddamned horse. The fact that he managed to dismount long enough to sire anything was a source of amazement.

Following the arrival of the new heiress and the shock of fatherhood, Branch Nolan climbed back on his horse and, cameras rolling, rode off into the sunset.

The divorce settlement agreed upon by Mimzee and her lawyers assured the aging cowboy star a succession of magnificent sunsets to ride off into.

The child from that unfortunate union was baptized Andrea Elizabeth Dawson Nolan.

Mimzee was definitely not motherhood material. She was embarking on marriage number three, the Italian jockey, and determined to keep her lusty young rider and her prizewinning horse under her watchful eye. Wherever jockey and horse went, Mimzee followed. Would she never get away from horses? she wondered.

But races were won long after the jockey had been retired from the Dawson stables and replaced by husbands four and five. While Andrea Elizabeth was left in the care of nurses, governesses, and a succession of other servants.

At seventeen, she ran off with the family chauffeur. At eighteen, she divorced him. For the next eight years, she matched her mother in collecting husbands. She bettered her by bearing two children from two different marriages.

Like her father, she retained a love of horses all her life. Unlike him, she was not so proficient at riding. She died of a broken neck at age twenty-six when the horse she was riding cleared the hurdle, leaving her behind.

Mimzee buried her daughter and repeated her method of child rearing with her grandchildren. They were attended by nurses, governesses, and a succession of servants. They were shipped off to prestigious schools almost as soon as they could stand up. Materially they wanted for nothing. Emotionally they were as starved as the mother they barely remembered.

Belinda Graham, at twenty-two, was a beautiful bulimic. Or anorexic. Mimzee never could get the two diseases straight in her mind. Her half brother, Howard "Howie" Caine, twenty-one, was extraordinarily handsome. He was also shiftless, a pathological liar, and a thief.

He would, Mimzee knew, steal her blind without a scruple to inhibit his greed.

These, then, were Mimzee's heirs. She despaired at the misfits life had bequeathed her, and tried to map out a workable solution.

Neither grandchild showed any indication of shaping up into material capable of steering the Dawson ship into fresh ports.

Clearly, something must be done.

Both children lived with her, another thorn in her side. Belinda, however, was malleable. If Mimzee could just get her married off, one problem would be settled. But, first, Belinda would have to gain thirty pounds so she didn't look like an Auschwitz reject.

Howie was the obstacle. Too lazy to hold down a job and too crooked to send into the company.

What the hell could she do with him?

* * *

All his life, women had fawned over him, petted him, fondled his golden curls, and marveled over his David-like beauty. So, early in life, Howie Caine concluded women were easily manipulated and gullible.

Except for his grandmother. Howie had respect for any woman he couldn't con. He was extremely cagey when he met someone who could read his number. And those beady blue eyes of his grandmother's could read him down to bare bone.

Despite the hot Florida sun beating down on him, Howie shivered. He picked himself up from the sand where he lay on his grandmother's stretch of private beach and dashed into the Atlantic, feeling exhilarated as he breasted waves and soared their heights into deeper waters.

He swam and fretted over his future.

He was in a bind. His trust fund from his mother's estate couldn't be touched until his twenty-sixth birthday. He'd be hanging by his balls until then if he didn't come up with something. No way could he manage on the monthly allotment his grandmother stintingly doled out. If he didn't deal a few drugs, he'd be up shit creek. But he needed dough, big dough, to deal on a scale that counted.

If he could just latch on to some of that big dough, he'd be off and sailing. He knew of a Miami connection who'd be suitably impressed with a real roll.

All he needed was a stake for starters.

Now, his grandmother was loaded. Up to her shriveled old kazoo in dough. And trinkets. But would she part with any? Fat chance!

Look at those jewels she decked herself out in. Jesus, she had so many goddamned tiaras, you'd think she was the bloody queen of England.

She'd never miss one. But she had them locked up in the goddamned vault, and only she knew the combination.

Maybe he could blow the vault up. When she was out one day. Just sashay in and grab a fistful of the stuff. Better still, a satchelful. Then he'd be on easy street. Without waiting until he was twenty-six. The gems could be taken out of their original settings, divided up, sold separately. He knew just the guy who'd unload them.

Howie floated on his back, shading his eyes from the bright Florida sun. Maybe it wasn't such a bad idea. Maybe the idea just needed some polishing.

In the meantime, he'd have to content himself with stealing and selling those things he found lying around that weren't anchored, vaulted, or sealed.

He'd been working on his grandmother's Fabergé collection.

One piece at a time.

Very carefully.

It was a magnificent collection. More than magnificent, it was one of the most extensive Fabergé collections outside the Soviet Union and the British royal family. Priceless. Irreplaceable. Painstakingly collected. Museum quality.

And Mimzee was missing several pieces.

Mimzee Dawson's Fabergé collection was displayed in the Fabergé wing connected to her bedroom suite. There, seated on her Louis XVI Brunschwig & Fils brocade upholstered settee, Mimzee was surrounded by vitrines containing her treasures.

Picture frames in gold or richly colored enamels. Music boxes, compacts, goblets, clocks, icons, fans, cigarette boxes, match boxes, pillboxes, a basket of lilies of the valley. Over 100 objects in all. With enamels mixed by Fabergé to produce colors of such voluptuous richness, women attempted to match those colors in fabrics for gowns.

The pieces were studded with semiprecious and precious stones. They blazed, glittered, and enchanted. They were exquisitely executed fantasies by the master goldsmith of his time—of all time—Fabergé, court-appointed jeweler to the imperial court of the Romanovs. Jeweler to Queen Alexandra of England, of whom it was said, "When in doubt of a gift to give her, give her Fabergé."

Queen Alexandra adored the fanciful animals Fabergé carved from hardstone. She gathered her own Fabergé menagerie.

Mimzee gathered one too.

In the late nineteenth century, a Fabergé animal cost between $100 and $300. Today it could fetch as much as $50,000.

One of Mimzee's animals, a rhinoceros, was missing.

But the pièce de résistance of Mimzee Dawson's collection were her three Fabergé Easter eggs. Only fifty-seven had been made.

Fabergé first proposed the Easter egg concept to Czar Alexander III in 1883 as a gift for the czarina.

The egg, Fabergé suggested, was a symbol of birth, renewal, perfection. It would symbolize a new beginning for the czar and the czarina who had witnessed the horror of the assassination of the czar's father, Alexander II. Inside each Easter egg would be a "surprise."

In 1973, one of Nicholas II's Easter eggs sold at auction for $200,000. Auctions were just about the only place a Fabergé piece could be picked up. Even then, only rarely.

Mimzee's three eggs were still safely ensconced in their vitrines. Missing were a rhinoceros, a gold picture frame, and an enameled pillbox.

She couldn't understand it. The vitrines were locked, the keys hidden in a jewel box used for minor jewels kept in her dresser drawer.

The pieces were indexed, photographed, cataloged. The vitrines were numbered. The pieces in each vitrine were accounted for.

It took Mimzee's sharp eye to realize three pieces were missing. She knew each piece well.

Mimzee interviewed the entire staff, one by one. Only a few had upstairs duties. Nevertheless, she pursued her course relentlessly. Someone had stolen from her prized collection. Who? Who would have the temerity to tamper with pieces of such value?

No one on her staff, certainly. Each one had been with her for years. Each was completely trustworthy. And her security force had initiated such stringent security measures that no stranger could possibly gain entrance.

Mimzee sent for Howie. She ordered him to sit down, faced him, and confronted him.

"Howard, three of my Fabergé pieces are missing."

"No!" Howie looked devastated at the announcement.

Mimzee eyed him shrewdly. "You wouldn't know anything about it?"

"Gee, Mimzee, how would I know anything about it?"

Mimzee stared at him.

Howie stared innocently back.

"Because you're a lying, conniving, little son of a bitch. That's why. Because you've got the lightest fingers accompanied by the least amount of conscience of anyone I know. Because you're greedy for anything and everything that doesn't belong to you. Because you have the motivation, the access, and the gall. Would you like more reasons, Howie?"

Howie's expression was total wonder. "I don't know what makes you suspect me."

She never dropped her eyes. "Don't you?" Despite her fury, Mimzee's voice took on an almost pleading note. "Howard, just tell me what you did with them. Do you still have them?"

"I never took them, Mimzee," lied Howie.

"Liar!" she shrieked, pleading no longer. The beady blue eyes glistened. "I bet you never even got a tenth of what those pieces are worth."

Howie opened his mouth to again defend his position.

Mimzee interrupted him. "And another thing. I want those pieces back. If you have to pay triple what you got to retrieve them, do it. Just get them back. One more thing. If you touch anything else of mine, I'll have you prosecuted. Don't for a minute delude yourself into thinking I won't send you to jail. And don't indulge yourself by underestimating me. And don't do battle with me. We're not in the same league, dearie. I'd gobble you up without a belch."

To the end of the interview, Howie protested his innocence. First, he was shocked at his grandmother's accusation, distressed by her suspicion of him. Second, didn't she know he would do anything for her? And third, he would personally undertake his own search for the missing objects.

"Balls!" said Mimzee to the first point. "Horseshit!" she shouted to the second. To the third: "Good. Get them back for me, Howard. And remember what I said. You won't like the hoosegow."

When the interview was over and Howie was dismissed, Mimzee prepared for the small dinner party she was giving. Nothing must interfere with the success of her dinner party. Especially a little shit like her grandson.

Outfitted in a splendid Elizabethan gown of heavy brocaded silk, with a lace ruff around her neck, Mimzee's spirits improved.

Ropes of pearls, rubies, and diamonds nested below the ruff. Rubies and diamonds glittered from her fingers and wrists.

She reached for a diamond, ruby, and pearl tiara and anchored it firmly atop her flaming red Queen Bess wig.

Resplendent in her imperial finery, she regally descended the stairs. Guests were gathered in the great hall, others in the drawing room. Mimzee was always the last to arrive at her own parties. An entrance was everything. A queen, after all, appeared only after all guests were assembled.

Marjorie Hunter, dressed in a peach Oscar de la Renta and smiling gaily at two escorts dancing attendance on her, turned to greet her hostess. "Mimzee, darling," she cried out with pleasure.

"Marjorie," noted Mimzee in response to her friend of sixty years, "you're wearing that same old Oscar de la Renta number, I see."

Marjorie's eyes glinted as she curtsied. "And you, Your Majesty, are still hanging onto that same old tiara."

Mimzee hooted, and patted it. "This one's new, dearie. The House of Graet whipped it up for me." She reached up, whisked off the tiara, and held it out for all to admire. "Feast your eyes and die of envy. Isn't it divine? Did you ever see so many pearls, diamonds, and rubies? It's so gorgeous, I can't bear it."

"Your Majesty dazzles us all," admitted Marjorie with humor.

"Damn right," agreed Mimzee, anchoring her tiara once more.

There were those times in life when you knew in your gut your number would come up a winner.

Earl Blakely knew that now.

He was long overdue. For too many years he'd been outside looking in. No more. Now he was cutting himself in for a large slice of the good-life pie.

To begin with, things were finally going his way.

First, there was Drucie Martin AKA Tami Hayes. Who ever thought little Drucie would turn up again in his life? A kid with nothing. Now, a big star.

Well, he'd managed to track her down. Soon he'd be calling her to let her know he was in town.

Yup, things were picking up. First, Drucie. Then—what was her name? The broad he'd picked up at the bar last night? Myra?

Myrna? Melba? Magda? He could have sworn she'd used all of them, teasing him with her silvery blue eyes, tossing her silvery blond hair back from a honey-tanned face.

A real classy chick. Fifty, if she was a day, but built like thirty, with the staying power of a twenty-year-old.

They'd really tied one on together, white magic and all.

She'd taken him back to her pad. Pad! Christ, it was a museum! She laughed when Earl's mouth fell open and told him she was the housekeeper there.

When he left four hours later, she was fresh as a daisy and he was dragging his ass. Still, his performance must have been up to par. She'd slipped 500 bucks in his jacket pocket. Five hundred bucks! From a housekeeper? Who the hell did she think she was kidding?

Jesus, this was the place to be!

And he had a date with her again tonight.

Earl whistled happily as he showered and soaped his head. He rinsed, stepped from the shower, toweled himself quickly, blow-dried his sun-scorched hair, and dressed with consummate care. A pale blue cashmere sweater that settled gracefully over his torso while still defining the breadth of his shoulders and the tightness of his gut.

Not bad for a thirty-seven-year-old!

He pulled on a pair of expensively faded jeans shrunk two sizes too small for him that hugged his ass and outlined his dick.

He thought of the TV feature he'd seen last night about fortunes made from cereal, soap, toothpaste, candy, sewing machines, and any service or product the public wanted badly enough to make the offerer rich.

Hell, he had a service the public would pay for too.

With his cock, he could fuck his way to a fortune.

4

There had never been a woman Mark Hunter couldn't handle. Lately, there didn't seem to be one he could.

First, there was his mother. Who had insisted on a command performance at her house where the riot act was read to him in no uncertain terms.

Marjorie had heard the gossip. Mark was to clean up his act, and stop seducing everything in skirts that struck his fancy.

"Remember, you're a Hunter, Mark. See that you act like one."

There was his wife.

Rosemary reached Mark in Washington. In a rush of agitation, she dumped all her anxieties about Carl on Mark.

Calmly, Mark relayed the incident in the library on Thanksgiving. Not the ultimatum Carl had delivered. Just the attack he suffered.

"Oh, my God," cried Rosemary. "Why didn't you tell me?"

He hesitated. "I don't know." He did know. Everyone tiptoed around Rosemary for fear of setting her off. "I suppose I didn't want to worry you."

"Well, I'm worried now. Worried sick." She started to cry.

"Don't, Rosemary," cautioned Mark. "Don't upset yourself." The last thing in the world he needed was for Rosemary to bathe her anxieties in booze. He didn't have enough energy left to see her through another extended rehabilitation.

In a reassuring tone, he said, "Your father's as strong as an ox, Rosemary. And stubborn as a mule." He forced a laugh. "He as much as promised me he wasn't going anywhere until he completed all the things he has lined up. And the list is impressively long. He's a long way from the end of his projects."

Mark didn't bother to tell Rosemary her husband was her father's prime project. The one project he vowed to stick around long enough to see through. "He'll be fine. You'll see."

"You really believe that?" asked Rosemary hesitantly.

"Of course I do. All he needs is to let go of the corporate reins and take things easy. It may be foreign to his nature, but I know he can do it."

"He can, can't he?"

"Sure, he can."

Rosemary was troubled on another score. "I haven't been able to find a place for them. One I think Daddy would be happy in."

"Have them stay with us, Roe. God knows, there's plenty of room." With Carl and Grace at Casa Miramar, absorbing Rosemary's attentions, Rosemary wouldn't be on his back so much, demanding his presence constantly.

"You don't mind?"

"Of course I don't mind. If they want a place of their own, you and your mother can look for one after they get there."

"That's just what Mamma suggested. Only she was thinking of looking from a rented house."

"Well, that isn't necessary. The important thing is to get them down there fast so Carl can begin to get well."

"Yes," agreed Rosemary eagerly. "That is what's important." Her panic eased, she sounded better.

"Good," said Mark. "Give them my best, Roe, and tell them I'm rooting for them."

There was a small silence. Mark waited. He and Rosemary had had a fairly rational discussion about a serious family problem. Mark didn't know what else to say.

Rosemary said it. "When are you coming down, Mark?"

"I think I can manage it soon, Rosemary."

"You think!" flared Rosemary. "Well, for Christ's sake, don't think, Mark. Do. Come down this weekend. I'm coming unglued over this situation with Daddy. I need you."

He sighed. "Rosemary, I've got a million things up here claiming my attention that I can't walk out on."

"I bet," snapped Rosemary, completely recovered from the dram of comfort Mark had proffered. "Well, you've got one edgy wife down here, buster, and if you don't want her to flip out, you'd better tidy up all your little *details* and come on down."

"I'll try, Rosemary."

"Don't try, Mark. *Do.*"

Then there was Reenie Boyd.

She had effectively reduced him to the status of whore while elevating herself to a position of power. She held all the cards. She called the shots. She demanded his presence. When the whim seized her. Apparently, it seized her weekly. On Tuesday. The implied threat was, if he didn't dance attendance on her, she would be forced to pick up her pen again and continue those spicy tidbits that enchanted her readers but set Mark's teeth on edge.

It was something she hated to do, she insisted. Still, she was a businesswoman first. An agreement was an agreement.

"Sugah, you're makin' such a fuss about nothin', workin' yourself up needlessly. You look positively peaked. Now, lie back and let Reenie relax you."

"Jesus, Reenie, the simple fact is, I can't fill in all the dance numbers on your little card."

She burst out laughing. "Oh, I like that. But who's asking you to, sweetie? Every Tuesday is not the whole damned dance card."

"I cannot be here every Tuesday. I have commitments. Responsibilities."

"Ah, I am impressed. But, you know, I'm not exactly idle myself. I run an empire and manage to squeeze in time for you. Seems to me your priorities need adjustin'."

"Screwing you is not my number-one priority."

"Well, then, I insist you rearrange things. Because that should be number one."

"Oh, for Christ's sake, Reenie, you've got a stableful of studs. Why me?"

"You suit me, darlin'. So hush up and let Reenie show you how much."

He accommodated her. Every Tuesday. Flying into New York in the evening. Flying back to Washington at dawn. It was not his favorite run, but he didn't know what the hell he could do about it.

Then Reenie announced a change in schedule.

"I'll be goin' down to Palm Beach, next week, sugah. We'll have to meet there."

"You've got to be kidding!"

"Stayin' at The Breakers until I can find something more permanent."

"Well, I'm sure as hell not going to prance through The Breakers, Reenie."

She laughed in delight. "Oh, you'll think of somethin', darlin'. A nice bright boy like you. Just improvise."

That's what his mother suggested.

That's what he'd been doing. And the strain of it was beginning to tell.

To offset the stress, Mark had started a relaxing little thing with his new secretary. He also relaxed with a Washington hostess and wife of a colleague of his, a California congresswoman, a black rock star, and a television executive from New York.

Never on Tuesday.

But beyond intrigues, assignations, and command performances was the thought of Kate. He couldn't forget her. He'd reached for the phone a dozen times since their last conversation. He'd even driven by her house once, late at night, over the Thanksgiving holiday, careful to make certain no one was following.

He didn't go in. He didn't stop the car. He just missed her. As he'd never missed anyone before.

Ben Gately's co-anchor at the station, Jenny McBain, was a gorgeous-looking blonde who had made several overtures in his direction. An invitation to a gallery opening. Two tickets to the theater. A weekend in Key West. Ben had deftly dodged all efforts to draw him in.

Ordinarily, he would have been tempted. Enough even to bend his rule about no hanky-panky on the job. Blonde, beautiful, brainy, and beckoning was a tough act to resist.

But that was B.K.C. Before Kate Crowley. Since Thanksgiving, Ben couldn't get the lady off his mind. He was in love, by God, and it was great.

Even when it hurt, it was great.

Even when he learned things about himself that surprised him. For one thing, he was jealous, a state of mind he'd never had before. But thinking about Kate in the arms of Mark Hunter crazed him.

He was possessive. Ever since he'd first had Kate, he wanted more. There was never enough. The lovemaking was terrific. Why, then, did he feel she was holding back?

Why did he sense a shadow between them?

The world was full of beautiful women. He'd had his share of them. What was there about this one that hooked him so completely?

She was wonderful, that was what. He'd been waiting all his life for her. His sisters were right. He was ripe. Ready. Past resistance.

Another thing surprised him. The guy with the long-range plans that didn't include entanglements wanted to make a commitment.

After an evening of intense lovemaking, he made his move. A finger lazily traced the length of Kate's thigh. "Marry me," he suggested lightly.

Kate stretched, smiled, then turned serious. "It wouldn't work," she said.

"Why not?" Ben asked.

There were too many complications. She was a poor risk. Not marriageable material.

She was all the material he wanted, Ben insisted. It would work. They would make it work. A little effort. A little humor. A lot of love.

His fingers worked their way across her stomach, rubbed gently at the smooth skin, slid expertly to the soft area between her legs. "It'll work," he repeated. "You'll see."

Kate sat up abruptly. "Oh, Ben," she said impatiently, "you make it sound so simple."

He eased her back against the pillows. "A piece of cake, sweetheart," Ben assured her.

It wasn't that simple. Everything was fine until Ben proposed. Why did he have to spoil things?

She loved him, yes. Being with him these past few weeks had been the best experience of her life.

Even the lovemaking was lovely. Gentle, caring, yet exciting.

Ben was a tender lover, not a greedy one. Her pleasure was his pleasure.

Unlike Mark, who took ruthlessly, certain his satisfaction was her satisfaction.

Why did she still think of him? He had put her aside without a second thought when their relationship threatened to tarnish his image. Why did she still love him? How could she love such a man?

Better still, how could she love two men at the same time?

What kind of woman was she?

Rosemary phoned her mother as soon as she'd hung up on Mark, told her she'd been unable to find anything suitable, and insisted her parents come stay at Casa Miramar. She asked her mother to have Carl call Rosemary as soon as he got home.

Carl called at nine that evening.

"Princess!"

"Oh, Daddy, how are you?" cried Rosemary, relieved to hear from him at last.

"Chipper as a pastor at a quiet Sunday collection, princess. How are you?"

"Now, Daddy, we're not going to joke together, are we? I'm very serious. And I'm angry with you."

"What for, sweetheart?"

"For not telling me you were sick."

"I didn't want to worry you. Besides, it was nothing."

"Of course it was something," said Rosemary impatiently. Then, "Did Mamma speak to you?"

"She did."

"When are you coming, then?" pressed Rosemary.

"In about a week. If there are any loose ends to tie up, I can tie them by phone from down there."

"Daddy, I will not have you undermining this whole plan playing giant of industry with seventeen telephones at your side."

"Just a few loose ends," cajoled Carl.

"You sure about that?"

"I'm sure."

"I wouldn't want anything to happen to my favorite person."

"It won't, sweetheart."

"I love you, Daddy. Know that."

"I love you too, princess. More than life."

"Love life too, Daddy," urged Rosemary.

"Oh, I do, princess. I do," insisted Carl.

5

Tami Hayes was not beautiful, even though Bordon Granger insisted she was. Tami gave the illusion of beauty, but, then, creating illusions was her business. At that, she was a pro.

What she was, was a superstar who made it to the top over obstacles that would have discouraged a less determined spirit.

She was small, but held herself so straight, she seemed tall. She was slender, but gave the impression of roundness. Her hair was brown and straight, her eyes round and brown, and she appeared almost plain. Until she opened her mouth to sing.

On stage or before a camera a metamorphosis took place. And the audience responded.

Critics hailed her as the greatest talent since Garland. She could make an audience cry, laugh, shout with joy, and beg for more of the same. But Tami always left them just a little bit hungry. With the promise she'd be back to give them just a little bit more.

The publicity releases listed the tragic accident that took the lives of both parents and left her orphaned in her teens with an infant sister to raise.

It didn't happen quite that way.

The publicity releases listed her age as twenty-four. She was thirty-one.

Aside from these untruths, Tami Hayes was as honest and candid as they come. A superstar without a super ego. A performer who drew praise from studio hands to studio heads. A professional lauded by her peers.

In a business noted for drug casualties, sexcapades, and suicides, Tami Hayes was as superclean as soapsuds without being super-sickening. Her image plus her talent sold records. Five gold labels. Four platinum. In only four years.

But her image was based on lies that could explode in her face any minute. That's what she couldn't tell Bordon. And that's why she couldn't marry him.

Funny, thought Tami. *You start with a few small lies to keep things simple. The lies turn on you, and things become complicated.*

From the time he was a kid, Earl Blakely was convinced the hospital made a mistake and gave him to the wrong people.

For parents, Earl got Lila-Jean and Billy-Roy. Losers, the pair of them!

Lila-Jean was a faded lush as far back as Earl could remember. The only time Billy-Roy touched him was when he hit him.

And when he wasn't beating Earl, he was beating up on someone else. Between assaults, passing bad checks, and other skirmishes, he was in and out of jail.

Earl split when he was ten. Only he was dragged back by a cruising cop who spotted him wandering about and delivered him back to Billy-Roy, temporarily out of jail, just in time for another beating.

The next time Earl left home, he made certain no one spotted him.

Street-smart, he survived. He scrounged from garbage pails, slept in hallways, and did whatever it took to get by.

There were pluses in his favor. He was a quick study and he was good-looking. Towheaded, bright blue eyes, and the face of an angel. Someone was always ready to help him, especially when he explained he was an orphan.

He had a series of surrogate mothers—all an improvement on Lila-Jean.

For six years he lived with a devout Catholic childless widow who lavished affection upon him and sent him to St. Bartholomew's Roman Catholic school, where a succession of childless nuns lavished even more affection on him.

But it was the young priest at St. Bartholomew's who had the most impact on Earl. An ex-musician, he introduced Earl to the saxophone, taught him how to play it, and opened new vistas.

Earl's aptitude on the horn was the young priest's delight.

Earl saw it as his way out of bondage. He was restless, ready to move on. He missed the excitement of life on the streets.

He had learned another thing during those six years. Too much affection and approval was more than he could deal with.

Besides, he had lucked into a band opportunity that looked too promising to pass up. Without a word to the widow, the young priest, or the nuns who lavished love on the luckless orphan, Earl split again.

The promising band deal fizzled. He was rootless once more. Until he made his next musical connection.

Only, the big break he knew was out there waiting for him somehow never came to pass. Only, the years passed. A succession of short gigs. An excursion into drugs that eased the frustration and disappointment. But the drugs brought busts. Stints in jail. Hustling for a buck outside of jail.

There were bright spots. Plenty of chicks for a good-looking stud. A fuckin' parade of chicks.

When he met up with Drucie Martin, he was twenty-two. She was sixteen. They stayed together three years.

The icing on the cake was his discovery that Drucie had a pair of pipes that could earn them a living. They were on their way to the big time. With his horn and Drucie's pipes, nothing could stop them.

Drucie Martin was the illegitimate daughter of an itinerant Tampa stripper. She never knew her father.

When Drucie was seven, her mother parked her with a neighbor for an hour while she went out to pick up some groceries. She never returned. Drucie was taken to the county orphanage.

At fourteen, she ran away. Fate favored her. At fourteen, she looked five years older. Just as, ten years later, and for the rest of her life, she would look five years younger.

Along her travels she met Earl Blakely. Sun-scorched yellow hair, bright blue eyes, semi-accomplished hustler, and jack-of-all-trades.

Earl Blakely's belief was that fortune lay just ahead. In the next town. Waiting for him. For two years, Drucie trailed after Earl in search of Earl's fortune.

One night in Toledo, Ohio, Drucie told Earl she was pregnant. He took the news calmly, lighting up his fifty-fourth cigarette of the day. Noting his supply was low, Earl said he was going out for a pack of cigarettes. He never returned.

Abandoned for the second time, Drucie made a vow. She would never depend on anyone else again. She never did.

In the county hospital where Erin was born, Drucie listed the father as deceased, having died in the car crash that also claimed the lives of both her parents.

When she left the hospital, the story changed. Erin became the baby sister left her when the tragic accident occurred.

For a year, Drucie waitressed and bartended in a small Toledo nightclub. When the female vocalist took off one night, Drucie offered to pinch-hit. The owner was wary. Drucie wasn't. She knew she could sing.

The audience reaction was so good, Drucie became the club's singing bartender.

When a group ready to go on tour and in need of a female vocalist approached her, Drucie never hesitated. She packed up Erin and joined them. They toured the country.

In Tarrytown, New York, an agent spotted her. He thought she had a terrific talent. He promised to do great things for her. He suggested a new look. And a name change. Tami Hayes.

It took ten years of pushing, packaging, promoting. Then, as if overnight, it happened. One song did it. Tami wrote it. A blues-rock number called "Baptism Blues," about the baptism of fire necessary to forge a person into the tempered steel required to sustain a big-time career.

The rest was show business history.

Ten years after he split, Earl Blakely could have kicked himself. Little Drucie Martin, AKA Tami Hayes, was on top of the charts, raking in the dough. While he had nothing. No record labels. No big deals. Only one-night stands, drug busts, and trips to the slammer. No future at all.

Until he spotted the picture of Drucie with her kid sister in the newspaper.

Sister, hell! That was his kid! She looked just like him. That was his meal ticket.

He managed to get hold of Tami's number.

Only the deal he set up with the bucks she gave him didn't pan out. He had to go back for more.

And more. Hell, was it his fault things didn't come together?

When he learned Tami had split to Florida, he was pissed. But when he saw her picture in the paper with her fiancé, he knew he had it made.

Bordon Granger! With his dough and his cable outfit, the sky was the limit.

With the money he'd get from Tami and the deal he was going to set up with Granger, there'd be no way he could miss this time.

He might luck onto a real live heiress in rich River City. And live happily ever after. Like in a real-life fairy tale.

Hell, if it could happen anywhere, this had to be the place for it to happen.

6

Howie Caine couldn't get the Fabergés back. No way. The fence told him they were long since gone. How much did he get for them? Howie wanted to know. Not much, responded the fence. Who wants old junk?

Howie groaned. He didn't know what they were worth, but if his grandmother made that much of a stink, it must have been a pretty penny. More than he let them go for.

Since he didn't want to rub his contact the wrong way, Howie didn't fuss about being shortchanged. "Shit," he said good-naturedly, "what the hell. Easy come. Easy go." His laugh was forced.

"Like I said, Howie, you bring me something real impressive, we'll make a bundle together. Meanwhile, I got some pure Colombian I can sell you if you're interested."

Howie was interested.

Howie had dinner with Belinda in the massive paneled dining room of his grandmother's Mizner mansion. Four El Grecos, pained or martyred, looked down on them from the walls where they were hung, adding a feeling of Spanish misery to the already oppressively Spanish room.

Mimzee was dining out that evening.

Belinda, poking absently at her food, looked up. "This room is positively lugubrious, don't you agree?"

Howie nodded. He didn't know what the word meant but he wasn't about to admit that to his half sister. Besides, he'd been brooding over how to tell his grandmother he hadn't located her missing Fabergés. "Positively," he agreed.

Belinda's turn to nod. She poked at her food again, then pierced a piece of meat with her fork, popped it into her mouth, and chewed interminably.

Howie watched, both fascinated and repelled. "Christ, Belinda, how long do you chew that thing before you swallow it?"

"Thirty-five times," said Belinda placidly. "Like Nancy Reagan. That's how we stay so thin. I read somewhere she chewed each piece of food thirty-five times. I tried it. It works."

"Maybe you oughta chew less and eat more. You look like you could use some padding."

" 'Never too thin or too rich,' " replied Belinda. "That was the Duchess of Windsor, Jackie Onassis, or Diana Vreeland, depending on your source. Actually, I suspect it's apocryphal."

Howie, impressed as usual by his half sister's fund of miscellaneous information, made no comment. Besides, he liked her. She never made fun of him. And she made him feel smarter than he was.

Belinda, weary of poking, dropped her napkin on her plate and pushed her chair back from the table before the butler could assist her. "Let's play some pool, Howie. I'm bored."

"What about dessert?" asked Howie, upset at having to forgo it.

"We'll have it later," she announced.

They played pool for about an hour in Mimzee's paneled billiard room until Belinda called a halt.

"I'm bored. Let's take a ride and get something to eat," she suggested.

"An hour ago you couldn't eat dinner," he pointed out.

"That was then," she explained. "I wasn't hungry. Now I am."

Belinda drove her red Mercedes convertible, canvas top down, fast and furiously down winding A1A to Boca Raton. Howie held his breath.

Until they almost collided with a northbound car. "You coulda killed us," yelled Howie.

"Nonsense," Belinda assured him. "It's all a matter of being in control. I have perfect control, Howie. At all times."

She steered the Mercedes into the Boca Mall parking lot, then led Howie to an Italian restaurant. "You can have dessert here. Cannoli. It's the best in Boca."

She ordered antipasto, lasagne, veal marsala, ravioli, bracìola, garlic bread, wine, and Howie's cannoli.

She ate slowly, methodically, and deliberately. Howie watched in awe.

Howie finished the cannoli and waited. He was getting sick from watching her pack it away.

"That cannoli looked so good, I think I'll have one," she told him. She had two.

Howie's gut ached from watching her. He breathed a sigh of relief when she motioned for the check.

They strolled along the mall, idly looking into shop windows. Belinda stopped short. "Pizza!" she cried. She turned to Howie. "The best in Boca."

"You gotta be kiddin'," he protested.

"Just one piece. So you can see how good it is," she urged.

Howie forced one piece down. Belinda polished off five.

On the way back to the car, she stopped short, grabbed his arm, and let out a yelp.

"Jesus Christ, Belinda! What is it now?"

Her eyes were glazed with anticipation. "Oh, Howie, look! An old-fashioned ice-cream parlor. The kind we used to go to when we were kids." He followed her inside reluctantly.

Howie ordered a small cola.

Belinda scoffed. She ordered a banana, hot fudge, pecan, and whipped cream supersize sundae. Two scoops of chocolate, two of vanilla, two of butter pecan. Smothered in hot fudge, piled high with sliced bananas, garlanded with whipped cream, festooned with pecans.

Belinda attacked it resolutely. Finished finally, she wiped her lips delicately with a paper napkin and turned to Howie. "Cigarette?"

"Huh?"

"Do you have a smoke, Howie?"

"Oh, sure." He reached in his pocket, pulled out a rumpled pack of Camels, offered one to Belinda, and lighted it for her.

She drew in and blew out a stream of smoke. "Dreadful things," she exclaimed. "Bad for you."

Howie nodded.

She settled the bill, left a meager tip, turned back to Howie, and told him, "I'll be right back, sweetie. I have to stop off in the loo."

She walked into the ladies room, entered a stall, locked the door, knelt by the bowl, and quickly purged her body of the accumulated food of the last two hours.

She flushed the toilet, exited the stall, washed her hands, repaired her makeup, and worriedly studied her reflection in the mirror.

Fat! She looked positively fat!

She found Howie in the mall, impatiently awaiting her return. He looked at her. "You okay? You look kinda pale."

Belinda managed a smile. "I'm fine. Terrific."

The smile faded. She tossed Howie the Mercedes keys. "Be a lamb and drive, Howie. I don't feel too great."

7

Over Rosemary's objections, Carl announced he was going to the House of Graet Christmas Ball and would brook no argument.

Rosemary had known since Thanksgiving she was in the running for the Kirsten. Carl had told her that weekend. Then, she had been thrilled. In light of her father's condition, the idea of owning the Kirsten lost its original luster.

"Oh, Daddy," cried Rosemary, "who cares about that old thing? You're the only gem that's important to me."

"I care," insisted Carl stubbornly. "I want you to have it. I want you to wear your prettiest dress to that shindig, and I want to be there when they slip that rock around that gorgeous neck of yours."

Despite her annoyance with him, Rosemary giggled. She thought of her Emanuel of London confection. Yards of bouffant skirt. Low scooped neck. A high tulle turban. She'd look like an ice-cream cone. Good enough to eat. "I have just the thing to wear, Daddy."

"Good!" beamed Carl, satisfied he'd won the round. "We'll all go in style. We'll light up this town with our splendor, won't we, Mother?" Carl grabbed Grace's arm playfully and proceeded to waltz her around the room.

"Now, Carl," warned Grace, "don't go getting yourself excited."

"Why not?" exulted Carl. "It feels good. And when you stop feeling, Mother, you're dead."

Mark flew down to Palm Beach several times to visit.

He found his father-in-law much improved. He told him so.

"Carl, you look terrific. Although, I must say, for a while you had us all worried."

Carl studied his son-in-law shrewdly. "Well, keep worrying, Mark. Because I want you on your toes. And I want you to toe the mark. As I told you before, I'm not going anywhere until you clean up your act. But even if I were struck dead tomorrow, I'd haunt you from the grave."

Mark smiled thinly. "You know something, Carl? I believe you would."

"Damn right," promised Carl. "You can count on it."

Mark observed Rosemary closely for signs of strain. God only knew how she was handling her father's condition. And only God knew when Rosemary would reach for her favorite prop.

She surprised Mark. She sipped her Perrier without resentment and coped magnificently. It was as though the presence and the need of her father infused her with new energy and purpose.

Mark was impressed. "You look marvelous, Rosemary. Better than you've looked in a long time."

"You think adversity becomes me?" asked Rosemary dryly. They were preparing for bed.

"I think it's bringing forth a part of you that is very attractive," Mark told her.

"Adversity builds character, darling. Isn't that what they say?"

He smiled. "That's what they say."

"Is it sexy?"

"Sexy?"

"Is my sterling character sexy, Mark? Does it give you a raging hard-on?" Rosemary leaned back against the peach satin bed pillows and struck a seductive pose.

He laughed. "I hadn't thought of it quite that way."

"Well, my sterling character is turning me on. Making me horny, darling. I suggest you take advantage of it." She slipped off her nightgown, folded down the blanket, and patted the bed invitingly.

"Besides," she added, "this is much more comfortable than the library floor."

* * *

There was one sensitive note in Mark's visits. The Kirsten. He wanted Rosemary to insist Carl withdraw her name from the list of contenders.

"I can't do that," Rosemary told him.

"You've got to. That damned diamond is creating the wrong kind of publicity for me. Jesus, Rosemary, you can understand that."

Rosemary was stubborn. "I only understand the Kirsten means a lot to Daddy. Getting it for me, that is. Personally, I don't give a hoot about it."

"Then tell him you don't want it."

"I can't, Mark. The way Daddy is, I won't do a thing to distress him. Besides, darling," said Rosemary cajolingly, "the odds I'll win it are slim."

"Suppose you do?"

"We'll worry about that then," Rosemary said calmly. She didn't want to upset Mark. They were getting along so well. The sex was so good. Better than it had been in a long time. And Mark was being so considerate of Daddy. She loved him for it.

She went to him and put her arms around him. "Darling, thank you for being so sweet with Daddy."

Mark, irritated over Rosemary's refusal to oblige him, sloughed off her embrace. "Rosemary, do me a favor. Stop calling your father Daddy. At thirty-nine, it's a little bit sick."

The rebuff was so unexpected, Rosemary was stunned. She blanched. Then rallied. "Thirty-eight, darling," she corrected. "And it's no more sick than being a frigging Don Juan at forty-three. That's what's lousing up your public image. Not the fucking Kirsten!"

8

Just as Louis-Philippe predicted, Consuela was no sooner settled at The Breakers than she was in the thick of the Palm Beach action.

She called Count Paolo Respighi at his Maurice Fatio–designed oceanfront cottage, reached Sheik Abu Kahli at his 112-room Joseph Urban–designed retreat, and Tony Owens at his Spanish-style hacienda.

After a few minutes of enthusiastic conversation, she informed each of some pieces of jewelry that had recently come into her hands. So *importante,* so *favoloso,* they must be seen to be believed.

In half an hour she had arranged appointments to show several million dollars' worth of jewelry.

She located Carl Schmittle at Casa Miramar, learned of his illness, and decided not to burden him with conversation about new merchandise. He had enough to contend with.

She reached Bordon Granger at his Wellington farm. She found him distracted. Most unlike himself.

"You are well, *caro?*"

"Fine, Consuela. A bit unsettled at the moment."

"Ah, *sì.* The wedding. *Naturalmente.*"

"Not that. A lot of other things."

Consuela tried to be more positive. "How is Tami?" she asked. "When is she coming out?"

"She's here," Bordon told her.

"Ah, that is good," Consuela said.

"You'd think so, wouldn't you?"

Consuela shifted the conversation. "Bordon, have you thought about the ball, about the raffle for the Kirsten?"

"No," he answered, despondent. Without Tami, what would he do with a goddamned necklace? "To tell you the truth, Consuela, I think I'm going to drop out of the raffle."

Drop out! Consuela found that truly alarming.

Something must indeed be wrong.

Derek wandered into the room. His expression registered distaste for the fine mechanics of commerce as practiced by Consuela. He wandered out again.

Dio mio! shrugged Consuela. What a pill! She should have left him in New York.

She spent part of each day either on the phone with Kate or popping in at the House of Graet. The jewelry from the New York store had arrived. The exhibit pieces by Louis and his staff were being readied for display. The pieces would be exhibited first at the store, then redisplayed and sold at the ball.

It did Consuela's heart good to see everything so splendidly arranged. She expressed her pleasure to Kate.

While she was checking out the jewelry, Consuela checked out the little redhead Derek had told her he met at Thanksgiving.

Consuela was also in daily contact with the New York store, either querying Suzy about sales or badgering Louis-Philippe to hurry down. She needed him. Did he not know that?

Louis promised to come as quickly as he could. He was looking forward to seeing her. He missed her, he said.

"Well, then, Louis, come quickly," urged Consuela tartly. "You need not deprive yourself one more minute. I am here."

9

Howie Caine faced his grandmother in her upstairs sitting room. "Well, Mimzee," he said, "I've come to make my report."

The beady blue eyes never wavered. "Oh?"

"You have no idea how much effort I've put into this investigation. I've explored every possibility. Looked everywhere."

The painted red eyebrows arched. The face beneath the curly red wig was inscrutable.

"Nothing, Mimzee. I can't imagine what ever happened to those things of yours."

"Fabergés, Howie. They are—were—Fabergés. Not things. Priceless pieces of art. Things, Howard, you see, can be discarded, thrown away, tossed off. Treasures are to be cared for, admired. Or cataloged and vaulted. Do you have any idea how long it has taken me to collect my treasures?"

"Well, I . . ."

"A lifetime. An entire lifetime. When one of my treasures is stolen, a piece of my life is stolen. I do not—I repeat, I do not—take that theft lightly. I consider it a sacrilege. And I am prepared to punish to the death the scoundrel who is responsible."

"Geez, Mimzee, all I know is, I didn't take them."

"Liar," she shrieked. "You are a goddamned liar. Of course you took them. Don't insult my intelligence by denying it."

"Honest, Mimzee, I swear . . ."

"Don't waste your breath. Or my time." She looked at Howie in disgust. "Go! Get out of my sight! But mark my words, grandson or no grandson, if I find one more item missing from my collection, I'll have you prosecuted. And you won't like prison, Howie. They devour tasty little treats like you."

Howie Caine opened his mouth once more to protest his innocence.

His grandmother's stare silenced him.

Howie exited quickly.

They were social bulwarks, bastions, landmarks, fixtures. Two women who formed the backbone of Palm Beach society. They chaired benefits, were photographed at all the major events of the season. They were admired, envied, and emulated.

They were very different. Yet, they had been close friends since childhood.

It was natural, therefore, following Howie's upsetting visit, for Mimzee Dawson to call Marjorie Hunter and suggest lunch. Mimzee needed to talk, she announced. Marjorie was happy to listen, she assured her friend.

Mimzee suggested the B&T. She preferred it to the Everglades. Much more casual. Who felt like dressing up at this hour? Besides, the B&T served the best lunch in town. For next to nothing.

Once more, Marjorie agreed.

Anywhere else in the country, a B&T might be a bacon and tomato sandwich. In Palm Beach, the B&T stood for the Bath & Tennis Club, one of the two most exclusive clubs in Palm Beach, the Everglades being the other.

The B&T, built in 1926, was formed in protest to the Everglades, a club owned by Paris Singer, heir to the Singer sewing machine fortune.

Singer insisted on reviewing each member's status every year, subject to his approval for readmittance. His arbitrary whims dictated a member's social future. Those who didn't pass Singer's muster found themselves outside the social pale. Membership was won only by the most socially impeccable. And only Paris Singer decided who was without social blemish.

The B&T provided an alternative option.

Both clubs were exclusively WASP. Later in their histories, a few anglicized Jews achieved membership, but both the B&T and the Everglades remained predominantly WASP. Jews settled into the Palm Beach Country Club.

Interestingly, the B&T, begun in protest to the exclusivity of the

Everglades Club, became itself more exclusive. Its membership was small, select, and conservative.

Mimzee Dawson and Marjorie Hunter held memberships in both clubs. Their parents were among the original members.

They dined on the terrace, ordered drinks and lobster salads.

Mimzee wore a flowing pink embroidered Indian cotton caftan and a huge pink cotton sunbonnet that covered her red hair and shaded her pale face. Only the blue eyes, sharp and piercing, glittered. Long cotton gloves protected her arms. She looked no more eccentric than usual.

Marjorie wore a pale lemon linen frock and a wide-brimmed natural straw hat. She looked crisply elegant.

Mimzee was in familiar form. Petulant and strident. The session with Howie had taken its toll. Belinda was an additional thorn.

Her friend of sixty years sympathized. "How are they doing?" Marjorie Hunter asked.

Mimzee chewed her lobster. "How do you think? Belinda keeps shoving her fingers down her throat until she throws up everything she's eaten and Howie keeps sticking his fingers into anything and everything that doesn't belong to him." Mimzee related the incident of the missing Fabergés.

"Perhaps he didn't take them?" suggested Marjorie kindly.

"Balls!" retorted Mimzee, loud enough to draw the startled looks of two guests, staid dowagers, at a nearby table. "Of course he took them. He's got sticky fingers. Miserable son of a bitch."

The dowagers at the nearby table pretended this time not to hear. Mimzee, itching for a fight, continued to stare at them.

Marjorie tactfully changed the subject. "This is the most divine lobster, don't you agree, Mimzee?"

Mimzee turned her stare toward Marjorie. "Marjie, don't cut me off with bullshit when I'm in the middle of letting off steam. It's damned annoying."

"Of course, dear," said Marjorie mildly.

"Did it not occur to you, Marjorie, and did I not make myself clear, I suggested lunch because I needed to unload?"

"Yes, dear."

"Then don't let those old biddies at the next table intimidate you." She raised her voice deliberately. "They're not even members. Only guests."

Marjorie kept her voice soft. "I'm not intimidated, dear. I just don't like to see you upsetting yourself."

"I feel less upset when I get it off my chest."

"Of course, dear. Whatever you wish."

"And don't patronize me, Marjorie. You're not the ambassador's wife anymore, dispensing charm and chocolates."

"Really, Mimzee," said Marjorie, finally annoyed, "if you're going to be in such a vile temper, perhaps we should lunch another day." She started to rise.

"Sit down, Marjie," ordered Mimzee, "and stop being so damned sensitive. You above all people should understand what it's like to have difficult offspring."

Marjorie toyed with her lobster salad, preferring not to comment.

Mimzee charged on. "According to the columnists, Mark's hobbies are catching up with him. He's just like his Dad, Marj. A finger in every tart. And Rosemary certainly reacts, doesn't she? Not like you at all. Nothing discreet about that girl."

Marjorie refused to be baited.

Mimzee pushed on. "How is she, by the way? Rosemary?"

"Rosemary is fine, thank you," said Marjorie stiffly, patting her mouth delicately with her napkin. "Her parents are living down here now. Carl's health hasn't been too good. As for Rosemary, ever since she came back from that health farm in Connecticut, she's been doing splendidly."

Mimzee hooted. "Marjie, don't pull that crap with me. That Connecticut health farm is a drunk farm. I know it and you know I know it. Spare me the euphemisms."

"Mimzee," said Marjorie in exasperation, "you were a mean, spiteful little girl and you've become a mean, spiteful old woman. How we've remained friends for over sixty years baffles me. Now, if you will excuse me . . ." Marjorie started to rise once more.

Mimzee reached out and grabbed her hand. "C'mon, Marjie," she said awkwardly; apologies did not come naturally to her. "I'm sorry. You know how I get. Howie has me so stirred up, I strike out at anyone."

"Well, don't take it out on me," said Marjorie, somewhat mollified by the unfamiliar apology. "I didn't do anything to set you off."

"No, you didn't," agreed Mimzee. She smiled. "You're a good friend, Marjorie Hunter, the best friend I've got. And we've been through a pile of crap together."

Marjorie smiled back. "That we have, dear."

Mimzee brightened. She decided to put the missing Fabergés behind her and concentrate her attentions on things that lay ahead. "You know I have a bid in for the Kirsten."

"I read about it," said Marjorie dryly.

"Your daughter-in-law has a bid in too," noted Mimzee. "Or rather her Daddy does."

"Mark would never permit Rosemary to have that thing," observed Marjorie.

"I certainly hope not. Because I aim to have it."

Marjorie shook her head in wonderment. "Mimzee, what on earth do you need with another jewel? For that matter, why would anyone want something so grossly conspicuous?"

"I want it," insisted Mimzee. "And I'll have it."

Marjorie sighed. "Mimzee, I was wrong. You haven't grown up at all. You're still the same little girl grabbing for all the marbles in the pile."

"I always won, didn't I? No matter what game I played, I always won."

"Because you cheated. Or bribed whoever was in your way."

"Winning is the bottom line, Marj. Not *how* you win. But *that* you win."

"Perhaps I never shall understand you, Mimzee."

"Oh, we're not so different," said Mimzee airily. "We just have different goals. You have your sights on your son's presidency. Mine are on the Kirsten."

They reached an impasse.

To avoid further dispute, they spent the remainder of lunch discussing an upcoming benefit they were both chairing.

Mimzee suggested a swim. They changed in cabanas, Marjorie into a sleek black maillot, Mimzee into a white one-piece pleated swimsuit. Under the suit she wore a long-sleeved, stockinged white leotard. She wore white gloves to protect her hands and kept on her sunbonnet to protect her face.

She submerged herself carefully into the water. "Watch that sun, Marj, or it will wrinkle you up like an old prune," she warned, splashing happily about.

Relaxed and refreshed from her afternoon with Marjorie, sipping her one predinner martini in her upstairs sitting room, Mimzee reviewed the situation.

It seemed to her her grandson's larcenous proclivities could be channeled for her gain rather than her disadvantage.

One fact was clear. Howie *owed* her. He had deprived her of her precious Fabergés. Protest though he might, Mimzee had no doubt Howie was the culprit behind the theft.

Well, she would think of something—some way Howie could repay her for the anguish and grief he caused her.

10

The Breakers interview with Ben was Consuela's last chance to promote the Kirsten. Kate knew how important it was. She called Ben to check out the details and to invite him to lunch at the beach club prior to the interview. The invitation was from the contessa, Kate told him. Ben accepted, then extended an invitation of his own. To Kate. For Sunday. On board the *Nellie*.

Sunday, they took the *Nellie* up the Intracoastal.

Two hours later, Ben set anchor.

They lay on deck, stretched out on blue denim–covered pads under a bright blue sky, Kate in a red bikini, Ben in yellow trunks. They lay silently, their fingers interlaced.

"Happy?" Ben asked.

"Very," murmured Kate.

He grinned. "You see how painless conversion is. You shouldn't resist so much."

Kate turned toward him. "Do I? Resist?"

"Lady, do you ever! Here I've been earnestly proposing for weeks, and you keep setting up obstacles." He raised one of her fingers to his lips and kissed it. "All you have to do is say yes."

"Oh, Ben, you make everything sound so simple."

"Most things are. Only most people complicate them."

"You believe that? Really?"

"Why not? It sure makes living easier." He reached for Kate and buried his lips in her hair. "We're a good combination, Kate. We'd make a great team. Why resist?"

Why, indeed?

Ben began to untie the strings to her bikini top.

Kate protested. "Ben, not here. The fleet's out practically."

"You don't want an audience, we'd better move elsewhere." His eyes glinted with an intensity she hadn't seen before.

He scooped her up easily, carried her below deck, and stretched her on the bed in his quarters.

He finished untying the straps of her bikini top, turned Kate on her side, pulled off the top, turned her on her back again, and yanked off the bottom.

He ran the palm of his hand down the length of her body, pushed her legs apart, and thrust his fingers in.

His mouth found a nipple, devoured it, then searched for the other until both were erect.

He yanked off his own trunks as Kate grasped for him. "Now," she cried. "Now, Ben."

He held back, watching her, working on her, his lovemaking suddenly less tender but strangely exciting.

Then, when she thought she could bear it no longer, he mounted her and thrust inside her. "Now," he insisted. "Now, Kate," as they exploded in climax together, the *Nellie* rocking rhythmically but no match for the crescendo that filled and echoed throughout the cabin.

They lay there quietly. The lovemaking had been different. More intense. Less tender. Less familiar. Unexpectedly forceful. Yet Kate felt wonderfully relaxed. She stretched languidly.

"Do you still think of him?" Ben asked, breaking the stillness.

She didn't answer at once. If she was startled at the question, she didn't show it. "Hardly ever," she said finally.

"Is he the reason you're resisting me?" probed Ben.

The good feeling was leaving her. "I'm not resisting you, Ben," said Kate, moving from the circle of his arm.

"Oh, you let me make love to you. That's true. But you always manage to hold back some part of yourself."

Somewhat stiffly, Kate said, "I'm sorry. I wasn't aware there were complaints."

"For Pete's sake, Kate, don't deliberately misread me. You know exactly what I mean. If I only wanted a body to make love to, there are a dozen women I could turn to."

"That many!" commented Kate dryly.

He ignored her. "The point is, I don't want anyone else. I want you."

"Maybe you want too much. More than I have to give."

"I think you underestimate yourself."

"Or you overestimate me." She moved off the bed, slipped back into the bikini pants, tied the top back on.

He watched her. "You are still in love with him, Kate. That's why you're holding back."

She turned angrily. "Don't be simplistic, Ben. I asked you from the beginning not to push me. I told you there are still things I need to work through."

His eyes searched hers. "Marry me, Kate. We'll work through them together."

Why, she wondered, why did he have to spoil things? She felt the familiar panic rising. "I'm trying, Ben."

The last thing he wanted to do was push her. Force her into flight. But he seemed unable to help himself. "Try harder, Kate," he urged.

11

The Breakers in Palm Beach rests on a section of its 200 acres with the insouciance of a dowager confident of the impeccability of her lineage.

It is massive, grand, awesome, and arresting. A stone twin-towered Italian Renaissance structure that rises imperiously toward the southern Floridian sky.

A stone Florentine fountain marks its entrance.

The Breakers is a visual rebuff to the standardized, sanitized American hotel structures now considered viable. Built in an era of American opulence, it remains sublimely resistant to transient tastes, a stunning reminder of a time when style and elegance were sufficient justifications for existence.

It was built three times. It burned twice. Once in 1905. Again in 1915.

It was first built in 1895 by Henry Morrison Flagler. A companion hotel to his then-famed Royal Poinciana. A resort hotel banking the Atlantic. His Breakers-by-the-sea. Only he called it the Palm Beach Inn. He changed the name to The Breakers when he rebuilt it after the first fire.

For almost 100 years, the three structures occupying that stretch of land have provided an appropriately grand setting for countless Palm Beach extravaganzas.

Inside the hotel, vaulted ceiling, archways, elaborate domed frescoes, marble floors, crystal chandeliers, richly loomed carpeting, graceful palms, and other well-tended greenery continue the note of elegance and opulence.

White wicker settees and white wicker barrel chairs placed in conversation groups add a less formal Palm Beach touch.

The hotel has two swimming pools, an ocean beach, a golf course, twelve tennis courts, restaurants, a bar and dance floor overlooking the Atlantic, and easy access to Worth Avenue, the shopper's paradise.

It is a city unto itself. A vacation spot that leaves little to chance. But The Breakers is more than that. It is one of the world's last grand hotels.

Following lunch in The Breakers Beach Club where Consuela was charmed by Ben, whom she insisted upon calling Benjamin, they adjourned to Consuela's suite to begin the interview.

Ben's camera crew joined him, followed shortly after by the House of Graet security chief.

He greeted the contessa and Kate, unlocked his attaché case, removed a flat leather House of Graet folder from it, and presented it to the contessa.

She nodded graciously, unsnapped the folder, removed the necklace, and allowed Kate to help her with the clasp.

The contessa wore a simple white cotton caftan, cut deep in the neckline. The Kirsten, red and resplendent, resting against her smooth bare skin, was given full prominence. As the contessa planned.

Her smile was brilliant. "We can begin, Benjamin," she told him.

Ben, who had never been that close to $15 million, was suitably impressed. What about security measures? he inquired. Is the contessa nervous about the safety of a piece of such value and renown?

No concern at all, Consuela assured him. Measures had been taken to ensure its protection. The Kirsten was already well-traveled. And had befallen no ill fate in all of its history.

Ben nodded. And asked which Kirsten the contessa would wear to the ball, the real or the replica?

The contessa smiled.

When the interview was over, the Kirsten was removed from the contessa, placed in the leather folder, given to the chief of security, locked in his attaché case, and returned to the House of Graet.

Consuela shook hands with the cameraman and the sound man and kissed Ben warmly on both cheeks.

She turned to Kate. "He is *perfetto*. I approve wholeheartedly."

And that endorsement, decided Ben, catching Kate's smile, would have to sustain him until the lady decided his fate. That, and the lady's gentle nod of encouragement when he left.

Watching the Kirsten on the TV screen, Mimzee Dawson was once again determined to have it. No one deserved the Kirsten more than she.

Mimzee thought of her grandson. Light-fingered, conniving, conscienceless Howie. All those miserable character defects should somehow be utilized to her advantage.

She sniffed as Consuela parried the question about which Kirsten she would wear to the ball.

"Balls!" said Mimzee aloud, taking a swallow of her martini. No way would that fancy former whore with those fancy airs wear a fake diamond to the ball. Mimzee knew damn well what the contessa would do. She would wear the real Kirsten. It's what Mimzee would do.

Her thoughts flashed back to her grandson.

Suppose Howie, who'd been stealing her blind, were induced to put those light fingers of his to work at lifting something worthwhile. Like the Kirsten.

Mimzee played with the idea like a cat with a spool of yarn.

Security measures would be tight. The ball would be crowded with a crush of people. The contessa would be wearing the Kirsten. In view of everyone.

Clearly, a plan would have to be worked out. A foolproof plan. To guarantee success.

A challenge for Mimzee to meet.

A project for Howie to execute.

Mimzee sipped her martini thoughtfully.

In his room at The Breakers, Earl Blakely watched the TV screen intently. What a rock! And they were going to raffle it off at some goddamned charity shindig.

Imagine that stone belonging to one dame. Or one guy. Jesus, this was the way to live. In a place where a $15 million rock was raffled off like a 50-buck watch. Big style! Big bucks! Big spenders! This place was so rich, it gave him a hard-on just thinking about it.

But right now, he had to think of other things. In exactly one half hour, his former girlfriend, the mother of his kid, was due to pay him a visit. Knowing Tami as well as he did, he knew she'd show up. She had too much invested in her future. And too much hidden in her past not to.

In Wellington, Bordon Granger watched the evening news in his den. Looking at the Kirsten on the screen, he remembered when life had been simply the decision of when to present the Kirsten to Tami. Before or after the wedding.

Now, it appeared there'd be no wedding. He and Tami had had the most awful row. Tami refused to tell him what was wrong.

He wasn't used to fencing in the dark. One of the finest things about his relationship with Tami had been the openness between them. That openness was gone. Replaced by a secrecy that threatened to tear them apart. And the knowledge that something was happening and that he didn't understand it was almost more than Bordon could bear.

~12~

Tami Hayes knew she had a lot of sorting through to do. The problem was, she didn't know where to begin. Or how.

When Erin was nine, Tami told her the truth. She wasn't Tami's sister. She was her daughter. Tami also told her about her own background.

She had no idea where Erin's father was. He took off before Erin was born. And as far as she was concerned, he could stay away. He was bad news.

Erin listened attentively. One thing puzzled her. "What's illegitimate?"

"Born out of wedlock."

"Like you?"

"Like me."

"Is that the same as bastard?"

"Bastard's a not very nice way of saying the same thing." Tami paused, then added, "I'm telling you this now because I think you're entitled to the truth, and because I want you to hear it from me." Her smile was shaky. "And because I love you." Tami shrugged helplessly. "The thing is, it'll have to be our secret. It's awkward to change stories now."

Erin digested the information with nine-year-old practicality. "What do I call you now?" she asked.

Tami smiled sadly. "What you've always called me, darling. Tami."

When she was thirty, Tami met Bordon Granger. He was fifty-two. He thought she was twenty-four. The age difference put him off at first. But not enough to prevent him from pursuing her.

He courted her resolutely and in style. Planes to fetch her,

292

exotic places to take her to, fascinating memories to delight her. She had never been so catered to or cared for. Besides, he was wonderful with Erin.

She agreed to marry him. And discovered she was in love with him.

"Will he be my brother-in-law or my father?" Erin asked.

"A bit of both," said Tami. However, Bordon didn't know about them.

Would Tami tell him?

Tami sighed. "I'd like to. It's just so complicated."

She started to tell Bordon several times. Then stopped. Where to begin? How to unravel the web of lies? When he lauded her for her spunk in raising a kid sister in the face of overwhelming obstacles, her resolve withered.

"Not many could have done it, Tami. You're an inspiration."

The truth, somehow, seemed less splendid in contrast.

The first call came six months after Tami and Bordon became engaged.

"Drucie?"

No one had called her Drucie in over fifteen years. "Who is this?"

"Earl, baby. Earl Blakely."

Tami sucked in her breath, let it out slowly, then asked calmly, "How'd you get my number, Earl?"

He laughed. "It wasn't easy, luv."

Always the hustler. She vowed to get another unlisted number immediately.

"I'd like to see my kid, Drucie."

"The name's Tami, Earl. As for your kid, call his mother."

"C'mon, Drucie. I saw her picture with you in the papers."

Few pictures of Erin were permitted, but every so often an enterprising photographer managed to snap one.

"That's my kid sister, Earl."

"Who're you kiddin', doll?"

"Earl, I'm not your doll. That's not your kid. So get lost." She hung up.

He was there waiting for her when she pulled into her driveway the next day. Ready to hurl himself in front of her car to get her attention. He got it. Her brakes screeched, barely missing him.

293

"You crazy?" she screamed.

He grinned. "Determined. Like I told you, I wanted to see my kid."

From inside the car, Tami glared at him. "And I told you you have no kid."

Earl's grin faded. "You'd better get off your high horse, babe. Or I'll be forced to give out interviews."

Tami, thinking ahead to interviews and aftermaths, studied him. "Get in," she said grimly. "We'll go for a ride."

She drove along the Coast Highway into the Malibu hills. She pulled over. Stopped the car. Turned to him.

"Earl, for the last half hour, I've listened to the sad story of the last ten years of your life. Fortune hasn't favored you. Fame has eluded you. What the hell do you want from me?"

He smiled winningly. "Ah, Drucie—I mean, Tami—look at you. Way up there. Riding the crest. One lucky break after another."

Tami thought of the ten-year struggle toward those lucky breaks. "So?"

Earl eyed her shrewdly. "I need a stake, Tami. I've got a friend looking for a partner for a real sure thing."

He wasn't interested in Erin at all. He hadn't changed a bit. "How much?"

"Ten thou, doll. Like I said, it's a real sure thing. You'll get it back fast. With interest."

She gave him the money the next day.

He was back in a month. The deal went sour, he said. He had a better one. This one couldn't miss.

Only, it did. Three months later, he was after her again.

Not for one instance did she entertain the thought of telling Erin Earl Blakely was in town. Never would she permit them to meet. Not in a million years. Not while there was breath in her body. If Earl Blakely was a deadbeat fifteen years ago, he was a miserable blood-sucking son of a bitch now. She'd see him in hell before she let him near her daughter.

13

She and Erin joined Bordon in Wellington. They rode, swam, picnicked, drove to Palm Beach, entertained, and were entertained. She felt better, freer. As though she hadn't a care in the world.

Until the call came.

"Earl here, Tami."

"How on earth did you get this number?" She was beginning to sound repetitious to herself.

He didn't answer her question. Instead he said, "You shouldn't have gone off and left me like that, Tam."

"For God's sake, what do you want?"

"I wanna see you, doll."

"See me? Where are you, anyway?"

"Palm Beach, baby, thirteen miles away. At The Breakers."

She felt faint. Then furious. My God, he had followed her. And he was staying at The Breakers. That scum was living it up on her money.

"I need to see you tonight, babe."

"That's impossible. We're having guests for dinner."

"Six-thirty. Unless you want your boyfriend to set an extra place at the table." He gave her his room number.

"I can't," she said desperately. "Not tonight."

"Six-thirty," he repeated. "And no fuck-ups this time."

Bordon came into the room just as Tami hung up the phone. "Who was that?" he asked.

"One of the publicists from the film," she told him.

"How did he get this number?"

"I left it with him. In case of an emergency." How glibly the lies came.

Bordon watched her quietly. "And is there one? An emergency?"

She smiled easily. "No. He's a classic worrier. Invents problems where none exist."

Later in the day, tired from wrestling with demons she could no longer control, and not wishing to involve Bordon in a scandal that threatened to erupt, Tami again told him she couldn't marry him. She couldn't tell him why. Yes, she loved him. If he really loved her, he wouldn't press her for an explanation.

"Does this decision have anything to do with that phone call you received?"

"No," lied Tami.

Bordon studied her. "I don't believe you," he said.

"I'm sorry, Bordon."

"Sorry I don't believe you?"

"Sorry it has to end this way."

"And you won't tell me why?"

"I can't."

Furious with her, he strode out.

At six that evening, Tami stopped by Erin's room. "I've got to go into town. But Bordon should be back any minute."

Erin looked surprised. "Will you be back in time? We're having guests, you know." Tami assured her she'd be back by eight.

She started down the stairs. Bordon was on his way up. He reached her, put his arms around her, and held her close. "Darling, I feel dreadful for giving you a difficult time. Whatever it is, we'll work it out."

For the first time, he noticed her attire. Her hair was pushed up into a white cap. Dark glasses covered her eyes. A long white coat covered her small frame. "Going somewhere?" he asked.

"Just for a short while, Bordon."

His expression tightened. "Does it have anything to do with that phone call?"

She touched his cheek gently. "Yes, it does."

He searched her face. "Tami, I want to help you."

She smiled sadly. "I know you do. Only you can't." Before he could say anything, she was gone.

She drove the thirteen miles from Wellington to Palm Beach in a state of agitation. She had no idea what she would say to Earl, or how she would handle him. One thing she knew, he had to be stopped. He couldn't continue to threaten her life and Erin's any longer.

She pulled into The Breakers' driveway and drove past the double rows of towering Australian pines that led to the hotel.

She parked the car, walked through the hotel doors, and headed for the elevator. She was certain no one recognized her.

Someone did. Reenie Boyd, who had just registered, was headed for the elevator to take her to her suite.

Wasn't that Tami Hayes behind those ridiculous dark glasses? What was she doing at The Breakers? Reenie had heard she was in Wellington with Bordon Granger. And where was Bordon?

Reenie's educated nostrils sniffed a story. She fell behind and waited as Tami walked into the elevator and seemed to meld into its interior. Reenie watched the elevator rise and noted the floor it stopped at.

She made a mental reminder to check out the occupants on that floor to see which one had clout enough to entice Tami Hayes to what appeared to be a clandestine encounter. At least, in that getup, it certainly looked suspicious. Why else the disguise?

It reminded Reenie of Mark. Which reminded her today was Tuesday. Which reminded her she hadn't heard from him.

The titillation of a possible scandalous item for her column was mitigated by the knowledge that perhaps she was being had by Senator Mark Hunter.

Or not being had. Depending on your point of view.

In her wildest imaginings, Tami could never have dreamed up the proposal Earl suggested.

"Now, hear me out, babe," he urged, "because I have this terrific plan. A partnership. Like old times. Only this time we'll make it. With my moxie and your connections, we can't miss."

She listened dumbfounded as he unfolded his proposal.

A video and record company. A Blakely-Hayes label. Or a

Hayes-Blakely. Hell, he wasn't above compromise. Tami would perform. Earl would produce, package, and promote.

Her boyfriend could sign them up on his cable network. A music video channel. The shit had been kicked out of the record business by video games. Video music was the shot in the ass it needed to revive it. Look at MTV. Cleaning up. Kids glued to TV screens with rock music and flashing images. It was a natural. They couldn't miss. They'd make a mint.

When the video company was off and running, Earl would buy out Tami's share. And, so help him God, he'd never bother her again. Hell, he'd even put it in writing.

Tami stared, speechless. Then reacted. "You know something? You're crazy."

He studied her coolly. "Not crazy, doll. Hungry maybe. Only now that I've had a taste of the good life, I'm not so hungry anymore. I just wanna make sure the feast lasts."

He lit a cigarette, blew out a long stream of smoke, and suggested, "Talk it over with your boyfriend and see what he says. I'm sure he's a sensible guy."

"What do you propose I tell him?"

"Anything you want. Just get the paperwork started so we can put this show on the road." He reached for Tami's hand. "It'll be great working together again, doll. Like old times."

Tami pulled her hand away. "What makes you think I'll go along with this?"

Earl picked up his drink and took a long swallow. "The way I see it, luv, you've got no choice. No choice at all."

Against her better judgment, Tami made one last desperate attempt to reach him. "Earl, how much would it take to get you to leave Palm Beach, tonight?"

His shock was genuine. "Why would I wanna leave? I like it here. I'm making out like a bandit, and I've only been here a week. You know the average age of the women here? Sixty. Hell, Tam, a young, healthy, single, good-looking stud can live like a king here."

Tami sat, stunned. Then wondered why anything Earl did should surprise her. "You disgust me."

The bright blue eyes glinted. "Yeah. Well, all I know is, babe, you gotta hustle fast in this world. Before the rest of the world outhustles you."

She sat in the car in The Breakers' parking lot. She needed time to think. Her whole world, carefully and painfully erected, threatened to come tumbling down around her unless she gave in to Earl's latest demand.

His *latest*. Because there would be more. She had no illusions. She was his golden goose. Filling his basket with golden eggs.

Suddenly, she made a decision. It was so simple, it was laughable. She had resisted the possibility before. Now, she had no alternative.

Bordon must be told. The rest of the world—her career—well, she would have to risk the consequences of that disclosure.

She had no choice but to reveal her deception. So she could begin a new life on a foundation of honesty.

With whatever was left her to begin it with.

Earl Blakely was exhilarated.

Shit, when he picked up his first check from the boyfriend, he'd have enough dough to find him an heiress. And court her in style.

He felt too good to be cooped up in a lousy hotel room. He grabbed a jacket, left his room, took the elevator down to the lobby, and walked out the door to where his rented Mercedes was parked.

The night was cool but pleasant. With the top down, Earl reveled in good feeling. All he needed to complete his image was a great-looking broad sitting beside him.

He decided to go to Peter's Pub, a small English tavern run by a transplanted Dubliner. Maybe he'd meet someone new.

The jukebox was playing a golden oldie—"Stardust." A tall, good-looking blond kid was dancing with a beautiful brunette. Except she looked as though she could use an extra twenty pounds easy. He liked his women lean, but not that lean. Still, she was a knockout. One classy chick. And she moved that skinny frame of hers like fire was lighting her ass.

Earl took a deep swallow of his Scotch, crushed out his cigarette, and strolled over to the beautiful couple.

"Mind if I dance with your girl?" asked Earl.

The good-looking blond kid blinked. "Girl! Hell, this isn't my girl. She's my sister."

Earl grinned and stuck out his hand before he whirled the girl away. "Earl Blakely," he called out.

"Howie Caine," Howie called back. "And her name's"—pointing to the dark-haired girl observing the exchange with customary cool detachment—"Belinda."

The guests were gone by the time Tami arrived home. But Bordon was waiting, his face grim.

Before he could say anything, Tami apologized. "Bordon, I'm very sorry. I really expected to be home in time."

She tried to smile. "Can we move out of the hall into the library? There's something I need to tell you. Only we might as well get comfortable, darling. Because it's going to take a little time."

In her suite at The Breakers, Reenie sipped her fifth bourbon and branch carefully. She had no intention of getting drunk. She needed her wits about her to blast Mark when he finally arrived. The nerve of him! Keeping her waiting like this!

Only he wasn't coming at all. She'd known that for some time now. He hadn't even had the grace to call with an excuse.

Humiliation choked her. Anger rose, along with the desire for revenge. Flushed and furious, Reenie plotted the excruciatingly painful end of Senator Mark Hunter.

When she was finished with him, there'd be little left. She'd dangle his scalp from her belt like a trophy. She'd shrivel his balls and wear them as charms around her wrist. She'd tear out his eyes, mount them in glass, and use them as paperweights. She'd finish him off until he was nothing more than the town clown. A party joke, with not a prayer in hell to help him.

Unless—unless he had a good explanation. Something acceptable to her pride. If he could persuade her his absence was unavoidable, she might forgive him. After a suitable period of torment.

Because for the first time in her life, she was in love. She hadn't planned it that way. Or wanted it that way. Only somewhere along the exquisitely exciting path toward humbling the son of a bitch, she had fallen head over heels in love with him.

How's that for a shaft, sugar? she thought derisively. With a toss of her head, and more than a touch of self-pity, she threw caution to the winds and proceeded to get thoroughly smashed.

Mark stalked his Watergate apartment restlessly. He was bored. And edgy. He didn't know why. Things were going well for a change. For a change there was order in his life.

The Senate hearing was moving ahead. Giving him the kind of popular press coverage he needed.

He'd even been working on his private image. Playing the dutiful, indulgent husband, catering to the demands of a beautiful, indulged wife.

He'd been treating Rosemary with kid gloves. Calling her often. Flying down when he could. Giving her the attention she required.

Whatever it took to keep her happy and sober, Mark was willing to do.

Even if it killed him.

He'd been right, though. With Carl and Grace in the house, Rosemary was better. And with Carl's health to absorb her energies, less energy was concentrated on Mark. So keeping Rosemary content was easier.

One area gnawed at him. Kate. He couldn't get her out of his mind. A dozen times he reached for the phone to call her, tell her he needed her, wanted her.

He reached for the phone now. Stopped himself once more. Kate was off limits. The relationship threatened too much. It threatened his political future. And it guaranteed to set off another relapse for Rosemary. That, he couldn't handle.

Better to keep his relationships casual.

Better to keep his head.

He'd brought some work home from the office he needed to have ready by Wednesday. Since today was Tuesday, he'd better get cracking.

Tuesday! Shit! He'd forgotten it was Tuesday. Forgotten Reenie Boyd's Tuesday night dance card.

She'd be in Palm Beach now. Well, he'd told her he wasn't about to prance through The Breakers' lobby to get to her.

Mark glanced at his watch, decided to give Reenie a call, then thought better of it. He didn't want to deal with her at the moment.

Hell, he told himself, anybody could forget one time.

Even Reenie wasn't so unreasonable she wouldn't grant him that.

14

Ben's second Palm Beach feature aired that evening.

A blow-up of one of society's greatest architects, Addison Mizner, filled the TV screen. A monkey perched on one shoulder, a macaw on the other. Various other members of Addison Mizner's menagerie surrounded him.

Ben Gately narrated.

"If Addison Mizner never existed, he would have been invented. He was that colorful a character.

"He was huge, well over six feet tall. Massive, rising at his top weight to 310 pounds. He was a raconteur, an entertainer, a showman, a hustler of indefatigable charm, a wit with a sharp tongue who knew where all the bodies in town were buried and who never hesitated to point them out with glee.

"According to Alva Johnson, author of *The Legendary Mizners,* the definitive work on the architect, Mizner was a sophisticated, cultured scholar, an expert on Spanish art and history, a sometime architect who could neither spell nor do basic arithmetic. Science was an enigma to him; math, an anathema. Yet he drew the praise of Frank Lloyd Wright, who compared him to Stanford White, and he changed the face of Palm Beach forever with his architectural innovations.

"He was the son of a socially prominent, if somewhat eccentric, northern California family, one of seven children. His background was as colorful as the figure he cut.

"He dug for gold in the Klondike, hustled his way through the Orient, wheeled and dealt in ecclesiastical wear in Guatemala, studied art and architecture at the university in Spain, fought in the ring in Australia, restored the deposed queen's ancestral portraits in Hawaii, and charmed New York society matrons with his stories and skills.

"In 1918, broke and desperately ill, he decided to die in Guatemala. Friends took up a collection and shipped him to Palm Beach.

"Two things happened to Mizner in Palm Beach. First, he met Paris Singer. Second, he elected to live.

"Paris Singer, handsome, six feet, three inches, former ward of the British court, named for the city he was born in, was one of the sixteen illegitimate children of the twenty-four (eight were legitimate) fathered by Isaac Merrit Singer, founder of the Singer Sewing Machine fortune.

"Paris Singer was a Renaissance man—scholar, art patron, amateur architect, student of medicine, devotee of all things cultural, and social arbiter.

"Paris Singer, too, came to Palm Beach to die. Stimulated by his meeting with Addison Mizner, he changed his mind.

"Cleveland Amory states that early in their friendship, Singer asked Mizner what he would do if he could do anything he wanted. Mizner responded, 'I'd build something that wasn't made of wood, and I wouldn't paint it yellow,' pronouncing without awareness the death knell of the Flagler era.

"The partnership was formed. Mizner, the architect. Singer, the entrepreneur with the bankroll.

"The first Mizner-Singer project was altruistic. Singer owned 160 acres of real estate there, and in the early days he kept trying to unload it. On it, they put up a home designed and built on what is now Worth Avenue for wounded soldiers returning from World War I. A sunny southern shelter to convalesce in. An architectural gem to soothe combat-frayed nerves.

"Many were invited. Few acknowledged.

"Only temporarily dismayed, the resourceful Singer turned his hospital into a social club and named it the Everglades. It became the most exclusive private club in Palm Beach.

"While recuperating World War I veterans never knew what they missed out on, Palm Beachers recognized at once what they had lucked into.

"El Mirasol, a thirty-seven-room house with garage provisions for forty cars, built for over $1 million for Eva Stotesbury, cemented the Mizner reputation. 'Queen Eva' was able to entertain masses of friends for an evening fit for a queen.

"Mizner's bastardized Spanish—'more Spanish than anything I've seen in Spain' was one comment—was *in*. Orange-tiled roofs, stucco facades, wrought iron, carved wood, stained glass, patios and balconies, turrets and fountains, proliferated.

"Mizner was socially and architecturally launched.

"One small error in the Stotesbury cottage. Mizner forgot to include a kitchen. The Mizner 'error' bĕcame a Mizner trademark. In each Mizner house, one major architectural detail was deliberately omitted. In one house, built for the Rasmussens, who had a grocery store fortune, it was the staircase leading from the first floor to the second. An outside staircase was added and, rain or shine, both Rasmussens reached their second floor from outside the comforts of their first floor.

"Mrs. Joshua Cosden, whose husband had once been a Baltimore streetcar conductor and who later redeemed himself by the fortune he made in Oklahoma oil, wanted a Mizner house bigger than Eva's. Plaza Riena, built in 1923 for almost $2 million, achieved that objective.

"But triggered a reaction. When 'Queen Eva' saw she had been outqueened, Mizner was called back to add the necessary wings to El Mirasol.

"To own a Mizner house became an indication of social status. New Palm Beach millionaires wanted big ancestral homes that looked old and reeked of old money. Mizner, with his shrewd understanding of psychology, gave them what they wanted. He once commented, 'These people can't stand anything that doesn't cost a lot of money.'

"Addison built big, and he supplied *old*. When he couldn't locate an ancient Spanish refectory table or an antique mantelpiece, he built them. He simulated age by burning, hammering, stomping, kicking, hacking, and mutilating pieces until they literally shrieked of antiquity. He even set up Mizner Industries to reproduce the antiquity clients required to establish their pedigree.

"Two incidents burst the Mizner bubble. The Florida land boom-bust and Addison's brother, Wilson, a man of equal wit and much talent who drew the protection of Addison only to bring about his destruction.

"Wilson Mizner was the wit who said, 'Boost a booster, knock a knocker, and use your own judgment with a sucker,' 'Treat a whore like a lady and a lady like a whore,' 'If you steal from one author, it's plagiarism, if you steal from many, it's research,' 'Be nice to people on your way up, because you'll meet them on your way down.'

"Wilson Mizner attracted success at the same time he thumbed his nose at it. More drawn to gambling, drugs, and the underworld, he alienated the very friends Addison needed to cultivate.

"Once asked by a judge he appeared on charges before if he was trying to show contempt of court, Wilson replied, 'No, Your Honor. I'm trying to conceal it.'

"At Wilson's urging, Addison became financially and artistically committed to creating a new Venice in Boca Raton, then Florida flatlands. Addison's imagination was fired with visions of the canals, gondolas, and medieval castles he would create in this new Venice-by-the-sea.

"When the Florida land bubble burst, Addison and Wilson were two of its casualties. They were left only with memories. They had become millionaires. For three short years.

"Addison Mizner and Paris Singer both died broke, but they left their mark on the face of Palm Beach. Tiled Spanish roofs dotted the landscape and glistened invitingly beneath the hot southern sun.

"But the vogue for Spanish was nearing its end. Palm Beach millionaires, suddenly rediscovering the WASP heritage they had abandoned with such fervor, opted for less ornate European structures to announce their presence on the Palm Beach scene. Many Mizner houses were torn down during the Anglo revival.

"Fifty years later, the Mizner craze is back. As Wilson Mizner might have observed with some amusement, 'You win some, you lose some.'

"It was called the Golden Age of Palm Beach—the age of style, flamboyance, elegance. Created by Addison Mizner and Paris Singer.

"Some Palm Beachers still remember Addison Mizner, massive, formidable, striding down Worth Avenue, shirttails flapping, monkey perched atop his shoulder. Addison was also known as the father of the sports shirt. He was a man who could devastate someone he disliked with the sharp edge of his tongue, or beguile someone he wished to cultivate with the smooth ointment of his charm.

"They remember Paris Singer, whose ever watchful social eye made certain those who entered the doors of his Everglades Club were worthy enough to remain inside.

"It was the day of the Palm Beach social hostesses, who not only lived conspicuously, but entertained that way. Entire Broadway casts and ballet troupes were brought down for an evening's diversion. European royalty was feted and entertained by American royalty, still shy, perhaps, of royal graces, but secure in the knowledge that their millions were impressive enough.

"When 'Queen Eva' Stotesbury retired from the social scene, she relinquished her mantle to Marjorie Merriweather Post, whose extravaganza Mar-a-Lago provided a suitable setting in which to continue to hold court.

"Today's Palm Beach, it is said, is different. Less flamboyant. More socially conscious. With young people turning their backs to the lavish entertainment, lavish life-styles, and rigid social structure of their elders.

"Only one hostess still glows with the aura left over from the Golden Age of Palm Beach—Mimzee Dawson, colorfully known as 'Queen Bess,' who despite fads, foibles, and fashions continues to hold court as though the Golden Age never ended, and, indeed, never will.

"But the questions remain. After 'Queen Bess,' what then? Will there be another queen? Or, better still, will there be another Palm Beach?

"This is Ben Gately, WKBQ, channel 9."

Mimzee Dawson was dining at home. Howie, who was avoiding her lately, was out. Belinda was dressing for a date.

Seated on the throne in the throne room of her Mizner oceanfront cottage, Mimzee reflectively sipped her predinner martini.

She wore a gold-threaded casual at-home caftan. There was nothing casual, however, about the jeweled crown perched atop her curly red wig. It was reassuring to know if anyone stopped by, she would be prepared.

Belinda breezed through the heavy carved oak doors, dressed

for her date in a sleeveless scoop-necked black wool dress that accentuated her gauntness.

Mimzee took another sip of her martini. "Switch on the TV news. Channel 9, honey pie," she instructed.

"What for?" asked Belinda. "It's just the same old grief."

"Turn it on, Belinda," ordered Mimzee. "When I want a philosophical observation, I'll hire a philosopher."

Belinda did as she was instructed. "Okay. It's your poison," she warned.

Mimzee pierced the olive in her martini glass with a solid gold toothpick, popped it into her mouth, and chewed on it thoughtfully.

Belinda shrugged again, perched on the edge of a chair, and watched the Ben Gately feature on Palm Beach unfold.

As scenes of twenties' balls, galas, and other extravagant entertainments flashed across the screen, Belinda shrieked. "Wild! Look, Mimzee! It's so Gatsbyishly decadent! So camp! Diamonds up to their doffles, sequined gowns shimmering like Waterford chandeliers, and champagne flowing like the River Seine. I love it!"

She glanced over at her grandmother. "Weren't you part of that whole scene, Mimzee?"

"Hardly," scoffed Mimzee. "In 1923, I was seven years old."

Belinda was disappointed. "Then you missed it all? All the fun?"

"Not bloody likely, dearie. There was enough fun left over in the thirties to keep me busy."

"But that was the Depression."

"Only for the unfortunate, chickie."

They watched the TV screen as "Queen Eva's" image was replaced by that of Marjorie Merriweather Post, whose reign was followed by that of "Queen Bess."

"You're famous, Mimzee," cried Belinda with delight.

"Damn right," asserted Mimzee.

Belinda laughed, then rose. "Say, Mimzee," she asked curiously, "when the time comes, who *are* you going to hand your crown over to?"

One of Mimzee's penciled red eyebrows flared upward. "When the time comes, dearie, I'm *not going.*"

Belinda hooted, then noticed the look of fierce determination. Mimzee meant it. She'd fight her way to the grave and beyond, by God.

Belinda had a sudden impulse to hug her grandmother. But in all her twenty-three years, she never remembered them touching.

"See you," she said breezily, sailing through the open massive carved oak doors as she exited.

Distracted, Mimzee failed to respond. She finished her martini, her thoughts elsewhere.

She rose, crossed the wide room to her desk, flipped open her personal directory, and dialed the private number of a New York jeweler who often made custom-designed pieces for her.

"Alain," she boomed into the mouthpiece.

"Ah, my dear Mimzee," responded Alain DuLac. Only one voice boomed that distinctly. No need for her to announce herself. "How good to hear from you. And what can I do for you, dear friend?"

"I need a necklace made up, Alain. I need it by next week. I'll be in New York tomorrow with the sketches. Can you manage it? You will, of course, be handsomely compensated for the rush."

He chuckled. "Bring me the sketches, dear lady. Then we shall see what we have to do."

"I know what we have to do, Alain. What I want to know is can you do it?"

He hesitated but briefly. Then said smoothly, "Of course we can, my dear. For you, we do the impossible. Always."

"Good," said Mimzee. "See you tomorrow. Two o'clock."

For the first time in days, Mimzee felt some of her old bounce and verve return. All this fuss and speculation about *two* Kirstens. Really!

Well, soon there would be *three* Kirstens. The third, of course, known only to her and Alain DuLac. And Alain, properly compensated, was Alain, properly mute.

The thought of outfoxing Consuela, the fox, cheered Mimzee. If a circus was what the Contessa Perrugia craved, a circus would be provided.

Only Mimzee, not Consuela, would be the ringmaster.

After all, Consuela was merely a contessa. By marriage. While she, Mimzee Dawson, was a queen. By right.

15

Ben received a number of congratulatory calls following his broadcast.

The first was totally unexpected. "Bordon Granger," announced the strong resonant voice. "I watched both those features of yours with interest, Mr. Gately."

Ben knew who Bordon Granger was, even if his face and name hadn't been on the cover of this week's *Time* lying in front of him on his desk. Bordon Granger, like Kellogg's Raisin Bran, was a household name.

"Thank you, Mr. Granger," said Ben, still flushed from his success.

"Bordon," suggested Bordon.

"Bordon," repeated Ben easily.

"I have something in mind I think might interest you, Ben. I'd like you to lunch with me tomorrow. Trouble is, I can't get away from my desk at home. Think you can make it out to Wellington?"

Ben said he could. Bordon gave him directions and said he was looking forward to meeting him. Ben said he was looking forward to meeting Bordon as well.

The second call was from Kate. As expected. She congratulated him, praised the feature, and allowed, of course, she was not surprised. It was a fine job. She knew good things would come from it.

They already had, Ben told her. At least, he thought so. He told her about Bordon Granger's call. Then he broke all vows.

Could he stop by?

Kate hesitated.

Not for long, Ben promised. But he was feeling so high, so good, and he hated to waste all those good, high feelings on a couple of the guys who'd offered to buy him a few beers to celebrate. He'd rather share them with her.

Kate laughed. How could she refuse such a request?

Ben's spirits soared. He'd be there in fifteen minutes. Ten minutes. Five, if he left right away. Hell, he was flying. He'd be right over.

Bordon Granger called Earl Blakely at ten the next morning. Bordon had been up since six. He had half a day's work done already, but the son of a bitch who answered the phone sounded as though the call woke him up.

Bordon had no patience with loafers. "Bordon Granger, here," he said tersely. "Earl Blakely?"

Earl struggled to rouse himself. "Yeah?"

"Miss Hayes tells me you have a proposal to discuss with me."

"Uh, yeah," mumbled Earl. Christ, he'd had only four hours sleep. That Belinda had been at him half the night. "Yeah, well, I . . ."

Bordon cut him off. "Be here at eleven, Mr. Blakely. We'll talk about it then. And be on time, please. I have a lunch appointment at 12:30." He gave him directions and hung up.

Jesus, thought Earl, Tami had really gone and done it. Laid it all out before her old man and enlisted his support. Holy shit, he was practically on easy street. The old guy had been so excited, he couldn't wait to call him. How about that?

Earl stumbled out of bed, groped his way to the shower, turned it on full blast cold, and stepped under it. He needed to be shocked awake. So he could be sharp. Quick-witted. He needed to look good. And he had only twenty minutes to get his shit together.

Be on time, the big man said. Well, Earl Blakely would be on time, all right. Never let it be said he wasn't there, sharp and sassy, when opportunity finally delivered his share of the goodies.

Earl was glad he still had the rented red Mercedes. He'd arrive at the boyfriend's in style.

* * *

It happened in the elevator on his way down to the lobby. This good-lookin' chick, all dolled up, dressed to kill, but looking like death warmed over, white as a sheet, suddenly started to keel over.

Earl grabbed her before the elevator operator could get to her. What the hell, she was standing closer to him, and if she fell and took him down with her, his jacket and trousers would probably be a mess.

He assured the operator he could manage, helped her out of the elevator, led her to a chair, and offered to get her a doctor.

She looked up at him incredulously. "Hell, sugah. I don't need a doctor. I'm just hung over."

Earl was relieved. The last thing he needed was to be held up by ambulances and police reports.

Reenie Boyd looked at the blond, good-looking stud standing in front of her, and smiled. "You the official Good Samaritan, darlin'? Riding the elevators rescuing ladies who've been naughty?"

Earl grinned. "My first rescue. Honest."

Reenie rose, unsteady at first. Then, with determination, she held herself erect. "And to whom do I owe this fortuitous impromptu intervention?"

"Huh?"

"Your name, sugah?"

"Oh?" Earl stuck out a hand. "Earl Blakely, ma'am."

Reenie held the outstretched hand. "Ma'am? You must be a southern gentleman." She released the hand reluctantly.

"No, ma'am." Another grin. "I'm from California. Hollywood."

Colored flags seemed to shoot up before Reenie's eyes. Hollywood! Tami Hayes, who had slunk into the hotel last night in that incongruous Garboish disguise, was from Hollywood too. Or Beverly Hills, darlings. A long shot, true. But long shots sometimes paid off.

She smiled winsomely. "Hollywood! Now, there's a wicked town. A person can't be too careful there." Blue eyes stared at blue eyes. "Care for a drink, Mr. Blakely?"

"Earl, ma'am," said Earl. Jesus! It was only 10:40 in the morning and she was hung over, and here she was ready to lap up more.

"I'd love to, but I'm in a rush. I have an eleven o'clock appointment in Wellington."

The colored flags spun round. Wellington was Bordon Granger country. Was it all a coincidence or had Reenie Boyd hit pay dirt without even lifting a finger?

She smiled up at Earl Blakely again. "Well, you're gonna love it out there, Earl. Very countryish. Tell you what. You take a rain check and give me a call when you get back. Reenie Boyd. Remember."

She fluttered thick blond lashes. "You call me now, heah? 'Cause it wouldn't be proper not to thank my rescuer properly, now, would it?"

"If you say so, ma'am."

"Reenie, sugah," corrected Reenie. "Only the butler calls me ma'am."

Nothing Tami told Bordon about her past had shocked him. If anything, he loved her even more. For the courage it took to come so far against odds that would have thrown most people. With no support along the way from anyone, except herself.

Of course, she'd had Erin. Bordon could appreciate what a motivating force that was.

What tore him apart was the pain Tami endured until she finally told him the whole story and allowed him to help her.

What infuriated him, what brought his blood to the boiling point, was the son of a bitch who caused it all. A no-good, do-nothing prick who figured he'd tapped into a gold mine. A low-down bastard who apparently saw Bordon as the kind of patsy who'd knuckle under at the first scent of scandal.

Well, that cocky SOB had a lot to learn. Bordon Granger hadn't built a cable empire by knuckling under to anyone. But neither had he built one by losing his perspective.

He kissed Tami, hugged Erin, and suggested they take off, enjoy themselves, spend some money, and not return till late afternoon. He would be busy until then.

"You're sure you'll be all right?" Tami asked. "Earl's not a nice person, Bordon."

Bordon put his arm around her. "Neither am I, darling, when it suits my purposes not to be. Don't worry. I've polished off little Earls with my breakfast grits."

Tami laughed. "You sound so fierce."

"I am fierce. I'm only putty in your hands. Ask anyone."

She rested her head against Bordon's shoulder. She felt secure, protected. She hadn't realized how tired she was from battling the world alone.

"I love you, Bordon."

"I love you, Tami."

Erin came up. "Hey, what about me?"

Tami and Bordon enveloped her in their arms. "You're loved too, darling," Tami said.

"By both of us," added Bordon.

"Okay," grinned Erin, "let's break this up before it gets any mushier."

16

Bordon Granger was a large man, broad-shouldered, with not an ounce of fat on him.

His face was broad. His brows, black and heavy, over clear gray eyes that could, when provoked, darken with anger. His thick dark hair was just turning gray. His nose was long and slender with strongly defined nostrils. His mouth was well-shaped, expressive when he smiled, generous when he laughed, but thin and tightly drawn when someone roused his wrath.

Even sitting at his desk with only the top portion of him visible, the impression of power Bordon Granger gave off was intimidating.

Seated there now, he shuffled through a pile of papers awaiting his signature, signed his name, and didn't bother to raise his eyes when his secretary led Earl Blakely into the study and announced his presence.

He let Earl stand there for a full five minutes, then raised his eyes to acknowledge Earl's presence.

"Mr. Blakely, please sit down," he said.

Earl, who had expected a more effusive welcome, sat in the chair Bordon indicated. What the hell, the guy was obviously getting stuff out of the way so they could really get down to the business of talking.

Earl wet his lips, somewhat uncomfortable under Bordon's steady stare.

"Cigar, Mr. Blakely?" Bordon pushed a box of expensive imported Havana cigars toward Earl. "Pure black market. Expensive as hell, but worth every peso. Each man to his weakness, don't you agree?"

Earl, who had never smoked cigars, accepted, then nodded. Jesus! Pure Cuban black market. This guy knew how to live. Earl watched Bordon go through the ritual of snipping off the tip with a lapis and gold cigar cutter, light the cigar, and enjoyably exhale expensive Cuban smoke.

Earl followed suit. "Nice," he approved.

"Glad you like it," replied Bordon. He leaned back in his swivel chair and smiled benignly at Earl. "Now that we're comfortable, Mr. Blakely, why don't you unfold this phantasm that seems to have beguiled you so."

"Huh?" asked Earl.

"Your proposal, Mr. Blakely. Tell me about it."

Heady from the feel of an expensive cigar between his fingers, Earl began to talk. For almost a half hour, he enthusiastically developed his proposal. He had some papers indicating figures and projections. He passed these to Bordon.

Bordon nodded, studied the sheets of figures and projections carefully and thoroughly, but made no comment. Earl tried not to fidget while he waited. He wanted to play it cool. The cigar helped.

He puffed away and casually glanced around the room. Nice. Expensive stuff. Classy. Nothing flashy. Earl puffed, and envisioned himself in such a setting.

Finally, Bordon looked up. Still, he said nothing.

Earl shifted in his chair. "Well, Mr. Granger, what do you think?"

"I think it's shit," said Bordon. "Pie-in-the-sky shit."

"Hey . . ." began Earl defensively.

Bordon cut him off. "Shit, Mr. Blakely." He rose from his swivel chair and Earl was amazed at the height of him. He came from behind the desk to the front and towered over Earl. "Did you really think I would go along with this greedy cockamamy scheme of yours?"

Earl flinched at the word *greedy* but desperately tried to keep things going. "It's all worked out, Mr. Granger. The figures are worked out for a two-year period. Although we'll be in the black long before then, as you can see from my projections. They look mighty good, if I do say so."

"Nothing about you looks good, Blakely," Bordon told him.

"Not you, or your figures, or your projections." In disgust, he picked up the box of Havanas. "Here, take a couple of these with you. That way the trip won't have been a complete waste."

Angry now, Earl started to rise. "Hey, listen you . . ."

Bordon pushed him back. "No, you listen. And listen good. You're small potatoes, Blakely. Why, I can get a contract out on you for 150 bucks. And don't for a minute delude yourself I wouldn't do it." Bordon looked at the box of Havanas. "I pay more than that for a box of these."

He grabbed hold of Earl's collar and brought his face up close. "Now, pay attention. Forget you ever saw or heard of Tami Hayes or Erin. And never—I said never—contact either one of them again. Not to threaten or intimidate or whatever. Or it will be the last mistake you ever make."

Bordon suddenly let go of his grasp and Earl fell back, stunned and shaken.

"You can go now, Blakely," Bordon said, turning away. "I'm finished with you." As though it were an afterthought, he added, "You can leave these papers. I'll dispose of them for you." He sat at his desk again and returned to work. It was as though Earl Blakely no longer existed.

Earl stumbled to his feet, dazed by the turn of events. He found his way outside to the rented red Mercedes. He couldn't believe it. His golden opportunity had come and gone without delivering any gold. It was over. Kaput. *Finito*. Earl had no doubt that bastard inside would never hesitate to go through with his threat.

He sat behind the wheel of the Mercedes, despondent. What the hell would he do now? He'd have to settle his bill at The Breakers and find some cheap place to stay while he figured out what to do. He'd have to turn in the Mercedes and rent a Pinto. He was almost broke.

All his plans had been geared to signing some papers and picking up a check today. Even a small one. Anything to keep him going until the big money rolled in.

His lunch with Ben Gately washed some of the bitter taste of Earl's visit out of Bordon's mouth. But every time he thought of Earl, he was sorry he hadn't flattened him. Well, he'd done more.

317

He'd scared the shit out of him. He knew that type. All bluff. One big scare and they folded fast.

Bordon deliberately forced his mind from revenge and concentrated on the business at hand. Ben Gately. He liked what he saw. Ben was a comer, bright, with a newsman's sound instinct for what constituted news, and an attractive way of presenting it.

They lunched on the terrace overlooking Bordon's much-photographed gardens. Beyond the gardens lay Bordon's much-photographed man-made forest.

Bordon outlined his proposal. Ben would serve as anchorman of his own nightly news program. With carte blanche to hire his own staff. To get out into the field—local, national, European, worldwide. To cover in-depth whatever scene he deemed politically newsworthy.

He would be based in New York City. A starting salary of $200,000 yearly. Stock options. All the usual fringe benefits.

Ben tried to assimilate the information with the sophistication of a man accustomed to being royally courted. Then he decided, *Oh, hell, why fake it?* This was everything he'd worked toward, suddenly hand-delivered ahead of schedule on a golden platter.

Timing. That's what it was all about. Being in the right place at the right time. *Ask not why Bordon Granger wants you,* Ben told himself. *Ask only how you can deliver for Bordon Granger.*

"Need time to think about it?" Bordon asked.

Ben grinned. "I'd be crazy if I did!"

Bordon nodded. "Good. Then we have a deal." He reached out and shook Ben's hand. "I'll have my lawyers draw up the contracts. You can have your lawyers check them over with you. Now, then, how long do you need to finish up here?"

"About a month should do it."

"Fine. I'd like you to start setting this up as quickly as possible." Bordon paused. "Have you any family to relocate?"

Ben thought of Kate. "Just some plans for one," he said more wistfully than he realized.

Bordon Granger smiled. "Well, good luck, then."

Earl Blakely was so agitated he completely forgot the raincheck Reenie Boyd extended. So eager was he to remove himself from the range of Bordon Granger's wrath, he settled his Breakers' bill quickly, turned in his rented red Mercedes for a blue Pinto, and located a cheap motel in Lake Worth. From here he could map out his future. What remained of it.

Earl thought of Belinda, the kid from last night, and her kooky brother, Howie. They seemed to have a fix on everything in town. Who was who. What was going down. What was coming up. A real weird duo, but he needed someone with a handle on things. A couple of bored richies might just have one. And baby Belinda was one hot number. Earl recalled the action in the Mercedes last night.

He reached in his pocket for the slip of paper she had slipped him and dialed her number.

Ben played and replayed the lunch meeting in his mind. He couldn't wait to share it with Kate. He loved her. And he had no intention of leaving her behind. Somehow, she must be made to see she needed him as much as he needed her.

Last night, she had let him stay over. Without any manipulation on his part. It happened naturally, simply. That was the way to Kate, light and easy. Some women wanted you to take over. Kate needed space.

His thoughts strayed from Kate to giving notice, tying up loose ends, covering the House of Graet Ball.

Then it would be Operation Big Time. Ben Gately, anchorman of his own nightly news show. Located in the Big Apple itself.

With Kate Crowley beside him to share his future.

Hell, it was their future, not his.

Tami and Erin came home laden with packages, mementos of an afternoon spent shopping on Worth Avenue.

"It was wild," Erin informed Bordon as the houseman helped her carry her parcels inside.

Tami remained behind. "I was so upset, I just kept buying. Crazy, isn't it? I bought things for both of us we didn't need and will probably never wear."

"Certainly you'll wear them," insisted Bordon.

"I was so anxious, it was like one extended nervous breakdown."

Bordon laughed. "Relax, sweetheart. It's over. The monster was immobilized."

"Was it awful?"

"A piece of cake."

"You're kidding!"

"Would I kid you?"

"The truth, Bordon. Please tell me every terrible thing he said and did."

He lifted her chin and looked at her. "There's only one fact you need concern yourself with, darling. That SOB will never bother you or Erin again."

Tami looked up at him. "Honest?"

Bordon grinned down. "Would I lie?"

Belinda was receptive when Earl called.

She'd been fretting over a small scene with Howie, who tried to hit on her for some more money. She refused the request, reminding him she was not a philanthropist. She felt no guilt. She was not sentimental about money. Still, it was always distasteful to be approached. The invitation to dinner promised to take her mind off the experience. If the dinner didn't do it, the sex would.

⚮17⚮

Reenie waited until late afternoon, then called downstairs and asked that Earl Blakely's room be rung. She was told Mr. Blakely was no longer registered at the hotel. No, he had not left a forwarding address.

Damn! thought Reenie, hanging up. She should have grabbed him while she had him in her hot little hands. To hell with his appointment.

Now, where would she find him? A needle in a haystack. He could be out of the state by now. Or the country.

She did two things. She called Julia Sheffield and told her she needed a favor. There was a young gentleman named Earl Blakely. Could Julia check around the area—all the hotels and likely places —and see if she could locate him? There'd be a real nice treat in it for her and yes, she was dying to have lunch. How about tomorrow? The Colony? Fine.

Then Reenie called her British secretary at her New York apartment. She said she wanted all and any information on Earl Blakely, lately of Hollywood, California.

Start with the L.A. Motor Vehicle Department. Get an address. Check with the L.A. Police Department. See if they had anything on him. Trace him back to the womb, if necessary. Reenie wanted a dossier on the dude and she wanted it like yesterday.

Yes, she understood that was a tall order. But tall orders command tall salaries. Since that's exactly what the British secretary was getting, how about earning it, sugah?

Reenie hung up and fixed herself a bourbon, then splashed more branch water in the glass than usual. She wasn't about to turn into a lush. She had neither the time nor the desire.

321

Besides, she had work to do. She was still waiting to see what Mark's next move would be. His period of grace, which she had graciously and unexpectedly extended, was drawing to a close. Love him or not, she was a businesswoman. What they had was an agreement, and if that arrogant bastard welshed on it, he'd have to pay the consequences.

Earl watched Belinda pick at her food. The bird was eating like a bloody sparrow.

Earl ate like a ranch hand.

Belinda met him at Peter's Pub, as Earl had requested. He ordered dinner for both of them. Belinda gave explicit instructions on how she wanted her filet prepared. Now, she wasn't even eating it. And at these prices. Earl tried not to look pained.

"You don't eat enough to keep alive," he protested. "That's why you're so skinny."

"Skinny!" scoffed Belinda. "I'm *huge.*" She poked at her food and announced, "I'm bulimic."

Earl tried to cover his embarrassment. "I never heard of it."

"It's fairly new. I wouldn't be caught dead with anything old." She pushed her food to one side of her plate. "I've had six psychiatrists, and not one's been able to break through my defense system. Guess I'm one of those no-win cases."

After she had pushed everything to one side, she began pushing it back. "But then my background is so bizarre, it's understandable. I mean, I suppose I compensated for nonaffection by erecting barriers of insurmountable impenetrability. And then, of course, I created a fantasy life that offered sufficient gratification to offset the deprivation I felt I had endured."

Jesus! She had to be kidding! He didn't understand a word she was saying.

Belinda sighed then. "Can you possibly know, Earl, what it's like to not remember one parent and never to have known the other?"

"Sure," said Earl. "I was an orphan myself."

She put her fork down. "You were?"

"Yeah. When I was three hours old, I was left on a convent doorstep in Trenton, New Jersey. The nuns took me in." There

322

wasn't a word of truth in it but Earl figured this weird chick liked weird stories.

"Imagine!" murmured Belinda with new interest.

"Yup," continued Earl. "They raised me. The nuns, I mean. And mean as hell they were too. Beat me, starved me when I wasn't good, played with my little prick. When it got bigger, they rode it. Sister Mary Margaret especially."

Titillation sparked Belinda's eyes. *"Really!"*

"Yeah, it was the pits there. I don't talk about it much. I figure what's in the past should stay there."

"How wise of you," approved Belinda. "I wish I had that kind of strength. To overcome so much."

"That's me," said Earl bitterly. "Overcome Charlie. Just when I think I'm landing on my feet, whammo! Another wallop in the gut."

"No!" cried Belinda.

"Yeah!" sighed Earl.

"Tell me about it," she urged.

So Earl told her.

He'd come to town for this big deal. Staked practically everything he owned on it. Had a meeting with this guy who stole the whole idea out from under his nose and then threatened to blow him away if he so much as showed his face anywhere near him.

"What will you do?" asked Belinda, all interest in food poking replaced by the drama of Earl's plight.

He explained he'd found a cheap room in a Lake Worth motel. He'd stay there until he worked out a plan of action. That bastard wasn't going to screw him out of what was rightfully his. No way.

Belinda was immersed in thought. Suddenly, she brightened. "Earl, I have the perfect solution to your dilemma."

"My what?"

"Your problem."

"Yeah?" asked Earl suspiciously.

"You can stay at one of the cottages at our place. The one way back by the lake. No one will look for you there. It has a kitchen, so I can bring your food. A bathroom. A bedroom. A living room and a sunroom. I used to play in it when I was little. When no one else was staying there. I can visit you and you'll have plenty of time to plan your strategy and plot your revenge. Oh, I think it's a fantastic idea. Don't you?"

"Fantastic," agreed Earl, stunned by his sudden good fortune.

"One small precaution," warned Belinda. "Stay away from my grandmother. She's the witch of Elsinore."

Earl didn't know what Elsinore was. But it sure sounded like heaven.

It looked like it too. He couldn't believe his luck. The grounds of Belinda's grandmother's house were a small park. The house was a castle. The dame was loaded. This kid was an heiress. He had it made.

The cottage way back by the lake was more luxurious than anything Earl had ever lived in.

"Jesus!" he said.

Belinda's eyes sparkled. "Like it?"

Earl hugged her. "You gotta be kiddin', baby. What's not to like?"

"Good." She toured Earl around the cottage. "Tomorrow I'll go over and pick up your things from the motel. And turn in your car. If you need one, you can take mine. The important thing is, you'll be safe here, Earl. Perfectly safe."

"God," said Earl. "How can I ever thank you, babe?"

Belinda smiled. "I'll be right back. I'm going to run over to the house and get you some extra blankets. I'll pick up some goodies too."

She was back in a half hour. With two blankets, a bottle of Scotch, some biscuits, cheese, and some grass.

She looked like a kid preparing for a party. More excited than Earl had ever seen her.

"Be back in a sec," she said, taking some linens from the closet into the bathroom with her. When she finally came out, Earl stared.

Belinda had cut a hole in one of the white sheets, slipped it over her head, and cut slits in the sides for her arms. She had cut another sheet into a head covering and taped it into place.

Her hair was hidden. Only the small thin face showed. Her eyes glowed with strange fire. In her hands, she held a rope.

Belinda looked sternly at Earl. "I am Sister Mary Margaret,

Earl, and I hear you have been a naughty boy. I'm afraid we're going to have to discipline you in the usual manner."

For the rest of the night, Belinda rode Earl as though he were Sunny's Halo being pushed toward the finish line at the Kentucky Derby. "We're going to make it, boy," shrieked Belinda, whipping him. "We're going to win."

Earl didn't know about the jockey, but Sunny's Halo was about to drop dead. The only thing that kept him going was the thought that this dame riding him was the heiress to all those millions.

If she could hang on, he could hang in.

Reenie Boyd lunched with Julia Sheffield at the Colony at a table with a view of the pool. Reenie ordered a chicken aspic salad. Julia ordered crabmeat. Both had glasses of white wine, which they sipped over gossip.

Julia waited until they were served before she delivered her news. "Well, darling, I did track your mystery man to Lake Worth. A seedy little motel, mind you. He'd been there briefly, is not there now, and no one had even the foggiest where he's flown off to."

Reenie nibbled on her salad, sipped her wine, and waited for Julia to continue.

"A young mystery woman, it seems, came to the rescue of your mystery man. According to the seedy, dreary little man at the desk, she paid the bill, settled his account, picked up his things, and disappeared into the distance."

Reenie toyed with her salad, then raised her eyes, looked at Julia, and smiled encouragement. "Why, that's just fine, sugah. You're makin' progress. Now go on back, get a description of the young lady, the car she drove off in, and anything else that will help us. You've made a grand beginnin', but it's only a beginnin', darlin'. We need more filler."

Julia looked shrewdly at Reenie. "Who *is* this mystery man, Reenie? I'm just dying of curiosity."

"I know, darlin'," replied Reenie smoothly. "In your shoes, I would be too." She offered no further explanation and Julia, receiving the message, returned to her crabmeat.

* * *

In the heat of passion, Ben forgot his recent insights about Kate.

Don't push. He was pushing.

Don't get possessive. He acted as if he owned her.

Give the lady some space. He needed to tie her down.

Love made him crazy. Or stupid. He didn't know which.

They'd just made love. The lovemaking was great. Kate acknowledged that.

"Well, then," pushed Ben. "Say yes. Marry me."

"There's more to a relationship than making love, Ben," Kate said.

"We've got more," he pointed out.

"Marriage is a big step."

"You won't be taking it alone," Ben reminded her. "There's someone here who'll help you through it."

"I need more time," fretted Kate.

"That's the one thing we don't have lots of," Ben told her. "Time's running out on us."

$\backsim$18$\backsim$

Derek put down his copy of Chekhov. He couldn't concentrate.

Consuela was out on the town. He had pleaded a headache, assuaging his guilt by reminding himself she was the one who insisted he come here to rest. Now even resting bored him.

He suddenly thought of Sandy Stone, remembered his offer to call her, recalled her tart tongue, and wondered whether he should. She didn't have the best of dispositions.

Still, he found himself thinking of her.

Why not?

One lunch. What could he lose?

He picked up the telephone directory, flipped to the S's, found Sandy's number, and dialed it.

He invited her to lunch. Tomorrow.

She surprised him by accepting. He had expected her to bark at him. She suggested the restaurant. La Famiglia.

Derek agreed. And felt his stomach lurch in protest at the thought of all that rich Italian food.

When Derek told Consuela the following morning he was having lunch with Sandy, she shook him off with an impatient shrug. She had a million things to do herself, she said. He should go enjoy lunch.

Derek walked past boxes of geraniums beneath the street windows of La Famiglia, passed under its red, yellow, and green awning, entered the restaurant, sat at the long bar, and ordered a seltzer.

He was halfway through it when Sandy arrived and strode toward him.

"Hi," she said.

Derek stood. "Hi." He indicated his glass. "Care for a drink?"

She glanced at her watch. "I think we'd better order. I only have an hour."

They were led to the rear room, seated at a red, white, and blue Cinzano umbrellaed table. A waiter came for their drink order.

"Would you like a drink now?" asked Derek, consulting the wine list. "A cocktail, or some wine? Asti Spumante. Frascati? Chianti?"

"Any white will do," Sandy told him.

He ordered wine for Sandy, milk for himself, explaining he rarely drank. Alcohol irritated his stomach. Could be an allergy.

"How odd," she noted. She sipped her wine and Derek drank his milk as they made awkward attempts at conversation.

They looked like brother and sister. Both tall, taut, thin to the point of reediness. Both had curly red hair, searching hazel eyes, and an intensity that sent off sparks.

They spoke at once.

"I think we'd better . . ."

"If you're ready to . . ."

"Let's order," decided Sandy. Derek signaled the waiter.

Sandy ordered veal and peppers, a side order of manicotti, a salad with the house dressing, garlic bread. The lunch might as well compensate for the company. Or lack of it.

Derek ordered plain pasta, dry salad, warmed bread with no butter or garlic. "Bad stomach," he explained to Sandy.

"You don't sound too healthy," she observed dryly.

He nodded. "I envy those people with cast-iron insides who can eat anything and everything in sight." His smile was apologetic. "I never could."

Sandy looked at him, noted a vulnerability she hadn't seen before, and found a physically flawed Derek less offensive than the superperfect oaf who had sat next to her at Thanksgiving. "Oh? Why not?"

"It's a long story," he said, strangely shy.

"So tell me," she encouraged. She rested her elbows on the table, cupped her chin with both hands, and surprised Derek with a smile. "Go on. I'm a captive audience all through lunch."

The waiter brought their food.

As Sandy ate with gusto, Derek surprised himself by telling her *why.*

He told her about forging out a career for himself and still not managing to lose the anxieties that plagued him since childhood.

He told the story without self-pity. He merely related the facts.

"My," sympathized Sandy. "No wonder you have stomach problems."

"You'd think by this time I'd have come to terms with it," mused Derek. "Actually, I think I have." He grinned, looking disarmingly boyish. "Only my stomach hasn't caught up with my insights."

"Well," observed Sandy with spirit, "that's not at all surprising."

"The funny thing is, when I'm working, I'm fine. No gut problems at all. It's all those other times that throw me. I get tense, my stomach knots up, and off we go."

"You're not tense now, are you?"

"No, I feel great," admitted Derek. He did.

"See," said Sandy. "You need to talk more about it."

Derek agreed.

Lunch was over.

"Well, there. That's it." She looked at her watch and gasped. "I have to run." Impulsively, she covered his hand with hers. "Listen, I really loved lunch."

Derek was suddenly embarrassed. "I didn't mean to spend it burdening you with my junk."

Sandy's hazel eyes shone with sincerity. "No burden. I enjoyed it." Seeing his confusion, she hastened to add, "Not your *stomach* troubles. But your opening up. Most guys never tell you anything real about themselves. They puff themselves up while they size you up. They spend the whole time playing games and trying to figure out how long it'll take them to get you into the sack."

"Well, I'm not like that," Derek assured her.

"I can see that," approved Sandy.

He motioned for the check, paid for it, and left the waiter a lavish tip. "Marvelous food," he told the astonished waiter.

Sandy smiled agreement.

Outside, he turned to her. "I'd like to see you again."

She paused, appraising him carefully. Finally, she spoke. "What about the contessa?" Their affair was no secret at the store.

Derek flushed. "I have no strings attached to me, Sandy."

She smiled sadly. "Derek, we all have strings binding us. The challenge is in the unraveling."

He persisted. "I really would like to see you again."

Again, she hesitated. Then, flashing him a brilliant smile, she said, "Okay. Give me a call. You have the number." She started to walk away, turned, and called back. "Let's make it dinner. My place. I'll cook you something that won't give you any indigestion."

When Consuela asked Derek how he enjoyed lunch, he said it was fine.

"What did you two find to talk about?" she asked curiously.

He couldn't tell her they'd spent lunch talking about his stomach. "Our families," he said. "They're great friends."

Earl Blakely couldn't believe his good fortune. A roof overhead. A fridge stocked with food. A stash of grass and booze to comfort him. And no sheriff pounding at his door.

The only thorn in this paradise he'd lucked into was Belinda. She was wearing him out. And kinky! Last night, she'd shown up dressed in a *real* nun's habit. Said she rented it from a theatrical costume place.

Jesus! He was a Catholic. Almost. He remembered enough of the hell-fire-and-brimstone sermons about sacrilege at St. Bartholomew's elementary school to feel uneasy.

He wanted to tell Belinda he'd made the whole fucking thing up. But he couldn't afford to blow it. He had to keep his heiress happy. He also needed some dough to do it.

He remembered the rain check that dame at The Breakers had offered him. Now, if he could only remember her name . . .

Mimzee Dawson took great pride in her prowess as a hostess. Her reputation was legendary, and deserved. For she paid attention to the minutest detail to ensure the comfort of her guests. A stay at Elsinore was more than a treat. It was an experience. Not since Marjorie Merriweather Post had there been a hostess so responsive to the sensitivities of her guests.

But Mimzee had allowed her preoccupation with the Kirsten to gain ascendancy over hostess duties. Now, however, arrangements had been made with Alain to provide her with a Kirsten replica. It would be delivered a day or two before the ball.

And her plan for retrieving the real Kirsten was firm in her mind. All that remained to accomplish the unbelievable was to enlist the services of Howie.

Thus, her energies were free to return to the duties at hand.

She studied her guest list, noted dates of arrival, lengths of stay, and guest preferences.

Each person who stayed at Elsinore was alphabetically indexed on a large white card which noted all pertinent information. Likes. Dislikes. Food idiosyncracies. Food preferences.

Also noted was the number of the cottage a guest stayed in. Certain of her friends, Mimzee knew, developed an almost childish attachment to a particular cottage and requested that one whenever they visited.

The Duke and Duchess of Embry, for instance, had the most irrational sentimentality toward cottage 12, the one closest to the lake. Mimzee couldn't imagine why. It wasn't the largest cottage by any means. Nor was it particularly lavish. It was, however, set apart, surrounded by a cluster of tall pines. And it had a charming view of the lake.

Mimzee tried to satisfy each request. She consulted her chart of guest accommodations, moved the name of the former Russian princess assigned to cottage 12 to cottage 9, moved the French count from 9 to 3, moved the former king of a small European country now absorbed by the Soviet bloc from 3 to 7, and penciled in the Duke and Duchess of Embry for cottage 12.

Over the summer, most of the cottages had been painted and redecorated. Mimzee had felt cottage 12 was perfectly adequate for the former Russian princess. Now that the Duke and Duchess of Embry had wired they were cutting short their stay in Scotland and would love to accept Mimzee's delightful offer, she felt obliged to have another look at it.

On her list of things to do in the upcoming week, Mimzee added a note to inspect cottage 12.

19

Carl Schmittle decided Grace had been right to insist he let go the reins of his corporate empire.

She had also been cagey. "For a while, Carl," she had cajoled. "Try it."

"I'll like it?" he had teased.

She smiled. "Maybe you'll love it. And I'll love you for it. Because you'll be around longer for me to love. That's what matters."

Grace had been right about that too. He did love it.

Few men, he decided, were as fortunate as he in the choice of a lifetime mate. And few were as fortunate in other ways. His blessings were many. His wife. His daughter. His grandchildren. Even, Carl thought wryly, his son-in-law, who seemed to be behaving himself lately and who, down for the weekend, was showering attention upon Rosemary. Carl wondered if this sudden show of husbandly affection was only that. A show. Put on for Carl's benefit.

No matter. Rosemary blossomed under it. She positively glowed as she bounded about the tennis court playing opposite Mark. No man, thought Carl, ever had a daughter so fair, so beautiful, so loyal and loving, as his. Now, if that shit of a husband could only see those qualities were also in Rosemary, the wife, Carl's uneasiness would be relieved.

Mark threw down his tennis racket and joined Carl and Grace at the umbrellaed table where they sat observing. Rosemary followed.

"Losing two sets in a row doesn't do much for my ego," Mark complained good-naturedly.

"Darling," Rosemary reassured him, "you're out of practice. I, on the other hand, have time for nothing else."

"She's too modest," interjected her father loyally. "Actually, between hovering over me and attending to all my needs, running the house, managing her charities, and painting up a blue storm, I'd say she was a phenomenon."

Rosemary's smile dazzled. "Build me up some more, fellas." She fetched a lemonade from the terrace sideboard, fixed a Scotch for Mark, and joined him and her parents.

"Darling," said Rosemary, handing Mark his drink.

He reached for it and grinned. "Thanks. There should be a reward for losing gracefully." He took a deep swallow and observed his father-in-law. "Carl, you look terrific. I don't know when I've seen you look so well."

Grace beamed. "Isn't it the truth? He looks ten years younger."

"Well," chuckled Carl, "you'd better watch out then, Mother. If I look that much younger, I'll start chasing you around the room again."

"Daddy!" cried Rosemary, shocked.

"Hell, Roe, I'm still a young man," Carl told her. "Your mother just said so. Don't slow me down. In fact," he added expansively, "I feel so good, I suggest a night on the town. We'll start with dinner at Café L'Europe, and from there . . ." He grinned, "Well, let's just play it by ear."

He patted Rosemary's hand. "Don't look so worried, honey. A little excitement won't kill me. Now, if you'll excuse me, I'll go make reservations."

Rosemary wore a black satin dinner suit with a sable collar. The skirt was knee-length with a deep slit. The jacket was open, revealing a white silk spaghetti-strap top and a narrow black satin belt. Her shoes were black satin sling-back high-heeled pumps.

She wore small pear-shaped diamond earrings and a slim diamond choker with a large pear-shaped pearl.

Her face was tanned a soft honey from tennis, her brown eyes glowed, and her blond hair shone.

She looked sensational. More than that, she felt sensational.

Taking a flat black satin evening purse from her drawer, Rosemary turned to Mark with a smile. "Dining out as a foursome should be fun."

He smiled back at her. "Maybe we ought to do it more often."

Rosemary reached up and kissed him lightly. "I'd like that."

"Good," said Mark. "We'll do it, then. We'll call this a practice run."

Afterward, Kate, who took a dim view of fate anyway, pondered the turn of events that fate provided.

Until two days before, she and Ben had planned to eat at La Vieille Maison in Boca to celebrate Ben's new job. Then Kate discovered she would be working late. She called Ben and told him it would be more convenient to eat closer to home. "Do you mind?" she asked.

"Not at all," he assured her.

"See if you can get a table at Café L'Europe," she suggested.

Ben called back in five minutes. "Not to worry. It's all been arranged. That's what happens when you have clout," he boasted.

They sat at the bar in the Bistro of Café L'Europe while they waited for their table.

Kate raised her glass of white wine. "Another toast to your success, Ben Gately."

Ben touched her glass with his martini. "Many thanks, Kate Crowley. And may I say you look particularly fetching this evening?"

She smiled. Although there were slight fatigue smudges under her eyes, the green of them was vivid enough to compensate. Her dark hair, center parted, fell to her shoulders. She wore a mandarin neckline sequined tunic, belted over a white wool pleated skirt. She wore no jewelry save a slim platinum diamond-bezeled House of Graet watch. She looked elegant.

Ben leaned across, brushed his lips against her hair, and whispered, "In fact, you look so fabulous, I don't see how I'll be able to concentrate on dinner."

Kate's eyes teased. "Food is a great neutralizer, Ben. You'll see."

Their table was ready. Kate and Ben stood.

And then it happened.

As they started to move, the front door swung open. Rosemary Hunter, the Schmittles, and Mark entered.

They stood, Mark and Kate, facing each other, and, in that moment, many futures were decided.

Kate paled visibly. Mark was the first to regain composure. He reached out a hand and smiled. "Kate. How good to see you."

Kate's own hand, as he grasped it, felt like ice. Her features felt frozen. She tried smiling, and nothing unusual happened.

"Nice to see you, Mark."

The introductions began. There was no way to avoid them. Mark turned to Rosemary. "Darling, I don't know if you've met Kate Crowley. She's with the House of Graet."

"How do you do," said Rosemary, her voice strained. She recognized Kate Crowley at once.

"And Mr. and Mrs. Schmittle, Rosemary's parents," continued Mark.

Kate nodded acknowledgments, then turned and introduced Ben.

Rosemary rallied quickly. "Heavens," she exclaimed, smiling charmingly, "we've formed a barricade here. I think we'd better move on in, darling, before we're given citations for blocking exits." She looked keenly at Kate, who towered over her, and said coolly, "So nice to have met you at last, Miss Crowley."

Kate nodded once more, then walked woodenly with Ben as they were led to their table.

Dinner was a disaster. Kate was all for leaving, but Ben put a hand over her wrist. "We'll stay," he said quietly.

Kate had no idea what she ate. Ben ordered for both of them and kept up a steady stream of chatter which required only minimal responses.

He even coached her at times. "Laugh, Kate. That was a funny one." Again, "Don't laugh now, sweetheart. I just told you a very sad story about the time I lost my first dog. I was only five years old, and . . ."

"Don't, Ben."

"Don't repeat it?"

"Don't tell me sad stories."

It was finally over.

The bill was settled.

Not once did Kate glance around the room to see where Mark

was sitting. Her eyes remained focused on Ben. Only their laughter reached her. Mark's deep, resonant laugh, Rosemary's bright one, Carl Schmittle's hearty roar, and Grace Schmittle's crystal-thin titter.

They appeared to be having fun together. A family affair.

When they arrived back at Kate's, Ben asked, "Do you want me to come in?"

She reached for the door handle. "Not tonight, Ben."

"Do you want to talk about it?"

She turned to him. "There isn't anything to talk about."

"Funny," mused Ben. "That wasn't the impression I got."

Kate leaned over and kissed him. "I'm sorry your celebration party was spoiled." She touched his lips lightly with her fingers. "Don't say anything, Ben. Anything nice or anything nasty. I'm just too tired to think up any more responses." She opened the car door, stepped out, swung it shut, ran up the walk, and fumbled in her bag for her house key.

She found it, opened the front door, closed it behind her, and leaned against it.

Carl Schmittle recognized her almost immediately. Even before Mark introduced her. A sixth sense.

He wanted to hate her, but looking at her, any feeling of ill will was dissipated. She looked more like a victim than a villainess.

She was very beautiful. But more. He saw character in her face. And something else. Kate Crowley seemed a very decent sort of person. Hardly a homewrecker.

Only, in the few seconds it took him to take Kate's measure, Carl noted his daughter's pain. Rosemary's ebullience was gone as quickly as it had come. Although her lips formed bright smiles and her laughter was rich and full, he knew his girl well enough to know an act when he saw one.

The conversation flowed through dinner. Flowed? Hell, it flooded. All holds were loosed as laughter washed over them.

Rosemary was flushed and desperately cheerful. Sipping her Perrier, picking at her veal, she regaled them with hilarious anecdotes. Topped only by Mark, whose good spirits surpassed his usual bonhomie.

The son of a bitch was an actor! But then the whole damned family were actors. Except for Grace, who seemed to be having the time of her life, oblivious to any undercurrents and unaware of the stellar performances enacted before her.

Even Carl was acting.

Smiling at that bastard opposite him when he wanted to punch him in the nose. Teasing Rosemary when he wanted to hold her. He drank more than he should have, ate faster than he normally did.

"A pretty girl," noted Grace.

"Who, Mamma?"

"That young woman Mark introduced us to. Really stunning. Didn't you think so, Rosemary?"

Rosemary's eyes were bright. "Actually, I thought her a frump."

"Rosemary!" said Grace, shocked.

"Well, didn't you see her, Mamma? Hair all scraggly. Stocking seams crooked. Dress two sizes too big for her."

Grace caught on. "Oh, you're kidding, Rosemary."

Rosemary laughed merrily. "That's right, Mamma. Only kidding. I thought she was quite breathtaking. Really. Don't you agree, Mark?"

Mark opened his solid gold cigarette case and offered Rosemary a cigarette. "Absolutely," he agreed.

Son of a bitch! thought Carl. How did a bastard like that attract two such women? Two! Hell, he probably had a string of them. Women of substance. Beautiful women. All eager to please him, blind to his deficiencies of character.

Women! Sometimes he wondered about them. They could be so goddamned practical in some things. Then completely lose their wits over someone with a good profile.

Rosemary had trouble sleeping.

She had said nothing to Mark about tonight. Somehow, she sensed this was far too important for her to scream and have tantrums over.

She noted at once the look that passed between Mark and Kate. She looked at Kate and knew. She had met her enemy and been vanquished. Then she looked at Mark and understood. It wasn't over. How could it be? It had never stopped.

She tossed restlessly in bed; slept fitfully, wondering when Mark was coming up. He said he'd had too much coffee with dinner to sleep. That he'd read in the library for a while.

He had kissed Rosemary absently and promised he would be up before long.

Carl woke in the middle of the night. Grace stirred beside him.

"Don't get up, Mother. A touch of indigestion. I'm just going to get some bicarb."

She started to rise. "Let me get it for you, Carl."

He pushed her back gently. "Stay. I just ate too much. Made a pig out of myself. When will I ever learn, eh, Gracie?"

He got up, and started toward the bathroom.

He never made it. Halfway there, a pain of such intensity hit him, he staggered backward from its force. He grabbed at his chest, cast a fleeting look of apology at Grace, and was felled suddenly like a massive tree struck at its base.

Her mother's screams woke Rosemary. She jumped out of bed without even bothering to look for a robe and ran down the hall to their room.

"What happened?" shrieked Rosemary. "Mamma, what happened?"

She stood immobilized inside the door, staring at her father's large inert form obscenely spread out on the Persian bedroom rug. Her mother sat beside him, stroking Carl's hand absently, re-arranging his pajama bottoms to cover him decently.

"Mother of God!" yelled Rosemary. "What are you doing? Call a doctor, Mamma. Call an ambulance. No, wait. I'll go get Mark." She started out the door.

"Rosemary," called Grace. "It's too late. He's gone."

Rosemary whirled about. "Sweet Jesus, Mamma, are you crazy? What do you mean *gone?*" She crossed the room, threw herself down, straddled her father's body, and began applying mouth-to-mouth resuscitation. "Goddamn it, Daddy, don't you dare die on me! You promised not to. Don't you dare go back on your promise. I'll never forgive you."

Her face was flushed, her eyes glazed, but she kept repeating the motions. In. Out. In. Out. In rhythmic desperation.

She turned to her mother. "Mamma, Mark is right downstairs. Go call him and tell him to get Bob Abercrombie. He's the best heart man in Florida. Call the hospital. Call the fire department. Only get Mark first." Rosemary fired orders wildly.

Grace pulled herself up and put both hands firmly on Rosemary's shoulders. "Rosemary," she said sternly, "stop that. Your father is gone."

Rosemary ignored her. She kept trying to breathe life into the still form beneath her. In. Out. In. Out. Pausing only to suck air into her own lungs. And direct her mother. "Call Mark, Mamma, and tell him to come right up here. And get the doctor. I think I'm making progress but I need help."

"Rosemary," commanded Grace, "let go. *Let him be. Please.*"

Rosemary stopped as suddenly as she had begun. She rose abruptly. Her hair was disheveled, her nightgown in disarray. Her breath was ragged. "All right, Mamma. I'll go get Mark, and we'll be right back. Now, don't do anything."

She rushed out of the room, ran down the long flight of winding stairs, opened the library doors, and flew inside.

She stood there, stunned; looked around, unbelieving. The room was empty. Mark wasn't there.

Frantically, Rosemary ran through the house, calling Mark's name, tears streaming down her face.

In Kate's dream, bells were ringing. Bells from a beautiful white stucco church. The church was built high on a hill, the highest hill in the surrounding area. The scene was tranquil, beautiful. The bells were glorious, breaking through the quiet of the morning with a purity that was stunning.

Only gradually, as consciousness returned, did Kate realize it wasn't a dream. She struggled awake and glanced at the clock on her bedside table: 3:20.

She flung a robe over her gown and groped her way sleepily down the stairs. Who on earth? But even before she reached the front door, she knew.

She looked through the peephole, unlatched the double lock, and opened the door.

Mark stood there, fatigue lines etched into his face. She thought she had never seen him look so defenseless.

"You win," he said. "I can't fight you anymore, Kate. I can't fight us. I only know I can't make it without you." He smiled crookedly. "May I come in?"

Silently, she stepped aside and let him in. And then, as the door closed behind him, she was in his arms and it was as though no time had elapsed since she was last there. It was as though this moment had been ordained from the beginning, destined to be, no matter how many barriers and obstacles were placed in its path.

Suddenly, all resistance left Kate as she allowed the moment to have its say.

BOOK THREE

The Price

1

The press had a field day speculating on the sudden death of Carl Schmittle. Could his be the first of a round of renewed Kirsten curses? Claiming new victims?

Carl Schmittle had been a vigorous sixty-five. Presumably with many active years ahead of him. Was his untimely death a portent of tragedies to come?

Did coveting the Kirsten, or owning it, unleash some mysterious force of retribution that was not satisfied until some mysterious need was met?

The names of its ten previous owners, and the list of disasters they met with, were recounted once again. Life had brought each of them tragedy. *If* the legend were to be believed.

New ownership of the Kirsten, the press concluded, would be announced at the upcoming House of Graet Christmas Ball to be held in Wellington.

"Che cosa chiassa!" What an uproar, exclaimed Consuela, not unmindful of the publicity value the increased exposure gave the Kirsten and the House of Graet. But her distress over the death of a dear friend claimed more of her attention.

How was it possible? She had spoken to him only the other day. He had sounded splendid. Surrounded and supported by the love of his family. She must call Grace and Rosemary at once to see what she could do to be of help.

Dio mio!

How ephemeral was life!

In Wellington, Bordon Granger read the press speculations and shook his head. "Poor bastard," he observed to Tami Hayes. "A

343

man spends his lifetime building an empire and he's memorialized for his involvement with a necklace."

Tami agreed. "Why anyone would even want that thing is beyond me."

But Bordon wanted it. For Tami. He still hadn't told her he was in the running for it. That, after all, was a surprise.

Which reminded him he had told Consuela he was dropping out.

Later in the day, Bordon went into his study, called Consuela, and told her he was back in.

At Elsinore, Mimzee Dawson read the press reports. "Horseshit," she exclaimed aloud. Bad luck happened to the careless. Or the stupid. She had patience with neither of these. Nor had she patience with reckless prophets of doom.

Besides, she was in a good mood and would allow nothing to mar it. Alain DuLac would soon bring her her very own Kirsten to play with. And that would keep her content until she had the real one to fondle.

At Casa Miramar, Rosemary Hunter attended to the business of making the funeral arrangements.

A part of her had died that would never live again. A light had gone out of her life that was forever extinguished. Nothing would ever change that. No prayer helped. No panacea existed to stop the pain. Even the memories of love hurt. It hurt to remember.

More than anything, she needed to forget.

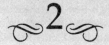

2

The funeral was held in Greenwich, Connecticut. Carl never really liked Florida, Grace explained. He had gone there for his health. He would be buried on land where they had built and lived and put down roots for almost thirty years.

Rosemary had her way too. The coffin was kept closed. "Daddy would have been appalled at people gawking at a waxy cosmeticized shell," insisted Rosemary. "No matter how professional the job."

Mark was amazed. Rosemary conducted herself with a poise and self-control he would not have thought her capable of. No tears. No hysterics. No histrionics.

"Daddy would have wished me to do this properly," Rosemary said when Mark complimented her.

Yet she barely paid attention to him. During the flight escorting Carl's body to Connecticut on the plane Mark had flown down in, Rosemary was civil to Mark. She answered when spoken to, but made no effort at conversation. Rather, it was Grace who nervously attempted small talk.

Late in the morning when Mark returned home from Kate's, Rosemary had been waiting for him.

"Daddy died early this morning, Mark," she told him in much the same tone she used to announce the evening menu.

"Oh, my God, Rosemary!" Instinctively, he reached out to her.

She stepped back. "No. It's all right. Mamma's with him now. We've made all the arrangements. We're taking him back to Greenwich."

"Of course. Whatever you think best." He still couldn't believe it. Death was the last thing Mark expected Carl to submit to.

Rosemary looked curiously at Mark. "Where were you early this morning? I looked all over for you."

"I couldn't sleep, Roe. I went for a drive."

"I see." If she didn't believe him, she didn't let on. She absently shifted a vase of flowers on the hall table from left to right, suddenly reminding Mark of Grace. But when Rosemary looked up at him again, her eyes were dark and undecipherable. "You know what, Mark? I learned something important this morning. We're alone. All of us. Isn't that funny? We cling to things, but we're really alone."

"Rosemary," said Mark, moving toward her again.

"Come," said Rosemary, stepping back once more. "Come see Daddy, Mark."

Marjorie Hunter flew up for the burial. So did Consuela. The church was filled to overflowing with friends, associates, clergy, politicians, senators, three governors, and the vice-president of the United States. All were people whose lives had been touched and affected by Carl Schmittle, the man, and Carl Schmittle, the generous contributor to ecclesiastical and political causes.

The Hunter girls were there. Kimberly standing close to Marjorie. Beth standing beside Grace. Rosemary and Mark stood together.

A high mass was said by the cardinal of the Washington diocese, another old friend of Carl's.

When Carl's body was lowered into the ground at his Connecticut estate, Grace swayed and had to be supported by Msgr. O'Leary, a friend of the family. Rosemary stood quietly watching the earth swallow up and claim the person who had the most influence on her life.

People offered the usual condolences to Grace and Rosemary.

"A blessing, Grace. Thank God, he never really suffered," said Father Ulrich.

"A tragedy, Rosemary. He had so much *energìa*. So much *amore* left in him," said Consuela.

Marjorie Hunter embraced her daughter-in-law. "I'm so very sorry, my dear."

"A good man, Grace," observed the cardinal. "He's with the angels now."

Is that where he is? wondered Rosemary. All her life she had accepted the teachings of the church and been comforted.

But now she felt empty.

She had done her duty. She had behaved the way her father would have wished. She had comforted her mother, greeted her father's friends and associates, officiated over the event with restraint and dignity.

But she was empty. And she was angry.

He had broken his promise.

He had left her.

And there was such a lonely aching core within her, she knew there were no words, no prayers, no comforts, to ever ease the pain that gripped her.

The girls had gone back to Palm Beach with Marjorie.

Mark had gone back to Washington.

Rosemary stayed with her mother for a few more days. There wasn't much more for her to do. There wasn't much for them to talk about. There never had been. And it seemed too late to begin now.

Rosemary was ready to go home.

Besides, she was beginning to feel edgy.

Earl was in the can when he heard someone thumping about. He opened the door and looked out, expecting to see Belinda.

It wasn't Belinda.

In the center of the room, an old lady with flaming red hair, wearing the wildest outfit he ever saw, stood pointing things out with a pearl-handled walking stick while barking commands to the nervous, fidgety spectacled dried-up prune of a dame with her.

"The curtains must go, Millicent. The furniture needs to be reupholstered and the room needs repainting," she commanded.

The fidgety dame took notes.

Mimzee, waving her walking stick, turned, spied Earl, stared for a moment, and asked, "Are you the groundskeeper's assistant?" Her stick was poised midair. Her eyes swept past him. "You aren't permitted to use the cottage bathrooms, you know."

Earl, stunned by the apparition before him, lost the powers of speech.

Mimzee's eyes bored into him. "What part of the grounds are you responsible for?"

"Huh?"

"Work! Where do you work, young man?"

"Uh, I don't work here, ma'am," stuttered Earl.

"You don't work here! Well, what the hell are you doing here?" barked Mimzee. "Speak up!" She poked her walking stick into one of Earl's ribs.

He jumped back. "Howie . . ." He was about to say Howie had introduced him to Belinda, who had invited him to stay there.

"You're a friend of Howie's?" interrupted Mimzee. Of course. Only Howie would find such riffraff and install it on her property.

"No. Of Belinda's."

"Belinda's? You are a friend of Belinda's?" Mimzee's red eyebrows flared upward. "Preposterous!" Earl stepped backward as Mimzee accented her words with sweeps of her stick. "You are telling me you are a guest here? Absurd. There are no guests at Elsinore unless they are specifically invited by me."

Elsinore! Now Earl knew. This was the witch Belinda warned him about. Jesus!

Mimzee turned to the frightened old bird with the note pad, who feared the intruder might have been a rapist and was relieved to learn it was just one of Belinda's friends, and barked, "Millicent, go fetch Belinda and bring her here at once."

"You," ordered Mimzee, directing Earl. "Stand over there, out of my way, until I get to the bottom of this."

She sat in a chair facing him. She did not invite him to sit. Instead, she continued to stare. She sniffed, "What is that odor, young man?"

Earl had just finished smoking a reefer.

Mimzee sniffed again. "Is that marijuana I smell?" She pointed the walking stick at him. "I do not permit smoking on these premises. I particularly do not permit joints." She looked at Earl suspiciously. "Are you a junkie?"

"No, ma'am," Earl assured her, keeping carefully out of range of Mimzee's walking stick. His rib still hurt.

"Humph," growled Mimzee, studying him with beady blue eyes.

Earl squirmed under the scrutiny.

Mimzee continued to stare and assess. Good-looking but weak. Crafty. He reminded her of one of her husbands.

Mimzee knew the type well. Hustler. Never did an honest day's work in his life if he could avoid it. No wonder he appealed to Howie.

But he'd said Belinda. Well, women were fools for good-looking parasites. She ought to know.

"Your name?" asked Mimzee at last. "What is it?"

Earl's first reaction was to lie. Under the spell of that fierce stare, he changed his mind. "Earl Blakely, ma'am."

"Obviously not related to the Blakelys of Sarasota."

"No, ma'am. Hollywood."

"That was a joke, dearie. No matter." Mimzee tapped her pearl-handled walking stick impatiently against the polished hardwood floor. The *thump, thump, thump* set Earl's teeth on edge.

What would she do? Call the police? Have him hauled into jail? He hadn't committed any crime. But this cuckoo obviously had clout. She looked as though she could get anyone to do anything she wanted.

Earl remained respectfully silent while becoming increasingly nervous. With relief, he spotted Belinda, followed by the weirdo who'd been sent to get her.

Mimzee waited until Belinda stood before her. With a withering look, she commanded, "Would you care to explain this *gentleman's* presence to me, dearie?"

Belinda remained unfazed. "Earl is the brother of an old school friend of mine," she explained. "He needed a place to stay for a couple of days."

Mimzee snorted. And pointed her stick in Earl's direction. "*That* creature is no relation to any school friend unless you all went to a reformatory."

"Really, Mimzee," protested Belinda. "It's the truth."

"Balls!" shouted her grandmother. She pointed her stick at Belinda. "Now, hear me out. Send your *friend's brother* packing. And I'll see you in twenty minutes in my rooms."

She rose, waved her walking stick at Millicent, commanded, "Follow me," and strode out.

"Poor baby," sympathized Belinda. "You look absolutely terrified. And no wonder. Isn't she the pisser, though?"

Earl allowed as though in all his travels he'd met no one quite like her.

"A witch," announced Belinda. "Didn't I warn you to stay out of sight?"

"I did. She didn't," complained Earl.

"Well," said Belinda. "Let me put on my thinking cap."

Following a less emotionally charged reaction to the situation, Mimzee had second thoughts. She reflected that perhaps providence had provided her with more of an opportunity than an irritant. The uninvited occupant of cottage 12 could prove useful.

Earl Blakely looked more experienced in nefarious pursuits than Howie. Probably because he'd been at it longer. The retrieval of the Kirsten was a delicate business.

Mimzee decided to introduce Earl into her plan.

But first, she had to keep him accessible.

And second, she needed to know more about him. She made one phone call and ordered a complete file on Mr. Earl Blakely of Hollywood. She suspected the information she gleaned would help keep Mr. Blakely in line.

When Belinda appeared for her command performance before "Queen Bess," she was prepared for a reckoning.

Instead, a benign Mimzee beckoned her closer. "I've been thinking, dearie. I may have acted hastily. That young man might need just a little help to straighten him out. I'm going to speak to the chief groundskeeper, Mr. Parkins, and see if he can use an assistant. I'm sure we can find something useful for him to do.

"Obviously, he can no longer stay in twelve. Parkins will find him suitable quarters in the servants' wing."

Thus was Earl Blakely given the opportunity to earn his bread by honest labor. It was not the course of action he would have chosen.

On the other hand, it was the only one offered him.

3

Polly Bowdin called to again extend the use of her cottage while she was in London. Consuela accepted. She was feeling cramped at The Breakers, and Derek was getting on her nerves. With more space between them, her nerves would improve.

What Consuela didn't know was that a call from New York had brightened Derek's spirits. There was a new play with a lead role custom-made for Derek.

A copy had been express-mailed to him.

It had just arrived.

There were, reflected Reenie, pluses and minuses in life.

At the moment, the minuses were in ascendancy. Julia Sheffield had come up with no new information on the mystery woman who whisked Earl Blakely away. The desk clerk Julia had talked to was off duty. A death in the family. He would be back in a day or so.

Reenie told her to keep on searching. She had complete confidence in Julia's ability to turn dead ends into thriving thorofares.

Another minus was Mark Hunter. The bastard never called to explain his Tuesday absence. Reenie was not a patient woman. She was, however, a vindictive one.

Her hunch had paid off and her persistence was rewarded. In her hot little hands she held the dossier on Earl Blakely, compiled and forwarded per her instructions to her British secretary.

Listed there were Earl's various skirmishes with the law. Scams. Swindles. Bad checks. Burglary. Drugs.

The beautiful tan that wicked boy sported was acquired re-

cently. Earl Blakely had spent the last twelve years in and out of
jails.

Also listed were the types of occupation he engaged in when he
was engaged. Bartending. Gambling. Ladies' escort. Male model.
Stints playing with small bands.

All in all, a checkered past. She wondered again if Earl Blakely
was the gentleman Tami Hayes visited. Reenie had nothing to go
on except a hunch. After all, lots of guys stayed at The Breakers
and went out to Wellington on business.

Still, the hunch persisted. A feeling of mystery persisted. Well,
hunches, plus a few other things, had got her where she was. And
mysteries, when they were explored, generally proved rewarding.

Consuela's move from The Breakers to Polly Bowdin's delighted her.

She luxuriated in the space. *"Molto grande! Maraviglioso!"* she
exclaimed, excitedly exploring the vast rooms.

Enthusiastically, she pointed out the advantages to Derek. The
gymnasium. The two pools. The ocean only a few hundred feet
away. Most of all, the space. Had he not felt cramped at The
Breakers?

He had not.

Ah, but this was a fine place for him to rest, undisturbed. He
would enjoy that. Trust her.

He'd been perfectly content at The Breakers, he pointed out.
And moving stuff from one place to another was not what he
considered restful.

"Dio mio!" complained Consuela to Kate, who helped with the
move. *"Che peso!"* What a burden!

What to do with him? She was almost sorry she had insisted he
come.

Now, if Louis were here, it would be a different tale. Louis did
not fatigue her with petulant demands and childish complaints.
She needed an escort, a companion, not a bearer of grievances.

Julia Sheffield called Reenie to report another hitch. The desk
clerk would be delayed one more day. Settling the deceased's affairs.

Julia did, however, have the juiciest bit of information to pass on. A dear friend of hers, Bebee Nolan, had dinner at Café L'Europe Saturday night. Drinks first at the Bistro bar. And Reenie would never guess whom Bebee saw and what she witnessed.

"I'm too damn hung over this mornin' for guessin' games, sugah," Reenie informed her. "Just spit it out."

Julia spat. All about Kate, Ben, Mark, Rosemary, and the Schmittles. "You know, of course, Carl Schmittle died early the following morning. Not that there's a connection. Still, it is a grisly coincidence. Bebee said the vibes between Kate Crowley and Mark Hunter were powerful enough to launch a missile and, during dinner, although neither of them looked at the other, the mood was *intense*."

"Darlin'," commented Reenie mildly while digesting the information, "sounds like your friend Bebee is given to hyperbole and an overactive imagination. But keep me informed. You never know. Meanwhile, follow up on that desk clerk. *That's* the information I'm really interested in."

When Reenie hung up the phone, she was anything but indifferent. She was furious. So that bastard had been in town with not even a phone call to announce his presence or explain his absence. Mark Hunter had to learn trifling with Reenie Boyd was a pursuit hazardous to his health.

But even more than fury, Reenie was staggered by the intensity of the pain she felt. Although she would admit it to no one, the knowledge that the *thing* between Mark and Kate Crowley still existed was the thrust that pierced. That there was someone else he cared about. Some *nobody*.

She vowed to undo Kate Crowley.

Reenie paced the floor wondering how to handle this new piece of information. Finally, she picked up the phone, called New York, spoke with her British secretary, and asked her to check out Kate Crowley. "Start with personnel, House of Graet. Find out where she's from. Tell them you have information on a legacy left her. Then check into her general background. Relatives, schools, that sort of thing. Look for the skeletons in her closet. And if you can't come up with any, a couple of live bodies will do. There has to be somethin' in her past. There generally is, darlin'. And I need this information quickly. Like yesterday."

353

* * *

It was exactly as though it had never ended. That's where her affair with Mark stood, thought Kate bleakly. She was exhilarated, buoyed up, enthralled. Lost in the feelings he aroused in her. She was also confused, helpless, and uncertain. Because she had relinquished control over her life once more.

Then there was Ben.

Who didn't take the news of Mark back in her life well at all.

"You certainly called the shots on that one," Ben told Kate harshly.

"Oh?" Kate wasn't sure what he meant.

"You said loving you could backfire."

"I didn't mean to hurt you, Ben," she protested weakly.

He didn't answer. What was the point? The lady never promised him a rose garden.

He hurt like hell. He wanted to throttle Mark Hunter, shake some sense into Kate, try to make her see what she was tossing aside.

And he was damned if he was into sharing. "I don't know about you, Kate, but I can't sleep with you while you're sleeping with someone else."

She flinched. "I'm sorry, Ben."

His smile was crooked. "Me too." He studied her quietly for a moment, turned quickly, and left.

4

Several days after returning to Casa Miramar, Rosemary accepted Marjorie's invitation to lunch at the Everglades.

Rosemary dressed with care. She looked pretty in an ivory silk shirtwaist dress belted in narrow brown crocodile. She wore matching crocodile pumps. An orange print Hermès scarf was looped casually around her neck.

Marjorie, as usual, looked elegant and crisp in a navy and red Adolfo suit.

Marjorie took her seat opposite Rosemary, noting with approval that Rosemary appeared in control of herself. "Sorry to be late, my dear. I was getting the girls off."

"How are they?" asked Rosemary wistfully.

"Marvelous. They're spending the day with the Kettle girls. And you know what an organized mother Amanda is. They'll come home refreshed but exhausted."

Rosemary nervously opened her silver and mother-of-pearl cigarette case. Then, remembering her mother-in-law's abhorrence of smoke, snapped it shut. "I miss them," she said somewhat plaintively.

"Of course you do, my dear. And they miss you. But if you'll indulge an aging grandmother for another week or so, I promise to return them intact. Besides, I really think it best you spend this time resting without bothersome interruptions."

"My children aren't bothersome," protested Rosemary.

"No, they're absolutely darling," agreed Marjorie. "But they do require a great deal of attention. And you, Rosemary, still look a bit peaked."

"I'm fine," insisted Rosemary.

"Of course you are, my dear. You need only allow yourself time to heal. The last thing we want to do is overdo."

The warning was implicit: *When you overdo, you get into trouble.*

Rosemary fiddled with the cigarette case. She was dying for a smoke. Maybe she could excuse herself and sneak into the ladies' room.

The waiter approached. Marjorie, knowing him, greeted him with just the right combination of charm and reserve.

"I think I'd like some wine, Rosemary. What about you?"

Rosemary was startled out of her reverie.

"A glass of wine will relax you," Marjorie assured her.

"Do you think so?"

"Of course, my dear." Marjorie ordered a bottle of Médoc '55, and the waiter departed. "One or two glasses a day of an alcoholic beverage are recommended. That's a known medical fact."

"Really?" mused Rosemary.

Marjorie nodded. "People who have one or two drinks a day live longer. Gracious, I'd be lost without my two nightly martinis." She smiled across the table at Rosemary. "It's only the *excesses* that get us into trouble."

Rosemary returned her smile. "You're right. The excesses cause trouble."

"And it isn't as though you were an alcoholic," added Marjorie.

"No," concurred Rosemary, "it isn't."

"Besides, you deserve to indulge yourself a bit." Marjorie leaned slightly forward. "I must tell you, Rosemary, how impressed I was with the way you conducted yourself at Carl's funeral. No one could have organized things better. Not to take away from your mother, of course. But you were a credit to your father's memory."

The waiter brought the Médoc, poured some for Marjorie, waited until she nodded, then poured for Rosemary.

"Thank you," said Rosemary.

She picked up her glass, raised it to her lips, and sipped thoughtfully. Marjorie was right. She had outdone herself. She deserved a reward. It wasn't as though she were an alcoholic.

It was much too early to go home. Besides, she had just begun to relax.

Lunch with Marjorie had been, as always, a trial, mitigated only by the introduction of that delightful beverage into the ordeal.

No excesses there, by God! Marjorie Hunter would never tolerate them. Everything was done in tasteful, moderate doses.

She, on the other hand, was a lady who *courted* excess. Nothing was done in moderation. When she did something, she did it big. And often.

She supposed she and Marjorie Hunter had little in common. Except for Mark. And the girls.

Well, the girls were just fine, but Mark, she decided objectively, left much to be desired as a son and father. As a husband, he was a complete dud.

The list of his lapses was endless. She ran through them. He was forever absent when she needed him. He was thoughtless, faithless, and conscienceless. What else? He was a cheat, a liar, a fornicator, a philanderer. And a rat. No doubt about it, Mark was a first-class rat.

So, who needed him?

Not she, for sure.

So Mark had a new tootsie in tow. So what? She had a little black book with a list of names. Men eager to bolster her spirits, warm her bed, make her laugh or tingle, or soothe her troubled soul. All she had to do was flip through the pages and make her selection.

The book must be getting mildewed. She hadn't opened it in almost two months.

For almost two months, she had been very, very good. And where did very, very good get you? It got you *very, very thirsty*.

Rosemary parked her Rolls convertible in the parking lot of Peter's Pub and checked her watch: 4:00 P.M. Almost in time for the cocktail hour. She had been driving aimlessly for over an hour. Now, she had a direction.

She smiled winsomely at the bartender-owner of Peter's Pub. "Hello, Pete."

His face registered pleasure at the sight of her. "Mrs. Hunter! Long time no see!"

"Long time," she agreed.

"How've you been, Mrs. H.?" He remembered reading about her father. "Sorry to hear about your dad."

"Thank you, Pete," she said. "I've been fine. And you?"

"Can't complain." He grinned. "Doesn't do much good, anyway."

"No, it doesn't," smiled Rosemary.

"What'll it be, Mrs. H.?"

Rosemary concentrated. "Something special. And festive."

"You celebratin'?"

"Let's say I've interrupted my mourning."

"How about a mimosa? You used to favor those."

She rewarded him with another smile for his inspiration. "Perfect. A mimosa it'll be."

She watched with interest as Pete prepared the champagne and orange juice, poured it into a frosted long-stemmed, wide-bowled glass, and served it.

She sipped delicately, then approved. "Delicious. As always."

He grinned, excused himself, and went to the other end of the bar to serve another customer.

Rosemary lifted her glass, took a longer, deeper swallow, felt the liquid slide easily down her throat, all her little nerve ends tingling with approval. She drank slowly, with satisfaction.

She removed the House of Graet silver and mother-of-pearl cigarette case and matching lighter from her purse, removed a cigarette, lighted it, and drew in deeply. She exhaled and studied her reflection in the bar mirror. Framed by a glistening array of labeled liquor bottles. She smiled at the effect with wry humor.

She felt lighthearted for the first time since her father's death.

The bar stool beneath her felt familiar and comfortable. The lighting in the bar was soft, diffuse. The atmosphere was warm, accepting. She experienced the old feeling of camaraderie, the sense of belonging so sadly lacking most of the time in her life.

"Another mimosa, Mrs. H.?"

Rosemary's eyes glinted. "Why not?" she said.

5

Mimzee Dawson read the file on Earl Blakely with intense satisfaction.

She'd been right. He was just the one to assist Howie in the Kirsten heist.

And she held in her hand the evidence that would keep him in line, should he entertain any thoughts of independent action.

She read through the file again. Earl Blakely could give Howie lessons in dishonesty.

Not that Howie needed any. He had enough crooked genes to manage quite nicely.

If it hadn't been for her sharp eye, the Fabergé theft would have gone undetected. How he managed to steal them in the first place was beyond her. And Howie was not about to enlighten her.

Well, let him put his fine hand to stealing *for* her, instead of *from* her.

One way or another, she would have her Kirsten.

With a couple of crooks on the premises like Earl and Howie, Mimzee was sure she could accomplish that.

All she had to do was work out a foolproof plan.

Howie Caine lay on his bed, arms folded behind his head, staring forlornly up at the ceiling. He needed $100,000 for a multimillion-dollar coke deal. The irony was the amount was a piss hole in hell compared to what he had in trust. Locked up and sealed away was a fortune that would one day make him a very rich man.

Who the hell could wait five years?

Not him! Not Howie Caine!

But there was no way he could get hold of any of that dough. Not until he was twenty-six. Nor could he borrow from Belinda. He'd tried that. She was not into philanthropy, she informed him.

As for his grandmother, Howie thought it hardly likely Mimzee would advance him a red cent. On any deal of his—honorable, questionable, or larcenous. And there was no way he could tap into her Fabergé collection again. That, and her jewels, were sealed off as tight as his trust.

The world was conspiring against him. The system was designed to stymie him. Fuck the system!

Ah, but the deal was sweet! A guy who called himself Joey Demarco, Howie's Miami connection, had the inside track on a Colombian shipment due in. Five hundred grand to buy. Five men to buy in at 100 grand each. Joey had three men lined up. He would make the fourth. If Howie could come up with his share, Joey would cut him in.

They could buy it for one half of a million. And sell it for $5 million. A 900-percent profit on the initial investment. Jesus, how often did you find a deal that sweet?

He could feel his palms sweat. To be so close to freedom and so far from deliverance was more than he could deal with. He needed that dough. Somehow, somewhere, he would have to get hold of it. No way could he let this deal slip through his fingers. No way at all.

Howie jumped off the bed and walked restlessly around the room trying to think of an angle, some way he could get hold of some scratch. But try as he might, he came up with nothing. Zilch!

His mind raced through a mental list of names of people he might approach. Again, nothing. Zero!

Frustrated, he grabbed his car keys, raced down the stairs and out the door, hopped into his 280 ZX, and steered the car out the long gravel driveway onto the boulevard. He drove aimlessly south along A1A for half an hour, then turned the car around and headed back toward Palm Beach.

He'd gotten himself into a state. He needed to get his mind off the obstacles that blocked him. Sometimes, just backing off a bit did the trick. You back off and then, whammo, out of the blue, a solution hit you. It had happened to him that way before. Pitch blackness one minute, then, bingo, the light.

He decided he needed a drink. He found a parking space in front of Peter's Pub, parked the 280 ZX, pocketed the car keys, and sauntered inside.

He sat at the bar.

"What'll it be, Howie, m'lad?" asked Peter Flannery approaching him.

Howie grinned boyishly. "A Heineken, Pete."

Rosemary Hunter picked up her drink, moved two stools down, and sat next to Howie. "Well, if it isn't little Howie Caine," she said, studying him intently. "Are you really old enough, Howie, to frequent dens of iniquity?"

Howie bristled. "Plenty old enough," he said indignantly. "I'm twenty-one."

Rosemary sighed audibly. "Are you really? You have no idea, Howie, how very old you have just made me feel. As penance for your indiscretion, I suggest you buy me a drink."

Howie had the feeling Rosemary Hunter was pulling his leg. But she was a real foxy lady. Even if she was pretty old. Way past thirty. Still, he was flattered by her interest. "What would you like, Mrs. Hunter?"

"Rosemary," corrected Rosemary. "Call me Rosemary, Howie. In dens of iniquity, Mrs. Hunter sounds a bit formal, don't you agree? And terribly, terribly stuffy." She thought for a moment about what she *would* like. Finally, "I'll have a Black Velvet, thank you."

"A Black Velvet for Mrs.—for Rosemary," Howie told Peter Flannery.

The bartender looked carefully at Rosemary. "You sure, Mrs. H.?" She had already had three mimosas before switching to champagne cocktails. She had also consumed three of those. Now she was planning to switch to champagne and Guinness stout. He knew from experience her hollow leg was not nearly as hollow as she liked to believe.

Rosemary stared back. "I'm sure." She turned to Howie. "Now, tell me, Howie, just when did you turn into this glorious vision of male perfection?"

Howie expanded under Rosemary's frankly admiring scrutiny.

Peter Flannery placed the Heineken in front of Howie, the Black Velvet reluctantly in front of Rosemary.

She lifted the glass, raised it toward Pete coolly, turned her attention once again toward Howie, and said, "Well, you haven't answered my question. Where *have* you been hiding these past few years?"

"Oh, I've been around," Howie assured her.

Rosemary continued to hold his eye. "Have you? Been around?"

They sparred back and forth over another drink while Howie craftily plotted where and how he would bed down this fox. The prospect was exciting. Most of the chicks he'd been laying lately bored him. He liked a woman with experience, and from what he'd heard, Rosemary Hunter had plenty of that.

When the bartender came to take new drink orders, Howie was surprised to see it was someone new. "Where's Pete?" he asked.

"Gone for the evening," replied his replacement.

"Well, he deserves a rest," noted Rosemary generously. "He certainly works hard enough." She raised her empty glass appealingly. "But we're still here, aren't we, Howie? And thirsty too."

When the drinks arrived, Rosemary drained hers quickly. Howie hoped she wouldn't get too smashed.

Suddenly, as though remembering something, Rosemary glanced at her watch and registered alarm. "Oh, my, I was due home hours ago."

She slid off the stool, opened her purse, fished out her wallet, removed some bills, and slapped them down on the bar. She also left a sizable tip. "My share," she said.

She leaned toward Howie, large brown eyes teasing, and whispered in his ear, "Thanks for the drink, you luscious thing. And give me a ring in a few years. We might be able to get something on."

Before he could respond, Rosemary weaved her way past him and out of the bar.

Howie sat there, dumbfounded.

The bitch had led him on. Laughed at him all the while. Tease! Cunt! That's what she was.

Well, one day soon, he vowed, Rosemary Hunter would learn what it cost to make a fool out of Howie Caine.

Rosemary walked to her car, drove it a block away, and parked it.

She walked to the rear entrance of the pub and climbed the stairs to the upstairs apartment.

She entered the apartment, weaving slightly, and stood there. Peter Flannery watched her. "Long time no see, Rosie."

Rosemary swayed slightly as she began unbuttoning the ivory silk shirtwaist.

Peter put his arms behind his head as he watched her. "Take it slow and easy, Rosie, m'girl. No need to rush. We've got the rest of the night."

She stepped out of her dress and, with a well-shod foot, kicked it aside. She slipped out of her panties; removed her bra.

Upright and naked, she walked unsteadily to the couch, stretched herself out beside him, and brushed her lips against his.

"What in hell took you so long?" he demanded.

"I was being circumspect, darling," she explained.

"The hell you were. You were playin' that kid like a harmonica."

Rosemary smiled lazily. "Just having a little fun. Passing time."

Peter slid a hand over Rosemary's breast. "Why waste time playin' with children, Rosie, when it's a real man you need?"

"But such a beautiful child, Pete," she teased.

She started to rise.

"Where you goin'?"

"For a drink."

He pushed her back. "You won't be needin' any more, Rosie. I've got somethin' far more satisfyin' for you than booze." He lifted her hand and pressed it over his swollen crotch.

Rosemary laughed. "Well, what are we waiting for, darling? Let's party."

6

Consuela's afternoon was productive. Two million dollars' worth. She had accomplished that coup by taking to Sheik Abu some *favoloso* pieces she knew he could not resist.

The entire parcel was purchased with a few strokes of Abu's twenty-four-karat gold pen.

The mission was conducted on board Abu's yacht, the *Kismet,* where she and Derek joined him and Danielle, Abu's Eurasian paramour, for a ride up the Intracoastal.

The entire day was glorious until Consuela and Derek were back at Polly Bowdin's and Derek began to complain.

"Jesus, Connie, you should take some of your own advice. You tell me to relax and you can't even go on a goddamned outing without dragging half the store along. You were supposed to relax, not sell."

Consuela was shocked. "Selling *is* relaxing, *caro.* It is always relaxing to do something you do well."

There was another argument following the evening at Count Paolo Respighi's, where Derek and Consuela joined Paolo and his Italian film starlet, Serafina Stolazo, for dinner.

Consuela had brought along some pieces she had promised to show Paolo. Serafina fell in love with them. Paolo purchased.

It was when they arrived home that Derek again upbraided Consuela for dragging merchandise with her everywhere she went. It was tacky. Offensive.

He was offensive, shouted Consuela. She did not drag merchandise everywhere. Only to special people. Did not Paolo thank her? Did not Derek hear Paolo say how he appreciated the trouble she, Consuela, went to to accommodate him?

Paolo hated shopping. Shopping was for peasants. Paolo preferred merchandise to be brought to him. So he could select in comfort. Did Derek know that?

Dio mio, he was a pill. Picking, protesting always. *Basta!*

"Enjoy, *caro,*" she admonished. "Before you are an old man and it is too late."

As an afterthought, she had another piece of instruction. Why did he not call his mother's friend's daughter again? He had been pleasant when he returned from that encounter.

Derek took Consuela's advice. The following night, when she was out, he called to invite Sandy to dinner.

She suggested her place, 7:00 P.M. She'd do the cooking. You never knew what herbs and spices the chef put into something when you ate out.

Sandy Stone walked to the ocean on her lunch break, sat on a bench facing the sea, and reflected on this unexpected turn of events.

She had actually invited him to dinner. Offered to cook for him. A man who, on first impression, seemed an insufferable conceited bore.

It was only at lunch that she saw another side of him. Shy. Insecure. Appealing.

There was a little boy in Derek Tracey that had never been nourished.

That was the part she found appealing.

Sandy's studio apartment reminded Derek of his first New York apartment. Only Sandy's view was better. From a corner of her bathroom window, you got a view of a corner of the Atlantic Ocean. From the one window in Derek's apartment, all you got to view was the back side of another New York tenement.

"I cooked the chicken with lemon juice," Sandy explained, serving it at a candle-lit table. "Butter is definitely a stomach irritant. The potatoes are boiled and the salad's covered with just a trace of lemon. So you can eat without worry." She smiled reassuringly as she poured milk for him.

Derek noted how pretty she was. The glow from the candles seemed to spark her red hair with gold; deepen the color of her eyes.

He didn't know when he'd felt so comfortable. Everything about Sandy was designed to cut right through trivia to basics. Like what was really important in life. And she was genuinely interested in what interested him.

Derek told her about the play with the part in it he'd barter his soul for.

Maybe that wasn't necessary, teased Sandy. Her smile was so engaging, his stomach did a flip-flop.

All through the lemon chicken (delicious, insisted Derek, as he accepted a second portion), he talked. About his plans, his goals, his ideals. He told Sandy things he had never disclosed to anyone. She was that easy to talk to.

Her comments were succinct, sensible, and insightful.

It was a relief to be freed from the tinsel of Consuela's world. Derek realized how turned off he was by it. And how desperately he needed an honest relationship.

Sandy served cheesecake for dessert. "My mother's recipe," she told Derek. She couldn't believe she was trying to entrap him with food. But her mother's words kept returning . . . "the way to a man's heart . . ."

Derek took a mouthful of cheesecake. "Say, this is terrific."

Sandy nodded. She wondered when he'd make his pass.

"You're terrific," Derek said, smiling the sincere Blaine Blandings smile that won him millions of fans.

Sandy joined their ranks. And wondered how she'd handle the pass once he made it.

Derek noted the flickering candlelight catching the red in Sandy's hair. Her eyes seemed even darker than before. But her quick bright mind was what intrigued him. "You're sure you're not a psychologist?" he asked.

Sandy shook her head. "No, but you'd be amazed at the insights you pick up in retail," she told him.

Sandy peered at her reflection critically in the mirror as she removed her makeup.

She examined her face, turned it, studied the nose.

Not bad!

So, what went wrong?

The first time she wanted a guy to make a pass, he didn't even try.

Maybe she'd been too domestic. Or too intellectual.

Next time she'd wear a scarlet dress, a smoldering look, and keep her mouth shut.

Would there be a next time?

Sandy sincerely hoped so. Because she was definitely interested.

And she had revised her opinion of actors. Not all of them were conceited dolts. Not even all good-looking ones. Derek Tracey was sensitive, and considerate, and sweet.

And sexy. Very definitely sexy.

Mark tried to reach Rosemary by phone. She wasn't home, nor had she told any of the servants where she would be. "Except for meeting the senior Mrs. Hunter at the Everglades," the house-keeper informed him.

He called Marjorie, who had absolutely no idea where Rosemary was.

"Well, I'm sure she's off somewhere with friends. She was in such good spirits, and we had a positively delightful lunch. Rosemary opened up and was quite chatty. We even had a couple of glasses of wine together. I was really pleased to see her unwind a bit."

He thought he hadn't heard her correctly. "You *what?*"

"*What* what, dear?"

"What did you say you had together?"

"Why, a couple of glasses of Médoc, dear. Perhaps three. I really don't remember."

"You gave Rosemary wine?"

"Well, you needn't sound as though I threw her to the floor and poured the liquid forcibly down her throat. I simply asked her if she would like a glass of wine, as I was having one. . . ."

"Rosemary does not drink wine, Mother," explained Mark patiently. "Rosemary does not drink anything alcohol-based. Because Rosemary is an alcoholic."

"Nonsense! I never for one minute believed that rubbish. Rosemary is a woman with many problems. Problems that are not to be blamed on alcohol, Mark. If anything, she perked up after a couple of glasses of wine."

"You're damned right she perked up," shouted Mark, losing patience. "And now that she's perked, she's probably off somewhere getting poured."

"Really! It was only a few glasses of wine. There is no need to dramatize."

"I'm not dramatizing, Mother. You just don't know what you've done."

Furious with his mother, he hung up.

Mark called Rosemary all night. At eight, nine, ten, eleven, twelve. Every hour on the hour. At 2:00 A.M., he woke the housekeeper and had her check Rosemary's room. Rosemary was not in it.

He called Kate. Of course he knew she was asleep, he said testily. He had a perfectly good Cartier quartz clock in front of him that provided him with accurate time. But he was going out of his mind and he needed to talk to her. She was the one sane element in his life. Outside of his kids.

Kate brushed the sleep from her eyes and tried to rouse herself. "Tell me what's wrong, Mark," she urged.

He told her. He was worried sick about Rosemary. He couldn't see her through another drunk. My God, she had to be crazy. Crazy like a fox. Difficult to track down. Remember the last one? When he'd tracked her to the Bahamas and confronted her, she didn't even remember boarding the goddamned plane to get there. One week she'd been there. One week in a blackout. Not remembering one goddamned episode. She was capable of anything because she was no longer responsible. She was not connected to reality. Not when she drank. No man in his right mind could stay with a woman like that.

Kate tried to calm him. They'd been through this before, she reminded him. She was certain Rosemary was all right. She'd probably turn up tomorrow, intact, and annoyed at Mark's lack of confidence in her. Rosemary was resilient. It was important to remember that.

There was no pacifying him. So Kate listened as Mark disgorged anxiety and spent his wrath.

Only it wasn't spent. In the midst of it, he made a decision. "I'm flying down."

Kate was alarmed. "At this hour? Mark, be sensible. Wait until morning. She'll probably be back by then."

"I can't wait. I have to find her before she does something god-awful."

"Mark, please," began Kate.

He had hung up. For Kate, there was no longer any possibility of sleep. She was wide-awake, every nerve in her body alerted. She would spend the rest of the night frantic with worry, she knew.

She rose, wrapped a warm velour robe about her, slipped her feet into fluffy mules, and padded downstairs to the kitchen to heat some milk.

She reviewed the conversation, wondering why she experienced a sense of déjà vu. Then she knew. Once again, she was cast in a scenario she had played before. All the characters were in place. All the attitudes were established.

Mark, crazy with worry over Rosemary's antics.

Kate, crazy with worry over Mark's reactions.

And Rosemary, drunkenly improvising the script.

Rosemary stole into the house at 3:00 A.M., showered, changed, packed two small suitcases, wrote a hurried note, and left.

The note read: "Mark. I've gone off for a couple days holiday with friends. Don't fret. Say hello to the girls for me and tell them I'll call them. Rosemary. P.S. I really need a change, Mark. Daddy's death upset me more than I let on."

In addition to the two suitcases, Rosemary took her little black book.

7

Shakespeare said it: "When troubles come, they come not single spies, but in battalions."

What he didn't say, decided Reenie Boyd, was that goodies come packaged the same way. Hers came in a batch of three.

Goodie #1. The clerk from the Lake Worth motel, having completed his postdeath duties, returned and provided Julia Sheffield with the information she requested. The young lady who bailed Earl Blakely out drove a red Mercedes, Florida license plate BG 12. He jotted the number down, something he did automatically, a result of thirty years on the New York City police force.

He thought the young lady and Earl Blakely an unlikely combination, worthy of his suspicions.

Julia Sheffield passed the information on to Reenie Boyd, who called her contact at the motor vehicle bureau in West Palm Beach. The owner of the Mercedes, license BG 12, she was told, was Belinda Graham.

It took only a minute or two for Reenie to riffle through her mental file and attach the name to the picture of the slender, dark-haired granddaughter of Palm Beach's reigning social queen, Mimzee Dawson.

Well, now, things were pickin' up!

Reenie set about locating Belinda Graham's unlisted telephone number. The process took only a few cursory phone calls.

The second batch of good news was delivered Federal Express from Reenie's British secretary—material gathered on the past and present of one Kate Crowley, currently vice-president of the House of Graet, Palm Beach.

Reenie pored over photocopies of old Worcester news clips,

reviewed the murder-suicide headlines of the socially prominent professional couple, noted the faded photographs of the solemn dry-eyed orphan at the burial site, flanked by the Springfield maiden aunts and bolstered by neighbors and friends.

Included in the file were the names and addresses of the two psychiatrists consulted by Katherine Crowley, college information, data on her career with the House of Graet, and sparse information on her personal life in her adult years. No mention of her liaison with Senator Mark Hunter. Kate Crowley and Mark Hunter had been successfully circumspect regarding their connection.

Reenie Boyd put the file aside. So that's who Mark was involved with! That's who her competition was!

One thing was clear. Mark was definitely not operating from a position of strength. Not only did he have a wife capable of providing banner headlines, he had a mistress who was a tabloid writer's dream. Accompanied by a well-documented past the press would have a field day with.

Mark Hunter could kiss his presidential aspirations good-bye. A man with a stick of dynamite in each hand was hardly likely to inspire the sort of public confidence required to pull voters to polls for him.

Reenie sat back, digesting the information, while she decided how best to utilize it.

Earl Blakely had a penchant for reading gossip columns. He never knew what piece of information he would pick up that he could convert into cash. Now he knew he'd hit pay dirt.

The *Palm Beach Daily News* was the paper that jogged his memory. A picture of a resplendent Reenie Boyd pictorially enjoying the festivities at a Palm Beach gala graced the paper. Gowned, jeweled, and surrounded by an attentive audience, Reenie seemed to smile up at Earl. Remember me? she appeared to ask.

Earl found Reenie's name printed among the list of names identifying the people in the photograph and remembered.

He might be late cashing in his rain check, but better late than never.

He hurried to the phone in the groundskeeper's quarters and dialed The Breakers.

He asked to speak with Reenie Boyd.

Thus was Reenie's third little bonus delivered.

Mark Hunter landed his twin-engine Cessna at Palm Beach International Airport, rented a car from a new Avis lady, and drove it frantically to his house. Fortunately, no police car was nearby to observe and detain him.

He was exhausted. He was also tense from flying under less than perfect conditions, and furious with Rosemary for putting him through this additional stress.

He barely greeted the staff, rushed upstairs to search the empty bedroom, and discovered Rosemary's note.

He read it once incredulously, read it again fretfully, then read it a third time with alarm.

He went downstairs to the library, poured himself a stiff drink, and collapsed in the wing chair facing the fireplace.

He picked up Rosemary's note and read it a fourth time. Very thoughtfully.

Now, if he were crazy like Rosemary, and he had the whole world to choose from, where would he choose to go?

Rosemary Hunter perched on the stool of the Lindbergh Field Airport Bar in San Diego and smiled at the good-looking dark-haired bartender.

He smiled back. "Perrier?" he asked. "In a frosted glass with a sliver of lime?"

Rosemary was pleased he remembered. "I'm off my diet. Let's make it a Scotch this time," she suggested.

He never expected to see her again. Chicks wandered in and out. Some hung around, others passed through. But this one had been different. Hard to forget.

He placed the drink in front of her.

Rosemary gripped it easily. "The last time we met," she told him, "we dispensed with the amenities. This time, let's not." She smiled again. "Your name?"

"Pete Reilly," he said.

Another Pete. Another bartender. Another Irishman. Another bender. Rosemary's world seemed suddenly filled with *anothers*.

"I'm Rosemary Stuart," said Rosemary. "It's nice to meet you, Pete Reilly."

"And good to see you again, Miss—Mrs.," as he noticed her ring, "Stuart."

"Rosemary will do," said Rosemary, lifting her Scotch for a long swallow.

"You on your way back to The Golden Door?" the bartender asked.

"No," said Rosemary. "I came here to see you, Pete."

He grinned. "You're kidding!"

"Do I look as though I'm kidding, Pete?" she asked.

He felt an unaccustomed flush settle over him, then collected himself. "What can I do for you—Rosemary?"

"First, Pete," she told him, "you can get me another Scotch." She smiled slowly. "After that, we'll see."

Whatever possessed her to get on a plane and fly all the way to San Diego to see someone she didn't even know? It was the sort of bizarre impulse Mark labeled crazy, inappropriate, alcoholic.

Except, she was looking for something. Something she had lost.

Now, if she could only remember what it was, she'd feel better.

8

Consuela spent the morning at the House of Graet. First, she wanted to make certain all the ball arrangements had been attended to.

Secondly, she wished to oversee the displays of jewels sent down from New York. She strolled the aisles, checked each vitrine, noted the guards standing discreetly by, and voiced her approval.

It did her heart good to see everything displayed to best advantage. It was rewarding to see how the jewel of the House of Graet crown outdid itself.

She praised Kate, complimented the House of Graet manager, and charmed the associates by chatting with each one individually. At last, she came to Sandy.

"Ah," said Consuela, flashing the famous dimple, "this is the little friend of my good friend Derek Tracey." She remembered Derek had told her he had dined with Sandy.

Not having the advantage of a dimple, Sandy smiled and raised her chin so Dr. Gruber's nose job could be seen to best advantage.

"Bella," approved Consuela.

Sandy, not certain whether she meant the nose job or the rest of her, responded charmingly. *"Grazie,"* she said.

Consuela looked at her shrewdly, then, convinced the little redhead was merely being polite, said *"Scusi,"* and moved on.

She lunched with Kate and learned that Ben was no longer in the picture. But that Mark Hunter was.

"A mistake, I fear, *cara.* I do not wish to interfere, but . . ."

"Don't, then," interrupted Kate sharply. Startled, she apologized.

"It is all right, Kate. You are quite right. It is none of my business."

"No, of course it is." Kate was genuinely shocked by her outburst.

Consuela nodded sympathetically. "I speak as your friend, *cara*. I do not wish to see you hurt." She paused. "And I did so like your Benjamin."

"So did I," confessed Kate.

Consuela sighed. "Life does not always present us with fair choices."

"No, it doesn't," agreed Kate sadly.

Back in Kate's office, Consuela placed a call to the New York store, chatted with Suzy, checked on sales, and asked to be transferred to Louis-Philippe's line.

"Louis," she cried. "I expected you to be here by now."

He apologized. "A last-minute delay. I'm getting things together so I can leave tomorrow with a clear conscience."

"You and your conscience," she rebuked. "How am I ever going to teach you to relax?"

He laughed, "I may be beyond redemption."

"Never," insisted Consuela. "Teaching you to relax may turn out to be my greatest challenge."

"I hope not. It's too small a challenge to hold your interest for long."

"To the contrary. I can see it will require a great deal of imagination and inventiveness."

She hung up the phone and turned to Kate. "That man is a trial sometimes. I can see he will require a great deal of attention." The dimple flashed wickedly. "But I suspect the effort will be more than a little rewarding."

Kate smiled back at Consuela, then asked about Derek. "Is he enjoying himself?"

Consuela's wicked smile turned wry. "Who can tell? He is a complainer. Complainers do not know how to enjoy. They only know how to complain. That, *cara,* they enjoy to excess."

She thought about the little redhead.

When Derek dined with her, he asked Consuela if she minded.

"Why would I mind?" she had replied. "It is good to have friends your own age."

Now Consuela decided to encourage the friendship.

Perhaps the little redhead could coax a smile out of him.

She, Consuela, was past caring.

Derek hated to admit it, but Consuela was right. It *was* better at Polly Bowdin's. He could rest undisturbed. And he did relax more.

But he wouldn't give her the satisfaction of telling her so.

He had told her about dinner at Sandy's. She hadn't minded. Derek wondered how she would react if he told her he was planning to see Sandy again.

Well, hell, he and Consuela weren't welded together. He was a free agent. So was she. That was the way she always wanted it.

It struck him more and more lately that he and Consuela were miles apart in life goals.

He couldn't get enthused about the things she got a kick out of. He didn't care about Kirstens and raffles and bushels of gems and what rock got sold to which count.

His sights were set on larger horizons.

Sandy seemed to understand that. She understood a lot of things about him. Things he didn't even understand himself.

Derek needed to see her again.

He was about to call and ask her out when his New York agent called with the news that the part in the play he had sent Derek was his. Without an audition. The author told him the part was written with Derek in mind. Now Derek was needed in New York for the necessary paperwork. And rehearsals would begin in a couple of weeks.

He couldn't believe it. The part he would have bartered his soul for. And it was his. Without any sweat.

He called the airlines, booked a flight, packed a small suitcase, and left a note to Consuela explaining the situation.

He'd call from the city. Let her know when he'd be back.

He didn't even have time to call Sandy.

But when he came back, Derek decided, he'd book himself into The Breakers. It didn't seem right to continue to date one woman from the borrowed house of another.

He was, after all, a man of principles.

Consuela found the note when she returned home from lunch. And shrugged.

Life without Derek would be simpler. She could come and go as she wished, without constant criticism about her life-style.

Dio mio! Who needed to be disturbed so?

Besides, Louis was due in tomorrow. What a pleasure to have a grown man around her again instead of a petulant little boy.

Louis had made plans to stay at The Breakers.

It was in Consuela's mind to install him in the quarters at Polly Bowdin's that Derek had just vacated.

That way, Louis would be close by.

So she could avail herself of all his expertise.

Rosemary woke up in a strange bed in a strange hotel room. She couldn't remember how she got there. A strange man lay beside her. She couldn't remember who he was.

Her head ached and her throat was parched. She reached for the half-empty bottle of vodka on the bedside table, splashed some into a glass, and swallowed it. It burned going down, and it didn't quench her thirst.

The body beside her stirred. The eyes opened. The gaze was sleepy but intimate. "A little early for that, isn't it, doll?"

Rosemary looked at him coldly. "I'm not your doll. And it's none of your business," she told him.

The stranger grinned. "Maybe you'd better have some. You were much nicer last night. Not so sharp-tongued." He stretched lazily, kicking back the sheet, his naked body lean but well-muscled, completely uncovered. "Last night you made everything my business."

Rosemary never took her eyes from his. "That so?" She wondered which name in her little black book fit his description. Or whether he was a new entry.

She looked around. Where was she? Crystal-clear blue water, fine white sand, glistened beyond the bedroom terrace. "Nice place," observed Rosemary carefully.

"You mean this hotel?"

"No—this place." She swept an arm out airily.

"Oh, you mean Acapulco."

"Yes—Acapulco." Now she knew where she was. But, still, not how she got there.

The young man placed the palm of his hand on Rosemary's belly, the fingers sliding into thick pale pubic hair. "Tell me the truth, babe. You don't know where the hell you are, do you?"

"Of course I do," snapped Rosemary.

"Or who I am? What my name is?"

Rosemary's eyes narrowed. "Your name is . . ."

His hand started to work its way downward. "Adam," he said. "And you're Eve, right? That's what you told me last night. So, what d'you say, Eve? Let's explore paradise again."

Despite herself, Rosemary was aroused. "What did you have in mind—Adam?"

"Why don't I show you, Eve? The way I showed you last night," responded Adam.

She wasn't a nice person. Nice persons didn't wake up in strange hotel rooms with strange men. Nice persons had control of their lives. Nice persons remembered things.

She was a nice person, once. A good Catholic girl. The kind her mother approved of. No, her mother never approved. Only her father loved her, listened to her, understood her, adored her, and approved of her.

Would Daddy be disappointed now? If she could talk to him, he'd understand. He'd listen. And help her.

If she told Daddy she'd lost something, he'd help her find it. If she told him she couldn't remember what it was, he'd help her remember.

She had to talk to Daddy.

So he could help her remember.

What it was she had lost.

9

Earl Blakely didn't know what he expected to gain from his call to Reenie Boyd, but he was desperate. He was tired of busting his ass on the grounds of Elsinore. Being assistant to the grounds-keeper was not his idea of upward mobility. It was hard work, something he tried to avoid as a matter of principle.

He had another problem. He needed courtin' money. He'd found his heiress, but he needed to wine and dine her in the style to which she was accustomed. That broad from The Breakers might just provide the dough he needed to keep things going for him.

He'd had plenty of experience with that type. He'd read the open invitation in her eyes the first time they'd met. All he had to do to have her eating out of the palm of his hand was to light her fire. All he had to do to separate her from some hard cold cash was to please her.

A piece of cake! Without a worry to deter him, and with more than a trace of his usual confidence, Earl Blakely waited while the desk clerk rang the number of Reenie Boyd's Breakers' suite.

Reenie expected to gain many things from Earl's visit. Her cultivated sense of smell had sniffed a story from the beginning.

She had accepted Earl's call with delight, warmly suggesting he come collect his rain check at her suite. "Long overdue, sugah," she told him. She had despaired of ever seeing him again. They must remedy that quickly.

Earl hesitated. The thought of the possibility of running into Bordon Granger chilled him. He didn't for one minute believe Granger's threat was an idle one. That bastard meant business!

Still, the probability of running into him was slim, he decided.

And worth the risk. He agreed to drinks at Reenie's suite at 5:30. He'd be off work by then—a point of information he did not share with Reenie. No way did he want this classy chick to know how he was earning his bread these days. Front was everything. You act poor, you're treated poor. Like shit. Earl intended to be treated royally.

And so he was. Reenie couldn't do enough for him. She poured his bourbon with a generous hand while she sipped hers slowly and deliberately. So mesmerized was Earl by Reenie's ubiquitous southern charm, plus all that expensive Jack Daniel's, he failed to notice. And made his first mistake.

He relaxed. His second mistake. He looked good, he knew. And prosperous. A combination hard to beat. He wore his $495 cashmere camel sports jacket over an Irish linen shirt with brown wool trousers. He stuck out his Gucci hand-stitched loafers and concentrated on Reenie.

Reenie wore her working clothes. Guaranteed to loosen tongues. A black silk charmeuse cocktail skirt with a deep center slit and a full-sleeved white silk blouse with a deep V neckline. When she crossed her legs and leaned forward to freshen Earl's drinks, Reenie's assets were boldly declared.

Earl's plan was to draw Reenie out, to get her to talk about herself. Women liked that. Then, when she was open and receptive, he'd make his play.

Reenie's plan was to loosen Earl's tongue. She counted on the Jack Daniel's to assist her. It didn't take long.

Seduced by his surroundings, beguiled by the lady's unflagging interest, and rendered increasingly defenseless by generous portions of bourbon, Earl began to talk.

Reenie listened raptly, making sympathetic sounds from time to time. Until, bored with Earl's meanderings, she steered the conversation to his Hollywood years.

Surely, with all his talents and his marvelous good looks, he had made *some* important contacts there. Why, she herself had been so impressed by Earl's presence, she had taken him for an important celebrity.

Earl preened. "Some," he allowed.

"Speaking of celebrities, darlin', Palm Beach is being overrun with them," commented Reenie. "Why, just the other night I practically bumped into Tami Hayes rushing toward an elevator in this very hotel."

Reminded suddenly of Tami's shabby treatment of him, Earl blurted out, "Yeah. She was coming to see me."

"You!" exclaimed Reenie. She poured herself a hefty bourbon.

"Tami and I go back a long way," boasted Earl. "You know, when I first met her, her name was Drucie Martin."

Reenie's skin prickled with excitement. "No, sugah, I didn't know. Now, how could I know that?"

Encouraged, Earl bragged some more. "I was the one who suggested the name change. And came up with the one she has now."

"Did you, now? Well, it's a mighty catchy name, darlin'. And look how far she's come with it! You certainly are one splendid picker!"

Earl swished his bourbon, then emptied the glass. "I made her what she is, you know. Spotted her talent. Gave her her start. She was just a green kid from the sticks. With a hooker for a mother who abandoned her when she was a kid and a father she never knew. Tami was raised in an orphanage."

"My!" sighed Reenie. She poured Earl another bourbon, took some more herself. "What a sad tale!"

Earl took a deep swallow. "You'd think being raised without a mother and father would have given her some sensitivity to other people's feelings. Instead, she hauls herself off one day without a thank-you, takes my kid with her, and never lets me see her."

"Kid? What kid?" asked Reenie.

"My kid."

"Your kid!"

"Yeah, *my* kid," repeated Earl with more than a touch of self-pity. Moved by his bad fortune, plus prodigious amounts of expensive bourbon, tears smarted his eyes. As the entire story of Drucie Martin AKA Tami Hayes, Erin, and Earl Blakely unfolded.

Reenie couldn't believe her ears. She got so excited she threw caution to the winds, poured herself another bourbon, poured one for Earl, urged him on, and listened, mesmerized, as he described Bordon Granger's entrance into the drama.

"Can you believe it?" whined Earl. "A guy with that kind of

power had to threaten me. When all I wanted was a chance to see my kid."

"He wouldn't let you see your child?" Reenie poured herself some more bourbon and freshened Earl's drink.

"Goddamn right, he wouldn't. Threatened to have me killed if I so much as went near her. Or Tami."

"Oh, my!" sympathized Reenie.

Earl suddenly grew quiet, hazily aware he was talking too much. He'd had more to drink than he realized. No way could he satisfy the lady. He doubted if he could even get it up.

He started to rise.

Reenie pushed him back. "Why, sugah, you're not plannin' to run off on me, are you?" She raised the bottle of Jack Daniel's and peered at it. "Not while there's some perfectly good bourbon left. And plenty more not too far away." She called down to room service and ordered another bottle of Jack Daniel's.

The bourbon may have affected Earl's performance, but it made Reenie horny. She smiled cozily at Earl. "Now, you wait right heah, darlin', and I'll be back in a sec. With a surprise."

She was gone a few minutes.

When she returned, she was wearing a white negligee, cut enticingly low. "Are you interested in medieval artifacts, sugah?"

Earl looked blank.

"Curiosities, darlin'," explained Reenie patiently. "Reconstructions of medieval conversation pieces. For instance, I happen to be wearing a simply marvelous example of a copy of the most wonderfully crafted piece of medieval workmanship."

She slipped off her negligee, allowed it to fall at her feet, and stood before Earl, a wondrous sight in all her voluptuous womanliness. She was naked except for two items. A gold chain around her neck with a solid gold key that nested between full and quivering breasts. And what appeared to be a replica of a twelfth-century chastity belt.

"What's that?" asked Earl thickly.

"Why, that's the surprise, sweetie. I had it specifically designed by the dearest little ironmaker in Vermont." She removed the gold chain from around her neck and handed the gold key to Earl. She spread herself out on the couch.

"What's this?" wondered Earl.

Reenie smiled knowingly. "Well, lovah, before you can enjoy the great mysteries of the universe, you need to release them."

It made sense. Earl rose to his feet unsteadily, accepted the key, then knelt before the recumbent Reenie.

With difficulty, he groped for the opening. "Can't find the damn thing," he muttered, too drunk to make the connection.

"Well, for heaven's sake, sugah, it's *there*. Keep tryin'," commanded Reenie fretfully.

The waiter from room service, with the fresh bottle of Jack Daniel's, knocked on the door, got no answer, knocked again more strongly.

"C'mon in," bawled Reenie drunkenly.

He entered, took in the tableau in one swift glance, then quickly rearranged his features into their customary blandness.

"Hi," welcomed Reenie. "We're searchin' for the secret door to one of the world's great mysteries." She smiled bleakly. "Only we can't seem to find the goddamned entrance."

Reenie planted her bombshells in her column, dated Palm Beach, deceptively nestled among familiar innocuous gossip about celebrities, jet-setters, and socialites. Along with details of who was being squired by whom, who was doing what at a current "in" café or private party, who was wearing what fabulous gown or new brilliant, and what delectable delights were served to select guests at the most exciting bash so far of the new season.

The pieces read:

What superstar about to wed a megabuck cable-empire tycoon must be shivering in her satin wedding slippers for fear a figure from her past will come forward, claim what's rightfully his, and put a damper on the nuptials? The gentleman's in town for the festivities with a story to tell that would cause the songster's apple-pie image to take a nose dive.

Speaking of images being overturned, what supercool jewelry emporium exec has a secret past that reads like a page from the Brothers Grimm? And what supercool senator would have his career blown sky-high if it were known?

Not only is that explosive tucked into the senator's basket of goodies, he has a wife who sends up her own flares. So who ever said life was simple, darlings?

The people involved began to react.

Almost at once, Earl Blakely spotted the reference to him, Tami, and Bordon Granger. Remembering Bordon's warning, he wondered nervously how the information got into a column. Then, he noticed the by-line, the dateline, put two and two together, and made the connection.

Reenie Boyd!

That bitch! That lying, scheming cunt! She'd filled him with bourbon and sucked him dry as a bone.

He'd been had! Hell, all the while he'd been trying to figure out when to screw her, she'd been screwing him.

He'd behaved like a goddamned virgin, that's what pissed him off. He'd given the cherry away for free. Under the influence of all that bourbon, he'd babbled away the entire stock of salable merchandise.

Well, it was time to collect what was due him. And it was time that cunt learned that while nice guys finished last, Earl Blakely was anything but a nice guy.

Tami Hayes's breakfast eggs had long grown cold.

What she had tried to avoid had happened. And this was only the beginning. Everything would come out. The story was too good to suppress.

Then she thought of Erin who would be most hurt by these disclosures. It was Erin who needed to be protected. She was the most vulnerable.

Bordon tried to distract Tami, but he was furious himself. "That son of a bitch! I was certain he'd left town. When I get my hands on him, he'll damn well wish he had."

Tami smiled wanly. "Isn't it a little late for threats, Bordon? After all, the damage is done. I should have settled with Earl. I should have known his was no idle bluff. I should have followed my gut instinct."

Bordon was only half listening. "And that bitch, Reenie Boyd.

384

When I'm through with her, she'll wish she'd never tangled with me."

For the first time since she'd read the item, Tami laughed. "Oh, Bordon, would you fight the entire world for me?"

His grin was sheepish. "Fight it, subdue it, win it, and present it to you like a trophy if that's what it took to make you happy."

Touched, Tami reached out for Bordon's hand. "All that for me?"

His grin deepened. "All that and more."

The mood at the table was lighter. Suddenly, there was hope. Because there was love.

"Then we'll be all right," Tami said. "Because I'd do the same for you. With a combination like that going for us, we can't miss."

Kate had no such combination going for her. She had not felt so violated in years. She reread the item in Reenie's column in stunned disbelief. It was a vicious blow, struck without conscience. Why?

She was so angry, she trembled. And so sickened, she gasped with pain. Everything she had worked for was threatened. What would happen when the rest of the story was revealed? She would be held up to scorn, ridiculed. She would be shunned as a freak. A participant in a macabre horror story too bizarre to be believed. Prurient tastes would be titillated and newspapers sold because of a scandal that was so private, so personal, so painful, it belonged to no one but her. No one had a right to invade that area of pain. No one!

Suddenly, Kate remembered Mark. This was even more damaging to him than to her. How would he react? And how could she explain she never told him because she wanted to spare him?

Well, there was no sparing him now. Mark was as inextricably bound to Kate's past as he was to Rosemary's future.

Ben, who never read gossip columnists, had the item brought to his attention by Jenny McBain, his co-anchor. "This could be interesting," she suggested. "What say we check it out?"

Ben recognized the reference at once. Jesus! How would Kate handle this?

385

He kept his voice light. "Why don't we leave the soap operas to prime-time drama?"

"Whatever you say, pal." Jenny grinned. "Are we on for tonight?"

Ben grinned back. "You bet."

He had broken his ironclad rule about not getting it on with anyone from work. Jenny was the perfect antidote to his agony over Kate. She was bright, beautiful, and sexy. All that a man could ask for.

Only it wasn't working. She wasn't Kate. Whose mark was buried so deep in Ben's psyche, he didn't know how to remove it.

After Jenny had left his office, Ben read the item once again.

What the hell, Kate had made her choice. How she was taking this was none of his business.

She belonged to someone else. She'd told him as much.

There wasn't anything he could do. Except get on with his own life.

The Eastern Airlines 727 was scheduled to land at Kennedy Airport in twenty minutes. Rosemary removed her rosary beads from her Hermès purse, slipped them into the pocket of her wheat-colored textured silk Halston jacket, and, resting her head against the first-class passenger seat, stared out the window into the sightless sky.

She had boarded the plane as Rosemary Winters. She had paid for her ticket with cash. Someone had been following her for days. Rosemary was aware of it, but she had cleverly given him the slip. So much for Mark's supersleuths, she thought with contempt. Amateurs, the lot of them.

She beckoned the stewardess imperiously and requested another Scotch. Easy on the ice.

Rosemary wore tinted glasses, a white scarf wrapped loosely around her neck, and her pale hair was tucked into a dark cap. She was satisfied with her disguise. She was certain she was unrecognizable.

The stewardess, however, recognized her. As she prepared Rosemary's Scotch, she turned to the co-stewardess. "Another for Mrs. Hunter," she announced wryly.

"Jesus!" the other exclaimed. "She must have a hollow leg."

The first stewardess smiled grimly. "Let's hope she can walk off the plane on it."

She brought the drink to Rosemary.

Rosemary thanked her and smiled, secure in her disguise.

Since she made her decision, a peace had settled over her. She had a direction now. She wasn't drifting aimlessly. That made all the difference. Knowing where you were going.

She was embarking on a pilgrimage. All the saints she had ever read about in her childhood embarked on pilgrimages to holy places to restore their souls. Not that she considered herself a saint. Not by a long shot. But she had once followed their direction so earnestly she was convinced if she did so now, she would find what it was she had lost.

And she was going to a holy place.

Rosemary sipped her Scotch, fondled her rosary beads in the pocket of her jacket, and sighed with contentment. Soon, everything would be all right. Soon, she would find the answer she sought.

She was going to visit Daddy's grave. She was going to rest there and restore her soul. And there, she knew, she would discover what it was she had lost.

Kate was shaken from her reverie by the ringing of the phone. She lay there for a moment, too numb to answer it. Finally, she rose dully, approached the phone, and picked it up.

"Yes?" she asked warily.

"I'm coming right over. You need someone with you," Ben told her.

Suddenly, she was no longer alone.

He was there in ten minutes. When Kate let him in, he took one look at her, opened up his arms, and Kate walked into them, grateful for the refuge they provided.

He held her close, stroked her hair, murmured reassurances. "It's all right, Kate. You'll be all right. I'm here to see to that."

He was, Ben saw, as helpless over his feelings for Kate as she was over the forces that threatened to engulf her.

❧ 10 ❧

Mark couldn't reach Kate. He tried her house. She didn't answer. He tried the store. And was told she hadn't come in yet. He tried the store an hour later and was told she had called in sick. When he tried the house again, he still got no answer.

He kept trying. No answer. Finally, in exasperation, he got the operator to try the number. And was told the phone was not ringing.

Damn! He'd have to run over to find out what the hell was going on. What the hell that nasty insinuation in Reenie's column was all about. As if he didn't have enough on his mind. He still hadn't located Rosemary. He cursed himself for underestimating Reenie's vindictiveness. And cursed her for the bitch she was.

Frustrated over not being able to reach Kate by phone, he decided to deal with Reenie first. He called her at The Breakers, hoping she was still there.

She was.

As soon as she picked up the phone, he lit into her. "What the hell was that item all about?" he barked without introducing himself.

He needed no introduction. "Well, hello, sugah," purred Reenie. "Tell me, lovah, why is it a few printed words on paper draws a response from you when nothing else will?"

"C'mon, Reenie, answer my question. What the hell is going on?"

She chose to deliberately ignore the question. "You've been missin' our Tuesday night specials, darlin'. Two of them," she added pointedly.

"Jesus Christ, Reenie," he fumed, "do you really believe I have nothing better to do than provide you with stud service?"

"What I believe, sugah, is that you had better get your priorities straight. We discussed that before. Remembah? We had a deal."

"That was no deal. That was a sentence." Realizing he had been maneuvered off the subject of his call, he returned to it. "Now, what the hell are you insinuating in that goddamn column of yours?"

Reenie ignored the question again. "Where are you callin' from, darlin'?"

"I'm at home. In Palm Beach. Why?" He had flown in last night, exhausted. Too tired to even think of calling Kate. He'd slept until almost noon. Then, at breakfast, he'd read the item in Reenie's column.

"Palm Beach!" She couldn't believe it. "Well, how about that! So near, and yet so far. Tell you what, sugah. Come on over and I'll fix you a drink. We'll talk then."

"No way am I about to walk through that lobby on my way up to your suite, Reenie," insisted Mark.

"No? Well, then, I'll come see you."

"Here?" Mark was startled.

"Why, certainly there. You do want to talk, don't you?"

Mark hesitated. He was figuring out the best way to stop her from coming over.

Reenie took the silence for assent. "I'll be there in half an hour, darlin'. Have something long and strong waiting for me." She laughed lightly. "I meant a drink, sugah."

Mark had no choice. He needed to find out what she knew. "Half an hour," he agreed.

"That's what I just said, lovah," Reenie told him.

The Hunter butler led Reenie into the library. "Mrs. Boyd," he announced.

Mark rose from behind the desk to greet her. "Good to see you again, Reenie," he said pleasantly.

"Good to see you, Senator," smiled Reenie. "And Rosemary? How is she?"

"Rosemary is fine," Mark said. "Visiting friends."

The butler exited.

Reenie's smile broadened. "How nice for us."

"Have a chair," offered Mark ungraciously. With effort, he added, "Something to drink?"

"Bourbon," ordered Reenie. "With branch. Long on the bourbon. Short on the branch."

He fixed it, handed it to her, and seated himself opposite her. "Okay, let's talk."

Reenie studied him, sipped her drink, and pondered. It was amazing. Mad as she was at him, she still had a thing for him. He'd humiliated her, mocked her, ignored her, and he still had her engine racing. No man she'd ever met had this effect on her.

"Well," urged Mark.

She crossed her legs carefully. She wore no undergarments. "Your girlfriend has a lurid past, darlin'."

"So you implied," noted Mark, trying not to react. She watched his face closely. He kept it guarded. "Now, tell me what the hell it's all about."

Reenie told him. About Kate's parents. About the murder-suicide of the perfect couple. The screeching Worcester headlines. The coverage of other city newspapers. "They had a field day, sugah. Describing the perfect way to celebrate a little girl's tenth birthday. Big party! Bang! Bang! Party's all over!"

"Jesus!" breathed Mark, shocked and sorry for Kate, then grasping the full ramifications of the story and the effect it would have on his career.

It was a disaster. Far worse than anything he could have imagined. Rosemary's peccadilloes were bad enough. But this! His Kate —his good, sensible Kate had skeletons in her closet ready to dance on his political grave.

Why in hell had she never told him? At least he'd have been prepared. This way, he was thrown for a loop. Vulnerable. Defenseless. A target for all the bastards who'd like to see him ruined.

Reenie knowingly watched a variety of emotions cross Mark's face. Fear. Self-interest. Survival. She read him like a book. But then subtlety was not the quality that had attracted her in the first place. "It wouldn't make good campaign copy for you, would it, darlin'?"

Mark turned his attention back with an effort. "You're not planning on printing any of that, are you?"

Reenie waited. "That all depends," she said finally.

"On what?" questioned Mark.

"On what you do," countered Reenie. "And how well you do it."

She undid the buttons on her jacket. She wore no blouse under it. And no bra.

Mark rose, strode to the library door, locked it, and returned to the chair opposite Reenie. "What must I do?" he asked coolly.

Reenie hitched up her skirt, spread her legs. "For starters, sugah, *you* can service *me*. Seems we spent too much time before pleasurin' you."

Mark knelt obediently in front of her. Before burying his face in the promising if much-used private parts of Reenie Boyd, he looked up at her. And smiled wryly. "But, Reenie, it's not even Tuesday."

She put both hands on his head and pushed him toward her. "Lovah, from now on, every day is going to be Tuesday for us," she announced.

Marjorie Hunter called just as Reenie was preparing to leave. She'd been trying to reach him, his mother said.

Mark apologized. He'd gotten in late last night. As a matter of fact, he was on his way over when she called.

He stretched out his legs, started to take out a cigarette, remembered his mother's distaste for them, and drummed his fingers idly instead. "How are the girls?" he asked.

Marjorie eyed her son shrewdly. He looked as though he'd been up to no good. "The girls are fine. At the moment, they're at their tennis lesson. And, speaking of the girls, I really think, Mark, it's time they were home with you and Rosemary. To pick up the normal threads of their lives again."

Mark agreed that was a splendid idea. There was only one obstacle. "Rosemary's not home yet."

"Not home! You mean you haven't located her yet?"

Mark assured his mother he had people working on it. "We've traced her to some of the places she's been. Only, we seem to have lost track of her in others."

Marjorie was appalled. "Good Lord, Mark, it isn't a piece of luggage we're discussing. How can you lose track of a full-grown woman?"

Mark's smile was rueful. "It isn't easy. Only, Rosemary's pretty devious when she gets like this."

Marjorie wasn't convinced. "There must be some explanation for her behavior, Mark. Something you said or did. Rosemary was perfectly fine when we had lunch. I haven't seen her in such excellent spirits in a long time."

Mark was spared describing Rosemary's relationship with spirits by Beth Hunter bursting into the room.

"Daddy!" she shrieked, almost throwing him off-balance by the intensity of her embrace. "I saw your car in the driveway, so I knew you were here."

"Baby," grinned Mark, steadying himself and holding her tight. He hugged her, then gently pushed her from him. "By gum, I think you've grown since I last saw you."

Beth giggled. "Oh, Daddy, I just saw you a short time ago. I haven't grown since then." Her eyes darted eagerly around the room. "Is Mother with you? Is she here, Daddy?"

Mark kept his smile even. "No, kitten. Mother's been delayed. But she'll be home soon."

"Oh," said Beth, disappointment coloring her voice.

Mark glanced at his watch. "Look, kitten, I've got some things to do. But how about a date for dinner tonight? I'll pick you and Kimberly up later. You too, Mother."

Beth was not about to let him out of her sight. "Let me go with you, Daddy. I haven't seen you in ages."

"Kitten, you just said it was only a little while ago," Mark reminded her. "Besides, I have business to attend to. I won't be long. And I'll be back for our date."

"Oh, but I won't be in the way," pleaded Beth. "I promise."

"Take her, Mark," urged Marjorie who felt the presence of the child would keep him out of mischief.

It didn't.

Earl Blakely finally reached Reenie Boyd at The Breakers. Following the renewal of her "contract" with Mark Hunter, Reenie was in an expansive mood.

Before he could begin to protest her shabby treatment of him, she assured Earl she had every intention of compensating him for the information he provided her with.

"I had a check to give you in the mornin', sugah," she told Earl. "But you were long gone." Her laughter forgave him his indiscretion. "I'm afraid we both indulged too much that night to conclude much pertinent business."

She invited Earl up for a drink around six. She'd give him the check then. She was certain he would find the compensation more than generous. And she had some release papers for him to sign.

Earl passed up on the drink. He'd just pick up the check and look at the papers she wanted him to sign.

"Suit yourself, sugah," said Reenie airily. "See you at six."

She hung up and whirled around the room, feeling giddier than she had in years. She was in love, an entirely new experience for her. And she was back in control, a very old feeling. And a very comfortable one.

She had Mark exactly where she wanted him. He wouldn't dare fool around with anyone now, not while she controlled all the marbles in the game. Pretty soon, he wouldn't even want to.

Obviously, Rosemary would have to go. She was a detriment to Mark's career. An albatross around his neck. But she, Reenie Boyd, with her vast communication network and her power, was a decided asset. She would do things for Mark's career he hadn't even begun to dream of.

As for the little matter of divorce, why, the man sitting in the White House now was divorced. That fact hadn't stood in the way of his election.

No, nothing could interfere with her plans. With Mark at her side, the world lay before them. And now that she had him in line, the possibilities for success that world offered were limitless.

Mimzee Dawson sat on the throne in her throne room. It was early evening and in front of her sat one very dry martini.

In her lap lay the Kirsten replica, personally delivered by Alain DuLac. An absolute marvel. It would keep her company until she replaced it with the real one.

There were a few more threads to be secured.

There was Earl Blakely, who needed to be acquainted with his role in her grand design, and Howie, who needed to be instructed in his.

There was one other matter.

Mimzee reached for the phone, dialed the Wellington Arms country club, of which she was a member, and asked to speak to the gentleman in charge of the parking concession.

Derek missed Sandy more than he thought possible.

The excitement of the new part, the thrill of stretching himself once again in an entirely new direction, the sweet smell of success already on his lips, all these experiences were as nothing, he learned, unless he could share them with her.

The knowledge stunned him.

He called Sandy from New York to tell her he'd gotten the part. The one he'd told her about.

That's why he hadn't called. "I just had time to pack a few things and grab the first flight out," he explained.

"It's okay," Sandy assured him. She added, "I'm really happy for you, Derek."

That made him happy. "I'll try to get back this weekend," he promised.

"This weekend's the ball," she reminded him.

"Oh. I forgot."

"I have to be there. I'm still a working girl. Remember? Besides," she asked quietly, "aren't you going with the contessa?"

"No," he said. "I don't care about balls. Anyway, it's you I wanted to see."

Sandy felt a small glow start in the center of her being.

"Maybe I could get there the night before the ball," suggested Derek. "I really need to talk to you."

The small glow widened.

"Terrific," said Sandy, remembering her decision to keep her mouth shut. The last thing she wanted to do was talk him out of whatever it was he was experiencing.

Derek hung up; started to call Consuela; thought about it; hung up.

How could he explain over the telephone that he'd found someone else?

Better to do it face to face.

When he got to Palm Beach, he'd check into The Breakers, call her, see her, and tell her then.

11

Mark pulled into Kate's driveway, drove toward the back of the house, turned off the ignition, and instructed Beth to wait. "I won't be long, kitten. The lady here does occasional typing for me, and I need to pick it up." He chucked her under the chin playfully. "You'll be all right?"

"I'll be fine, Daddy," Beth promised.

"Good. If you get bored, you can sit by the pool."

Kate heard the car drive toward the rear of the house and knew instinctively who it was. Mechanically, she reached for a faded quilted gown, slipped her feet into mules, and was downstairs by the time the doorbell rang.

She opened the door.

Mark stepped inside and closed the door behind him. His eyes appraised Kate. "You're not dressed."

"I wasn't feeling well."

Mark got right to the point. "Why didn't you tell me, Kate?"

"That I wasn't feeling well?"

"You know damn well that's not what I mean. I'm talking about those innuendoes in Reenie Boyd's column."

"Oh. That . . ." Kate's voice trailed off.

"Yes. That." He grabbed her shoulders to shake some life into her. His eyes blazed with fury. "Why the hell didn't you tell me about it? The Grafton special. Murder-suicide on a slow news day in a sleepy little New England village."

Kate blanched. "How did you find out?"

"Not from you, certainly. Reenie Boyd filled me in." His eyes raked Kate. "Why, Kate? For God's sake, why didn't you tell me?"

She broke from Mark's hold and turned away from him. "Somehow, the moment of truth never came," she said.

She turned back to face him. "You were the one with problems, Mark, remember? You were the burdened one. I was the strength and support you needed when everything was falling in on you."

She raised her chin and looked coldly at him. "If I had told you, do you think you could have handled the information?" She laughed shortly. "I doubt it. You don't seem to be handling it too well now. But, then, why should *you* be any different? I have trouble handling it myself."

Looking at her standing there, more vulnerable than he had ever seen her, a rush of emotion overtook Mark. His invincible Kate was no longer invincible. The knowledge touched him rather than repelled him, and suddenly all thoughts of his own welfare disappeared, replaced with the unfamiliar urge to protect her from whatever forces threatened her.

He crossed quickly to her and gathered her into his arms. "I love you, Kate."

Her smile was bitter. "Sometimes that isn't enough."

The doorbell rang, startling them both.

Kate stiffened, then left the security of Mark's arms to open the door.

A child stood there. Large solemn brown eyes. Thick bluntly cut wheat-colored hair. Kate recognized Rosemary's daughter at once.

Beth spotted her father and rushed to him. "Daddy! I'm sorry to bother you, but I was getting worried."

Mark smiled easily. "No problem, baby." He turned to Kate. "Oh, Kate, this is my younger daughter, Beth. Beth, this is Miss . . . Bromley."

"How do you do," said Beth politely, redeeming herself for having burst in uninvited.

Mark tousled her hair fondly. "I think we'd better go, kitten." He smiled wryly at Kate. "Thank you, Miss . . . Bromley. I'll be in touch."

Kate smiled woodenly. The materialization of Beth Hunter was a dramatic reminder that Mark came with some ties that would never be severed.

She thought of Ben. Who came unencumbered. Who made no

397

demands upon her. And who was somehow always there when she needed him.

She recognized she was torn between two needs. Her dependence upon Mark and her reliance upon Ben.

She was trapped. In the middle. Unable to choose sides.

Ben had made his decision to resume his own life. Then, as though he had no will of his own, he had called and rushed over to ease Kate's anxieties as though no one were capable of taking care of her but him.

What was there about this woman that caused him to lose his perspective?

His number-one priority was finishing his Palm Beach assignments.

His goal was to move to New York and take advantage of the opportunities offered him.

Everything had been clear, unclouded, and uncomplicated.

Until Kate refused to go with him into that bright, beautiful future.

Part of her was still bound to Mark Hunter. Which left Ben Gately where? Damned if he knew. Any more than he knew why he tolerated this unholy mess.

His only excuse was he was in love.

Well, if this was love, and love was so terrific, why was he so miserable?

Ben made another decision.

Kate would have to make a choice. The senator or him.

One way or the other.

Mark was just as preoccupied on the drive back from Kate's as he had been driving over. The only difference was that Beth was quiet now too.

She broke the silence. "When will Mommy be coming home, Daddy?"

"Soon, kitten," he promised.

And she would, he vowed. Come hell or high water, he'd find Rosemary and bring her back.

Everything was going to be all right. He had a handle on things again. He knew where he stood. And he was a born juggler. He knew how to manage his mother, and he knew he could deal with Kate's stigmata, now that he was aware of them. All he had to do to keep the lid on that can of worms was to see that Reenie remained content. No problem. For now.

But he had to find Rosemary. Rosemary was sick and sick people needed to be treated. But he also needed to be free of her. He'd had enough to do with sickness.

His usual optimism in the midst of seemingly unsurmountable obstacles returned, and his spirits rose.

Everything would work out.

Rosemary leaned her head against the simple Vermont granite slab that marked the Connecticut resting place of Carl Schmittle.

She felt as though she had been on a long journey. Only, she couldn't remember where she had come from. Or where she had been.

There was a reason she'd come here. She was certain of that. But what was it?

She was tired, more tired than she'd been in a long time.

She must have traveled far to be this tired.

Where had she been?

There was something she wanted to ask her father. What was it?

A cold wind whipped across her face, and a wet snow began to fall. Rosemary shivered.

Where was her coat?

She opened her large burgundy Cartier shopping bag and saw that she had stuffed it with airline-size liquor bottles. She took out a Wolfschmidt, broke the seal, and drained it in one swallow.

She shivered again and opened a second one.

"Little dead soldiers," said Rosemary mournfully, laying the empty miniatures side by side.

The alcohol would make her forget what she needed to remember, but she was cold.

When there were ten little dead soldiers, Rosemary felt warmer. She laid them, labels up, alongside her father's grave.

"Never mind, Daddy," Rosemary assured the marker. "I'm sure I'll remember what it was I wanted to ask you."

She rose, brushed herself off, got back into her rented car, and drove the quarter mile on her parents' estate to the main house.

Maybe her mother would help her remember. Maybe the answer was at the main house. If she were patient, just a little longer, she was certain it would come back to her.

Earl Blakely presented himself at Reenie Boyd's suite exactly at six.

"How prompt you are," approved Reenie. She invited him in and offered him a drink.

Once again, Earl refused. "I really gotta get goin'."

"Heavy date?" teased Reenie.

Earl thought of Belinda. A March wind would blow her away. "Not so heavy," he noted.

Reenie smiled. "Well, then, to the business at hand, darlin'." She crossed to the desk, opened a drawer, removed an envelope and some papers, and crossed back to Earl.

She handed him the envelope. "Open it. The check's inside."

He opened it and stared at the cashier's check. "Jesus!" he exclaimed. It was for $5,000.

Reenie smiled again. "I told you I'd do right by you. Now, aren't you ashamed at all those nasty little thoughts you harbored about me?" She wiggled a finger at him. "No, don't deny it. I know you thought I'd taken advantage of you."

Earl looked sheepish as he wondered how much more he could have jerked out of her.

"That's it, lovah," Reenie said, as though reading his mind. "I may be generous. I'm not crazy. Your information was worth every penny in that check. But not a cent more."

He recognized a dead end when he faced one. "What about those papers you mentioned?"

Reenie placed them in front of him. "Just put your John Hancock on these, sweetie, and we're all through."

Earl started to study them.

"I wouldn't strain my pretty blue eyes, lovah, on all that tiresome small print. They're just standard release forms concluding our deal." She handed him a pen.

He took it, signed the papers, handed them back.

"Thank you, sugah," smiled Reenie. She raised her chin slightly and studied him. "Sure now you don't want to change your mind about that drink? We could settle in here and celebrate. Kick off our shoes, let down our hair, and get to really know each other." Her look was challenging. "We didn't quite manage that the other night."

Earl hesitated, flashed back to a picture of a naked Reenie.

One thing he hated was unfinished business.

Besides, she'd been pretty decent with him. Fair and square.

Earl grinned. "Why not?" he said.

A night to remember, that's what he'd give her.

Hell, it was the least he could do for her!

Bordon Granger was not about to let up on Earl Blakely. Without informing Tami of his plans, he put out feelers for information on Earl's whereabouts. Bordon was lying, of course, about taking a contract out on Earl. Not that the idea wasn't tempting. But at least he'd put a scare into Blakely he'd never forget. A couple of hired muscle men to rough him up and hurry him out of town. That should take care of Blakely.

Reenie Boyd was another matter.

The rumor on the Street was a substantial block of Boyd Enterprises stock was unexpectedly available.

Bordon reached for his office phone and made four brief calls. Within two hours, he had quietly purchased enough stock in Boyd Enterprises, in New York, Chicago, Denver, and Los Angeles, to give him absolute control.

There was only one way to deal with the Reenie Boyds of this world. That was to place yourself in a position of power.

Bordon Granger had just collected the bargaining chips he needed to win the game.

❦12❧

Derek was back in town. He couldn't get space at The Breakers, but managed to find a room at the Colony.

He called Consuela.

"Where are you?" she demanded.

He told her.

"Here? You are here in town? What are you doing *there?*"

He needed to talk to her.

He was making an appointment? Like a stranger? *Pazzo!* "Wait," said Consuela. "I will check my book." She put the phone down and tapped her fingers in annoyance. She picked up the phone. "Come in ten minutes. I have some free time," she told him.

When he arrived, Consuela studied him carefully. "So, talk," she directed.

He began by telling her how much he admired her, what a wonderful woman she was. . . .

"Spare me the eulogies, Derek," protested Consuela. "When I am dead, you have my permission to recite them."

He told her about the new play. And the lead role that was his. Consuela told him she was happy for his good fortune.

Then he told her about Sandy. He'd fallen in love. At least, this must be love. He couldn't get Sandy out of his mind. And he felt he had to tell Consuela. As a matter of principle . . .

"*Sì,*" said Consuela. Derek's principles, she remembered. She was quiet for a moment, then broke through the suspense. "I am happy for you, *caro.*" She opened her arms wide. "See. There are no strings to bind you." The dimple flashed. "There never were."

Consuela reached out and kissed him on both cheeks in the

Roman fashion. "Be happy, *caro,* that you have found true love. That happens only to the most fortunate. I ought to know." She smiled again. "And the little redhead? What does she say to all this?"

Derek looked sheepish. "I haven't told her yet," he admitted.

Consuela shook her head in wonder. Derek, who was so precise about his pajama tops and his career, was helpless in all other areas. "Go at once," she urged. "Go tell her."

She pushed him gently toward the door, then thought of something. "But, *caro,* do not marry her before the ball. I need her there. It is too late to get a replacement."

Consuela called Louis-Philippe, who was staying at The Breakers. Even though he had been firm in refusing her offer to stay at Polly Bowdin's, at least he was nearby. She needed him now.

"Consuela!" He sounded delighted to hear from her.

"Louis, how would you like to take an abandoned lady to dinner?"

His hesitation was momentary. "Who abandoned you, Consuela?"

"Derek, *caro.*" Her laugh was light. "He has discovered his life's *amore,* and the discovery has stunned him."

"I'm not surprised," noted Louis-Philippe. "The discovery is stunning. I can empathize with him. I know how he must feel. I found mine a long time ago."

"You found yours?" A flicker of jealousy flashed over Consuela. *Who could it possibly be?*

Louis-Philippe's voice was reassuring. "I'll tell you about it to-night, Consuela. Over dinner."

Consuela lay down on Polly Bowdin's elaborately detailed four-poster bed. Witch hazel pads covered her eyes. But rest eluded her.

Louis-Philippe was an innocent in the realm of romance. An unscrupulous woman could easily take advantage of him.

She, Consuela, must protect him.

But first she had to find out who the woman was she would protect him from.

Consuela decided she and Louis would eat in. Her fingers itched to sink into pasta dough.

She gave the Bowdin cook the night off.

She dug her hands into the dough, kneading, pounding, rolling, and cutting. The mechanics of the work freed her mind for other concerns.

She was relieved the affair with Derek was over. It was the business with Louis that disturbed her. It was the ultimate betrayal.

What kind of woman would inspire such an *extended* devotion? *For years? A long time ago, he had found his* amore, *he said.*

Clearly, she would have to take things in hand. For Louis's own good.

They had after-dinner brandy in Polly Bowdin's downstairs sitting room. A fire blazed in the hearth.

Louis-Philippe was quiet, savoring the moment.

Consuela, too, seemed reflective as she gazed at the flickering flames.

He turned to her. "For someone so recently abandoned, Consuela, you appear remarkably restored."

The dimple flashed. "Good food restores me, Louis."

"You're not desolate, then?"

"Not at all."

Suddenly, her nearness and his unrequited love for her proved too much. Almost unconsciously, he sought refuge in something less threatening. "There are some things I thought we might discuss about the ball tomorrow night, Consuela."

She put her brandy glass down. "No. There is something far more important on my mind."

"More important than business?" he teased.

"I do not always put business first," snapped Consuela. "First, I am a woman."

"I never for a moment doubted that," he assured her.

She ignored the assurance. "And I am curious about another woman."

"Another woman?" Louis-Philippe was confused.

"I must confess, *caro,* I had no idea such a one existed," said Consuela testily. "You always seemed so satisfied with your life."

He finally understood what she was getting at. "So I did."

She sighed. "Still water runs deep, they say, Louis. They are right."

She saw she would have to be more direct. "We are beating the trees, Louis. Can you not bring yourself to tell me who this paragon of a woman is?"

He couldn't believe her obtuseness. "Don't you know?"

"How would I know unless you tell me? Am I clairvoyant?"

He smiled slightly. "I thought everyone knew, Consuela. I suspect many did. I wasn't terribly effective at concealing it." He looked directly at her. "Come, now, a woman as discerning and sophisticated as you must easily recognize a man so smitten with love he is defenseless in the lady's presence. It was written all over me. How could you miss it?"

Recognition finally dawned. Consuela stared at him, stunned. "The woman is I, Louis?"

"How could it be otherwise?" he responded.

"But why did you never tell me?" she demanded.

He shrugged. "You were always surrounded. By other men. In the midst of a new affair. Or a new business venture. Somehow, the timing was always off."

Consuela appraised the situation quickly. Her practical nature took over. "Well, Louis, the timing is right now. There are no distractions to interfere. You have my undivided attention. And my unqualified approval." Her smile of encouragement was all he needed.

As he reached to gather her into his arms, she tilted back her head and said, "About the ball, Louis. There was something you . . ."

"Don't talk, Consuela," he instructed roughly. "Don't say another word."

Sandy sat very quietly and listened to Derek.

He loved her.

He'd discovered that fact while he was in New York.

He'd come back to Palm Beach to tell her that. And to attend to another matter. Sandy guessed what that was.

He'd never been in love before. Never wanted to share his life with anyone before.

Sandy still didn't speak.

That's what he wanted to share with her. *Needed* to share.

Sandy remained silent.

"I love you, Sandy. I need you. I want to marry you. Don't you understand?"

Sandy broke her silence. "Oh, yes. Yes. Yes to all three of the statements. And I love you too, Derek."

When they made love, it was everything Sandy hoped it to be. The waiting had been worth it.

Even without rockets bursting, balloons soaring in the air, and music crescendoing throughout the room, it was, as Derek would say, terrific.

Afterward, somewhat awed, Derek observed, "You didn't tell me."

Sandy smiled. "It's not the sort of thing you bring up over lemon chicken."

He pulled her closer, stroked her gently. Sandy sighed with contentment.

She traced a finger along the side of his face. "Derek?"

"Yes?" he said tenderly.

Sandy's eyes were soft dark pools. "I want to find out if love's as wonderful the second time around."

Obligingly, he proceeded to demonstrate the veracity of the song title.

13

Mimzee Dawson summoned Earl Blakely to her study. She explained she had arranged a job parking cars tomorrow night for him at the Wellington Arms country club.

She knew he could use the extra cash.

She also had another job for him. A delicate business. She was sure he was up to it.

At a certain point in the evening, he was to meet Howie by the terrace on the club grounds.

Howie would give him a parcel.

Earl was to take the parcel, leave the club grounds, and return to Elsinore.

He was to wait with the unopened parcel at Elsinore until Mimzee returned home. At that time, she would give him a check for $2,000. A more than fair sum, she felt, for a few hours' work.

Mimzee lifted a folder from her desk and stared at Earl with beady blue eyes. This folder, she explained, contained a complete dossier on Mr. Earl Blakely. She would not hesitate to use the information, if necessary.

Did Mr. Blakely understand?

Earl chewed the inside of his lip.

Then told Mimzee he understood perfectly.

Howie Caine still hadn't raised the money for his Colombian coke deal that would guarantee him independence. "But," he explained to the guy who called himself Joey Demarco, "I'll have it for you in a couple of days." Howie's voice was cool and confident.

"You gotta have it now, man," the guy insisted. "We're ready to move. You think we just sit around here jerkin' off waitin' for you? No way, man." He paused. "I got someone else interested."

Howie kept his voice smooth and easy. "I'll have it for you in two days," he promised. "No sweat. I have my source all ready to hand over the cash."

A longer pause. Howie held his breath. Finally, reluctantly, "Two days. No more. You hear, man?"

Howie let his breath out slowly. "You're on," he said cheerfully.

It was only after he hung up that his cheer left him. Where in hell would he get $100,000 in just two days?

A knock on the door interrupted his reverie. His grandmother wished to see him immediately. In the library.

Mimzee was regally seated on her throne, loftily looking down on her subject.

Howie wondered if he were expected to kneel.

Mimzee smiled craftily at him. "I have something very pretty to show you, Howie."

He waited.

She carefully unsnapped the leather case in her lap. When the flaps were opened and the contents revealed, she grandly announced, "The Kirsten diamond. What d'ya think, dearie?"

The necklace of red and white diamonds blazed, sparkled. The huge red center stone surrounded by smaller diamonds stunned Howie with its brilliance. It must have cost her a fortune!

"It must have cost a fortune," he said, giving voice to his thoughts.

"It would have," his grandmother informed him, "if it were real. As it is, it cost a tidy sum. Not a fortune."

Howie looked from the necklace to Mimzee. "It's a fake?"

Mimzee's eyes narrowed. "A replica, dearie. A work wrought by a master. Exquisitely executed down to the minutest detail. But you're right. A fake."

Howie recalled the mountains of publicity that followed the travels of the Kirsten. He remembered something else. There was another Kirsten. *Another replica.* "Doesn't this make three Kirstens?"

"That it does," observed Mimzee merrily.

Howie wondered why his grandmother wanted to own a replica of a replica.

She explained why. Howie stared at her.

"You want me to steal the *real* one?"

"Hardly steal, cookie," Mimzee informed him tartly. "I merely wish to retrieve that which is rightfully mine."

She outlined her plan for achieving this goal in specific detail.

At some point in the evening, Howie was to lure the contessa, who would be wearing the real Kirsten, out on the terrace, out of sight of the others.

He was to render her unconscious, just long enough to remove the real Kirsten from her person and substitute Mimzee's replica.

He was to wrap the necklace in brown paper and secure it with tape. Mimzee would see to it these were in place behind the large tub of geraniums on the terrace.

Earl Blakely would be positioned nearby. Howie was to hand him the parcel and return to the ball with the contessa, who would, by then, be fully recovered. Howie's explanation to her would be, she had suffered a dizzy spell.

When the raffle was held, the winner would receive the replica.

"What if you win?" wondered Howie.

"If I win," said Mimzee airily, "I shall simply be the owner of two Kirstens."

"And if you don't win?" he queried.

"Then I'll own only one. The one that counts."

"What does the winner do about the fake?" asked Howie.

Mimzee smiled. "The winner will never know the difference. It will be assumed the raffled Kirsten is the real one. Why should it be otherwise?"

"What if they test?" persisted Howie. "For authenticity?"

"They won't," Mimzee assured him. "Why would they? Everything will appear normal." She shrugged. "But if they do, so what? It will merely be a matter between the House of Graet and their insurance companies."

It sounded almost plausible. All he had to do was charm the contessa out on the terrace for a few minutes. Not too hard. Everyone knew she had a thing for young men.

"How do I knock her out?" asked Howie.

Mimzee produced a small atomizer from the pocket of her gown. "I purchased this the last time I was in the Orient. One whiff and it renders your opponent momentarily unconscious. In your case, Howie, long enough to conduct the switcheroo."

At Howie's dubious look, Mimzee picked up a small napkin and sprayed it. "Spray some on a handkerchief, cookie," she instructed. "Tell the contessa she's got a spot on her nose. Offer to remove it. Works like a charm.

"I'll prove it to you, Howie." Mimzee's beady blue eyes eagerly searched the room; rested on the black Persian. "We'll practice on the cat."

Howie had one last question. "What do I get out of this, Mimzee?"

His grandmother's eyes raked him. "You get restored to my good graces, dearie. That's the closest state to my pocketbook there is. Isn't that where you've always wanted to be?"

He couldn't believe her gall. His grandmother wanted him to steal a necklace worth $15 million, with nothing in it for him.

She had to be off her fuckin' rocker!

Well, if he was going to risk his neck, he might as well go for broke. Steal the goddamned thing for himself.

He'd been stealing things all his life and getting away with it. Except for the Fabergés. Well, he'd managed to lift them right out from under his grandmother's sharp little nose. One at a time. And if she hadn't counted the goddamned things, he'd have gotten off scot-free.

His one mistake, he decided, was he'd been stealing too small most of his life.

This time, he was going to steal big. He'd turn the necklace over to a fence, pick up the dough, and deal himself into the drug deal. That way, he'd make out both ways.

And what could his grandmother do about it?

She couldn't very well accuse him of stealing something she was planning to steal herself.

14

It did not occur to Grace Schmittle that Rosemary was drunk. But she was appalled at her condition.

"Good heavens, Rosemary. You're soaked right through. Where have you been?"

"Visiting with Daddy," announced Rosemary.

"In this weather? That was foolish."

She insisted she get out of those wet clothes, fixed a hot bath for her, gave her clothes to the maid to clean, and prepared a tray of good nourishing food for her.

She liked doing it. She hadn't taken care of anyone but herself since Carl.

"Eat some of this good food," she said, placing the wicker tray carefully on Rosemary's lap. "You'll feel much better with something in your stomach."

She didn't want any food. She wasn't hungry. She wanted a drink. And her mother's fussing was getting on her nerves.

Rosemary picked listlessly at her food.

"You must eat, Rosemary," urged Grace.

"I'm not hungry, Mamma," insisted Rosemary.

Her nerves were rubbed raw. She was tired. Terribly tired. There was something she had come here to find. But for the life of her, she couldn't remember what it was.

Suddenly, Rosemary looked bleakly at her mother. "Mamma, I've lost something." Her voice was very small.

"Oh? What was that, Rosemary?"

Rosemary looked troubled. "I don't know. I can't remember."

"Well, if you can't remember what it was, dear, it can't have been terribly important." Grace picked up the tray. "If you aren't

411

going to eat anything, I think you should rest. You'll feel better after a while."

Rosemary nodded. "Yes," she agreed.

Grace walked to the door with the tray; stopped; turned; looked back. "It's nice to have you home, Rosemary," she said.

"Thank you," said Rosemary politely. "It's nice to be home."

But home was far away.

Home was where she should be.

Once she was rested, she would go there. Right now, she was tired. Confused. She needed a drink to help her sort things through.

She stumbled out of bed, groped for her Cartier shopping bag, fumbled through its contents, and discovered six more airline-size bottles of Wolfschmidt.

She picked up her cup of honey and lemon, emptied it in the bathroom sink, filled the cup with vodka, and climbed back into bed.

When she finished the vodka, she rested her head once again upon the pillows. And passed out.

Toward dawn, she woke suddenly, bolted upright in bed, and stared straight ahead.

Where was she?

When she remembered where she was, she wondered what she was doing there.

She needed to be home. With Mark and the children.

She reached for the phone, called the airlines, and reserved a first-class seat on the next Eastern flight to Palm Beach. Name: Rosemary Hunter.

She dressed quickly in the freshly cleaned clothes Martha had returned to her closet, scrawled a quick note of apology to her mother, and went downstairs.

The house was still.

Everyone was asleep.

Rosemary pulled the collar of her jacket high around her neck as she stepped outside. She got into the rented car and drove to the airport.

* * *

Halfway between New York and Palm Beach, Rosemary suddenly remembered the House of Graet Christmas Ball. Tonight. For no reason at all, it came to her.

She remembered her gorgeous bouffant David Emanuel ball gown, purchased for that memorable event.

She remembered the Kirsten diamond and the raffle. For the first time in days, Rosemary seemed visibly cheered.

Wouldn't Daddy be pleased if she won the raffle? Winning the Kirsten meant so much to him. He wanted so badly to win it for her.

All at once, Rosemary was determined to win it. And to wear her beautiful gown to the ball, where everyone would admire it and tell her how beautiful she was.

Wouldn't Daddy be proud of her!

When the stewardess stopped by to ask if she wanted anything, Rosemary ordered a screwdriver. "With a lot of *drive* in it," she instructed.

When the screwdriver arrived, Rosemary nodded. She sipped her drink and stared out the window of her first-class seat.

Her face suddenly clouded as she remembered something else. She had been looking for something. Only she couldn't remember what that was.

Maybe the answer was at home. At Casa Miramar.

Rosemary was certain that was where she would find it.

As soon as she woke and had her breakfast coffee, Grace Schmittle called Mark to tell him Rosemary was there. "We had such a nice visit," Grace said, "although Rosemary does look a bit peaked."

Mark couldn't believe his ears. "Rosemary's there!"

"Sleeping soundly," Grace assured him. "She came to pay a visit to Carl's grave. That was so thoughtful of her, don't you agree, Mark?"

Mark was no longer listening. His mind was racing wildly. "Keep her there, Grace. If you have to sit on her, do it. Whatever you do, don't let her out of your sight."

"Well, I . . ."

"Do it," yelled Mark. "If you've never done anything right

before, do this. I'm leaving for the airport now. I'm flying my own plane. I'll be in Connecticut as quickly as possible. Lock Rosemary in the goddamned room if necessary. Just make certain she stays there. I'm on my way."

Grace spent time puttering about in her greenhouse, tending to her roses, brooding about Mark and the phone call. Mark's attitude was inexcusable. There was no need for him to shout at her that way. She had only been trying to tell him Rosemary was visiting.

Maybe Rosemary was right about Mark being difficult. He did appear to have a terrible temper. It must not be easy to live with someone like that.

Grace decided to wake Rosemary and tell her Mark was on the way.

But Rosemary wasn't in her room. Grace searched the closet. Rosemary's freshly cleaned clothes were gone. Then she noticed the envelope propped up against the bedside lamp. She opened it and read Rosemary's hurried note.

Rosemary was on her way home!

Grace Schmittle put in a call to Mark at once to tell him not to come. She certainly didn't want him shouting at her again when he discovered Rosemary wasn't there.

She was informed by the Hunter butler that Senator Hunter had already left for Connecticut.

15

Kate received two calls in quick succession. One was from Mark, who sounded fretful and frantic. He was flying to Connecticut to pick up Rosemary. Maybe he could finally settle things, he said, and have a normal life. Whatever the hell that was. Kate made soothing noises to calm him.

The other call was from Ben. Who needed to see her. He sounded most unlike himself.

The last thing Kate expected was an ultimatum. She stared at Ben, noted the tight line of his jaw, and saw that he meant what he said.

"I can't concentrate. My moods are erratic. My temper is short." His drawn face tore at her heart. "I love you, sweetheart, but this can't go on. This crazy yo-yo up-and-down seesaw situation is driving me nuts. It's either him or me. You have to make a choice."

"I can't do that," protested Kate.

"You're going to have to," insisted Ben.

"I need time, Ben."

But she had asked him for time too many times before. His eyes were suddenly steely. "There's no time left, Kate."

Rosemary took a cab from the airport to her house. She was welcomed home effusively by the staff and informed that Senator Hunter had left unexpectedly for Connecticut.

Why on earth would Mark do that? wondered Rosemary.

"Where are the girls?" she asked.

She was told they were with the senior Mrs. Hunter.

415

Rosemary called Marjorie. "I just got back," she announced breezily. "How are the girls?"

"The girls are fine," replied Marjorie with an edge to her voice. "Where have you been?"

Rosemary was silent.

Where had she been? She couldn't remember. How long had she been gone? She wasn't certain.

Then she recalled her flight. "In Connecticut. I've been visiting Mamma."

"Are you aware that Mark just left for there? He's been desperate for word of you. Worried sick."

Rosemary couldn't remember when Mark had been desperate or worried about anyone other than himself. "That was foolish of him, Marjorie," she replied. "But, then, Mark does have a flair for high drama. And he exaggerates so."

Marjorie chose not to comment. "Your daughters have been worried too, Rosemary. Especially Beth."

Rosemary's expression softened. "Tell them I'll be over as soon as I freshen up," she said.

She studied her face critically in the mirror. It was puffy. Her eyes were red. Her hair was a mess. She was a mess. And she had to look beautiful for the ball tonight.

She had to look beautiful so everyone would admire her. So no one could criticize her. So no one would know there was anything wrong.

Rosemary showered, washed her hair, blew it dry, put eye drops in her eyes, and dialed downstairs for some thinly sliced cucumbers and a bottle of chilled white wine.

When they arrived, she lay down on the bed. She placed the cucumber slices on her eyelids, and, as the wine chilled in its silver bucket, she made some decisions.

She would look beautiful tonight.

She would drink only white wine.

She would drink sparingly.

She needed to remember what she was doing.

She needed to be in top form when she won the Kirsten for Daddy.

* * *

Earl Blakely didn't know what was going on, but he knew whatever it was, it was shady. The whole thing reeked. The job setup. The meeting with Howie. The parcel he was to pick up, return home with, and turn over. Without a peek, by Christ! Yes, something was definitely not copacetic at Elsinore.

And Earl was definitely interested.

Where there was a deal to be made, he wanted in.

After all, he had an heiress to court.

To do that, he needed courtin' dough.

Mimzee Dawson had two things on her mind. The Kirsten diamond and her grandson. If Howie messed this one up, she'd have his head. They didn't call her Queen Bess idly.

Everything for the ball had been attended to. Her new red wig, bouffant and blazing, had arrived. Her ivory satin pearl-and-diamond–encrusted Elizabethan gown was ready. Her jewelry for the occasion had been selected.

As for the Kirsten coup, she had worked with Howie over the Kirsten clasp until he was nimble-fingered.

Figuring out the mechanics of the switch was a challenge. Howie had worked on it for hours until he'd come up with an idea. A chamois pouch. He'd pinned straps on it to tie it around his waist and thighs.

He experimented. He slipped the replica into the chamois pouch, dropped his trousers, tied the straps around his waist and thighs. The pouch, with the Kirsten in it, fell right over his pecker. Just thinking about all the dough the real Kirsten would bring gave him a raging hard-on.

He pulled up his trousers, zipped himself up, and studied the effect in a full-length mirror.

The Kirsten made a slight bulge, but with his evening jacket on, Howie bet no one would notice. And without the hard-on, it wouldn't even be visible.

The plan was simple. He reviewed the steps in his mind. He'd wear the pouch with the replica to the ball, lure the contessa onto the terrace, knock her out, take the real Kirsten off, drop his pants,

417

take out the replica, make the switch, pull up his pants, revive the contessa, and return her to the ball.

Timing was essential.

Howie set up a timer and practiced the procedure. He took the Kirsten off a dummy stand, dropped it into the pouch, dropped his trousers, took the Kirsten out of the pouch, dropped in a string of beads, pulled up his trousers, zipped up his fly, and put the Kirsten back on the dummy.

Finally, he had the whole performance down to two minutes. It wasn't good enough.

He needed to practice some more. One minute—at most—was all he'd have.

Mark was livid when he reached Greenwich in late afternoon and discovered Rosemary wasn't there.

"I tried to stop you," protested Grace. "I called, but you had already left. As for Rosemary, she was gone before breakfast, apparently."

Mark called Casa Miramar. Rosemary had gone out, he was told. He called his mother. Rosemary had already left with the girls. "But, Mark," noted Marjorie reassuringly, "Rosemary seemed fine. I mean, she wasn't . . ."

Mark cut his mother off. "Listen, Mother, if you can get hold of her, tell her to stay put until I get back." He hung up before Marjorie could reply.

He tried the house again, but Rosemary and the girls hadn't returned. Jesus H. Christ, he couldn't hang on the phone all night playing games. He had to get back there.

He looked terribly tired, Grace thought. It was foolish of him to fly up here so impulsively in pursuit of Rosemary. Really, his behavior was becoming increasingly bizarre.

"Why don't you stay the night?" she urged. "You'll be better rested for the trip back."

Mark stared at her and wondered how anyone so loose-ended could have kept Carl Schmittle in line all those years. She seemed to have no idea whatsoever of the gravity of Rosemary's condition.

"I have to get back tonight, Grace," he said, keeping his temper in check.

"Well, at least take Carl's plane back. His pilot will fly you and you can sleep all the way. You look much too tired to fly yourself."

That made sense. He was tired. And he needed to be in shape for the upcoming marathon with Rosemary. He agreed.

But when Grace called to make the arrangements, she was told it would be several hours to ready the plane for flight.

Mark couldn't wait that long. He called and booked a seat on an Allegheny Airlines flight out of Westchester Airport connecting with a TWA flight leaving Newark in an hour and a half.

Grace offered the use of her chauffeured limousine to Westchester Airport.

Mark accepted.

~16~

The House of Graet Christmas Ball was the splashiest event on the December calendar. All over town, women prepared for it with anticipation and excitement.

While the woman responsible for the gala took the occasion in characteristic style.

Consuela stood before the floor-length mirror in Polly Bowdin's bedroom and studied her image.

The ivory satin Geoffrey Beene ball gown was elegantly understated, but exquisitely detailed. A perfect setting for the Kirsten diamond.

Even for the Kirsten replica.

The necklace was absolutely beautiful. A wonder. Who would think it was not the real one? Louis was a genius. He was also a magnificent lover.

With effort, she forced her thoughts to the evening ahead.

Everyone would assume she was wearing the real Kirsten. As she wished them to. When the raffle was won, she would make the announcement she was wearing the replica.

One person would win that raffle. That person would be delighted. The rest would be disappointed. Mimzee Dawson would be furious. Who knew what hysteria she would exhibit, should she lose? Who could fathom the behavior of such a neurotic woman?

But Mimzee, along with the other losers, would have their checks returned. Let her buy something else with the money.

Meanwhile, the drama had yet to be played out. And nothing, nothing must mar the perfection of the production.

It was pure theater. The excitement, the suspense, the color.

And the pleasure of the participants. The praise she would receive was incidental to the pleasure she brought to others.

The contessa would perform magnificently tonight. This was her finest role. After all, Consuela reminded herself dryly, she had plenty of practice. She had been playing it for years.

Kate wore a white chiffon gown she had bought in Paris three years before. The sleeves were full with tiny pearl buttons at the wrist, the skirt was layered, the neckline was scalloped. She wore pearl and diamond drop earrings, from her mother's collection, and a double-strand pearl and diamond necklace, from the House of Graet. Her dark hair, brushed and glossy, gracefully touched her shoulders.

Despite her elegant appearance, her face was strained. She hadn't heard from Mark since his morning call. She had no idea where he was.

And the situation with Ben—or without him, to be more exact —had taken a toll. Why would he choose this moment—when she was feeling so pressured—to force a decision from her?

Still, she missed him. More than she thought possible, she missed him.

Like Kate, Marjorie Hunter selected a Paris gown she had worn before to wear to the House of Graet Ball. Only, Marjorie's was a Balmain. And it was forty years old. She had first worn it in 1946 when her husband was ambassador to France.

The gown still fit perfectly. Not many women could claim that distinction. Marjorie was pleased she could.

Mimzee decided she had never looked more regal. Diamonds sparkled from her neck, fingers, wrists, and ears, and atop her head.

She adjusted the diamond tiara on her curly red wig, studied its effect, admired the ivory satin, pearl-and-diamond–encrusted Elizabethan gown, and smiled.

She was ablaze with light.

Later tonight she would be ablaze with glory. One way or another, she would have her Kirsten. Whether she won it or Howie heisted it, it would be hers.

Tami Hayes, Erin, and Bordon didn't have far to go for the ball. Bordon's estate bordered the club grounds.

They met for drinks in the huge entrance hall before leaving for the ball. The housekeeper had set up a tray with a champagne bucket, chilled Dom Pérignon, and three crystal flutes.

Bordon uncorked the champagne and poured. He handed each of the ladies a glass, then took one for himself.

He looked at Erin, unbelievably lovely and almost grown-up in a strapless white organza ball gown embroidered with pale pink flowers and seed pearls, and at Tami, beautiful in a sapphire-blue halter-necked chiffon gown, a hand-beaded mandarin-collared floor-length coat casually draped over her shoulders.

He lifted his glass. "A toast—to the two most beautiful women in town."

How he'd love to tell Tami he'd tracked Earl Blakely to the Dawson estate; bought up enough shares in Reenie Boyd's publicity empire to give him the clout to silence her once and for all. But Tami looked unusually free from care tonight and he had no wish to spoil her evening with unpleasant reminders of a past that continued to haunt her.

When everything was attended to, he'd tell her. When his mission was successful. When it was completed. He'd tell her then.

Reenie Boyd, in a glittery beaded white Neil Beiff gown that flamboyantly accentuated her much-photographed endowments, was furious. Mark hadn't called her or even sent a thank-you note to her for calling back the vultures from his senatorial doors.

Earlier, she had called his house to see if he was there. "Senator Hunter," she was told, "has gone to Connecticut."

Now, why would he go to Connecticut on the day of the House of Graet Ball? wondered Reenie.

"Do you wish to speak with Mrs. Hunter?" she was asked.

Now, why the hell would she wish to do that? "Thank you, no," replied Reenie.

While she waited for George Martinson, the junior senator from North Carolina, to pick her up for the ball, Reenie bolstered her spirits with a couple of stiff bourbons.

George Martinson wasn't the senator she wanted, but she was damned if she was going to a goddamned ball without an escort.

No decent southern lady would be caught dead doing that.

Sandy Stone glumly studied her reflection in the mirror.

She looked good. Too bad it was wasted.

She wore a green taffeta dress that hugged her body and highlighted her hair. The dress had cost her three weeks' wages. Bought to impress Derek.

But Derek had gone back to New York. He didn't think he should appear at the ball. As a matter of principle. Besides, he needed to get back to the city, find an apartment, get things ready for their new life together.

Sandy had agreed. Reluctantly. It was the sensible thing to do.

She modeled the dress for him anyway, and he had fallen in love with it, and they made love one more time, after Derek insisted Sandy take the dress off and hang it up so as not to crush it.

Love, Sandy decided, was a series of unveilings. And sex, well, sex was terrific.

Rosemary was her own most severe critic. She studied her reflection in the mirror and frowned.

The David Emanuel ecru and net gown swirled gracefully around her hips; nipped in at her slender waist; exposed a delicate swell of bosom, creamy neck, and arms. The gown was airy, bouffant, totally feminine, utterly enchanting.

Why, then, was she vaguely dissatisfied?

Rosemary added diamond drops to her ears, several diamond bracelets, and a huge emerald and diamond ring. She left her neck bare. Ready to receive the Kirsten.

She stepped back once again to view the effect. And frowned again.

She was dissatisfied with the way her hair looked. She paused, fretted, remembered the high puffed turban she had purchased with the gown, looked for it, removed it from its box, and put it on.

Ah, that was better. The turban gave her a look of hauteur and unapproachability that was comforting.

Because she was feeling edgy and apprehensive.

She sipped white wine from a French crystal wineglass and studied her reflection even more critically.

The eye drops and the cucumber slices had done some good,

but there was still a slight puffiness around the eyes that disturbed her. Impulsively, she withdrew a pair of pavé diamond–framed tinted glasses from their House of Graet case and put them on.

There! That was better! In addition to feminine enchantment, hauteur, and unapproachability, she had added a note of mystery.

And the slight puffiness beneath her eyes was completely concealed.

But there were butterflies in her stomach, and her feelings of apprehension increased.

She sipped from her French crystal wineglass and turned to look at her daughter.

"Well?" asked Rosemary uncertainly.

Beth was in awe. "Will I be as beautiful when I grow up?"

"More beautiful, darling. Much more," Rosemary told her. She added, somewhat wistfully, "And much, much nicer."

"Never!" vowed Beth.

"You'll see," insisted Rosemary, adjusting a turban that needed no adjusting. "Now, go see if your sister is ready."

Beth paused at the door. "When will I be big enough to go to balls?"

"Soon enough," said Rosemary. "Too long for you, perhaps, but much too soon for me."

The Allegheny Airlines flight from Westchester County Airport, scheduled to connect with TWA flight 702 to Palm Beach, was rerouted to Binghamton, New York. Both New York City airports and Newark were closed due to heavy storm conditions.

Mark Hunter couldn't believe his bad luck. He would miss his connecting flight to Palm Beach. He had a mind to go up front and offer to fly the goddamned plane himself. God knows, he'd flown through worse, hundreds of times.

And why the hell reroute to Binghamton? He needed to be in Palm Beach, not Binghamton. He had no idea what was going on at home. He hadn't been able to get through to either Rosemary or his mother in the few minutes he'd had before the Allegheny Airlines plane took off from Westchester Airport.

The thought that Rosemary was on the loose while he was trapped in a plane en route to Binghamton, a city he had no desire to visit under the best of circumstances, irked him.

He drummed his fingers in frustration, stared unseeing into the stormy sky outside the plane window, and helplessly contemplated the callous indifference of fate, which saw fit to wreak such havoc with his plans.

~17~

Ben narrated his last segment on Palm Beach, live from Wellington.

"Art Buchwald once observed that 'it's gauche to give a party in Palm Beach just for the sake of a party. Therefore, everyone's in the business of giving a party for a cause.' The challenge, he suggested, was to find enough causes.

"The House of Graet, hosts of tonight's Christmas Ball, came up with three.

"The site of the ball is Wellington—more precisely, the Wellington Arms Squash and Tennis Club.

"Wellington is a man-made phenomenon, thirteen miles from Palm Beach and the sea. Once farmland, it now attracts the rich and famous from all over the world.

"Whereas most of southern Florida is scrubby, sandy, and flat, Wellington is green, rolling, meticulously man-tended, lovingly cultivated, heavily wooded.

"Its landscape is dotted with towering pines, riding trails, sweeping paved roads, narrow dirt trails. Still largely undeveloped, it looks rustic, countryish, but pampered. Like Virginia horse country.

"Indeed, horses are a large part of the Wellington ambience. Polo is a big attraction. Enough of an attraction to draw the enthusiastic participation of England's Prince Charles and the enthusiastic encouragement of his beautiful princess during their visit.

"Low white fences outline acreage. Stables, barns, thoroughbred horseflesh, establish a mood.

"Sophisticated condos and ranch-type units at the Palm Beach Polo and Country Club attract the rich and famous.

"The tone in Wellington is bucolic but chic, wholesome but exclusive. It attracts the young, spirited international rich more open to a casual life-style than the structured one dictated by Palm Beach dowagers.

"What brought about the transformation from farmland to resort chic?

"Two groups were responsible.

"Gould, Inc., a Fortune 500 Chicago electronics firm, purchased 11,000 acres in the mid-seventies, built the Palm Beach Polo and Country Club on 1,650 acres of it, brought in the only $100,000 world championship polo matches, and in a short time created a resort complex with an international ambience.

"Bordon Granger, founder of a communications empire, purchased 12,000 acres back in the sixties. In the late seventies, he, with a small group of investors, built the Wellington Arms Squash and Tennis Club, and made Wellington the squash capital of the world. The rest is resort history.

"Cartier, Piaget, Rolex, Boehm, Gucci, and Michelob sponsor the PBPCC polo matches. The House of Graet sponsors the WASTC squash and tennis matches.

"The Cartier March Polo Ball, held at the PBPCC, is a highlight of the Palm Beach social season.

"The House of Graet Christmas Ball, held at the Wellington Arms, is another of the season's prime events.

"A highlight of the Christmas Ball tonight is the highly touted raffle of the highly publicized Kirsten diamond—a diamond that rumor suggests brings only misfortune to its owners. The myths surrounding the Kirsten, however, fail to deter continued interest in its acquisition.

"Tonight, there are ten contenders for the legendary diamond, none of whom seems frightened off by its grim history.

"But even without Kirstens and causes, the House of Graet Christmas Ball is a spectacular event.

"Vitrines of priceless jewels enhance club rooms, and the huge white tent erected for the evening on club grounds will be where cocktails are served. The festivities begin here.

"Pinkerton men discreetly guard the several hundred million

dollars' worth of jewelry on display this evening. Most of the gems on display are for sale. Ten percent of the sale price of the pieces will benefit the several charities the ball honors. And provide tax deductions for the purchasers.

"Three orchestras have been engaged for the gala. Glorious Food has been flown in from New York to prepare the gourmet dinner that will be served later.

"The club itself is handsomely decorated with Swiss-made House of Graet ornaments, tubs of poinsettia plants, silver and gold balloons, and three twenty-foot Christmas-festooned Norfolk Island pines.

"But most spectacular are the designer-gowned and -jeweled crème de la crème of Palm Beach society and their black-tie escorts. They will drink, dine, dance, and wait to learn who among them is the lucky new owner of the famous—or infamous—Kirsten diamond.

"The woman responsible for all this excitement and elegance is the elegant Contessa Consuela Perrugia, president of the House of Graet, New York.

"Contessa," said Ben, spying Consuela and approaching her. "Are you prepared for the evening's festivities?"

Consuela smiled into the camera. *"Naturale!* As prepared as one can be."

"And are you ready to relinquish that fabulous Kirsten diamond for good?"

"Of course. That is what this is all about." Consuela waved her jeweled hand expressively outward. "I will be only too happy to turn the Kirsten over to its new owner."

"What about the losers tonight?"

Consuela sighed. "Ah, it is a pity that everyone cannot win it. But that is the way of life, no?" Her smile was apologetic. "You know, of course, the Kirsten will begin its world tour after the presentation this evening?"

"Won't it be difficult for the new owner to let go of it? Once he —or she—lays hands on it?"

"I do not think so. The arrangement was understood from the beginning. And all the moneys collected from the tour will be used for very important charities." The famous dimple flashed. "That is a great satisfaction, *sì?"*

"Of course," agreed Ben, falling under Consuela's spell. "I notice, Contessa, you're wearing one of the Kirsten necklaces. I must say it's a stunner." He paused; leaned toward Consuela. "Are you prepared to tell us now which Kirsten this is?"

Another sigh escaped Consuela. "I am sorry. That information will be announced when the raffle has been conducted."

Ben grinned boyishly. "You mean, we still have to wait?"

Consuela's jeweled fingers stroked the replica. "Only a bit longer, *caro*. Now, if you will excuse me . . ."

"Certainly. Thank you for your comments, Contessa. And may I say no one could possibly display that necklace to better advantage."

Consuela's smile rewarded him. *"Grazie, Benjamin."*

Ben turned back to the cameras. "It looks as though the suspense will last a little longer. I'll be reporting on the festivities throughout the evening. And I will be covering the raffle. So, as soon as I know, you will know.

"This is Ben Gately, WKBQ, live from Wellington. Covering the House of Graet Christmas Ball."

Bordon Granger came up to Ben. "Nicely done, Ben."

Ben thanked him.

Bordon grinned. "All prepared for the move tomorrow?"

"As prepared as I'll ever be," Ben told him.

"Good. I'll talk to you before you leave." He smiled encouragement. "It's a whole new life you're beginning, son."

Ben nodded. "A whole new life," he agreed.

Only after Bordon left did Ben allow himself to brood. Without Kate, what life would there be?

There was a nip in the December air. But Earl Blakely kept warm parking the cars of the very rich. Those that weren't chauffeur-driven, that is. Just the feel of a Rolls wheel beneath his fingertips kept his blood circulating merrily.

He'd just finished parking one Rolls when the chauffeur-driven Dawson Rolls rolled right up to the red carpet. Earl watched the witch of Elsinore alight, followed by Belinda.

Earl's eyes slid from Belinda to Howie, who trailed after them.

At some point in the evening, Howie would meet Earl and hand over the parcel.

Earl recognized his future lay in Howie's hands.

And that knowledge made him nervous.

But not so nervous he didn't have wits enough to keep an eye out for that bastard, Granger. No way did Earl want to lock horns with that SOB.

Because if he locked horns with Granger, there'd be no future for Earl Blakely.

18

The huge white tent was carpeted in rich red. Lighted colored lanterns attached to ceiling poles provided soft light. A twelve-piece band played a seemingly uninterrupted medley of music from the forties and fifties.

Poinsettias flowered against tent walls. Bougainvillaea bloomed and twined on tent poles. Vitrines of jewels glittered from the branches of a twenty-foot Norfolk Island pine. Other vitrines around the room displayed more important pieces from the House of Graet collection.

The center vitrine housed the Kirsten diamond. Guarded discreetly by Pinkerton men.

Black-tie waiters wearing immaculate white gloves passed silver trays holding glasses of Dom Pérignon and Perrier.

Bowls of Beluga caviar over cracked ice sat on white-clothed tables alongside silver baskets of thin-sliced black bread, sliced lemons, silver baskets of hard and soft salamis and sausages, veal tartare, baskets of crudités, a variety of sauces.

People mingled, ate, and drank.

The House of Graet Christmas Ball had begun.

The Kirstens were the focus of attention. The one around the contessa's neck and the one in the center vitrine.

Consuela was everywhere. Chatting warmly with guests, greeting friends. Tony and Angie Owens. Paolo and Serafina. Abu and Danielle, Bordon, Tami, and Erin, the Duke and Duchess of Embry.

Mimzee Dawson, flanked by Belinda and Howie, swept imperially into the tent.

She peered intently at Consuela's necklace. "Tell me, that is the real one, isn't it?"

Consuela's eyes glittered. "What do you think?"

"I'd know the real one anywhere," boasted Mimzee.

Consuela shrugged helplessly. "You are impossible to fool."

"Damn right," bellowed Mimzee.

Consuela marveled at the exquisiteness of Rosemary's David Emanuel gown, at how elegant Marjorie looked in her blue chiffon—"Balmain, is it not?"—and how beautiful Kimberly was.

"But where is Mark?" inquired Consuela.

Rosemary responded sotto voce. "Off somewhere. Ferreting out national secrets."

Marjorie frowned. "We're hoping he'll be here before the evening ends."

"*Sí,* I hope so too," said Consuela smoothly. "It would be sad for him to miss all the festivities."

"Sad," agreed Rosemary, helping herself to a glass of Dom Pérignon from the tray of a passing white-gloved waiter.

Reenie Boyd, her arm linked through the arm of the junior senator from North Carolina, George Martinson, strolled into the tent, trailing her ermine wrap.

"Darlin'," she said, handing it to the senator, "take care of this like a love. And bring me a bourbon on the way back. That's a good boy."

She walked up to Consuela. "I see you're wearin' that fabulous rock, Consuela. Or is it the fabulous fake?"

She looked at Consuela shrewdly. "Depend on you to do the unexpected. I'd say it was the fake. Right?"

Consuela merely smiled.

"Not telling? Oh, well," said Reenie, bored with guessing games, "I honestly don't give a damn." Her eyes restlessly roamed the room. "You wouldn't by any chance know where the senator from Connecticut is, darlin', would you?"

Consuela said she did not.

"If the senator from North Carolina comes lookin' for me with my bourbon," Reenie told Consuela, "tell him I'm circulatin'. Will you do that, darlin'?"

Howie Caine's eyes bulged at the dazzling display of jewelry.

Jesus! There were enough rocks in this room to finance a dozen drug deals.

But it was the rock around the contessa's neck that claimed his attention. Getting it off her neck and into the pouch over his pecker was the order of the evening.

Consuela extracted Louis-Philippe from a cluster of women eager to meet and speak with the designer of the newly designed Kirsten.

"Such a throng, Louis." She smiled up at him. "Without you, I could never manage this. You are my total support."

"Consuela, you know as well as I you don't believe a word of that," he responded, somewhat testily.

The dimple flashed. "Well, part of it is true, *caro.* You are my support, and I do manage better when I know you are nearby. Besides," she added, "you are the star tonight. Everyone is marveling at your Kirsten. And its replica. No one can guess which is which. Not even I."

He smiled at her, not believing even that, but realizing he could never change her. Nor would he want to. Perfection was not to be tampered with.

Consuela was forced to relinquish Louis-Philippe to some Palm Beach matrons who insisted on a complete verbal recounting of the Kirsten legend by the man who was expert on the subject.

She circulated the room, and noted that Sandy Stone, looking quite fetching in green taffeta, was without Derek.

She must take time during the evening to wish her luck.

Dio mio, with Derek she would need it, thought Consuela philosophically.

Kate performed her duties with consummate skill. Only two times during the evening was her poise threatened.

The first incident was her confrontation with Rosemary Hunter.

Suddenly, Kate, parting from one group, turning to join another, found herself facing Rosemary Hunter.

For a second, Kate didn't recognize her. The turban. The tinted glasses. The elaborate ball gown. "Mrs. Hunter," said Kate, at last recovering her senses.

The gracefully shaped head enveloped in the high puffed turban tilted speculatively. "Hello," responded Rosemary. She weaved slightly. "Are we waiting for the same man, Miss Crowley?"

Kate paled.

Rosemary smiled. "Well, he won't be here," she told Kate. "He's off somewhere chasing shadows." She turned to her group of admirers and, lifting her glass high, beckoned them on.

The second unpleasant confrontation of the evening was with Reenie Boyd.

Reenie's restless eyes appraised Kate. "I don't believe we've met, Miss Crowley. But I understand we have mutual interests. Oh, by the way, this is Senator Martinson of North Carolina. And, speaking of senators, where is ours?"

"Ours?" managed Kate.

"Mark, sugah," explained Reenie impatiently. "Mark Hunter. Who else? I've been lookin' for that bastard all over town. Do you know where he is?"

Kate was stunned. "Why don't you ask his wife?" she suggested coolly. "Perhaps she knows."

Reenie raised an eyebrow. "Why, thank you, darlin'. I might just do that. I can't believe I didn't think of that myself."

Rosemary drifted around the great tent, peering at vitrines of jewels, smiling, chatting, sipping from her ever-filled wineglass, accepting the attentions of the group of admiring males that drifted with her.

Julia Sheffield passed by. "Love your gown, Rosemary. And your turban."

"Thank you," smiled Rosemary sweetly. *Bitch! First-class, fucking, hypocritical bitch, that's what Julia Sheffield was!*

Buddy Bigelow, an old beau of Rosemary's, peered at her intently. "Rosemary? Is that you behind those tinted shades?"

"None other." She laughed gaily.

Buddy Bigelow looked around. "Where's Mark? I haven't seen him."

"Out looking for me," said Rosemary. "But he hasn't caught up with me yet."

She had no idea where Mark was. What's more, she couldn't care less. Mark was a madman. Off on a witch hunt.

She felt freer without him. Less constrained. All he did was criticize her. Put her down. Hold her back.

Maybe Mark was the cause of her problems. Maybe Mark was the greatest weight attached to her. Maybe without him . . .

"Let me freshen your drink, Rosemary," offered Buddy Bigelow.

He was rewarded with a beguiling smile. "Yes, do that," said Rosemary, handing him her wineglass.

The Allegheny Airlines plane with Senator Hunter on it landed in Binghamton, New York. Barely. It was grounded until weather conditions improved.

Mark Hunter headed for the airport bar and downed several Scotches in frustration.

He looked at his watch: 6:00 P.M. At this rate, he'd be lucky to be in Palm Beach by dawn.

He finished his drinks, slapped some cash on the bar, and went in search of the plane's pilot.

The pilot recognized him. A taciturn Texan, he was neither impressed nor awed by the presence of an irate United States senator. "What can I do for you, Senator?" he asked lazily.

"How soon can we get this show on the road?" demanded Mark. "Or, more precisely, this plane in the air?"

The Texan didn't smile. "Your guess is as good as mine. Certainly not before this mess clears up. You were there. We were lucky to get her down on the ground."

Mark tried his famous charm. "Look," he said, "I just need a goddamned plane to fly. Mine's stranded in Connecticut. I've got to get to Palm Beach tonight. Got any suggestions?"

The pilot shifted in his chair. "Senator, I'm plumb out of suggestions. I'll tell you this, though. You may as well relax. Nothing's going up in this stuff. I don't care who the pilot is."

Mark shrugged in surrender. "What in hell is there to do in the meantime?"

The Texan finally grinned. "I don't know about you, Senator, but I'm going to get laid. I happen to know a little lady who lives real close by."

Mark slid into an adjoining chair and stretched out his legs. "Why don't you ask her if she's got a friend?" he suggested.

19

Each of the 100 round tables in the club dining room was set for 10 people. Cloths on the table were layered—red over silver. Napkins were red. China was white, gold-rimmed with a center *HG* gold crest. Silver was Georgian. Crystal was Baccarat.

On each table, branches of juniper entwined with holly and boughs of pine formed a circle around a miniature silver-sprayed pine tree. Ten elegantly wrapped boxes of table favors decorated each tree. Inside the boxes—sterling silver compacts for the ladies, lapis and silver cuff links for the gentlemen.

Baccarat chandeliers hung from the ceiling. Silver candelabra glowed from sideboards. Colored votive candles on each of the round tables cast soft shadows, erasing lines from faces of designer-clad dowagers. Every woman looked ageless. Every gentleman appeared beguiled.

The room buzzed with the sounds of conversation, the rise and fall of laughter, the discreet movements of 150 black-tie waiters serving courses, pouring wine, removing dishes.

A blonde vocalist in a beaded red dress caressed the room with her rendition of "Embraceable You."

The House of Graet Christmas Ball dinner was under way.

Mimzee Dawson couldn't take her eyes off the Kirsten around Consuela's neck. Soon, soon, it would be hers. The pleasure of imminent ownership brought a satisfied smile to her face.

"You look like the cat that ate the canary," noted Belinda.

"Damned right," exulted Mimzee. She looked sharply at her granddaughter, who barely touched her soup. "You'd better stop eating like a canary, or even the cat'll turn up his nose at you. Why you think skinny is attractive is beyond me."

"I'm hardly skinny," defended Belinda.

"You're hardly there. One good puff of wind and you'd disappear."

"Really!" said Belinda, laying down her spoon in annoyance.

"Really!" repeated her grandmother. "I've got big plans for you, Belinda. But I can't market a bag of bones for beans."

"I'm not a piece of meat you can market, Mimzee."

"Damn right, you're not. Not enough meat there," said Mimzee, chewing heartily on a mussel from her cold mussel soup.

If she doesn't get off my back, decided Belinda, *I'll spite her and marry the groundskeeper's assistant.* He had asked her. Belinda had laughed at him. Being good in the sack was not the highest matrimonial priority in her book, she informed him.

Still, if Mimzee continued to bug her . . .

On her way through the club dining room, Reenie, trailed by the junior senator from North Carolina, stopped at Rosemary's table.

"Darlin'," said Reenie, "how divine you're lookin'."

Rosemary's eyes beneath tinted pavé-framed glasses moved from Buddy Bigelow's face to Reenie's. She neither acknowledged the compliment nor returned it.

Nonplussed, Reenie rushed on. "Could you tell me, sugah, where that wicked husband of yours is? I've been lookin' all over for him."

Rosemary lifted her wineglass, sipped from it, put it down. "Why don't you ask his mistress?" she suggested pleasantly.

"But, honey," explained Reenie, "she asked me to ask you."

"Well, then," observed Rosemary blandly, "any other suggestion I have for you would cause these dear gentlemen with us to turn scarlet."

Considering the conversation terminated, Rosemary turned her attention back to Buddy Bigelow.

Reenie moved on.

During dinner, Rosemary switched from wine to vodka.

The wine was giving her a slow lugubrious buzz. If she didn't watch out, she'd soon be crying into her Baccarat.

How could the French drink it all day?

Rosemary picked up her vodka, tossed it down. That was more

like it. Bracing. Stimulating. As it slid smoothly down her throat, her eyes smarted, then cleared.

Suddenly, everything looked brighter.

It was an unfortunate mix-up in placement that put Reenie Boyd at the same table with Tami Hayes, Erin, and Bordon Granger.

Not unfortunate for Reenie. She reveled in the seating arrangement. She particularly relished the opportunity to study Erin. Damned if there wasn't a decided resemblance to Earl Blakely. The color of the eyes and hair. The shape of the face and nose. Everything looked softer on Erin, but then she hadn't had her features sharpened in the school of hard knocks. Things had come easy for her.

"You look mighty like your daddy, you know," Reenie said to her.

"You know my father?" asked Erin, startled.

Across the table, Tami froze. Bordon tensed.

"I've met him," said Reenie. "In fact, I met him here."

"Here?" cried Erin.

"A decidedly handsome man," noted Reenie. "Don't you agree, Tami?"

In her agitation, Tami moved jerkily, upsetting her espresso and dessert, spilling the contents of both into her lap. Pain and humiliation brought tears to her eyes as she jumped up.

"Tami!" cried Erin, rising in alarm to help her. Several waiters stationed nearby rushed forward. But Bordon was there first, grabbing some ice from the champagne cooler, wrapping it in a napkin, applying it to the scalded area, while wiping up the remains of a custard and cream dessert with another napkin.

"My dress!" cried Tami absurdly.

"Let's get you out of it, love, and see to that burn," said Bordon, calmly taking charge. He turned to Erin, refusing to leave her behind, unprotected from Reenie Boyd's malice. "Erin, you had better come with us," he said tightly.

Bordon fixed Reenie with an icy stare. "You're skating on thin ice," he told her, drawing comfort from the knowledge she was still ignorant of his Boyd Enterprises takeover.

Reenie Boyd was through.

At the appropriate moment, he'd make that fact known to her.

George Martinson, the junior senator from North Carolina, turned to Reenie. "An unfortunate accident," he noted.

"Know of any fortunate ones, sugah?" asked Reenie.

He laughed. "What was all that badinage about?"

"That wasn't badinage, darlin'. That was information bein' disseminated," Reenie told him. "Some people just overreact to good news."

The burn was minor. Bordon attended to it. The ball gown was a disaster. The housekeeper whisked it away, insisting she could remove the stains. But Tami's emotions were not so easily attended to, not so quickly restored.

There was the business with Erin, who was due an explanation. Tami knew she would have to tell her about Earl, that he was indeed in town, that he had made no effort to see her, that he really didn't care.

Whatever needed to be said, she would say.

She looked over at Bordon. "If you'd like, darling, after I've talked with Erin, we can return to the scene of the crime."

Reenie's eyes slid over Kate with uninterest. She was bored. Bored with baiting Kate and Tami Hayes. Bored with antagonizing Rosemary. And bored with the junior senator from North Carolina.

Only one thing would relieve her boredom. The sight of Mark Hunter easing his way gracefully into the room.

It wasn't to be.

Mark Hunter still hadn't arrived and Reenie Boyd fretfully wondered why the hell not.

❧20❧

The club ballroom was strung with festive colored lanterns. Another huge decorated Norfolk Island pine stood in one corner of the room, surrounded by vitrines of House of Graet jewels.

The Kirsten diamond had been moved into the ballroom, where the raffle would be held later in the evening. Preceded by the presentation of several door prizes—a diamond necklace, sapphire earrings, 18k and diamond cuff links and studs, a diamond and pearl brooch.

A thirty-piece forties' band played golden oldies—"Up a Lazy River," a Mills Brothers favorite. "Don't Sit Under the Apple Tree," "Day by Day," "I'll Get By," "Call Me Irresponsible," from the Broadway show *A Delicate Condition.*

Several bars around the room, manned by black-tie bartenders, filled orders.

People drank, danced, flirted, laughed. Some bickered.

The House of Graet Christmas Ball gained momentum.

Rosemary danced and flirted with each of the partners clamoring for her favors. Her feet barely touched the floor. Her body floated.

She was weightless.

She soared.

She was a bird in flight.

She could do anything.

Nothing could hold her back.

Men kept cutting in on Buddy Bigelow. Buddy Bigelow kept cutting back in.

"I think you're a bit snorkeled," laughed Buddy.

"Nonsense," replied Rosemary. "I'm in transit."

"In transit? From where?"

"From here. To there." She let herself drift with the music. "There's where I haven't been yet. Here's where I'm at."

Buddy Bigelow pulled her closer.

Marjorie Hunter, observing them, frowned.

Kimberly Hunter, feeling the familiar mortification coupled with fury at her mother's drunken exhibitionism, smiled brilliantly at the inane chatter of her dance partner.

Consuela was dancing with the Duke of Embry. Louis-Philippe cut in.

"You see," he confessed, taking her into his arms and pulling her close, "I cannot bear to be apart from you for a moment."

The dimple flashed. "Ah, Louis," she said throatily, "that is only as it should be."

They danced expertly to the music. As though they had been dancing together for years.

So content was she in Louis's arms, Consuela did not even ask him how he thought the ball was going.

Ben cut in on Kate. No longer lovers, they were still friends, he reminded himself.

He pulled her gently into the circle of his arms. There were so many things he wanted to say to her. This wasn't the place. Besides, he had said them all.

But her scent, her nearness, her body enveloped in his arms, were too potent a reminder of what they'd had for caution. "You feel awfully good, sweetheart," he told her huskily.

Her eyes were soft. "Oh, Ben, I missed you," she admitted.

It didn't have to be this way. Couldn't she see that? wondered Ben.

From her table at the edge of the dance floor, Mimzee Dawson monitored Howie's every move. She watched him sashay from partner to partner, wondering irritably how long it would take him to get to Consuela and waltz her out onto the terrace.

Suspense made her testy.

Her eyes moved restlessly from Howie to the Kirsten—so close and yet so distant. It hung around the contessa's neck like a reproach. It belonged to Mimzee.

Her dependence on Howie to successfully complete his part in the mission was another reproach. Mimzee preferred to be in sole charge. Results were more predictable that way.

Howie Caine hadn't forgotten his mission. He was gearing up for it.

He danced and flirted with dozens of beautiful young things. And a score of older ones. Female flesh floated in and out of his arms and, although he was properly appreciative, he never lost sight of his goal.

He danced with Kimberly Hunter, a vision of virginity in pale blue tulle.

"You look good enough to lick," whispered Howie in her ear.

Kimberly pulled back and stared at him coldly. "You're such an ass, Howie. Particularly when you try not to be one."

Howie relinquished Kimberly to a callow youth who seemed to deserve her and cut in on Kimberly's mother.

"Well, well," crooned Rosemary, "if it isn't little Howie Caine."

"Not so little," corrected Howie.

He swept Rosemary into his arms. Pulled against the bulge of the Kirsten replica, Rosemary reflected, "You're right, Howie. You're not."

He knew he shouldn't be wasting time on her. He should make his move toward the contessa. But he hadn't forgotten the short shrift he'd received from her. He was determined to pay her back.

Later, he promised himself. After he'd taken care of the other.

He looked down at Rosemary. "Why're you wearing those shades?"

Rosemary swayed in his arms. "It's a cruel world out there. Everybody needs a little protection."

"Yeah," agreed Howie. "That's for sure." He looked past her. "Say, where's your husband? How come I never see you with him?"

Rosemary shrugged. "Only The Shadow knows. And he isn't telling."

Why was everyone interested in Mark, anyway? What did it matter where he was?

The Allegheny Airlines pilot had left the phone number of hi friend's town house with the flight office. When the call came hi

442

plane could take off, he patted the sleeping blonde's rump affectionately and slipped out of bed.

He padded naked down the hall to the door of the other bedroom and knocked.

He opened the door. Mark was awake. The redhead was asleep.

The Texan leaned lazily against the open door. "You're in luck, Senator. Looks like things are movin' again."

Mark grinned, then glanced at the redhead. "What do we do about the ladies?"

"Leave 'em a thank-you note. And some cash. That oughta clear us for next time. If there is a next time." The pilot padded back to his room.

Mark dressed quickly, took his pen and a small pad from his inside jacket pocket, and scribbled a short note. He took a $100 bill from his wallet and folded it around the note. He put the two items under the pillow of the sleeping redhead.

What the hell, he thought. Binghamton wasn't such a bad place to be stranded in after all. That is, if he had to lose time, it certainly helped to be able to make time.

The layover was worth every penny of the 100 bucks.

Earl paced the stretch of graveled driveway at the entrance to the club restlessly. Waiting for Howie played havoc with his nerves. Earl preferred action.

All he needed to court his heiress properly was some dough.

All he needed to waltz her to the altar was a little more time.

Earl had a hunch the parcel Howie would deliver contained the means to provide Earl with both.

He couldn't miss. The lady had an itch. He had the itch scratcher. That was a combination difficult to beat.

⸙21⸙

It was time to make his move.

Howie Caine edged his way through the maze of dancers as the music stopped.

Consuela and Louis-Philippe parted. Consuela's face was flushed, her color high.

"May I borrow the contessa for the next dance?" asked Howie, smiling boyishly. Louis-Philippe reluctantly released her.

Dancing with the lady, Howie was dazzled by the nearness of the Kirsten as he wondered how the hell he was going to waltz her out onto the terrace.

"That's some beautiful rock you're wearing, Contessa."

Consuela smiled. "Some very fortunate person will shortly own this rock."

"Must be tough to part with," he suggested.

"Not so tough," she allowed. The dimple flashed. "Perhaps your grandmother will be the one to win this great prize tonight. That would give her great pleasure, no?"

Howie grinned. "You can say that again." *But not,* he thought, *as much pleasure as it's going to give me.*

The music stopped. They stood there, Howie's mind working feverishly as he planned his next move.

"It is so warm in here, *caro.* Take me out on the terrace for a bit of air before I expire," directed Consuela.

Howie's grin was broad. Someone was looking out for him, he exulted. Things were picking up.

He walked Consuela out onto the terrace and steered her toward a secluded spot overlooking the lush, meticulously tended club grounds.

She walked ahead of him to the white wrought-iron railing, her back to him.

Howie quickly removed the handkerchief from his breast pocket, the atomizer from his inside pocket, and surreptitiously but thoroughly sprayed the handkerchief with the mists from Mimzee's token of her last Far Eastern jaunt. He replaced the atomizer and the handkerchief, and moved closer to the contessa.

"Ah," said Consuela, breathing deeply of the moist southern air, "much better."

"You warm enough?" Howie asked solicitously.

"I am fine now, thank you, Howie." She turned, spied the floral-cushioned wrought-iron bench nearby. "Let us sit for a moment. My feet are protesting the abuse I have put them through." The dimple flashed again. "Dancing at your age, *caro*, takes no toll. That comes later."

They sat together in silence, Consuela content for a moment's respite from her duties as hostess.

Consuela turned to him. "This is nice, no?"

"Nice," agreed Howie. He leaned over and peered intently at Consuela. "You have a spot on your nose, Contessa."

"A spot?" Consuela's hand instinctively flew to her nose.

"Here, let me get it for you," he offered, whisking out the handkerchief from his breast pocket.

He cupped the handkerchief so the drug-saturated section covered her nostrils, dabbing diligently at the imaginary spot.

"There," said Howie, satisfied. "All gone."

So was the contessa. Out like a light. Her head lolled against the back of the floral-covered cushion, her mouth slightly ajar.

Howie went into action.

He dropped his trousers, ripped Mimzee's Kirsten replica from the pouch over his crotch, jammed it into his jacket pocket, and reached for the clasp on the Kirsten around the contessa's neck.

He struggled with it, jiggled it, groped at it, tried to pry it open.

He couldn't get the goddamned thing off her neck!

This clasp was different from the one Mimzee had him practice on!

At her table, Mimzee Dawson was the center of attention. This did not, however, prevent her from noting the departure of her grandson as he accompanied the contessa from the ballroom to the terrace.

"What were you saying about Hollis Pane, Mimzee?" the Duchess of Embry, the former Betsy Armstrong, asked.

Mimzee adjusted her tiara. "He's on fire, dearie. That's what. A flaming queen."

"But he just married the Wilson girl," protested Betsy.

Mimzee's look was scornful. "A cover, cookie. In a conservative business like investments, what did you expect him to do? Dress in drag for the wedding?"

The clasp wouldn't budge. It had an extra little doohickey on it. Goddamn! Fiddling with it was using up time. And time was what he was running out of.

Howie sweated. Consuela's head lolled forward. Howie pinched, pulled, and picked at the opening. It refused to give.

In desperation, he gave one last final tug at the clasp and tried to wrench it open. Nothing! The goddamned thing must be riveted in place!

Howie fell back on the bench next to Consuela, flushed and exhausted.

The contessa stirred.

God Almighty, she was coming to!

Hastily, he stepped to the rear of the bench, took the replica from his jacket pocket, dropped it back into the pouch, pulled up his trousers, zipped up his fly, stepped back in front of the contessa, and solicitously bent over her stirring form.

"Are you all right?" he asked.

The obvious concern on his face touched Consuela. To ease his distress, she made light of the incident. "To swoon like a Victorian lady is most unlike me, *caro*. I must apologize for frightening you."

"I'm just glad you're okay," Howie assured her. He helped her to her feet.

"*Grazie.*" She smoothed her sleek chignon and slipped her arm through his. Her rich laugh rang out. "Perhaps I needed a little rest, no? Now that I have had that, you can see I am properly returned to the ball, *caro*. In time for the raffle."

Howie dutifully returned the contessa to the ball.

The Kirsten replica, secure in its pouch over his pecker, no longer gave him a hard-on.

But he wondered how much the fake was worth.

Mimzee cornered Howie under cover of a large potted palm.

"Did you get it?" she stage-whispered.

"Get what?" queried Howie, knowing full well what she meant.

"You know what," she hissed.

Bitterness gnawed at him. "A breeze! That's what you said, right? Well, the damned clasp was different. I couldn't get it undone. Unless you wanted me to hit her on the head with a hammer and saw the damned thing off her neck."

Mimzee paled. "Dunce!" she spat.

Howie glared. "Thanks," he sneered.

Rosemary spotted Howie Caine across the room. He looked so irresistibly young, so breathtakingly beautiful, it almost broke her heart. Such youth and beauty lasted for so fleeting a moment.

She needed someone young to revive her flagging spirits.

She was tired. Depressed. Edgy. Her earlier mood of exuberance was dimmed.

And there was something else. Something she had been looking for. If only she could remember what it was.

She weaved her way to Howie's side and smiled at him brilliantly. "You look so delicious, I had to come claim you. I want you with me when they raffle off the Kirsten." She linked her arm through his. "You're going to bring me luck."

She would win. She had to win. Daddy was counting on her. It would please him, and pleasing Daddy was what she wanted most of all.

And it would piss Mark off. That thought was sufficiently gratifying to dispel all gloom.

"You can wear it in the tub, Roe," Daddy had said.

The hell she would! She would wear it to the Palm Beach supermarket if she pleased. Except she didn't go to supermarkets. But she would wear it anywhere, anytime she wished. No matter what Mark said. No matter what image he said he had to protect.

She would never play the subdued socialite again. For anyone.

447

She was going to shine. At last.
In spite of Mark.
To spite Mark.
No. To satisfy herself.

The connections, it seemed, were made effortlessly this time. There was a flight from Newark Airport, nonstop, to take him to Palm Beach.

Now that he was on his way back, Mark began to face up to the problems that awaited him.

Rosemary. It was time to get off the treadmill.

His mother. All of his life, she'd been trying to manipulate him under the benevolent guise of family responsibility, honor, duty, destiny. That would end.

His kids. They deserved a better shake than the one they were getting. He would see that they got one.

Kate. The only one who asked nothing of him. And whom he'd given so little in return. That would change. Kate deserved more. He determined she would get it.

His career? Other divorced politicians made it to the White House. So could he. And if he didn't make it there, there were other challenging ways to make a contribution in this world.

Things were looking up. There was a light at the end of the tunnel.

22

The moment everyone was waiting for was at hand.

Consuela made the announcement. "And now, ladies and gentlemen . . . the raffle of the Kirsten." She turned toward an elderly gentleman in black tie. "Mr. Angus Broderick has kindly agreed to assist us on this momentous occasion."

A burst of applause acknowledged the announcement.

Consuela raised her hand, diamonds flashing on wrist and fingers. "One last item before the long-awaited raffle." The other jeweled hand moved gracefully to the Kirsten around her neck. "To answer the question that has been on the minds of many as to which Kirsten is which," she paused dramatically, "the Kirsten I am wearing . . . is the . . . replica." Gasps of astonishment from the audience. "The one on the form in the center vitrine is the real one." A huge burst of applause.

"And now, Mr. Broderick, if you will kindly do the honors and end our suspense . . ."

Drums rolled.

Angus Broderick dipped his hand into the House of Graet crystal bowl, withdrew one folded slip of paper, and handed it to Consuela.

The room was suddenly stilled.

Consuela opened the folded slip of paper and read the name written on it. Her face gave no indication of what the contents revealed.

She raised her eyes, held up the slip of paper, and made the announcement. "The winner of the Kirsten is—" another dramatic pause, followed by another brilliant smile—"Miss Mimzee Dawson."

The announcement was greeted by a few inelegant hoots, wild applause, sighs of disappointment, and one lone shriek of joy.

"Hot damn!" yelled Mimzee, slapping her thigh with delight. "Some things just have to be!" She turned to Marjorie and confessed, awe in her voice, "It almost makes me believe in God."

She rose, drew herself up regally, adjusted her diamond tiara, and stepped forward to claim her prize. Her face wore a smile of victory and vindication. Her thoughts were clear and precise.

The blunder committed by Howie was forgiven. Thank God, he hadn't come home with the replica!

The Kirsten was clasped around her neck. For the duration of the ball, she would wear it. At evening's end, it would be returned in preparation for its world tour.

Meanwhile, Mimzee pranced about, showing off her Kirsten to awed and envious viewers, discreetly followed by Pinkerton men. "Don't hang over me," she snapped. "The only way anyone will get this off me is to kill me. And I don't anticipate that happening."

Ben Gately wrapped it up. He was finished with the House of Graet gala. Finished with the last Palm Beach segment.

There was one final bit of business he needed to attend to. He searched out Kate. "I'm on my way," he told her.

She walked outside with him.

The night air was soft. Stars glittered perfectly in the sky above them. A sliver of moon beckoned brightly. "Well," observed Ben wryly, "the best and worst is over."

Kate looked puzzled. "Oh?"

"The winners and the losers. Everyone can go home now. Some satisfied, others not."

"Ah," mused Kate, smiling. "I see."

"Somewhat like life," added Ben.

The smile faded. "I'm sorry, Ben."

He raised her chin and looked directly into her eyes. "Don't be. Be happy, Kate. There are too many miserable people around." He ought to know, he thought ruefully.

Tears filled Kate's eyes. "Oh, Ben," she said wistfully. "I do love you."

He bent; kissed her lightly. "I know," he said before he turned and walked away from her.

Rosemary was crushed at having lost out on the Kirsten. She wanted to win so much. As a prize for Daddy. As an irritant to Mark. As an affirmation of her own value for herself.

Mimzee Dawson, flaunting ownership, paused to preen in front of Rosemary. "Well, dearie, what d'ya think? Ain't it grand?"

Defeat was gall in Rosemary's mouth. "Grand," she smiled back.

She was damned if she'd let anyone know how much she cared. How much it bothered her.

The plane was scheduled to land in fifteen minutes. Mark psychologically geared himself for what lay ahead.

First, he'd track down Rosemary. Either at the ball or at the house. He'd try the house first. He could shower and change.

He'd deal calmly with Rosemary. If he came on strong, she'd get ornery. But if he handled her with kid gloves, maybe they'd be able to work things out reasonably.

He'd suggest one more trip back to that Connecticut farm for her.

And when Rosemary finished her treatment program this time, the split would be final. An amicable divorce. Reasonable custodial rights for Rosemary, contingent, of course, upon her sobriety and the consistency of it.

He'd find Kate, tell her how much he loved her, needed her.

He'd make it up to Kate. No more random redheads. No more easy ass. He was beginning to tire of it anyway.

All at once, the world was a beautiful, fantastic place. Filled with hope. Ripe with promise.

And the light—the light at the end of the tunnel seemed so bright, it was almost blinding.

23

Reenie Boyd was bored with the ball and tired of the prolonged ado over the Kirsten. She didn't give a fig who won or who lost out on that monstrosity. She had come to this event solely to see Mark. Since he obviously wasn't coming, she saw no reason to remain.

But she did feel the need to stir things up before she made her exit.

Her eyes restlessly covered the room. She saw that Tami Hayes and Bordon Granger had returned, even though they kept their distance from her. But she had lost interest in baiting them. Her eyes came to rest on Rosemary Hunter.

Suddenly, Rosemary became the focus of all the discontent Reenie felt surfacing. It was really quite simple. Rosemary Hunter possessed that which Reenie wanted most—Mark Hunter. Were it not for Rosemary, Mark would be free to marry her. And Reenie would be free to set in motion her plans to foster Mark's political career.

Rosemary Hunter was the obstacle to all her dreams.

When she saw Rosemary head for the powder room, Reenie stood.

"My nose needs dustin', darlin'," she explained to the junior senator from North Carolina.

She followed Rosemary into the pale peach silk striped ladies' lounge with its mirrored walls, lacquered vanities, and rattan lounge chairs.

Rosemary passed through the lounge into the toilet area and entered one of the stalls.

Reenie, waiting outside, listened impatiently as the vast

amounts of fluid Rosemary had consumed during the evening exited her body in seemingly endless cascades.

At last, the toilet flushed, the door opened, and Rosemary wobbled unsteadily out. She looked surprised to see Reenie. "That may well be the longest pee in history," she announced. "Were you timing it, darling?"

"No," replied Reenie. "I just happened to be in the neighborhood."

Rosemary weaved past her, plopped her evening purse on the sink counter, washed her hands, turned, and with a nod accepted a towel from the matron standing solicitously but silently nearby.

She dried her hands, returned the soiled towel to the matron, picked up her purse, opened it, removed a bill, and put it in the dish on the counter.

Reenie observed the ritual without comment.

Rosemary weaved her way into the lounge, surprisingly empty, sat before one of the lacquered vanities, and with diamond-framed sunglasses still on, inspected her face.

She opened her purse, removed a lipstick brush, and outlined her lips with a remarkably steady, practiced hand.

Reenie continued to observe the ritual quietly. But Rosemary was too much in her cups to be bugged by a silent presence. She ignored her.

Finally, Reenie spoke. "So sorry to hear about your loss, sugah."

The lipstick brush poised in midair. "Oh? Did someone close die I haven't heard about?" she asked.

Reenie laughed. "The Kirsten, darlin'. That loss. What is it they say? Unlucky in raffles, lucky in love?"

Rosemary returned to the business of outlining her lips. "I believe it's cards that's said of."

"Oh? So it is. But then, you're not, are you? Lucky in love, I mean? I notice you seem to have a great deal of difficulty keepin' that enticin' husband of yours in line." Reenie studied Rosemary carefully. "Offhand, I'd say accomplishin' that is a woman-sized job bein' handled by someone not big enough to manage it."

Rosemary turned around slowly. It took a second or so to focus on the face before her. "And I'd say, offhand, how I manage or do not manage my affairs—including handling my husband—is none of your goddamned business."

"Oh, but it is, sugah," insisted Reenie. "You see, when you divorce that darlin' man, I intend to marry him. And I have no doubts at all about my ability to keep him in check."

Rosemary stared at Reenie, then burst out laughing. *"Marry you!"* She stopped laughing and stared at Reenie once more. "You really think Mark would marry *you?* Oh, my dear, you are laboring under delusions. Mark would no more marry you than he would swallow snake oil. He has too much class to marry a slut like you."

Rosemary snapped her purse shut and rose unsteadily. "Tell you what though, *sugah*. If I were to divorce him—which I'm not— Mark might marry someone like—what's her name? Ah, yes. Kate Crowley. Now, whatever else my opinions of the lady are, she does have class. While you—" Rosemary drew herself up to her full height and stared at her rival with contempt—"you're just a cunt."

Reenie's face drained of color. "You're drunk," she said.

Rosemary nodded. "That may very well be true," she agreed. "But when I wake up in the morning, I may or may not be sober. You'll still be a cunt."

She walked out, leaving Reenie behind in the lounge with the matron, who blended innocuously into the decor, seemingly rendered oblivious to the scene just witnessed.

Reenie sucked in her breath, defiantly tossed back her head, and flounced out to look for her escort.

She found him where she'd left him. "Let's go to my place, sugah," she commanded. "There's gotta be more action there than here."

Kate went through the motions expected of her. She circulated; chatted; charmed. She looked beautiful, untroubled, and in full command of herself. And as vice-president in charge of public relations, she received her share of compliments for the success of the ball.

"It has gone well, Kate," observed Consuela, pausing for a moment to savor the fruits of her efforts.

"Beautifully," agreed Kate, her eyes following Consuela's as they swept the room.

Consuela turned back to Kate. "And you, *cara*. How have you weathered this evening?"

Kate's look was steady. "Very well, Consuela."

"I am glad," murmured Consuela, pressing Kate's hand fondly before she moved on.

It wasn't true, of course. She wasn't doing well.

She felt sorry to see Ben go. She would miss him. And she did love him.

The trouble was, she loved Mark too.

Someone asked her to dance. Kate smiled acceptance. But as she stepped into her escort's arms, her eyes made contact with Rosemary's, dancing by.

The look in Rosemary's eyes chilled Kate. The message seemed to say, "There is no future for you and Mark. There never will be. So why waste time making plans?"

Kate tensed, then turned away. She resolved to stay clear of Rosemary Hunter for the rest of the evening. Rosemary was unpredictable, unstable, and obviously drunk. A highly combustible combination that could only spell trouble.

Trouble, decided Kate, was the last thing she needed.

The scene in the john left a bad taste in Rosemary's mouth. All scenes, she thought, took a toll.

Imagine that bitch confronting her like that! And having the gall to tell her she was drunk!

Well, she might be drunk, but she was still ambulatory. And so long as she was ambulatory, she was functioning. And so long as she was functioning, no one had a right to criticize her.

She weaved her way again to Howie Caine. She gave him a quizzical, slightly lopsided smile. "I'm ready to leave," she announced. "You may take me home, Howie."

Howie had been busily trying to figure out how much cash he could parlay the replica into.

Looking at Rosemary, it suddenly occurred to him she might like to kick into the kitty.

Hell, that bracelet she was wearing must be worth a fortune. The rest of the junk must be back at her house.

"Sure thing, Rosemary," said Howie agreeably.

Marjorie Hunter pressed a hand fretfully to her forehead. She couldn't believe Mark hadn't shown up. More alarming, though, was her awareness Rosemary was no longer in attendance.

"Kimberly, have you seen your mother?" asked Marjorie.

Kimberly, who had observed Rosemary leave with that creep, Howie Caine, nodded. "She went off to repair her makeup."

"She's all right, then?" asked Marjorie, seeking reassurance.

"She's fine," replied Kimberly, supplying it. Rosemary Hunter would always be fine, thought Kimberly bitterly. It was everyone else who was affected.

Mark strapped himself in for the approach to Palm Beach International Airport.

He glanced at his watch: 12:45. Rosemary was probably still at the ball. She never left a party while the booze still flowed. He'd stop at the house first. Better still, he'd wait for her there.

He needed to collect his thoughts some more before he confronted her. It was important to remain in complete control. It was imperative to think clearly.

Something else occurred to him. If Rosemary were drunk, maybe he should wait until morning before issuing ultimatums. He wanted a minimum of fuss. To achieve maximum results.

His thoughts strayed to Kate. He needed to see her. But he knew she'd be tied up at the ball until the very end. There was no chance of seeing her now.

When he worked things through with Rosemary, he'd call Kate. Go over to see her. Tell her all his plans. Their plans.

How he needed her. Kate was his oasis of sanity in a world of confusion and stress.

More. Kate was his life. Indeed, Kate was the light at the end of the tunnel.

24

Howie swung the car up the long driveway to the Hunter house and stopped in front of the entrance.

Rosemary leaned toward him provocatively. "Come in for a nightcap, Howie. Such proficiency in seeing me home safely deserves a reward."

Howie helped her out of the car. A few more belts of whatever she was taking in and he could help himself to the rocks she was wearing.

Rosemary led him down the wide tiled entrance hall to the library, opened the door, stepped inside, and announced, "The library. Also known as the meditation room. Also known as the assignation room. Also known as a neat little place to find a drink."

He sat on one of the two library couches and watched her prepare two drinks at the bar. Idly he wondered where in hell she put all the booze she consumed. She must have a hollow leg. Christ, she must have a hollow torso too.

Rosemary crossed the room unsteadily, handed Howie his drink, and sat next to him on the couch.

She clicked her glass to his. "To friendship," she toasted. "Ours. Long may it thrive."

She was still wearing those damned shades. "Why don't you take those glasses off, Rosemary?" Howie asked petulantly. "How can you see anything with them on?"

"I can see well enough to see what I like," she told him.

She finished her drink, refilled her glass, her eyes carelessly flicking over the room.

They paused at Howie. *So delectable,* thought Rosemary. *Such a tasty sight. And so very, very young.*

She had been that young once. And beautiful. Breathtakingly beautiful. Everything had been waiting for her then. Everything offered to her. All she had to do was reach out her hand for something and it was hers. It was that easy.

She had been desired, envied, admired, adored.

What went wrong?

Rosemary turned and studied her reflection in the mirror behind the library bar. She still looked beautiful. The David Emanuel gown. The high gauze turban. The diamond-framed tinted glasses.

> *Mirror, mirror, on the wall.*
> *Who is the fairest one of all?*

She turned again. "Do you think I'm beautiful, Howie?"

"Yeah," he said, strangely aroused by the sight of Rosemary narcissistically admiring her own reflection.

She smiled. "So are you. Very, very beautiful. Two beautiful people, Howie. That's what we are."

She crossed to the couch, put her drink down, took Howie's glass from him, and put that down too. "Two beautiful people," mused Rosemary, "should make beautiful love together." She removed her glasses and Howie found himself drowning in the depths of Rosemary's soft brown eyes.

Her scent, her perfect body, her imperious air, the closeness of her, suddenly overpowered him. He felt himself grow hard.

Before he knew it, Rosemary was on top of him, smothering him with kisses, tearing at him, unbuttoning his shirt, her hands light, feathery, but hot and demanding as they spanned his chest, moving over it with practiced ease.

One hand moved down, deftly undid his fly, expertly groped within for the prize she sought.

And discovered a different prize.

Jesus! He had forgotten the pouch!

Puzzled, Rosemary looked at it, quickly undid it before Howie could stop her, and withdrew the Kirsten replica.

"Mother of God!" cried Rosemary in disbelief. "You not only

have your own set of family jewels, Howie, you carry a spare." She started to giggle.

"Gimme that," he demanded angrily, but Rosemary, even in her cups, was too quick for him. She darted from the couch to the other side of the room, holding the Kirsten aloft and waving it enticingly at him.

"It's mine," she laughed. "Finders keepers." She looked at the necklace again, dazzled by the brilliance of the red and white diamonds flashing fire. The necklace looked familiar. Rosemary looked more closely. Then she knew.

"Dear God in heaven!" she breathed in awe. *"You've stolen the Kirsten, Howie!"*

"It's not the Kirsten," insisted Howie heatedly, lunging at her.

Rosemary moved quickly aside. *"Not the Kirsten!* What the hell is it, then?" she demanded.

"A replica," he told her breathlessly. "It's a replica. My replica. Now, give it back to me, Rosemary."

"A replica?" repeated Rosemary. *"Your replica?* I don't believe you." She waved it at him, tantalizing him. "Besides, it's mine now. I dug for it. Buried treasure," singsonged Rosemary, running from Howie, enjoying the game.

He caught up with her, grabbed at her. "Listen, Rosemary," he panted, "that *is* my replica. And I need it."

He pulled the necklace from Rosemary's fingers, breaking one of her fingernails.

Furious, Rosemary stared at him. Then, with an almost super-human strength nourished by years of frustration and nurtured by prodigious quantities of alcohol, she pushed at him, hitting him full power in the chest with the flat of both palms, catching him off-balance. "Mine," she insisted. "It's mine. I found it."

Stunned by the intensity of the attack, Howie stumbled backward, lost his footing, and fell, hitting his head against a marble table foot.

He lost consciousness.

Rosemary stared at the inert form lying before her, stooped, bent her head to Howie's chest, and listened for a heartbeat.

He was all right. Rendered temporarily helpless. Nonthreatening. But soon he would awake and demand his Kirsten once more.

He couldn't have it.

Rosemary loosened Howie's fingers from the necklace, took it, rose, walked to the library bar, looked in the mirror, and fastened the necklace around her neck.

She stood back to admire the effect.

Beautiful. Exquisitely beautiful. Just as Daddy knew it would be. The Kirsten was made for her. Daddy had known that too.

And now that she owned it, no one would ever take it from her. Not Mark. Not little Howie Caine.

Rosemary turned; walked unsteadily out of the library and up the winding hall staircase to her bedroom. She withdrew a .38 caliber Bijan pistol protected in its mink case in her bedside table drawer. Daddy had bought it for her, insisting she keep it nearby when there was a series of burglaries in the area a year or so back. Then she walked unsteadily back downstairs to the library.

She picked up the tinted glasses, put them back on, poured herself another drink, and took a seat at the library desk, pointing the pistol at the unconscious form of Howie Caine.

When he awoke, he would see at once the futility of arguing with her.

Little Howie Caine would understand that the Kirsten rightfully belonged, not to him, but to Rosemary Hunter.

The House of Graet Ball was winding down. And not too soon for Sandy Stone. Between selling jewelry and smiling, she was wearing out.

But every man she chatted with paled in comparison to Derek. Each was either vapid or oafish, offensive or macho. Only Derek was sensitive, brilliant, accomplished, wonderful, and sexy. He was sexily wonderful. Or was it wonderfully sexy?

Sandy wasn't sure which. But she could hardly wait to research the subject some more.

Consuela cajoled Tony Owens over the loss of the Kirsten, enticed Sheik Abu with hints of other gem treasures, and commiserated with Bordon Granger.

So much empathy took a toll. She sought out the comforting presence of Louis-Philippe. "Pleasing everyone is a trial, Louis," she brooded. "How attractive obscurity appears."

"You would tire of it fast," he observed dryly.

Consuela surveyed the scene she had created; noted the color texture, and vibrancy. Even in its ebbing moments, it was a marvel.

The dimple flashed. "No doubt you are right, Louis," she admitted. "As always."

Louis-Philippe let the observation pass without comment.

Mimzee Dawson couldn't bear the thought of the ball ending. When it was over, she would have to relinquish her magnificent Kirsten. Like Cinderella. Really! She must speak with Consuela about the absurdity of this ridiculous tour.

Meanwhile, Mimzee circulated, showing off her Kirsten and beaming with delight at the unmasked envy in the eyes of the less fortunate.

Belinda, who had picked at food sparingly all night, was ravenous. She could have shoveled tons of food into her mouth to relieve the tedium of this dreary ball.

What idiocy! Imagine her grandmother getting her rocks off because of some dumb rock.

There were better things to be turned on by.

There was a void in Belinda that ached to be filled. Suddenly, she recalled just the thing to fill it. And it wasn't even fattening.

She slipped outside the tent and went in search of Earl. Maybe they could get it on in the back of one of the cars.

Earl surmised Howie was a no-show. Shit! What a rotten piece of luck!

His luck improved when he saw Belinda beckon.

When she indicated what she wanted, Earl hesitated. "Here?"

"Not here, dopey," said Belinda. She told him where.

In the back of the Dawson Rolls? Where was the chauffeur? wondered Earl.

He always went off with his buddies for some poker at these things, Belinda informed him. They'd be done in plenty of time.

Earl digested the information, then shrugged. Hell, the lady had an itch. And he knew how to scratch it. Why fight fate?

"You don't care, darling?" Bordon Granger asked Tami.

"About the Kirsten?" She laughed. "Of course not." She smiled at him contentedly. "It's people, not things, that bring the ultimate pleasure, my love."

"What a fortunate man I am to have won such a wonder," teased Bordon.

"And think how much money you're saving to boot," shot back Tami happily.

She felt wonderful.

The business of explaining Earl to Erin had been attended to. Thank God, Erin had taken it so well. And expressed no desire to see her father. "What father?" asked Erin, dispatching Earl forever.

Thus was the chapter on Earl Blakely closed.

Except . . .

Tami could have sworn she saw someone who looked like Earl parking a Rolls in the club lot.

Absurd.

Imagine Earl working for a living.

Fat chance!

25

Kate was eager for the evening to end. Anxiety gnawed at her, accompanied by a vague premonition of something she couldn't pinpoint. She tried to shake the feeling. She couldn't. She tried to turn her thoughts into more productive channels. She failed.

She was tired, she told herself. But what tired her, she knew, was the pretense that all was well. The pretense her life was in order. The pretense her future was assured.

All was not well. Her life was in chaos. And her future did not look too promising. Not as far as Mark was concerned, certainly.

So much for honest assessment, thought Kate.

Yet maybe that's where change began. First, you admitted the problem. Then you made the changes.

But you had to think clearly to make changes. That's where the difficulty lay. She wasn't thinking clearly. She hadn't been for a long time.

And yet she must begin somewhere. She must begin to put some order into her life.

Howie stirred.

Rosemary watched.

It took him a minute to get his bearings. Where in hell was he? His head hurt. What happened? He rubbed at it gingerly.

Then he remembered. And raised his head. Right away, his eyes met Rosemary's. She was wearing his grandmother's replica. And she was pointing a pistol right at him.

"You hit your head," she explained. "When you fell." She said nothing about pushing him.

The pistol made him nervous. "Could you put that thing down, Rosemary?" he asked, struggling to his feet.

"No," replied Rosemary, observing him closely.

He wobbled to the couch and sat down unsteadily. He looked at her, his mind racing. He had to have that necklace. He needed it. He had to get it back from her. Hell, it was his.

He tried persuasion. "If you let me have that necklace, Rosemary, I'll be on my way. And I won't mention a word of this to anyone. I promise." He started to rise.

"Stay back!" cried Rosemary. "Stay back or I'll have to shoot." She looked grim. "Protection of property. Mine."

Shoot him! Protection of property! Jesus, she was as nutty as a fruitcake. And drunk as a skunk.

He tried boyish charm. He grinned, ran his fingers nervously through his golden curls, and opted for a crestfallen expression. "Christ, Rosemary, my grandmother'll have my head if I go home without it. Besides, it's only a replica. Who'd want a replica? Except her."

Rosemary's laugh tinkled gaily. "Don't try to trick me, little Howie. I know you stole the Kirsten. The replica is back in its case at the ball."

"But that's *another* replica," blurted Howie.

"*Another* replica?" echoed Rosemary in wonder. "Such a vivid imagination, little Howie. What lies will you think of next to trick Rosemary?"

He saw that she didn't believe him, wouldn't believe him. He grew desperate, rose quickly from the couch, and lunged toward the desk.

Deftly, Rosemary swiveled the chair out of his range, stood up, and pointed the gun directly at him. She was no longer laughing.

"Don't try that again," she warned, "or I'll have to shoot you. Even at a distance, I'm an excellent marksman. Up this close, you don't stand a chance."

She waved the gun in the direction of the door. "Now, get out and don't try anything funny. As I said, I'm a pretty good shot, but I'd hate to have to prove it to you."

Rosemary was right. Howie saw the futility of arguing with her. Juiced up as she was and waving that fancy weapon in his face, he knew he was no match for her.

He'd better kiss that necklace and anything else good-bye.

Rosemary watched from the library door as Howie walked the length of the entrance hall and let himself out.

She went back into the library, put on a Frank Sinatra album, and, arms outstretched, danced around the room, the Kirsten replica flashing brilliantly as she moved.

She caught sight of her reflection in the bar mirror and smiled at it.

No one would take the Kirsten from her now. No one.

She paused before the mirror, arms still outstretched, as Frank Sinatra vocalized "I'll Do It My Way."

"That's it, Frankie," crooned Rosemary, "that's us. We'll do it our way."

That was the trouble. The root of her problem. All her life she'd done it everybody else's way.

But that was in the past. From now on, she'd be in charge. And she'd do it her way.

"Remember this, Rosemary Hunter," Rosemary instructed her mirror image, "you can be anything you want to be."

What did she want to be?

Ah, that was the sixty-four-dollar question.

If only she knew, the next step would be easy.

Rosemary moved back to admire the red glow of the Kirsten diamond accented by the high puffed tulle, the embroidered sleeves, of her David Emanuel gown. So beautiful! Oh, so beautiful! And it was hers!

> *Mirror, mirror, on the wall.*
> *Who is the fairest one of all?*

"You, Rosemary Hunter," giggled Rosemary. "You are."

She turned, crossed her arms in front of her body, closed her eyes, and swayed to the music as Frank Sinatra began his rendition of "Dear Heart."

She stumbled and fell onto the couch, the full tulle skirt of her David Emanuel gown spreading crazily about her.

She was so very, very tired. Maybe she should rest a bit.

Rosemary noticed the Bijan pistol on the bar where she had tossed it after Howie Caine left. She rose, retrieved it, and tucked it under one of the couch's cushions. Howie might come back and try to take the necklace from her. She wanted to be prepared. She needed to protect herself.

Rosemary leaned back against the cushions and passed out.

Mark took a taxi from the airport to his house.

He paid the driver, let himself into the house, and paused in the entrance hall. He saw at once that the doors to the library were open, noticed light flooding the entrance hall, heard the sound of music drifting from the room, and grew immediately angry. Jesus, Rosemary was throwing a party!

He strode quickly down the hall, stood in the entrance to the library, and took in the sight of Rosemary sprawled on the couch, one leg on, one leg trailing the floor. A ridiculous gauze thing on her head was half off, and sunglasses were hanging down over her mouth. Christ Almighty, she was drunk!

But it was the necklace that drew Mark's rage and caused him to lose sight of his resolves to remain calm, think clearly, not act impulsively. The Kirsten diamond on Rosemary's neck suddenly became the symbol of everything wrong with his marriage. Rosemary knew how he felt about it. Yet she had accepted it nonetheless and now deliberately flaunted it.

Fury mounted in him. He crossed the room, bent over Rosemary, and shook her until both the turban and the glasses fell off. Mark angrily swept them away.

"Goddammit, Rosemary, wake up," he shouted. "Wake up so we can have this out once and for all."

Rosemary's eyes opened, tried to focus with difficulty, as she stared at the creature attacking her.

"That necklace," yelled Mark. "Tomorrow morning I will take that goddamned atrocity personally back to whoever will accept it and that's that. Do you understand?"

Rosemary's hand flew instinctively to her necklace.

"And another thing," Mark told her. "Tomorrow you will be shipped off to a permanent restricted nuthouse where they will keep you confined for the rest of your life or until you decide to shape up. No more of that Connecticut country-club crap for you. You're too far gone." Mark, exhausted from the two-week chase Rosemary had led him, stepped back and stared at her with disgust. "Look at you. You're a disgrace. A scandal. You're not fit to

466

raise children. You're not fit to be my wife. You're not fit for human society. You're nothing but a goddamned drunk."

He wanted to take her necklace from her. He wanted to send her away. He wanted to spoil all the good things that were going to happen to her.

She wouldn't let him. She couldn't let him.

With a movement too quick for Mark to comprehend or intercept, Rosemary reached behind the cushion, picked up the Bijan pistol, aimed it at him, and fired the gun twice.

He looked at her in bewilderment. "Oh, my God, Rosemary," he cried out, "what the hell have you done now?"

He fell in front of her, twisted with pain. A light, a blazing white light opened before him. The light at the end of the tunnel, he thought reassuringly. That's what it was.

But as another pain grabbed him, he remembered the rest of the scenario about light and deliverance.

Suppose the light at the end of the tunnel wasn't light from the opening, but light from the headlight of an oncoming train?

In that case, thought Mark wryly with his last conscious breath, the goddamned train was headed right for him. And it was too late to get out of its path.

Dazed, Rosemary stared down at Mark. The sight of his life-blood spilling out before her confused her.

What had she done?

She had done something wrong again.

In one sudden, startling moment of clarity, Rosemary remembered what it was she was searching for. What she had lost. And not been able to find in all the many places she had looked.

She had lost faith, and along with it, hope. Hope that tomorrow might be better, brighter, more promising, less painful.

Numbed into apathy, Rosemary raised the pistol to her head, fired once, and, looking somewhat startled by her act of decision, fell to the floor next to Mark's body.

The shots that rang through the house woke the servants sleeping in the back. They also woke Beth, sleeping upstairs.

She bolted out of bed, raced downstairs, and arrived first on the scene.

She stared in horror at the crumpled bodies of her parents.

They looked like rag dolls, she thought. Soiled rag dolls. They looked unfamiliar.

She stood there, frozen with horror. She was there when the servants rushed in. She refused to move. She was there when the police arrived, and only with the gentle but persistent ministrations of a female police officer did she allow herself to be led from the grisly scene. But she knew that, however long she lived, she would carry that scene with her. Wherever she went. Wherever she was. As long as she was.

Ben was doing his final packing when he got the call from the studio. "Say, Ben," his colleague asked, "you know the Hunters, don't you? Senator Hunter and his wife?"

"Sure," Ben said. "Why?"

"We just got the news. There's been a double shooting. Mrs. Hunter shot the senator, then turned the gun on herself. No further word yet on their condition."

Ben sucked in his breath. Good God! He'd just seen Rosemary Hunter. He had film on her in that gorgeous getup. The senator hadn't been at the ball; that he'd known too. But Rosemary hadn't let that stop her from enjoying herself.

Kate! Did Kate know? The Hunter daughter had discovered them. What horrors would that resurrect in Kate?

"Hey, Ben. You there?"

"I'm here," Ben told him.

"Rough break. Sorry I had to be the one to tell you."

"Somebody had to," Ben said slowly. "Thanks, anyway."

He went out on deck and stood there for a few minutes, staring at the dark waters of the Intracoastal. He knew what he had to do. He didn't relish the task. But just as someone had told him, he had to tell Kate.

26

Forever after, Kate would wonder about the vague premonition that had clouded her evening. Nothing she could pinpoint or identify. Yet it persisted.

Consuela had finally insisted she go home. "Go," she commanded. "There is nothing more to do here that we cannot handle, and it is obvious you are exhausted."

"But . . ."

"No buts. I insist. Go home, rest, take a couple of days off, and when you are renewed, come back to work."

"You're certain you won't need me?"

"I am certain," Consuela assured her. She embraced Kate. "Call me tomorrow or if you need to talk. Promise?"

Kate promised.

The streets were almost bare of traffic as Kate drove home.

She thought of Mark, wondered again where he was and why he hadn't called her.

She thought of Rosemary; remembered the look of scorn and proprietorship Rosemary had worn. *Mark is mine,* Rosemary's look informed Kate. *He's always been mine. He always will be mine. Not yours. Never yours.*

Ah, but Rosemary was right, thought Kate. Mark never had been hers. He had always belonged to somebody else.

Maybe that was part of the appeal. Perhaps knowing that Mark would never demand a full commitment from her had been a kind of protection. A buffer from pain.

What about Ben? Hadn't she run in terror from him because

staying with him would demand exactly the kind of commitment she was too frightened to make?

Kate pulled the car into the driveway. She felt more tired than she had in years.

The headlights of the Mercedes picked out Ben's Karmann Ghia. He stood beside it.

Her first thought was that he had come to say good-bye to her once more. Her second, that he had come to insist she go with him.

It was only when he walked over, opened the car door, and quietly said, "Let's go inside, Kate," that she sensed something was wrong.

With no inkling of what was troubling him, Kate led the way into the living room, flicked on the lights, and turned to him with a smile. "Well, Ben?"

"Sit down, Kate," he directed quietly.

She sat.

He sat beside her, took her hands in his, and said simply, "There's something I have to tell you, Kate."

Everything in her resisted. *No,* she thought, she couldn't go with him. She thought she'd made that clear. *Dear Ben,* she brooded, *don't make me say it again.*

"Can't this wait, Ben? I really am exhausted," she said.

"I'm afraid it can't," he told her.

Still, she had no premonition. All she felt was a slight increase of pressure from Ben's hand holding hers.

Finally, he spoke. "There's been a shooting, Kate." He told her the rest then, quickly. "Rosemary shot Mark, then herself. Beth found them."

Kate couldn't believe her ears. Her reason told her this couldn't be happening again, not twice in her lifetime. Not to her.

Dully, she searched Ben's eyes. "Is he—are they—alive?"

"We don't know anything more at this time."

Something suddenly occurred to her. Ben wanted her back. He'd made this up. "I don't believe any of this," she said.

"It's true," Ben told her quietly.

Her reason returned. Of course it was true. Why would Ben lie about something so terrible? Ben, who lied about nothing.

She felt numb. If she allowed herself to feel, the pain would be intolerable. But if she remained very still and held herself aloof from what was happening, she would feel nothing.

She pulled her hands from Ben's, folded them in her lap, and retreated into a place inside herself where nothing outside could reach her.

Minutes passed. Finally, in desperation, Ben grabbed Kate's shoulders and shook her furiously. "Goddammit, Kate, react. Scream. Cry. Yell. Pull at your hair. Beat your breasts. Wail. Do something. Anything. But don't sit there like some goddamned marble statue."

The pain startled her. Ben had never been rough with her. He had hurt her. And he was swearing at her. He'd never sworn at her before. Or yelled at her. Tears formed in her eyes, spilled over, and trickled down her cheeks as she stared at him in disbelief.

She rubbed at the shoulder he had squeezed at the hardest. Didn't he know he had hurt her? Didn't he know how much he had hurt her?

Furious with him, Kate raised her hands, formed them into fists, and pummeled him in the chest. "Damn you, Ben, damn you," she cried out, hammering at him. "Who do you think you are? God?"

As she struck at him repeatedly, something strange happened inside her. Ben was no longer Ben. He was her mother and father, Rosemary and Mark, and all the people who with their senseless actions inflicted intolerable suffering on innocent victims, and left them a legacy of anger and frustration, and a persistent guilt that would torment them all their days. *What had they done? What hadn't they done? What might they have done to avoid this?*

Ben became the surrogate perpetrator and Kate was not only Kate but Beth and all the other faceless, nameless victims. She was the avenger demanding a pound of flesh in return for wounds and indignities suffered.

Until, finally, spent, exhausted, no longer able to protest, she fell into Ben's arms and surrendered.

"I'm sorry," she sobbed. "I'm so sorry, Ben."

His arms enveloped her, his hands gently stroked her hair. "It's all right," he assured her. "I understand."

He lifted her in his arms, carried her upstairs, undressed her, slid her between the sheets, and covered her. "Rest, sweetheart," he told her.

Her eyes widened with fear. "Don't leave me, Ben," she pleaded.

"I'll be right here when you wake up," he promised. "And if there's any more news, meanwhile, I'll wake you."

He went downstairs to make some calls. He called the station and left Kate's number. Officially, he was off the payroll, but he left the number in case someone wanted to reach him for a last good-bye.

He called Bordon, waking him. He apologized, explained the situation, and asked if he could postpone his departure a day or two.

Bordon told him to take what time he needed and to let him know if there was anything he could do. He would call New York about the delay. Not to worry.

Nancy, Kate's secretary, called, offering support and anything else Kate needed. Her call was followed by Consuela's. The contessa wanted to come right over to take over. Ben assured her everything was under control.

He put on a fresh pot of coffee and was reaching for a cup when the phone rang.

It was the colleague who had given him the information about the Hunter shooting. "Turn on your TV," he instructed tersely.

Automatically, Ben tensed. "What's up?"

"Senator Hunter's not dead. His wife is."

Ben hung up without another word, strode into the living room, switched on the TV, and focused on the words of his former co-anchor, Jenny McBain.

"We interrupt with this bulletin. Senator Hunter, who was reported involved in a shooting early this morning, is in critical condition. Repeat. Senator Mark Hunter is in critical condition. Rosemary Hunter, the senator's wife, is dead.

"Senator Hunter has been in surgery for the past two hours here at Spencer Garvey General Hospital in West Palm Beach.

"Our hospital source tells us one bullet has been successfully removed from the senator's chest cavity. A second bullet, however, is lodged close to the heart. There is discussion on how best t remove it. Two specialists have been flown in from Washington, D.C.

"Marjorie Hunter, Palm Beach socialite, widow to a former American ambassador, and mother to Senator Hunter, is in attendance at the hospital. She is accompanied by the senator's older daughter, Kimberly Hunter. The senator's younger daughter, Beth Hunter, who discovered the tragedy, has been sedated, we are told.

"For those tuning in late, we repeat that Senator Mark Hunter, who was shot early this morning at his Palm Beach home, is fighting for his life.

"Rosemary Hunter, wife of the senator, is dead. Apparently by her own hand. Details about the tragic finale to one of Palm Beach's most glittery galas, the House of Graet Christmas Ball, which Mrs. Hunter attended, and about what precipitated this tragedy are not available at this time.

"This is Jenny McBain at Spencer Garvey General Hospital for WKBQ-TV, channel 9, West Palm Beach. More details will be forthcoming as we receive them."

Ben flipped off the TV and sank into a chair.

God Almighty! What a mess!

He felt nothing either way about the life or death of Mark Hunter. He was sorry about Rosemary Hunter. And the family. But his main concern was Kate.

What the hell was the best way to prepare her for this latest development?

27

It turned out the best way to tell her was straight out.

After she awoke and had her first cup of coffee, Ben broke the news. Kate took it calmly, almost as though she expected it.

Funny, she thought, despite all her premonitions of doom, she had never really believed Mark was dead. She was so accustomed to his bouncing back from disaster that she was unable to picture him defeated. How could someone so favored by the gods be so abandoned?

A new bulletin had been issued while she slept, Ben told her. The second bullet had been successfully removed. The senator had regained consciousness. He was very weak, but the medical prognosis looked more promising.

Kate's prognosis looked less so. It was immediately clear to her that Rosemary had had the final say.

There was no possible way for Kate and Mark to continue their relationship. The specter of Rosemary would stand between them always. Rebuking them.

And Rosemary's daughter, who had come first upon the scene, would bear scars too similar to Kate's own for Kate not to feel tormented by guilt.

Her expression was tight. "Not a very encouraging picture," she observed to Ben.

He knew immediately what she meant. "No," he acknowledged.

"You know something?" she said bleakly. "I don't feel anything."

It was true. She felt neither pain nor pity. The feelings were all used up.

"Don't be too hard on yourself," Ben advised gently. "It'll take time."

Kate grasped at the word. Time. That was what she needed. Time to assimilate the horror. Time to sort through it.

Ben suggested a change of scene. He had a friend with a cottage on the Keys they could borrow.

Kate nodded.

Ben told her he'd call Consuela, talk to Nancy about canceling Kate's appointments, see about the cottage, and make the rest of the arrangements.

Kate managed a smile.

Someone had to take charge.

She was too numb to think clearly.

She was grateful Ben could.

The cottage was perfect. The setting—sea, sand, clear crisp air —guaranteed to heal.

They stocked up on food and settled in. And at Ben's insistence, although she was rarely hungry, Kate ate.

They swam, stretched out on the sand, and walked along the water's edge. One night, they slept out on the beach and watched the sun rise.

They talked, and when there was no talk left, they rested in a silence easily shared. They talked of everything but Mark. Ben waited for Kate to broach the subject. She never did.

Yet it seemed to Kate in those few short days that she was beginning to heal.

She had started to put things together. She needed more time.

She hadn't yet sorted out her feelings for Mark or for the events that had taken place. But she had made a beginning.

She had begun to stop brooding about the waste of lives that lay wrecked by the tragedy. There was nothing she could do about it. Nothing she could do to change it. She had to accept that. She had to let go. So that she could move on. It was that simple.

Just as she had to accept and let go of the tragedy that blighted her own life. In time.

She longed to comfort Beth, to tell her she, Kate, understood what she was going through. The thought of the child's trauma was a heavy weight, as heavy as the knowledge there was no

475

possibility of ever sharing her experience with Beth or consoling her.

Kate's own participation in the drama was another burden. What triggered Rosemary's reactions? Was she, Kate, in any way responsible?

Once again, she had to let go.

She also had to face some hard truths.

She discovered some of these on walks alone along the water's edge. Shoeless, hands dug deep into the pockets of her windbreaker, wind whipping through her hair, sea foam sprayed into her face, Kate began to look at them.

She had allowed herself to drift—just like that piece of wood bobbing about in the sea out there.

She had turned control of her life over to others. Given away pieces of herself she needed to reclaim. So that she could become a whole person. For the first time.

It would take time and work. She had the time. And work was never something she shirked.

There was another unpleasant truth to swallow. Just as Mark had used her, she had used him. To shield her from taking responsibility for her own life.

And she had used Ben. She was still using him.

Kate squatted on the sand and stared out at the expanse of sea. How peaceful, how simple, everything seemed from here. How far away and pointless balls and benefits and Kirstens seemed in the midst of such tranquillity. She wished she could have that tranquillity inside her always.

But soon she must leave. There were decisions to make. People would be hurt. People she cared about. Still, a new beginning must be made.

Kate rose quickly and began walking back toward the cottage. She wanted to share these thoughts with Ben. To thank him for being there when she needed him. Dear Ben. Tender lover. Trusted friend. Providence had sent him into her life. Providence would keep him there.

But if there was to be a future for them, Kate needed to be a whole person. Ben deserved nothing less. And nothing less would satisfy Kate.

∾Epilogue∾

Marjorie Hunter stoically kept her vigil outside Mark's hospital room. Only when the doctors informed her the second bullet had been successfully removed and that the prognosis was encouraging did she allow herself to unbend. And then, only some.

It was necessary, she informed Kimberly, to be wary with the press. Rosemary's behavior had become more and more erratic of late. No need to discuss this. The less said, the better.

To herself, Marjorie acknowledged the futility of planning Mark's political future. He could forget the presidency. Rosemary's death had issued the death knell. The press would never let the public forget.

Mark could thank Rosemary. Taste and timing were never her strong points. That was evident right up to the end.

Mimzee Dawson generously offered to share Marjorie's vigil. The thought of Mimzee pushing her presence about was unnerving. Marjorie thanked her, but declined to accept.

There was another matter about which Mimzee might be helpful. The Kirsten diamond discovered on Rosemary's body.

Mimzee explained that it must be the replica she'd had made for fun. How Rosemary got hold of it was beyond her. No doubt Howie had stolen it and given it to her. He had such sticky fingers.

Mimzee had no further use for the necklace. After all, she already had two. Since Rosemary had such a passion for it, perhaps she'd like to be buried with it.

Marjorie paled at the thought and icily pointed out that Rosemary was beyond liking anything. Marjorie would see that the replica was returned to Mimzee. She could give it to the maid, for all Marjorie cared.

Mimzee said there was no need to get huffy. She was only trying to help.

Reenie Boyd tried every which way to get into the hospital to see Mark. She used clout, and when that failed, she tried bribery. She threatened, screeched, and screamed. She cajoled and pleaded.

Nothing worked. Marjorie Hunter would allow no one near.

Reenie sent her a note. She explained she was a dear, very dear, close friend of the senator. She knew Mark would want her near at a time like this.

Marjorie frowned. Reenie Boyd? The name sounded vaguely familiar. When Kimberly pointed out Reenie was a columnist, Marjorie became incensed. Under no circumstances was any member of the press to be allowed access to this floor. Was that clearly understood?

Frustrated and furious, Reenie plotted and planned anew how to reach Mark. To no avail.

At last, she surrendered. At least he was alive. And a widower. Now, there was nothing to stand in the way of their future.

Mark's name might be mud at the moment, but she had the power to turn him into a fuckin' saint. Lordy, she had a communications empire at her disposal.

With power like that, Mark would surely see the light.

Whatever else he was, Mark was a realist.

And Reenie knew that for a fact.

She learned another fact when she called her New York office and found herself talking to Bordon Granger.

"I must have the wrong number," fretted Reenie, somewhat confused.

"No, *sugah,*" Bordon informed her. "You've got the right number."

Then he told her he was in charge and she was the unemployed former head of Boyd Industries.

Consuela was devastated. First Carl and now Rosemary. In so short a space of time. What a tragedy! But thank God, Mark was spared. How awful for Kate! *Dio mio,* it was a good thing she did not believe in omens! Was that not so, Louis?

Louis-Philippe said he, too, did not believe in omens. The Kirsten was a gem of great beauty. Not a bearer of disasters. It was the flaws in humans that forged their fates, not the diamonds they wore or coveted.

Consuela sighed. Ah, how true. How wise Louis was. What a great comfort he was.

She forced herself to be more positive. "Aside from all this, Louis, the ball was a great success, *sí?*"

Louis agreed the ball could not have been more successful.

For some time after the Rosemary Hunter suicide, the press continued to speculate on the disasters wrought by the Kirsten curse. It reprinted the names of previous owners and retold the grim fates that had befallen them. Rosemary and Mark Hunter's names were added to the list of victims, despite the fact that Rosemary never owned the Kirsten and Mark never wanted it. Nor had he died. But pride, greed, and avarice were sins that demanded an accounting. Besides, they were sins that sold papers when committed by the rich.

Better be satisfied with the simple life, suggested the press. The rewards might not be so lavish, but the reckoning was not so horrendous.

With the return of the Kirsten diamond at year's end to its rightful owner, Mimzee Dawson, speculation dimmed. Aside from the misadventures of her grandson, which continued to plague her, Mimzee Dawson seemed to thrive.

As did Palm Beach.

Seasons come and seasons go in Palm Beach. Longer now than they were when Henry Morrison Flagler rang out the season's end at his elaborate George Washington's Birthday Ball, less flamboyant than they were during the colorful Mizner-Singer reign, they still hold an irresistible attraction to those who savor the rich life and those who love to watch those savoring the rich life.

Yes, Virginia, there is a Palm Beach. And so long as there is, it may be assumed the story continues.